# AFTER SHE'S GONE

Camilla
Grebe

ZAFFRE

Originally published by Wahlström & Widstrand, a division of the Bonnier Group

First published in Great Britain in 2019 by Zaffre
by arrangement with Ahlander Agency, Sweden

ZAFFRE
80–81 Wimpole St, London W1G 9RE
www.zaffrebooks.co.uk

A CIP catalogue record for this book is
available from the British Library.

Hardback ISBN: 978–1–78576–470–7
Export Trade Paperback ISBN: 978–1–78576–473–8

*Also available as an ebook*

1 3 5 7 9 10 8 6 4 2

Typeset by IDSUK (Data Connection) Ltd
Printed and bound in Great Britain by Clays Ltd, Elcograf S.p.A.

Zaffre is an imprint of Bonnier Books UK
www.bonnierzaffre.co.uk
www.bonnierbooks.co.uk

# AFTER
# SHE'S GONE

*Also by Camilla Grebe*

The Ice Beneath Her

*To Åsa and Mats,*
*for showing me there's a way out*
*of even the deepest darkness*

Those who sow the wind, harvest the storm.

—BOSNIAN PROVERB

# ORMBERG

*October 2009*

# Malin

I held on tightly to Kenny's hand as we walked through the darkness and the woods. Not because I believed in ghosts. Believing in ghosts was for idiots. For people like Kenny's mother, who spent her days in front of the TV watching pathetic shows about so-called mediums searching through old houses looking for spirits that didn't exist.

Still.

The fact remained that almost everybody I knew had heard the sound of a baby's cry near the cairn—a sort of prolonged, mournful whimpering. They called it the Ghost Child, and even if I didn't believe in spirits and other stupid things like that, why risk it, so I've never been out here alone after dark.

I looked up at the sharp tops of the spruces. The trees were so high they almost hid the sky and the bright, round, milky moon. Kenny pulled me forward by the hand. I could hear beer bottles in the plastic bag clinking, and smell his cigarette and the moist soil and the rotting leaves. Just a few meters behind us, Anders lumbered along through the underbrush, whistling a song I recognized from the radio.

"Come on, Malin."

Kenny jerked me by the hand.

"What?"

"You're slower than my mom. Are you drunk already?"

The comparison was unfair—Kenny's mother weighed at least four hundred pounds, and I'd never seen her walk anywhere besides from the couch to the bathroom. And even that left her out of breath.

"Shut up," I said, hoping Kenny could tell I was joking. Hoping he'd know I meant it with love and respect.

We'd been together for only two weeks. In addition to the unavoidable and awkward make-out session in his bed, which stank of dogs, we'd devoted our time to establishing our roles. Him: dominant, funny (sometimes at my expense), and at times overcome by a precocious, self-centered melancholy. Me: admiring, pliable (usually at my own expense), and generously supportive when he was depressed.

The love I felt for Kenny was so intense, unreflective, and, of course, physical, that it sometimes left me completely exhausted. Still, I didn't want to leave his side for a second, as if I were afraid he'd turn out to be a dream, a sweet figment of my imagination that my yearning teenage heart had somehow cobbled together.

The pine trees around us seemed ancient. Soft pillows of moss spread out around their roots and a gray beard of lichens grew from the thick branches closest to the ground.

Somewhere in the distance a twig snapped.

"What was that?" I asked, perhaps a little bit too shrilly.

"That's the Ghost Child," Anders said in a dramatic voice somewhere behind me. "It's here to take you awaaaaay."

He howled the last.

"Damn it, don't scare her!" Kenny hissed, overcome by a sudden and an unexpected urge to protect me.

I giggled, stumbled over a root, and came close to losing my balance, but Kenny's warm hand was there in the darkness. The bottles in the bag made a muffled clinking sound as he shifted his weight from one foot to the other to support me.

The gesture made me warm inside.

At that point, the trees thinned out, as if stepping to the side. Made room for a little clearing where the stones of the cairn stood. The stones resembled an enormous, stranded whale under the moonlight—overgrown by thick mosses and small ferns that swayed gently in the breeze.

Beyond the clearing the rest of Orm Mountain's dark silhouette rose toward the night sky.

"Ugh," I said. "Why could we not just go to somebody's house and drink beer there instead? Do we really have to sit in the woods? It's freezing out here."

"I'll keep you warm," Kenny said with a grin.

He drew me so close I could smell the beer and snuff on his breath. Part of me wanted to turn my face away, but I stood still and met his eyes because that's what was expected of me.

Anders just whistled, sat down on one of the large, round stones, and reached for a beer. Then lit a cigarette and said:

"I thought you wanted to hear the Ghost Child."

"There's no such thing as ghosts," I said, and sat down on a smaller rock. "Only idiots believe in ghosts."

"Half of Ormberg believes in the Ghost Child," Anders countered, then cracked a beer and took a swig.

"Exactly," I replied.

Anders laughed at my comment, but Kenny didn't seem to hear me. He rarely seemed to listen to what I said. Instead he sat beside me, running his hand over my butt. Stuck an ice-cold thumb inside the waistband of my pants. Then he brought his cigarette to my mouth. I obediently took a deep drag, leaned my head back, and looked up at the full moon as I exhaled. All the sounds of the forest seemed louder: the rustle of the breeze through the ferns; muffled cracking and snapping, as if thousands of unseen fingers were being dragged across the ground; and the ghostly hoot of a bird somewhere in the distance.

Kenny handed me a beer.

I took a drink of the cold, bitter liquid and stared into the darkness between the pines. If someone was hiding in there, squeezed behind a tree trunk, we'd never see him. It would be a breeze to sneak up on us here in the clearing, like shooting deer in a cage or catching goldfish from an aquarium.

But why would anyone do that, in Ormberg?

Nothing ever happened here. That's why people made up ghost stories—to keep from dying of boredom.

Kenny belched quietly and opened another beer. Then he turned and kissed me. His tongue was cold and tasted like beer.

"Get a room!" Anders said, then belched. Loudly. As if the belch were a question he expected us to answer.

The comment seemed to trigger something in Kenny, because he pushed his hand inside my jacket, groping his way under my shirt and squeezing my breast hard.

I repositioned myself to accommodate him and ran my tongue along the sharp teeth in his upper jaw.

Anders stood up. I pushed Kenny away gently and asked:

"What is it?"

"I heard something. It sounded like . . . like someone crying, or sort of whimpering."

Anders let out a mournful cry, and then laughed so hard beer sprayed out of his mouth.

"You're mentally disturbed," I said. "I need to pee. You guys can stay here looking for ghosts."

I got up, walked around the cairn, following the stones to just a few meters away. Turned around to make sure neither Kenny nor Anders could see me, then unbuttoned my jeans and squatted close to the ground.

Something, maybe moss or some plant, tickled my thigh as I peed. The cold snuck around my legs and under my jacket.

I shivered.

What a wonderful idea to come out here to drink some beer.

Truly inspired! But why didn't I say anything when Kenny suggested it?

Why didn't I ever say anything when Kenny suggested something?

The darkness was compact, and I pulled a lighter out of the pocket of my jacket. Flicked the little wheel with my thumb and let the flame shine onto the ground: autumn brown leaves, velvety moss, and those big gray stones. And there, in a crevice between two nearby stones, I caught a glimpse of something white and flat that looked like a hat on a big mushroom.

Kenny and Anders were still talking about the ghost, their voices animated and slurred. The words tumbled out quickly and on top of each other, sometimes interrupted by laughter.

Perhaps it was curiosity, or maybe I just wasn't that keen to go back to the boys yet, but I felt a sudden urge to examine the mushroom more closely.

What kind of mushroom would it be, at this time of the year, in the middle of the woods?

The only mushrooms I'd ever picked here were chanterelles.

I held the lighter closer to the crevice between the stones so that the dim illumination slowly revealed the object. Peeled off a few leaves and pulled a small fern out by its roots.

Yes, there was definitely something there. Something that . . .

Still in a squat with my jeans around my ankles, I pushed my free hand in and poked the white smoothness. It felt hard, like stone or porcelain. Maybe an old bowl? Definitely not a mushroom.

I stretched a little more and rolled away the stone that lay on top of the bowl. The stone was smaller than the others and not very heavy, but still landed with a thud in the moss beside me.

And there it lay, the bowl or whatever it was. It was the size of a grapefruit, cracked on one side, with some kind of fibrous brown moss growing from it.

I stretched out my hand and felt those thin, dark threads.

Rubbed them between my thumb and forefinger for a moment before my brain finally put the pieces of this puzzle together, and I realized what it was.

I dropped the lighter, stood up, took a few stumbling steps straight into the dark, and started screaming. A scream that came from deep inside and seemed to have no end. As if terror were pushing out every atom of oxygen in my body through my lungs.

When Kenny and Anders came to my rescue, I still had my pants down and my lungs had given new life to my scream.

The bowl was no bowl. The moss was no moss. It was a skull with long dark hair.

# ORMBERG

*Eight years later—2017*

# Jake

My name is Jake. I'm named after Jake Gyllenhaal—one of the best actors in the world. It's supposed to be said in the English way, but most of my classmates say it wrong on purpose. They call me Yake or even worse, Yakuh, exaggerating the Swedish pronunciation. It makes me wish I had another name, but there's not much I can do about that. I am who I am. And my name is my name. Mom really, really wanted me to be named Jake, and Dad did what Mom wanted, probably because he loved her more than anything else in the world.

Even now that Mom is dead, it's as if she's still with us in some way. Sometimes Dad sets a place for her at the table, and when I ask him a question it takes him a really long time to reply, as if he's trying to figure out what Mom would say. Then comes the answer: "Sure, you can borrow a hundred kronor" or "Okay, you can go to the movies, but be home by seven."

Dad almost never says no to anything, though he's gotten a little stricter since TrikåKungen, the old textile factory, was turned back into housing for asylum seekers.

I'd like to think it's because he's kind, but Melinda, my big sister, says it's because he's too tired to say no. When she says it it's usually with a meaningful glance at the empty beer cans on the kitchen floor, then she smiles crookedly and blows a perfect smoke ring, which slowly rises toward the ceiling.

I think Melinda's being ungrateful. I mean, she's even allowed to smoke at home. Mom never would have allowed that, but instead of being thankful, she says stuff like that. It's ungrateful, unfair, and, above all, unkind.

When Grandma was still alive, she used to say her son-in-law probably wasn't the sharpest knife in the drawer, but that at least we lived in the prettiest house in Ormberg, which is something. I don't think she realized I knew what a sharp knife was, but I did. In any case, it was clearly okay to be a dull knife as long as you had a nice house.

Ormberg's prettiest house lies five hundred meters from the highway and goes straight into the forest, next to a creek that flows all the way to Vingåker. There are two reasons the house is so nice: first, Dad's a carpenter, and second, he rarely has any jobs. That's lucky, because it means he can work on the house almost all the time.

For example, Dad's built a huge deck around the whole house. It's so big you can play basketball on it or ride your bike. If you really got a good start, and there wasn't a fence, you could jump straight into the creek from the short side. Not that anyone would want to do that—the water is ice cold, even in the middle of summer, and the bottom is full of sludge and seaweed and slimy, disgusting worms. Sometimes, in the summer, Melinda and I blow up an old air mattress and float down the stream to the old sawmill. The trees lean over the creek, making a ceiling of green lace, like the tablecloths Grandma used to knit. When you're on the creek, the only thing you hear is birds, the rubbery squeak of the air mattress, and the rushing sound of the little waterfall that flows into a pond near the old ironworks.

When my grandfather, whom I never met, was young, he worked at the ironworks, but it closed long before Dad was born.

The dilapidated building was burned down by skinheads from Katrineholm when Dad was my age—fourteen—but the blackened ruins remain. From a distance, they look like fangs sticking up between the bushes.

Dad says that everyone had jobs in Ormberg back then: either on a farm, or in the ironworks, or at Brogrens Mechanical or at TrikåKungen. Now, only the farmers have jobs. All the factories closed, and the jobs moved to China. Brogrens Mechanical stands silent and abandoned, a skeleton of corrugated sheet metal on flat land, and the castle-like brick building of the TrikåKungen textile factory has been converted to refugee housing.

Melinda and I aren't supposed to go there, even though Dad normally lets us do whatever we want. He doesn't even seem to think about what Mom would have said either, because the answer comes in a flash if we ask. He says it's for our safety. What exactly he's afraid of is unclear, but Melinda always rolls her eyes when he brings it up, which makes him angry, and they start talking about caliphates, burkas, and rapes.

I know what burkas and rapes are, but not caliphates, so I've made a note of it to google later—I usually do that with words I don't know. I like words, especially hard ones.

I like collecting them.

That's another secret I can't tell anyone. You get beaten up for less in Ormberg, like listening to the wrong music or reading books. And some people—like me, for example—get beaten up more often than others.


I walk out onto the deck, lean against the railing, and stare out over the creek. The storm clouds have thinned out and exposed a sliver of blue sky and an intense orange sun just above the horizon. Frost, which makes the wooden deck look hairy, glitters in the last rays of sunshine, and the creek flows by dark and sluggish.

The creek never freezes—because it's always moving. You could swim it the whole winter, but of course nobody does.

The deck is littered with branches that blew down during the storm late last night.

I should probably gather them up and throw them onto the compost pile, but I'm hypnotized by the sun, hanging there like an orange just below the edge of the clouds.

"Jake, come inside for fuck's sake," Dad shouts from inside the living room. "You'll freeze your ass off out there."

I let go of the railing, stare at the perfectly shaped wet imprints where my hands just lay, and go back into the house.

"Close the door," Dad says from the massage chair in front of the huge flat screen.

Dad lowers the volume with the remote and looks at me. A wrinkle appears between his thick eyebrows. He runs a freckled hand over his bald head. Then he absently moves his hand to the massage chair's control panel, which no longer works.

"What were you doing out there?"

"Looking at the creek."

"Looking at the *creek*?"

The wrinkle between Dad's eyebrows deepens as if I've said some hard words he doesn't know, but then it's as if he decides he doesn't care anymore.

"I'm going to Olle's for a while," he says, unbuttoning the top button on his jeans to make room for his belly. "Melinda made some grub. It's in the fridge. Don't wait up for me."

"Okay."

"She promised to be home by ten."

I nod and go out to the kitchen, grab a Coke, go up to my room, and feel butterflies in my stomach.

I'll get at least two hours to myself.

• • •

It's dark when Dad leaves. The door slams so hard that my window-panes rattle, and after a moment the car starts and I hear him drive off. I wait a few minutes to make sure he's not coming back, then I go to Mom and Dad's bedroom.

The double bed is unmade on Dad's side. On Mom's side the blanket is stretched neatly across the bed and the pillows stand perfectly fluffed against the wall. The book she was reading before she died still lies on the nightstand, the one about the girl who gets together with a rich guy named Grey. He's a sadist and can't fall in love, but the girl loves him anyway, because girls like when it hurts. At least that's what Vincent says. I find it hard to believe—I mean, who likes getting whipped? Not me, anyway. I think the girl probably likes Grey's money, because everybody loves money and most people would do anything to get rich.

Like take a whipping now and then or give a blow job to a disgusting sadist, for example.

I walk over to Mom's closet and pull the mirror door aside. It sticks a bit and I have to give it a shove before it glides open. Then I run my hands over her clothes: sleek silks, sequined dresses, soft velvet, tight jeans, and wrinkled, unironed cotton.

I close my eyes and swallow.

It's so beautiful, so perfect. If I were rich, as rich as that Grey, I would buy a walking closet or whatever it's called. I'd fill it with handbags for every occasion, every season, hang them on special hooks, and my shoes would be lined up on their own shelves with special lighting.

I realize, of course, that's impossible. Not just because it costs tons of money, but because I'm a guy. It would be totally preposterous to get a closet full of women's clothes. If I did, it would truly prove I'm a freak. That I'm worse than that weirdo Grey—because it's okay to hit women and tie them up, but not to dress like one.

At least not in Ormberg.

I take out the gold-sequined dress, the one with the small shoulder straps, and the slippery lining. Mom used to wear it on New Year's Eve, or when she took a cruise to Finland with her girlfriends.

I hold it up in front of me and take a few steps back so I can see myself in the mirror. I'm skinny and my brown hair is like a crown around my pale face. I gently lay the dress down on the bed and go to the dresser. Pull out the top drawer and select a lacy black bra. Then I take off my jeans and my hoodie and put on the bra.

It looks kind of bulky, of course. There's nothing where the breasts should be, just a flat, milky white chest with small, stupid nipples. The bra cups stand straight out from my chest. I put a rolled-up sock in each cup and then slip the dress over my head. As always when I try on the sequin dress, I'm struck by how heavy it is—heavy and cold against my skin.

I observe my image in the mirror and suddenly feel uncomfortable. I'd rather use someone else's clothes beside Mom's, but I don't have any women's clothes of my own, of course, and Melinda mostly has jeans and tops. She'd never wear something this pretty.

I ponder which shoes would go best with the dress. Maybe the black ones with pink jewels on them? Or the sandals with blue and red straps? I choose the black ones—I almost always choose them because I love the sparkling pink jewels. They remind me of expensive jewelry, like what the girls wear in those YouTube clips Melinda watches.

I back up and examine my mirror image. If my hair were just a little longer, I'd definitely look like a girl for real. Maybe I can let it grow out a bit, at least long enough so that I can put it up?

The thought is titillating.

When I walk into Melinda's room, I leave imprints on the thick carpet. Dad put in wall-to-wall carpet in all the rooms except the kitchen, because it feels nice to walk on. I love the feeling of that softness under high heels; it's almost like I'm walking on grass, like I'm outside.

Melinda's makeup bag is huge and messy. I take a look at the clock and decide I have time. I paint thick black lines around my eyes like Adele and color my lips with wine red lipstick. The heat spreads inside of me when I look in the mirror.

I'm beautiful, for real.

I'm Jake, but not, because I'm prettier and more perfect and more like myself than before.

In the hall I pull on one of Melinda's sweaters—it's freezing outside and even if I wanted to, I couldn't go out in just the dress. The black wool is scratchy and the buttons have fallen off, so it won't stay closed. The chill nips at my legs as I lock the front door, put the key under the empty, cracked flowerpot, and head for the road. The gravel crunches under my weight, and I have to concentrate on keeping my balance in these high heels.

The night is dark and colorless and smells like wet earth.

A light mixture of snow and rain has started to fall. The dress makes a sound as I walk, a sort of rustling. The trees are silent along the path, and I wonder if they see me and if so, what they think. But I don't think the spruces would have any objection to my attire. They're just trees.

I take off on a smaller path.

A country road lies about a hundred meters in front of me. I can walk there, but no farther, because someone might see me and that would be the worst thing that could ever happen. Even worse than death.

I love walking by myself in the woods. Especially in Mom's clothes. I usually pretend I'm out on the town in Katrineholm, on my way to a bar or restaurant.

When I'm a few meters from the road, I stop. Close my eyes and try to enjoy this as much as I possibly can, because I will have to head back soon. Back to Ormberg's prettiest house, back to the flat screen and massage chair and my bedroom with all the movie posters. Back to the fridge filled with fast food and an ice machine that works if you bang your fist against it a few times.

Back to Jake, who doesn't have a dress or bra or high heels.

Cold raindrops fall on my head, flow down my neck and in between my shoulder blades.

I hunch over, but really the weather isn't that bad. Not compared to yesterday, when the wind blew so hard I thought the roof would fly away.

I hear a thud coming from somewhere; maybe it's a deer—there's a lot of them around here. Once, Dad came home with a whole deer that Olle had shot, and he hung it upside down in the garage for several days before skinning and butchering it.

More sounds.

A twig snapping and then something else—a stifled groan, like an injured animal. I freeze and peer into the darkness.

Something moves between the trees, creeping through the brush toward me.

A wolf?

The thought scares me, but I know there are no wolves here. Only moose, deer, foxes, and hares. The most dangerous animals in Ormberg are human beings; that's what Dad always says.

I turn around to run back to the house, but one high heel sticks in the ground, and I fall backward. A sharp rock penetrates the palm of my hand and pain pierces my lower back.

A moment later a woman crawls out of the forest.

She's old. Her hair hangs in wet strands around her face, and her thin blouse and jeans are soaked through and torn. She has no jacket or shoes and her arms are streaked with blood and dirt.

"Help me," she says in a voice so weak I can barely understand the words.

I slide backward on the ground in complete terror to escape her. She looks exactly like a witch or an insane murderer from one of the horror movies I watch with Saga.

The rain has gotten heavier and a big puddle spreads out around me. I get up onto my haunches, take off my shoes and hold them in my hand.

"Help me," she mutters again, trying to get to her feet.

I realize that she's not a witch, but maybe she could be crazy. And dangerous. Last year, the police arrested a mentally ill guy in Ormberg. He'd escaped from Karsudden Hospital in Katrine-holm and hid for almost a month in somebody's empty summer cottage.

"Who are you?" I ask, still backing up, my feet sinking into the wet moss.

The woman stops. She looks surprised, as if she doesn't know how to answer that question. Then she looks at her arms, pushes away a branch, and I see she's holding something in her hand, a book or maybe a notebook.

"My name is Hanne," she says after a few seconds.

Her voice sounds steadier, and when she meets my eyes, she tries to press out a smile.

She goes on:

"You don't need to be afraid. I won't hurt you."

The rain whips against my cheek as I meet her eyes.

She looks different now, less like a witch and more like some-body's aunt. A harmless old woman who's ripped her clothes and fallen down in the woods. Maybe she got lost and can't find her way home.

"What happened?" I ask.

She looks down at her ripped-up clothes and then looks up and meets my gaze. I can see the despair and horror in her eyes.

"I don't remember," she murmurs.

At that very moment, I hear a car approaching in the distance. The old woman also seems to hear it, because she takes a few steps toward the big road and waves her arms. I follow her up onto the edge of the highway and stare into the darkness toward the oncoming vehicle. In its headlights, I can make out Hanne's bare feet, which are covered with blood, as if she'd scratched them on sharp twigs and stones.

And I see something else, too: I see the sequins of my dress glitter and sparkle like stars in a clear night sky.

Who knows who might be sitting in that car—could be a neighbor or a friend's big brother or the crazy old man on the other side of the church—but the likelihood that it's someone I know is pretty high.

The terror spreads inward, twisting my intestines, squeezing my heart tight.

There's only one thing worse than witches and mental patients and insane murderers—being discovered. If people in Ormberg found out you might as well just shoot me now.

I back up into the woods and squat down behind a few bushes. The driver must have seen me, but hopefully didn't recognize me. It's dark, the rain is pouring now, and I am in a costume of sorts.

The car stops, and the window glides down with a hum. Music flows out into the night. I hear the old woman talk to the driver, but I don't recognize the woman inside or the car. After a minute, the old woman opens the back door and jumps in. And the car disappears into the night.

I stand up and walk down the path, which runs like a dark, shining snake through the woods. The only sound is the rain.

The old woman whose name was Hanne is gone, but she left something on the ground—a brown book.

# Malin

huddle over against the wind in the parking lot, staring down at the shiny black asphalt, my mind still on the question Mom asked just before I got the call.

*Why did you become a cop, Malin?*

When I get that question I usually laugh and roll my eyes. I make some joke about how it's not for the money, or the car, or the hours. In other words: I deflect. I don't *want* to consider the question seriously, examine my motives or myself. If I were to try to explain it, I'd say it's in part because I like helping people, that deep down I really believe I can make a difference. Also, I've always had the urge to create order, put things in their proper place, like that feeling you get when you clean your house or weed your garden.

Besides, going away to study at the Police Academy in Sörentorp, just north of Stockholm, was an easy way to escape. A free ticket out of Ormberg, and an excellent excuse to avoid having to visit on the weekends.

And the skeleton that Kenny, Anders, and I found in the woods eight years ago—did that have anything to do with my career path?

I don't know.

At the time, it was exciting to be at the center of a high-profile criminal investigation. Even if the victim, a little girl, was never identified. And the perpetrator never found.

It definitely didn't occur to me that I might work that very case one day.

A bitterly cold gust of wind blows an empty plastic sack and some leaves in the direction of the one-story brick hospital. Someone exits the reception area, stands with his back to the wind, and lights a cigarette.

Manfred Olsson, my temporary colleague, called me less than an hour ago.

I remember the surprise on Mom's face when I took the call. Her eyes flicking between the clock and me, and then her realization that something serious had happened, and I was going to have to leave. Even if it was the first Sunday of Advent, and she had a roast in the oven.

Manfred sounded out of breath when I answered the phone, as if he'd run the three-kilometer track near the church. But he often sounds out of breath, probably because he's carrying around an extra fifty kilos. And I was completely unprepared for what he said: Hanne Lagerlind-Schön had been found in the forest yesterday—alone, suffering from hypothermia, and confused. Could I head to the hospital and meet her with him?

It apparently took the local police almost a day to connect her to us and contact Manfred. Not so strange, I suppose—there's no police station in Ormberg. The closest one is in Vingåker, and we don't have much contact with them. Plus Hanne couldn't remember what she was doing in the forest, or that she'd ever been in Ormberg.

Of everyone I've ever worked with, Hanne is the last person I'd expect something like this to happen to. She's a kind, quiet, and pathologically precise criminal profiler in her sixties, from Stockholm. She never comes late to a meeting and takes constant notes in a little brown book.

How is it even possible? How can you forget where you are and who your colleagues are?

And where the hell is Peter Lindgren? He never leaves her side.

Hanne and Peter are two of the five people investigating the murder of the girl in the cairn. Since the arrival of our new national police commissioner, there've been a number of new initiatives: We're going to get tougher on vandalism. Our clearance rate is supposed to increase. Special teams will focus on gang violence in vulnerable areas. And a new task force has been set up to revisit cold cases related to deadly violence. The statute of limitations for murder was abolished in 2010, and now there are stacks of murder cases lying unsolved all over the country.

The murder of the little girl in Ormberg is only one such cold case dug out of storage for a new review. We've been working on it for just over a week. Hanne and Peter are here from the National Operations Department. If I understand correctly, they're also a couple—an odd couple, since Hanne must be at least ten years older than Peter. Manfred came down from NOD as well. He's been working with Peter for a long time. Besides them, Andreas Borg is in our group—a police officer in his thirties who's stationed in Örebro usually.

And then there's me, Malin.

That I would end up working on the investigation into the murder of the girl at the cairn is unforeseen to say the least—not just because I was the one who found her that autumn night eight years ago, but also because I've been working at the Katrineholm police station since graduating from the academy. But there's a logic to it: I was sent to Ormberg because I grew up there. I'm expected to contribute my local knowledge. I think I might be the only police officer in all of Södermanland who grew up in Ormberg.

The fact that I discovered the body wasn't even a part of the calculations when my superiors made this decision. They wanted someone on site who knew their way around the seemingly endless forests in this area, and who could to talk to the old people who live inside them.

They have a point.

Ormberg isn't exactly welcoming to strangers, and I know this village inside and out, know everyone who lives there. The few that are left, that is. Since the TrikåKungen factory and Brogrens Mechanical plant closed, most people have moved away. All that's left are the people who own summer homes, the old folks, and the unemployed.

And the refugees, of course.

I wonder who came up with the brilliant idea of putting hundreds of asylum seekers into a depopulated small town in Södermanland. It's not the first time, either. When the Balkan refugees came in the early nineties the old TrikåKungen building also served as a refugee camp.

Manfred's big German SUV swings into the parking lot, and I head toward him.

He parks the car, and his solid, hunched figure begins to trudge in my direction. The wind grabs hold of his reddish blond hair and blows it up and back so it forms a halo around his head.

He's dressed elegantly, as usual, wearing an expensive coat and a red scarf of thin, slightly wrinkled wool. He's wrapped it around his neck with studied nonchalance. He has a briefcase in cognac leather tucked under his left arm, and his steps are hurried.

"Hello," I say, and jog to keep up with him.

He nods reservedly toward me as we enter the hospital.

"Is Andreas coming, too?" I ask.

"No," says Manfred, running his hand through his hair, trying to force it back into place. "Apparently he's at his mother's place in Örebro. We'll have to brief him tomorrow."

"And Peter—have you heard anything?"

It takes a moment for Manfred to answer.

"No. His phone seems to be turned off. And Hanne doesn't remember anything. I've filed a missing person report. The police and the military will start searching the forest tomorrow morning."

I don't know how close Peter and Manfred are, but you can tell they've worked together for years. They seem to agree about most things and communicate with very few words. A look or a short nod seems to be all that's required.

Manfred must be worried.

No one's heard from Peter since Friday, when he and Hanne left our temporary office in Ormberg at half past four.

As far as we know, I'm the last person who saw them.

When they left they seemed more animated than usual, as if they were headed for something fun. I asked where they were off to, and they said they were thinking about going to Katrineholm for dinner—they were tired of food that tasted like cardboard, something to that effect. After that, neither of us heard from Hanne or Peter—which wasn't so strange, since it was a weekend, and we'd decided to take a few days off.

We enter, go to the front desk, and get directions to her room. The bright hospital lights shine off the linoleum floors of the corridor. Manfred looks tired, his eyes bloodshot and his lips pale and chapped. But he often looks tired. I suppose the combination of his stressful job and the demands of being a fifty-year-old father to a young child must be quite draining.

Hanne is sitting on the edge of her bed when we enter. She has on a hospital gown and an orange blanket wrapped around her shoulders like a cape. Her hair hangs down over her shoulders in damp wisps, as if she's just showered. Her hands are covered with small scratches, and her feet are bandaged. There's an IV stand next to her, and a tube runs from the dropping-bottle to her hand. Her eyes are glassy, her face expressionless.

Manfred goes over to her and gives her a clumsy hug.

"Manfred," she murmurs in a raspy voice.

Then she turns her eyes to me, tilts her head a little, and stares uncomprehendingly.

It takes a few seconds for me to realize she doesn't recognize me, even though we've been working together for more than a week.

The realization chills me.

"Hi, Hanne," I say, touching her arm gently, suddenly afraid my touch might rip her like a paper doll—she seems so desperately frail.

"It's me, Malin, we work together," I continue, trying to keep my voice steady. "Do you recognize me?"

Hanne blinks several times and meets my gaze. Her eyes are watery and bloodshot.

"Yes, of course," she says, but I'm sure she's lying because her expression is one of tormented concentration, as if trying to solve a difficult equation.

I grab a stool and sit across from her. Manfred sinks down on the bed and puts his arm around her narrow shoulders.

Hanne seems so tiny and thin next to him, almost childlike.

Manfred clears his throat.

"Do you remember what happened in the woods, Hanne?"

Hanne's face crumbles. She wrinkles her forehead and shakes her head slowly.

"I don't remember," she says, burying her face in her hands.

For a moment, she seems embarrassed, as if she'd like to push this whole situation away.

Manfred catches my eye.

"It doesn't matter," he says, squeezing her shoulders, and then continues in a steady voice:

"You were in the woods south of Orm Mountain last night."

Hanne nods, straightens her back, and puts her hands on her knees.

"Do you remember that?" I ask.

She shakes her head and scratches absently at the surgical tape holding her IV needle in place. Her nails are cracked and black-rimmed.

"You were found by a young woman driving through the forest," Manfred says. "And apparently you were with another young woman. She was wearing a cardigan and some kind of glittery dress. Do you remember?"

"No, sorry. I'm so sorry, but . . ."

Hanne's voice breaks and tears start running down her cheeks.

"It doesn't matter," Manfred says. "It's okay, Hanne. We'll find out what happened. Do you remember if Peter was with you in the woods?"

Hanne buries her face in her hands again.

"No. *Forgive me!*"

Manfred looks distressed. Gives me a pleading look.

"What's the last thing you remember?" I try.

At first I don't think she's going to answer. Her shoulders are rising up and down violently, and every breath seems like it takes great effort.

"Ilulissat," she says, with her face still buried in her hands.

Manfred meets my eyes and mouths: "Greenland."

Hanne and Peter came here straight from Greenland to participate in the investigation. They'd been on a two-month-long trip of a lifetime, which they took after solving a very complicated murder case.

"Okay," I say. "And then you came to Ormberg to work on the investigation of the skeleton in the cairn. Do you remember that?"

Hanne trembles and sobs.

"Do you remember *anything* from Ormberg?" Manfred asks quietly.

"Nothing," Hanne says. "I remember *nothing.*"

Manfred takes her thin hand and seems to ponder something. Then he stiffens, turns her palm upward, and stares intently at it.

At first I don't understand, but then I see something's been written on Hanne's hand. Sprawling numbers in ink, pierced by small wounds, visible on her pale skin. I'm able to make out "363," but then the text becomes blurry and impossible to decipher, as if it were scrubbed away along with the forest dirt.

"What's this?" Manfred asks. "What do these numbers mean?"

Hanne stares at her hand uncomprehendingly, as if she'd never seen it before. As if it were a wild animal that's snuck into the hospital and settled there on her knee.

"I don't know," she says. "I haven't got a clue."


We're sitting in the lunchroom with a doctor named Maja, who seems to be my age. Her long blond hair falls in soft curls on her white coat. She reminds me of the kind of woman I wanted to be when I was younger: tiny, curvy, and sweet—everything I've never been. She's wearing jeans, and a pink T-shirt peeks out from under her lab coat. A blue pin with the word "Doctor" written on it sits on her chest, and a few pencils stick out of her pocket.

The room isn't large. It contains a couple of refrigerators, a dishwasher, and a round table with four birch-veneer chairs. There's a poinsettia sitting in a plastic pot in the middle of the table. A thank-you card filled out in wobbly handwriting is stuck between its leaves.

Two nurses enter, grab something from one of the refrigerators, and then head back out to the corridor again without saying a word.

"She was suffering from extreme hypothermia and dehydration when she arrived," Maja says, pouring a splash of milk into her coffee. "And, she was found wearing nothing but a thin blouse and pair of pants, even though it was freezing out."

"No coat?" Manfred asks. Maja shakes her head.

"No coat, no shoes."

"Was she able to tell you anything about what had happened?" I ask.

Maja gathers her long, light hair into a knot at the nape of her neck. Her perfectly shaped lips form a small pout. She sighs, and shakes her head.

"She couldn't remember anything. We call it anterograde amnesia. That's when you're unable to form new memories after a certain point in time. At first we thought she might have suffered head trauma. But there's no evidence of that. She has no external damage and the head X-ray revealed no bleeding or swelling. But, of course, we might have missed something. You need to do an X-ray within six hours of a head trauma in order to be sure you catch any bleeding. And we don't know how long she was out there in the woods."

"Could she have suffered something so terrifying that she's repressed it?" I ask.

Maja shrugs slightly and takes a sip of her coffee. Then grimaces and slams the cup down onto the table.

"Sorry! The coffee around here tastes like shit. You mean could she have suffered psychological trauma so intense that it caused the memory loss? Perhaps; that's not my area of specialty. But we're beginning to think she might have some underlying form of dementia. Perhaps it's become more acute as a result of what she experienced. Her short-term memory is severely impaired, but she remembers everything that happened until a month ago quite clearly."

"Could we check her medical records?" I ask.

"You mean her medical records in Stockholm?" Maja asks. "Hanne has given us her permission, which we require legally. But we don't know where she's been receiving treatment, and she doesn't remember. Records are often kept by the health care providers themselves."

Manfred clears his throat, seems to be hesitating. Strokes his beard.

"Hanne *did* have some trouble with her memory," he says quietly.

"*What?*" I say. "Why didn't you tell me before?"

Manfred squirms and looks embarrassed.

"I didn't think it was very serious. Peter mentioned it, but I got the feeling she was more scatterbrained, not that it was . . . well, not that she was suffering from *dementia*, in the clinical sense."

He falls silent, starts fiddling with his expensive Swiss wristwatch. His confession astonishes me. Could he seriously mean that Hanne was allowed to work on a murder investigation even though she was ill? That a person suffering from dementia had been entrusted with matters of life and death?

"We still don't know why her short-term memory is so impaired," Maja inserts diplomatically. "It *could* be due to underlying dementia, but she also could have experienced some form of trauma, either physically or psychologically."

"What happens to her now?" Manfred asks.

"I don't really know. Apparently, social services is trying to find a temporary placement for her, because the rest homes are full. But she's not sick enough to stay at the hospital. Not if you ask me, anyway. She's having problems with her short-term memory, but everything else is fine."

"Could her memory come back?" I ask. "Could it be temporary?"

Maja smiles sadly and tilts her head. She lays her small hands on the table and folds them.

"Who knows. Stranger things have happened."

# Jake

On the school bus ride home, I sit down next to Saga. No one else wants to, but I like sitting with her.

I like Saga.

She looks different, and she is different. It's like she's made from a completely different material than everyone else. Something tougher and softer at the same time.

"Hi," she says, and pushes a strand of her pink hair away from her face. The ring in her nose sparkles in the dim evening light.

We ride through seemingly endless fields. Black, plowed, lying there waiting for winter. We start to pass by some woods, then we'll go by the gas station near the exit to the big highway, and after that it's pretty much forests all the way to Ormberg.

Ormberg itself is basically a forest. And then there's Orm Mountain, of course, and its Stone Age ruins. We've taken field trips there, but there's not much to see, just some rocks in a circle on the top of a hill. I remember feeling disappointed. I was expecting runes or bronze jewelry or something.

Saga grabs my wrist. Her touch sends a shock through my body, and my cheeks burn.

"Can I see," she says, turning my palm upward to reveal words written in ink.

*Proposition*
*Bouillon*
*Conjunction*

I collected them from my classes in social studies, home ec, and Swedish.

"I'm planning to google them later," I explain.

"Sweet," Saga says, then closes her eyes as if lost in thought.

When she does, I see her shiny, pink eye shadow. It looks like crushed jewels have been gently brushed onto her eyelids. I'd like to say something, comment on it. Or maybe run my finger over it.

But, of course, I don't.

And that's when Vincent Hahn throws himself on my knee. The smell of cigarette smoke and mint gum slams into me, and my breath is knocked out. His face is so close to mine, I see the sparse hair of his beard, the whiteheads of his pimples, and his downy mustache. His Adam's apple juts out from his neck, as if he's just swallowed a whole egg. His eyes are full of hate—and I don't know where it comes from.

I've never done anything to him, but he loves hating me. In fact, there's nothing he likes more.

I'm his *favorite* person to hate.

Vincent holds my hand in his iron grip.

"*What the fuck,* look what the fag wrote on his hand!" he screams. "*Conjunc . . . Conjunction.* What the hell does that mean? Is that when you fuck somebody in the ass?"

Vincent grinds his pelvis and sneers. Scattered laughter comes from behind us. As for me, I don't say a word—that's the best strategy. Sooner or later he'll stop.

Vincent drops my wrist and stands next to me, grabs my neck and pushes my head slowly toward the seat in front of me.

*Thud. Thud. Thud.*

It hurts my forehead, and his grip on my neck stings.

There are two options: Either he gets bored and goes back to his friends at the back of the bus or it get worse. Much worse.

"Leave him alone, you *freak*," Saga says.

Vincent stiffens.

"Did you say something, whore?"

His voice is sharp and mean, but his grip on my neck slackens and the thumping stops.

"I told you to leave him alone. Are you deaf? It's pathetic to pick on somebody smaller than you."

Vincent releases me, and I glance at Saga from where I'm sitting with my head bent forward. I know she's deliberately putting me down to make him stop.

That's fine by me.

I'm used to putting myself down. Making myself as small and uninteresting and cooperative as I can so it stops being fun to spit on me, or hit me, or mess with me.

I'm very good at it.

A few seconds later Vincent loses interest and returns to his place at the back of the bus. The skin on my neck burns like it was touched by fire.

"Fuck him," Saga says. "He's so fucking twisted. Are you okay?"

I run my hand over the skin on the back of my neck, trying to massage the evil away.

"That was definitely not nice."

Saga close her eyes and leans against me.

"When he does stuff like that, you should just imagine him taking a shit."

"*What?*"

Saga giggles and seems pleased with herself.

"That's what my mom always says. If somebody's being an asshole at work, or if they think they're so fucking important, just think about them while they're taking a shit. It's hard to be afraid of them after that."

I consider it for a moment.

"You're right," I say. "It works."

Saga smiles, and I feel butterflies return to my stomach.

"You coming over tonight?" she asks. "I downloaded some new horror films."

"Probably. But I have something I need to do first."


Everything's quiet when I get home. Except for the forest: the whisper of swaying treetops, a snap and a creak from the invisible creatures that lurk in the darkness. The air is thick with the scent of spruce, rotting leaves, and the wet charcoal in the grill that stands in front of the house.

Dad's old navy blue Volvo is parked diagonally across the driveway, as if he were in a hurry when he got home.

I unlock the door and go inside. Throw my school bag under the coat rack and kick off my shoes.

Light flickers from inside the living room: The television is on, but the sound is off. Dad's asleep on the couch, snoring soundly and with one foot on the floor, as if he fell asleep just as he was about to stand up. Empty beer cans litter the coffee table.

I gently lift his foot onto the sofa and drape an old checkered blanket across him. He grunts and shifts his position, turning so that he's facing the back of the sofa.

I turn off the TV and go out to the hall. I sneak up the stairs, into my room, and very carefully close my door. Then I go over to my bed, lift up the mattress, and take out the brown book beneath it. Sit down on the floor with my back propped against the bed.

I know who she is now—Hanne, the woman I met in the forest. I read it online in the local paper last night. According to the article, she was "suffering from memory loss" and was in the company of "a young woman" when she was found. The police would like to find the young woman, it said. There was even a phone number you could call. They wrote that "any information could be useful" and that the woman's colleague, a police officer from Stockholm named Peter, was still missing. Then there was a description of him, and of what he was wearing at the time of his disappearance: a red-and-white-checked flannel shirt and a blue winter coat.

When I read it, I actually considered calling that number. But if I did, they'd figure out I was the one standing there in a bra, a dress, and high heels. And that's just not possible. In fact it's completely fucking impossible. I even thought about going to the police station and dropping off the book, but the police station is in Vingåker, and it's open only one day a week.

Plus: How would I explain how I had it?

I've thought about it a lot, and I've come to the conclusion that the best thing I can do is go through those spindly notes and see if I find something important in there, something that might help them find the missing police officer.

So that's what I'm doing now. I open the still damp book. On the first page is the word "Diary" written in an old-fashioned, forward-leaning style. And then, just below: "Read morning + night."

Strange.

Why would you write a diary that you need to read morning and night, like it's a medicine prescription? Besides, the only one who reads a diary is the person who wrote it.

Did Hanne write that for herself?

Read morning + night.

It seems totally mentally disturbed.

I flip past a couple of blank pages and come to something that looks like a long alphabetical list. It takes up four pages. Numbers appear after every word or name.

I run my finger over the text, stop at the letter *M* and read:

M

Malin Brundin, police: 5, 6, 8, 12, 20

Mode: 12, 23, 25

Metal plate, in skeleton: 12, 23

It takes me a while to realize this must be an index that references page numbers.

I flip through more pages. In the lower right corner of each one, Hanne has written a number.

Why?

It's a diary, not a freaking cookbook.

I can't figure out any good reason for it, so I flip past the index and start reading.

ILULISSAT, NOVEMBER 19

Are you allowed to be this happy?

I'm finally where I most want to be. And I'm here with the man I love.

When I woke up this morning, P served me breakfast in bed. He'd been down to the village and bought the bread with seeds on it that I like so very much. It's not a big deal, going to pick up some bread. But the thoughtfulness of the gesture makes me feel warm inside.

We lay in bed for a long time. Made love. Read the newspaper. Ordered more coffee up to our room.

Then: a long walk and lunch under the sun until it went down around two.

The weather is still beautiful, but much cooler than a couple of weeks ago. The days are shorter now, only three hours long.

In ten days it will start to be dark 24 hours a day. And the sun won't come back until January.

P thinks that's "creepy," but I wish we could stay.

Everything I want is here! For the first time in my life, everything is perfect. Even though my memory's getting worse, it's as if nothing can touch me in my perfect Greenland bubble.

So yes, you are allowed to be this happy.

But only for a short while, I suspect.

ILULISSAT, NOVEMBER 20

Last day in Greenland.

The weather is beautiful for those short periods when the sun's up. The water is like a mirror. The icebergs bob in the bay. Some are gigantic, a kilometer long. Others are small, like cotton balls. Their color ranges from the purest white to a faded turquoise.

I'm going to miss the icebergs. Those and the old settlement, Sermermiut, which we visited again today.

I put my hands on the rocky hills that the inland ice has carved into roundness over millions of years, tried to imagine what life was like in that valley: how generation after generation of Inuit people lived here without leaving a trace—so unlike we modern people, who wreck the earth wherever we decide to settle.

Tomorrow we're going back to Sweden.

I love this place and would stay here if I had the choice. Ride out the long, dark winter in the glow of an open fire.

But there is no choice.

We have to go home. Our vacation is over, and two weeks earlier than planned. We're headed to Södermanland to work on a cold case in a small town called Ormberg. Eight years ago they found the skeleton of a five-year-old girl there. Now they've reopened the investigation.

Life, always headed somewhere you need to be, always someone who needs you.

In this case: a dead girl in a cairn.

I look up from the book's spindly text and ponder. Hanne's talking about the girl they found in the cairn eight years ago. I was only six at the time, so I don't really remember what happened, but Dad told me how Malin and her friends went up to the cairn to look for the Ghost Child and ended up peeing straight onto a human skull.

I try to imagine what that must have felt like—standing out there, in the middle of the night, under a full moon, then stumbling onto a corpse—but I can't. It's too crazy. Too fucked up.

Things like that only happen in movies, or in some other place, like Stockholm.

But not in Ormberg.

I keep reading.

I'd rather not leave Greenland earlier than we planned.

We argued about it. Or: I argued and P sulked.

I asked if the dead girl needed him more than me.

He said I was being pretty childish for a sixty-year-old. He'd expected more understanding.

My age, yes.

P says I'm beautiful. But I don't see anything beautiful in my wrinkles & loose flesh. At the same time: There are worse things than the decline of the body.

For example, losing your memory.

It's getting worse and worse every day. Maybe I should call the doctor at the Memory Clinic, but I don't want to. There's nothing they can do. I'm already taking all the medication. There's no other help available.

I sat on my bed last night and tried to remember what we did during the day. And I couldn't! It was as if the hours had been erased from my mind, rinsed away by some powerful solvent.

Memory like a sieve.

But the doctors say my cognitive abilities are "surprisingly well-preserved."

Cold comfort, but it's something.

I'm COGNITIVELY INTACT, despite the wrinkles, the gray hair, and the dementia.

Not really something you'd write in a personal ad: "Cognitively intact 60-year-old woman seeks an outdoorsy type for cozy evenings at home & long forest walks."

Yesterday: P noticed something was wrong, but I didn't say anything when he asked. He's the last person I'd tell—for entirely selfish reasons. I don't want to give him up—the man I love, the body I desire.

But I know how this will end. I'm getting worse. P won't be able to be, won't want to be, with me.

And I'll have to give him up.

No, P can't find out.

KEFLAVIK ISLAND, NOVEMBER 21

At the airport. Waiting on our flight to Stockholm. We flew from Ilulissat to Nuuk early this morning, and then from there to Iceland.

P's happy, full of anticipation. He always is when a new, interesting murder investigation begins. Strange that death could cause such high spirits!

Though honestly, I suspect P felt we'd been in Greenland long enough when they asked him to join this investigation. Because it's not the most thrilling case. It's not just cold, it's as ice cold as the snowy glaciers of Greenland.

BUT, it's a good pretext to skip the last two weeks we were planning to stay for.

And really that's fine by me, too. Perhaps Ormberg will offer a nice change of scenery.

P's reading through the preliminary investigation on his laptop. I'm eating chocolate. Watching our fellow travelers. Wondering if I'll ever sit at a gate again, my bag checked, & my sights set on some remote location.

Have to stop now. We're boarding.

Night.

The flight from Iceland was turbulent. The flight attendant spilled coffee in P's lap. She was very embarrassed, apologized profusely, and tried to wipe it off. P just smiled, assured her it was no problem.

In that moment . . .

I saw it on P's face, how he looked at her. His eyes wandered over her body as if she were a foreign land. A new, exciting continent he was considering emigrating to.

I wanted to scream at him: I'm sitting right here—look at me

instead! Maybe I'm not as young and beautiful, but I am COGNITIVELY
INTACT!

Of course, I said nothing. He would have thought I was crazy, not
just demented.

We head for Ormberg tomorrow.

P & Manfred say I can assist with the investigation. I'm not sure they
really need help. I suspect they're being kind. (Still, I'm looking forward
to seeing Manfred.)

Anyway. I think P wants me close by to keep an eye on me.

P clearly loves me, but I'm not sure he trusts me.

I can hardly blame him for that.

I don't even trust myself anymore.

## ORMBERG, NOVEMBER 22

Ormberg is so tiny. You can hardly call it a town. Two dirt roads that
cross in the middle of nowhere. A few run-down buildings. The largest—
yellow-brown, two-story, stucco—was once a general store.

Manfred has set up a temporary office there. He calls it "Chateau
Ormberg." Very funny—the last thing it looks like is a castle. Next to it:
the old post office. It's no longer a post office, of course—an
e-commerce company that sells dog clothes & dog beds on the
Internet rents it. Finally: an apartment building, empty for ten years.
Windows and doors nailed shut, its walls covered in graffiti.

Around the buildings: fields, overgrown with high grass and brush-
wood.

A few hundred meters farther away, on the other side of the overgrown field: a church. It's abandoned as well. In need of repair apparently. Some problem with the stucco.

Behind the church: forest, forest, and even more forest. Here and
there stand tiny, charming red cottages—most situated along the
creek or near the church.

There are about a hundred permanent residents in Ormberg and its
surroundings. In other words, a very small town, even in comparison to
other depopulated areas.

Manfred introduced us to Malin Brundin: a newly commissioned police officer who's usually stationed in Katrineholm. Malin grew up in Ormberg. She knows everyone and can find her way around the woods.

Malin isn't even twenty-five yet. She has long, dark brown hair. Slim, fit, and beautiful in a very ordinary way—as some young women are without any effort or even realizing it.

Before life & time catches up with them.

Malin briefed us on the case. Took out a map, pointed out where the body was found on October 20, 2009.

Malin, then fifteen, was one of three teenagers who discovered it.

Quite the coincidence, but as Malin said: Ormberg is so small unlikely coincidences happen naturally.

We looked at photos of the skeleton. Long wisps of hair still clung to the skull.

The probable cause of death was blunt force trauma.

Malin showed us more pictures: magnifications of the cracked skull, fragments of bone next to a ruler. A few teeth found near the skeleton. Tiny broken ribs, which looked like the sun-bleached sticks you'd find washed up on a deserted beach.

Death is rarely beautiful, but dead children make me feel dizzy & nauseous. I had to grab hold of the table to keep from losing my balance.

Things like that aren't supposed to happen to children. Children are supposed to play, hurt themselves, and cause trouble. Then grow up and have children of their own who play, hurt themselves, and cause trouble.

And above all, they're not supposed to die.

P seemed affected, too, but not as shaky as me. He's used to it—he's seen most everything in his twenty years of investigating murders. He's also a man. (Call me heteronormative, but I do think men are different.)

They were never able to identify the child, despite successfully extracting DNA from her femur and the extensive news coverage of the case. The media dubbed her the Ormberg Girl.

That's somehow even more tragic: A child dies and no one misses her.

Then another colleague arrived: Andreas Borg—a fairly handsome man in his thirties. He's the representative for the local police on our team, usually works in Örebro.

I noted Malin's reaction. She became stiff when Andreas arrived. I couldn't decide if she disliked him, liked him, or was just annoyed he was late for our meeting, but there was an energy there that affected the entire balance of the room.

I don't think P noticed it. (And yes, I think it's because he's a man.)

Have to stop. Time for lunch.


I close my eyes, envisioning the cairn, conjuring up the outlines of the stones under moonlight with black spruces standing in a circle around them. Can almost feel tall ferns tickling my legs and soft moss beneath my shoes.

*The Ormberg Girl.*

People here still talk about her, just like they talk about everything else that's gone: the ironworks, TrikåKungen, and Brogrens Mechanical.

I've never thought about it before, but most of the conversations in Ormberg are about the past.

My phone rings and interrupts my thoughts.

It's Saga.

I look down at the palm of my hand.

*Cognitively intact*

*Inuit*

*Heteronormative*

I'll have to google them later.

# Malin

It's Monday, December 4th, and no one's seen Peter since Friday. I think of the confusion on Hanne's face when Manfred and I visited her yesterday, and the wounds covering her hands and feet.

What happened to them in the woods?

It's started snowing. Heavy flakes wind down from a darkening sky and land silently on the blueberry bushes and the moss.

I'm at the old ironworks that sits next to the creek, just a few hundred meters north of the cairn. It's a good distance from where Hanne was found last Saturday, but since Peter is still missing, the search area has widened. Police officers, national guard, and volunteers are methodically combing the forests in search of him.

It's no easy task: The area is vast and inaccessible, and the forest is full of fallen trees and branches after the storm last Friday.

The local police are in charge of the investigation into his disappearance, but we're cooperating with them closely—in part because Peter is our colleague, and we were the last people to see him and Hanne before their disappearance, but also because we can't rule out that his disappearance is connected to our investigation.

Svante, a man in his fifties who comes from Örebro, is leading the task force. Apparently, he works with Andreas most of the time.

Svante looks like Santa Claus—gray hair and big, bushy beard. He wears a thick, homemade stocking cap and an oversized puffy coat that reminds me of Dad.

"Well," I say. "Find anything?"

"Nothing," Svante says, pulling his colorful knit cap farther down over his ears. "We've searched the woods and every unlocked house. Even the dogs are starting to have a hard time. It's been three days and a hell of a lot of people have tramped around out there now."

Soon it will have been two weeks since Peter and Hanne arrived in Ormberg. We only worked together for a little more than a week before they disappeared, but it feels like I've known them much longer. And even though Peter's been gone three days, it feels like he just disappeared yesterday.

It's as if time itself has warped in protest of what's happened.

I show Svante around among what's left of the buildings, pointing out the blast furnace, the roasting furnace, the coal house, and the smithy.

The brick buildings are surprisingly intact, though most of their windows gape open with no glass, betraying the fact that the ironworks has been closed a long time. The coal house, on the other hand, which was built of wood, is just a pile of boards.

We climb over some large branches and head toward the old roasting furnace, which consists of a beautiful octagonal house with a tall brick chimney.

The creek flows, black and tranquil, beside us. The gleam of our flashlights plays across the surface of the water, and the occasional leaf floats by.

"Why did you stop the helicopter search?" I ask, wiping a snowflake off my nose.

"We searched the entire area with an infrared camera yesterday," Svante says, looking up to the sky. "Didn't help one bit. And it's not easy to see anything from above with all these trees. The best method we have is to search on foot."

I hesitate before asking the question that's been on my mind since this morning.

"Could anyone survive three nights in this cold?"

Svante stops, meets my eyes, and shrugs his shoulders.

"Outdoors, with no sleeping bag or tent? No, I don't think so. But we don't even know if he's in the woods."

He takes a step over some rocks at the water's edge.

"You have to be careful not to fall in," he says, nodding to the creek.

"Yes. If you don't know the way."

As for me, I could find my way blindfolded. When I was a teenager we hung out here in the summer. Swam in the creek, drank beer, and grilled. Made out and smoked. Testing our newly won freedom and getting a taste of the adult life that seemed to stretch in front of us like an endless buffet.

Then we all got jobs somewhere else and moved away.

*Everyone except Kenny.*

We stop at a wall of black stones, and I run my hand over it, brushing off some snow.

"My great-grandfather worked here from the age of sixteen until the ironworks closed in the thirties," I say. "He built this wall."

I try to imagine what it looked like here in the early part of the last century, when the ironworks was still in operation. It must have been magnificent and bustling with activity—but now everything's dead, dilapidated, and overgrown with bushes and moss.

"Strange rocks."

"It's slag tile," I say, pointing to one of the black rocks in the wall. "It's a by-product of iron manufacturing."

I look at the wall and then over at the roasting furnace.

"Where did the ore come from?" Svante asks.

I'm still looking at the wall when I answer, my hand resting on one of the black rocks.

"Bergslagen, mostly. But also from Utö in the Stockholm archipelago."

"Why'd they close it down?"

"The economy, I suppose. It wasn't profitable to produce iron anymore. Just like the textile factory or Brogrens Mechanical. The jobs disappeared, and we were left behind."

"And all the people who worked here?"

"It was tough. My grandmother and grandfather were children during the Depression, and the stories they told me . . . you wouldn't believe. They lived on bark bread and bottom feeders from the creek for several years. There weren't many jobs in Ormberg when the ironworks and sawmill disappeared. Most people moved, of course. But my grandparents didn't want to leave their land. It was all they owned."

"Is that so," Svante says, looking like he's ready to leave.

"People move away from Ormberg; no one moves here."

Svante turns around and meets my eyes. Wipes his nose with the thumb of the glove.

"What about the refugees?" he says. "The new arrivals. Maybe they'll breathe new life into Ormberg?"

"You can't be serious? A bunch of Arabs in the middle of the forest? That won't go well. They don't know anything about life around here."

"But they'll get help, right?" he ventures. "Learn the language, find a job?"

I don't answer, because he's right. They get plenty of goddamn help. Help that the people of Ormberg never received, despite the fact that the factories closed and the village slowly withered away.

Even though we were born here, there was no help for us when we needed it.

But you can't say that out loud. Especially not if you're a cop, and you're supposed to represent a good and just society.

. . .

By the time I leave the task force leader and walk the short distance through the forest to my car, it's already dark. Inside, a growing unease gnaws at me. I knew the search effort would be complicated, but I was expecting we'd find something. Anything: a glove, an old receipt, a tobacco container—some sign that Peter and Hanne had been here.

But all we've seen are trees and more trees. Orm Mountain's dark, slippery slopes, and the creek silently winding its way through the woods.

Just before I get to the road, I hear a snap. Like a branch breaking behind me.

I turn around, take out my flashlight and shine it into the trees. All I see are shadows playing across the enormous trees as the beam of light moves.

I continue back toward the road, but more quickly.

The snowfall is heavier now.

The flakes wind down between the spruces, dancing in the light in front of me. It occurs to me that the flashlight offers a false sense of security—outside its beam the darkness is impenetrable, and it leaves me as visible as a lighthouse.

Just as the trees are thinning out in front of me, making way for the road, I hear something again. A scraping sound, as if someone was dragging a heavy object over stones.

I turn around quickly and aim the flashlight at where the sound came from, but see nothing, just the falling snow reflecting light. I turn off the flashlight, close my eyes, and wait for them to adjust.

Slowly the contours of the trees become visible.

Odd: no deer, no pursuer, no confused colleague who got lost on the way to the road.

Still, I'm sure someone was there.

*Someone or something.*

"Hello?" I shout. "Anybody there?"

No answer. The only thing I hear is the sound of my own breathing.

Just as I'm about to go on, I hear footsteps behind me. That and something else—it almost sounds like laughter. The steps are getting closer, and now I hear someone panting loudly.

A large dark figure appears ten meters in front of me.

A man. He moves clumsily and slowly over the terrain.

Just behind him I see three smaller figures, running. Children. The first one is wearing a red stocking cap and carries a long stick in his hand.

The big man trips and falls face-first into the snow. He groans as he hits the ground with a thud.

The boy with the stick screams:

"We got him!"

The other two boys catch up and circle the man lying in the snow. Then the boy with the red hat starts hitting the large body with a stick. Striking it over and over again until the figure begins to whimper.

Something cold spreads inside me as I realize who the man on the ground is.

It's Magnus.

*Ballsack-Magnus.*

That's what they call him. Once when he was a child he was kicked in the crotch, and his scrotum swelled up to the size of a soccer ball. He had to go to the hospital and have an operation. Drain out a lot of blood. After that, everyone called him Ballsack-Magnus, and that was that.

Once you get a nickname in this village, it's not easy to escape it.

Magnus is my cousin, and Ormberg's village idiot.

I don't think he's actually mentally handicapped—his problems seem more social. But he's clearly different, though I've never really been able to put my finger on what's wrong. And I've always felt fiercely protective of him, plus a kind of awkward affection, even though he's twenty years older than me.

Not so strange, I guess. The little brats of Ormberg have made terrorizing him into a sport. They throw rocks at him, leave firecrackers in his mailbox, and string trip wire across the stairs outside his small house.

Now and then Margareta—my aunt and Magnus's mother—catches a few of them in the act and boxes their ears. Or calls their parents, threatens them, gets her way like she always does. And it works. For a while. The kids come over and apologize: their eyes filled with shame, their cheeks red.

But in a few weeks it starts all over again.

That's one of the reasons I loathe Ormberg—there's no way to get away from the assholes, no place to hide.

In a small town you're always fully exposed to other people.

And to yourself.

I run toward Magnus and his tormentors.

"What are you doing?" I scream.

"What the hell," the boy with the stick shouts, then drops his branch in the snow and takes off running toward the road.

Within moments the other two boys run off behind him.

". . . just a joke," I hear one of them say as he disappears between the trees.

I hesitate, but decide to stay. I sink down beside Magnus and gently grab him by the shoulders.

"Magnus, it's me, Malin. Are you okay?"

Magnus sniffs loudly. His heavy body heaves up and down, but he doesn't say anything.

"Are you okay?" I ask again, stroking his back.

"Nooo," he whimpers.

And then:

"Don't tell Mom. Please!"

I promise not to say anything, then help him up. Brush off his coat and give him a hug.

Magnus leans over and sobs against my shoulder—a two-hundred-pound, forty-five-year-old man who's just been chased down and beaten by a bunch of middle school boys.


As soon as I drop Magnus off my pulse slows. My rage starts to fade, which allows the rational part of my brain to function, my ability to reason and analyze. The part of me that says you can't thrash those boys, especially if you're a cop.

Apparently they ran into Magnus by chance near the ironworks—half the village was there for the search effort—and started to chase him through the woods.

Magnus knew who they were, but he wouldn't give me any names.

I suppose he feels too ashamed.

Halfway between the ironworks and downtown I stop, like always at this location. Sometimes I even park, get out of the car, and sit for a while next to the ditch.

But not today—I have to get back to the office, and I still feel uneasy.

I stare through the car window at the dark woods and take a deep breath.

This is what happened to Kenny.

I close my eyes and sit for a moment, silent and unmoving with the engine still idling. Then I straighten up and start driving back to the office.


Mom calls just as I'm turning in to downtown. She has some questions about the wedding. Or, rather, suggestions for how to cut costs and save some money.

Mom's always afraid things are going to cost too much, and even though I've told her a hundred times she doesn't have to spend a cent on the wedding, I still hear that worry in her voice.

"Stop nagging me about money," I say. "I'm paying. It's important to me to do this in the right way."

She doesn't answer, but I can see her in front of me, sinking down onto the couch and putting her head in her hands. She's never understood why my wedding is so important to me. I suppose it didn't used to be like this. Getting married wasn't a big deal. It was just expected, or maybe you did it because you got knocked up.

If it were left to me I wouldn't have the wedding in Ormberg—I've spent most of my life trying to get away from here. But it would break Mom's heart, and of course I don't want to do that. And it is lovely here in the summer, so the wedding will be beautiful.

I park outside the old grocery store with my phone pressed against my ear.

"Malin," Mom says in a small voice, and I sense the unspoken reproach. "Sweetheart, with that kind of attitude you're just setting yourself up for disappointment. Try to relax a little. Everything will work out. We can talk about it more when you come home tonight, okay?"

I agree, and hang up. Then I unlock the door and enter the temporary office we've set up in the old grocery store.

There's no longer a grocery store in Ormberg—there's no customer base. When Mom was little, there was a general store, and in the eighties the Karlman family sold it to a grocery chain. That closed ten years ago and the building's been empty ever since, other than occasionally being used by teenagers for parties. I've come here to drink whatever alcohol we could pinch in flickering candlelight. It was the logical and inevitable consequence of growing up in this backwater.

I take off my coat and sit down in front of the computer. I throw a glance at the pictures of the Ormberg Girl's skeleton, which are taped to the wall, a reminder of an investigation we've barely mentioned in two days. Then I take out a notebook and flip to the last page.

My phone beeps and I take it out, a text message from Max: "Gray or beige plaid for the sofa?"

Max is my boyfriend, or actually fiancé. He's a lawyer at an insurance company and lives in Stockholm. After we're married, I'll move there, too. Then I won't have to have anything to do with Ormberg anymore. All those fragile threads that keep me tied to this place, those thousands of tiny umbilical cords, will finally be cut.

And Max is the pair of scissors to do it.

It feels good.

Of course, I'll stay in touch with Mom. Visit a few times a year, or even better, bring Mom up to Stockholm.

The door opens and cold air pours in, along with a few leaves and the smell of wet soil. Manfred stands in the doorway.

"Hello," he says. "How did it go?"

"Not so well," I answer. "I just came from the ironworks. They didn't find anything."

He closes the door behind him and takes off his coat. Sinks down onto the chair opposite me. He looks dejected—dejected and on his way toward furious. Fear and stress seem to bring out something hard and aggressive in him that I haven't seen before.

"*Damn it.*"

I nod quietly and look at him. His red-blond hair is glued to his head, and he's wearing a tweed suit.

He looks like he came from another planet.

Nobody, and I mean *nobody* in Ormberg would ever dress like that. Not even the Stockholmers who moved into the old manor house on the other side of the creek, who breed weird little horses that are too small to ride, or the Germans who bought the old summer cottages in the forest to live closer to nature.

When Manfred arrived here with his colleagues, I considered suggesting to him that he change how he dresses, make things easier for himself, so to speak. People out here won't respect a person dressed like an English lord on his way to a foxhunt. But I kept that to myself. And then Peter disappeared, and Manfred was pushed so off balance that I didn't dare bring it up.

He's still off balance.

So am I.

We're worried about Peter, and a bevy of journalists have started showing up asking questions we couldn't answer if we wanted to. I wonder where they're staying—there are no hotels in Ormberg, just a campsite near Långsjön that's closed this time of year.

"Tell me," Manfred says, placing a thermos on the table and nodding to the map lying in front of me.

Ormberg is situated in the ancient province of Södermanland. It's just a few thousand hectares of rocky woodland, which, unlike the rest of the province, aren't suitable for farming. It was once a small, thriving industrial center, but now it's mostly depopulated. The map of this area shows forest, forest, and then more forest. Along with a few farms scattered as if by chance along the creek that flows all the way to Vingåker.

We've drawn a grid on top of it and marked a few important places: the cairn where we discovered the body, the old ironworks, and the place where Hanne was found.

"The task force and the national guard searched this area today," I say, pointing my pen to two of the squares on the map. "I talked to Svante, the task force leader."

"And?"

"Nothing. But the terrain's rough, it's easy to miss . . ."

I'm about to say "a body" but manage to stop myself in time. Neither of us wants to think of Peter as "a body"—not that friendly, handsome police officer from Stockholm. Handsome, that is, if you like older men. He is fifty years old, after all—I learned that information during the search. I also know he's 185 centimeters tall, weighs eighty kilos, and *is* in a relationship with Hanne. He has a teenage son named Albin, whom he almost never sees, and an ex he can't stand.

When people become the subject of a police investigation, nothing about their life remains private. It doesn't matter if you're the victim or perpetrator. We dig up all your dirty laundry, everything you'd rather leave in the closet, and hang it up for all the public to see.

I wonder what Peter will think when he finds out about our sitting here, in the old grocery store, talking about his height and weight and whom he's sleeping with.

*If* Peter ever finds out, that is.

As far as we know, he's been missing since Friday, and the temperatures have dipped far below freezing at night.

Plus there was a storm late Friday. It knocked down several trees, and apparently took the roof off a barn ten kilometers north of Ormberg. It's not so unlikely that Peter might have suffered an accident if he got caught out in that.


Manfred unscrews the lid of the thermos and reaches for the paper cups. Pushes his damp hair off his forehead.

"Coffee?"

"Please."

He pours a cup of steaming liquid and hands it to me.

"I spoke to Berit Sund, the woman who's helping social services take care of Hanne."

"Is Hanne with *Berit Sund*?"

Berit, who lives in an old cottage just beyond the church and the ironworks, was old even when I was a kid. I find it hard to imagine her capable of taking care of someone else these days, especially someone who's confused and traumatized. Though I do remember she used to work with the handicapped.

"Yes. Hanne has been placed there temporarily. Until social services finds another solution. I think that's a good thing—it means we can go talk to her if we need to. If and when she starts to remember."

"Does she?" I ask. "Remember anything, I mean?"

"Not a damn thing."

Manfred looks down at his coffee cup. He looks sad; his entire walrus-like body radiates grief.

I want so much to comfort him, but I don't know how.

"I still don't understand how she kept it from us," I say. "I mean, if you can't even remember where you are, you must be pretty sick. How could you hide it?"

Manfred shakes his head, then says, "I know. It's strange. But I think she had her strategies for managing life. Remember the journal she always had with her?"

I nod.

Of course I remember the brown book. When it wasn't tucked under Hanne's arm, she was writing in it. When she wasn't writing in it, she was reading it.

"You think she wrote things down?"

"Yes," Manfred says, and takes a sip of his coffee. "I'm pretty sure she did. Otherwise, she never would have been able to handle the job."

"Then she must have documented everything. What people looked like, what the . . ."

Manfred doesn't answer. Instead, he stares out through the small, dirty window. Outside, day has surrendered to night, and darkness reaches inside as well. A bare lightbulb, hanging from a temporary cord in the ceiling, and the faint glow of the laptops are the only illumination.

We're sitting in what used to be the back office of the grocery store. The adjacent room was the actual store part. Shelves still stand there, and an old checkout counter. The walls are covered with graffiti, and we had to clean out piles of empty beer bottles, cigarette butts, and used condoms when we moved in. At that point we thought it was sort of fun. Manfred called it *Chateau Ormberg,* the house of sin in deepest Södermanland. And Hanne . . . Well, Hanne took out her book, probably to write down what he said.

Manfred pushes a broad finger on the map. When he pulls it away, a small coffee stain sits on the paper.

"Hanne was found here on the road that goes south of Orm Mountain. We searched the forest within a one-kilometer radius and talked to the people who live nearby. The Brundin family, relatives of yours, were apparently in Katrineholm on Friday night. They were home on Saturday, but didn't notice anything out of the ordinary. And what about the Birgersson family—they didn't see anything, either? Right?"

I shake my head, then add, "I talked to the father, Stefan Birgersson. And the daughter, Melinda, who's sixteen. They didn't see anything. The daughter was with her boyfriend on Saturday night at the time Hanne was found, and the father was at a friend's playing video games."

"Video games?"

"Yep. And then there's the son, Jake. He was home alone on Saturday night. "

"Jake. *Jake Birgersson?* That's his name?"

I nod.

"Classic Ormberg name," I add.

Manfred smiles uncertainly, as if he's afraid to insult me by laughing.

We've gotten to know each other over the two weeks we've worked together, but not well enough to navigate where the fine line between joke and insult lies. Especially when it comes to a sensitive subject like my hometown.

I smile a little. Not a cheerful smile, but rather an I-think-we-should-change-the-subject smile.

Manfred takes the hint and says nothing more.

"What about the woman who found Hanne?" I ask. "Has anybody followed up with her?"

"Yes. She lives in Vingåker. I called her this morning. She confirmed everything, but had nothing new to add. She was on her way to a friend's home in Ormberg at eight o'clock on Saturday night, took the wrong turn by mistake just before Orm Mountain, and turned around when she realized she was on the wrong road. On her way back, she encountered Hanne, stopped, and then picked her up when she noticed something bad had happened to her."

"And the girl she saw?"

"She still claims Hanne was with a woman. Young, maybe in her twenties, wearing a gold dress or skirt and a dark top, which she thinks might have been a cardigan. No coat as far as she could make out."

"I don't get it. Why would you be dressed like that in the middle of the forest at this time of the year? And in such awful weather?"

We both fall silent while we consider it.

"Maybe we should talk to Hanne again," Manfred says, in a quieter voice.

My thoughts return to Hanne: Peter's lover, a behavioral scientist who specializes in criminal profiling. Manfred told me quite a bit about her during those three days we were working on the case before Hanne and Peter arrived. He said he'd never met anyone as sharp. That it was almost uncanny how accurate her predictions were—apparently she was called the "witch" by some of their colleagues in Stockholm.

She really fooled us: Neither of us saw any sign of her illness or sensed the depth of her handicap.

I'm not sure what I think about Hanne.

I often felt like she was staring at me strangely, especially when I spoke to Andreas. Those eyes, stuck to me like chewing gum, made me feel vaguely uncomfortable.

"We have to at least try to find Hanne's book," Manfred says. "If she wrote everything that happened down maybe it can help us find Peter. I did call and ask her where it was, but she didn't remember. And Berit had no idea, either."

"It's not here, and it wasn't at their hotel," I say. "Svante and I went there to check."

"Maybe she had it with her when they disappeared," Manfred suggests. "Could have dropped it in the woods."

"It'll probably show up in the spring, after the snow melts."

Manfred sighs.

"And Peter's car?"

I nod and take a look at my notes.

"It hasn't been found yet, but they've issued a description. They're tracking Hanne's and Peter's cell phones as well. And checking to see if Peter's bank or credit cards have been used."

Manfred falls silent. He looks angry again, closes his eyes and takes a deep breath.

"I'm still wondering about Hanne's hand," I say.

"The numbers, the ones she wrote in the palm of her hand?"

"Yes. If she was the one who wrote them. It said '363' and then something illegible. What could it have meant? We have to try to figure it out."

The door flies open and Andreas comes in. He's wearing jeans, a fleece shirt, and a puffy vest. His dark curly hair is damp and his shoulders and upper arms are wet.

"Burning the midnight oil, I see," he says, and stands with his legs wide, just a little too close to me for comfort.

Andreas is the kind of guy who thinks he's God's gift to women, just because he was born with a penis dangling between his legs. He probably thinks I find him irresistible.

I don't.

I'm not the least bit attracted to Andreas. I think he's pathetic, or more so, pitiful. He's like a little boy screaming for his masculinity to be confirmed, but I won't give him the satisfaction.

I look down at the map again. At the squares that represent houses and the winding line of the creek. At the height lines that illustrate the topography and which get tighter and tighter around Orm Mountain.

Andreas clears his throat and takes another step closer to me, so that his leg almost grazes my arm.

"I just came from the task force center. They found something in the woods, right next to the place where Hanne was picked up. I have no idea if it has anything to do with her and Peter, but . . ."

He leaves his sentence unfinished and roots around in the pocket of his puffy jacket. Pulls out a small plastic bag that looks empty and lays it on the table next to me.

A drop of water falls from his sleeve onto my hand.

We lean forward to see what the bag contains while Andreas continues:

"I sent the technicians there to be on the safe side. The guy from the task force claimed he saw footprints there. They put some sort of blanket over them, so the snow won't cover them again."

I squint at the little bag, scrutinizing it. Something glitters inside it.

A tiny golden sequin.

# Jake

The Eiffel Tower is 324 meters high, weighs nearly ten thousand tons, and consists of twelve thousand iron beams, which are joined together by over two million rivets. They were all produced in Värmland. It took them two years to build it, and only one worker died during construction—and he wasn't even working when it happened. He was showing the tower to his girl a few days before it opened in 1889, trying to impress her, but fell down from the second floor and died.

He must have been very surprised. The girlfriend, too, of course.

I read all of that online.

It's important to know the background in order to make a really good copy of the Eiffel Tower.

I stare at my miniature tower, still not quite satisfied. There's something about the top section that doesn't work. It seems a little lopsided, and when I try to straighten it out with the pliers, it slants in the other direction instead.

It's really, really difficult to make it perfect, even though I've googled pictures and drawings and spent hours building this tower.

The door swings open, and Melinda comes in. She's wearing a

tight black dress that ends mid-thigh. It's cute, really cute considering it's Melinda. So cute the thought of trying it on pops into my head as soon as I see it. And then I can't stop thinking about it.

That's how it works with *The Sickness*.

It won't leave me alone. It's like a stubborn puppy who follows me around all the time, nipping at my legs. And it doesn't matter how many times I tell it to stop. That just makes it more eager, as if I were playing a game.

That's not what I want.

I want *The Sickness* to go away. Leave me alone and disappear into the forest, like that cop did.

Melinda throws her hands in front of her mouth and stops midstride. She smells like perfume and hairspray.

"Oh my God. What the hell. That's amazing! Did you build that all by yourself?"

She takes a few steps closer and trips over the mountain of butchered beer cans on the floor. They rattle around, and she grabs the edge of the desk to keep her balance.

"It's for school," I explain. "We're supposed to build something famous from recycled material."

Her eyes shine with excitement as she bends over my homemade Eiffel Tower and gently runs her finger along the top.

"It looks so real. How did you do it?"

I point to the ragged beer cans.

"Smart," Melinda says, and smiles crookedly. "Very smart. We have plenty of those around here. How do they stick together?"

"First, I built a kinda frame thing for these parts."

I point to the seam that runs around the upper edge of one of the beer cans and continue:

"It's stronger and more stable than the metal in the cans. I pounded that part down and wired those parts together with steel thread. Then I cut up pieces of thin metal and glued them to the frame."

"That's insane. You should be . . . What's it called when you draw buildings?"

"Architect?"

"Exactly. You should be an architect."

The realization that I might grow up someday hadn't occurred to me yet. And the thought of becoming an architect seems almost unimaginable.

"There are no architects in Ormberg," I say.

That's the truth.

There are only old people and the unemployed in Ormberg.

And the Stillmans, who sell dog clothes on the Internet, and the Skogs, who breed those ridiculous tiny horses. And then in the summer the Germans and Stockholmers come. They wander around in the woods in military-style clothes and paddle canoes down the creek.

And they grill.

On windless summer evenings the smell of roasted meat hangs over Ormberg, a giant cloud of smoke that stinks of BBQ.

It smells like city slickers, Dad usually says, and wrinkles his nose.

"Could you help me straighten my hair?" Melinda asks.

"Sure," I say, hoping she doesn't notice how happy that question makes me.

Boys aren't supposed to straighten hair.

Only gay hairdressers in Stockholm do stuff like that, or maybe pop stars, who want all the teenage girls to follow them on Instagram.

I go with Melinda to her room. Her floor is covered with clothes: thong underwear in bright colors and lacy bras. There's a pair of inside-out jeans draped on the chair. She picks them up and throws them across the room and they land at the foot of her bed.

The scent of perfume is even thicker in here, and the desk is covered in makeup.

So much beauty: glittery rouge, eyeliners, eye shadow in every possible color, and small mysterious tubes, all of it piled into a makeup bag with the word "Bitch" written on it.

I wish I had one just like it.

At the same time: I know that would be totally fucking mentally disturbed.

I swallow hard and grab the straighteners from the floor, get a slight whiff of burned hair and feel the warmth of the handle.

"Okay," Melinda says. "Let's go!"

She puts the top layer of her hair up in a clip, and I start to straighten. It's become a ritual of sorts for us, me helping Melinda with her hair before she goes out.

"You're sweet," she murmurs, and reaches for the nail polish.

"Where are you going?" I ask.

"Meeting Markus," she says absently while opening the nail polish and starting to paint her long pointed nails.

Markus is Melinda's boyfriend. He's eighteen and he drives an old Ford he restored himself. He bought it at the scrapyard a year ago. Melinda usually says it started as a *rust bucket,* but he turned it into *a sweet ride.*

I don't really know what I think about Markus. He never says a word when he's here, just sits with his hair hanging in front of his face. I don't even know what he looks like under that hair. Dad doesn't like him, because I've heard him and Melinda fighting about Markus many times. But I think he's mostly afraid of Melinda getting pregnant. Or that's what he yells at her. ". . . and don't expect me to support your damn kid."

"And what are you gonna do tonight?"

"Don't know," I say. "Stay home, I guess."

"You're not gonna go meet Saga?"

The thought of Saga makes my stomach flutter. As if a very small insect were crawling around in there.

"She's going to the school party."

Melinda puts down the nail polish with a bang.

"Why are they having a party in the middle of the week?" she asks. And then, more gently:

"Aren't you going?"

"Don't want to."

I don't feel like explaining it to Melinda. Don't feel like telling her what Vincent and his buddies would do to me if I went. But as usual, she understands anyway. That's Melinda's superpower. She always knows what I'm thinking, even before I do. As if my thoughts are radio waves she can receive and listen to in her head.

I suppose my superpower is building things out of old beer cans.

"It's Vincent, right?" she asks.

I don't respond. It sizzles a little as I press a damp strand of hair between the metal plates of the straightener.

"I'm gonna kill that asshole if he doesn't quit it," she growls.

"Please. Don't do anything!"

"No. I *will* kill him if he doesn't leave you alone."


After Melinda leaves, I go down to the kitchen to grab a Coke. Dad's asleep on the couch again, so I turn off the TV and throw a blanket over him. Grab a couple of empty beer cans and take them to my room.

They'll end up recycled.

But first I'm going to read some more of the diary.

I take out the book and curl up in bed. Run my hand over the brown spine.

It's really weird. When I read it, it feels like I'm *inside* Hanne's head. It's almost as if I become her, even though she's really old and a woman. As if I had Melinda's superpower and could read thoughts.

I don't even know if I like Hanne, but I feel sorry for her. It must be horrible to lose your memory and have to write down everything that happens. But she's smart—it took me a while, but then I figured out why she made the index. She can't read through the book every time she forgets some little thing.

Yes, Hanne is smart. Smart and lonely, because she can't tell anyone what she thinks.

Especially not P.

It's just like *The Sickness*, I think.

You have a secret, Hanne, and I do, too.

We've just been to the site where the body was found.

The road there: narrow, full of potholes, lined by large spruces. No buildings.

No people.

The cairn itself was two, maybe three meters wide, and twenty meters long. It consisted of tall moss-covered rocks of varying sizes.

Behind it: a slope, which turned into a steep hill—Orm Mountain.

On the other side: the dark water of the creek.

We hunched down in the moss. Trying to take in the incomprehensible. That the skeleton of a five-year-old girl was found under the stones of this cairn, with her hands clasped across her chest.

I note that the perpetrator must have been very strong, because the stones are quite large and heavy. Probably, the perpetrator had local knowledge and knew about the cairn before he buried the girl here. Finally: the fact that the girl was buried with her hands clasped says something about the perpetrator's relationship to her. It's almost tender, as if the perpetrator liked her.

We were silent for a while, until Andreas said we should go back. I noticed once more that Malin was annoyed by him.

It can't be my imagination.

No, I don't think she likes him.

ORMBERG, NOVEMBER 23

It's 3:05 A.M.

I'm sitting in a small chair, staring out the window. Puddles are growing larger on the uneven asphalt. Small, dirt-brown ponds that the clouds wrung out. They glow under the lights of the parking lot. The only car outside is ours.

I don't even know if there are any other guests here.

Beyond the parking lot: only darkness. No animals, no people, no cars passing by.

Manfred's staying at a hotel in Vingåker. He probably has the right idea. Our hotel is in the middle of nowhere, halfway between Ormberg and Vingåker.

I woke up with strange palpitations. I couldn't figure out why. Then realized it was terror, because I didn't know where I was.

My first impulse: to wake up Peter. Shake him and ask where we are. Why we're lying in this strange bed.

But I calmed down, realized that was the last thing I should do.

P absolutely cannot find out!

I concentrated on trying to remember. Got only as far as Ilulissat: the icebergs, the cold, clear air. The silky feeling that everything was perfect.

I never should have left Greenland. I was strong there.

I slid out of bed with my diary. I sat down in the chair and read. Waited for the text to provoke something, a flow of images and memories.

But not this time.

It was like reading a book for the first time. As if I hadn't experienced any of it, as if it were someone else.

Am I becoming someone else? Is that what this is? Or is it an isolated incident, an anomaly, the result of overexertion?

I couldn't sleep. Read about the investigation instead.

The police initially believed that the Ormberg Girl's death was accidental, perhaps a traffic accident, which someone tried to cover up by burying the body. But when the girl couldn't be identified, they changed their minds.

If somebody had been injured in an accident, that person would be missed—but there are no missing children in the area. Not in any neighboring towns either.

The girl isn't from Ormberg. And this was no accident.

I put the book on my lap and look at the Eiffel Tower. It shines dully in the light of the desk lamp.

Cold spreads from my stomach to my chest. What Hanne writes isn't exactly news to me, but it still makes me feel ill to think of that little girl buried in the cairn.

It's hard to understand that Hanne wrote this less than two weeks ago. That she sat in that old grocery store talking about the Ormberg Girl with her colleagues. With Malin, whom I know, even if I don't know her well. She's a lot older than me, but I know what she looks like and where her mom lives.

Hanne's story has affected me somehow. I don't really know why, but my life doesn't feel quite so hopeless anymore. Vincent and his buddies are just pathetic idiots, and though *The Sickness* is truly terrible, it's not as awful as what happened to the Ormberg Girl.

Or what happened to Mom.

*The Sickness* isn't cancer or dementia, but I still wish it would go away.

I reach for my phone to google the word "anomaly."

# Malin

I don't really know what I was thinking when I agreed to work on this investigation. It didn't really occur to me that it would mean moving home again—moving in with my mother—even if only for a short period.

But what's the alternative? The hotel in Vingåker?

No.

It would have crushed Mom. And that's the last thing I want to do. I love her. And in a strange way, I love Ormberg, too, even if I never want to live here again. The forests are magnificent, and the summers are magical—a pastoral idyll of red cottages, dark woods, and the shiny, warm water of Långsjön Lake.

And yet, I want to leave.

I can't handle all Mom's questions, can't stand the worry in her eyes every time we talk about my job.

And it's sad to see how the property has deteriorated.

I don't think anything's been done to the house since Dad died just over three years ago. Paint's peeling off outside, the window casing is hanging loose, and the yard's turned into a jungle. A drainpipe fell off, and it's still lying in the high grass, like a snake in the undergrowth, ready to strike as you pass by.

And then there's the barn.

The barn is full of Dad's old stuff. He never threw anything away. He collected everything from old home appliances to transistor radios, moth-eaten clothes, tires, broken instruments, old cross-country skis, cans of paint, and every edition of the Swedish Tourist Association's yearbook dating back to 1969. He even died carrying an old washing machine out to the barn—his heart just gave out. When Mom found him in the grass, he was still holding on to the old Electrolux, as if he were shipwrecked and the machine were his lifeboat.

Mom hasn't been able to get rid of any of the old junk stacked in the barn. It's a lifetime of rubbish, and when I go inside it's like watching an old movie. All my memories come rushing back: When I see my old bike I can still feel the pain in my wrist from driving into a ditch near the ironworks, and when I smell the fabric of the tent, I remember having sex for the first time in my sleeping bag. Feel Kenny's warmth, the scent and cold of the ground beneath the thin camping pad.

And there's the washing machine.

Mom never threw it away. She just parked it next to all the other junk in the red barn.

My sexual awakening sits next to my father's death.

The first time I brought Max to Ormberg I felt so ashamed. Even felt ashamed of my shame. I find Mom somewhat annoying, but I love her, and really there's nothing in Ormberg or my upbringing to be ashamed of. But Ormberg is everything I don't want: It's sparsely populated, unemployed, elderly. It's crumbling houses, yards littered with junk cars and rusty bathtubs that cows drink out of. And above all it's people who won't let go of the dream of what was.

I want so much more than that.

Max and Mom got along immediately, which didn't surprise me. Max is very socially gifted when he wants to be. He has the ability to ingratiate himself with people, make them feel comfortable, get them to babble on about themselves, even when they don't really have much to say.

He would have made a damn fine police officer.

But that's definitely something I don't want—a relationship with another cop. In fact, Max thinks I should go to law school when I move to Stockholm, and I think I will.

Apparently, he doesn't want to be in a relationship with a cop, either.

I park the car outside the old grocery store. A thin layer of snow covers the ground. Everything is white, and the reflection of the sunshine off the snow makes me squint. The chill nips at my cheeks. Small clouds chase each other across a mostly clear blue sky, and the wind makes the new snow dance along the ground.

It's Tuesday, and Peter will soon have been missing for four days.

I picture that friendly, trim police officer, with his grayish blond hair. His checkered flannel shirt, and his gaze that never gave an inch, no matter whom he was speaking to.

After he disappeared, we put the investigation into the Ormberg Girl aside. A murder that happened more than twenty years ago can wait a few more days.

Even though the local police are responsible for investigating Peter's disappearance, we've done everything we can to help. We joined the human search chain, met the task force leader several times, and searched Peter's and Hanne's papers for clues that might reveal what happened Friday evening.

We haven't found a thing.

Maybe that's a clue—maybe Hanne and Peter were up to something they wanted to keep from the rest of us for some reason.

Andreas waves to me as I enter. The remains of his saffron bun lie on the table. He's leaning back on his chair with his feet on the table. He's taken off his shoes, of course, but still. This is an office, an improvised one, but still a workplace, not his fucking living room. He has one arm draped over the back of the chair next to him, and he's holding his tobacco container in the other hand.

I detest men who chew tobacco.

"Hi there," he says, smiling widely so that a bit of tobacco peeks out from under his upper lip.

"Hi," I say, shrugging off my goose down jacket.

We don't get further than that before there's a knock. The door opens and a slim woman in her seventies comes into the room. Her thick gray hair sticks out like sheep's wool all over her head, and her enormous glasses fog up immediately as she enters the warm room.

Ragnhild Sahlén.

Ragnhild lives on the other side of the field, near the old TrikåKungen factory, which now houses asylum seekers. And right next to the green house where Kenny used to live.

As usual when I think of my former boyfriend, my stomach twists uneasily. We were together from the time I was fifteen until that rainy night in October 2011. I was seventeen and not at all mature enough to handle something like that.

But could you ever be?

"Hello, Ragnhild," I say.

Ragnhild takes off her glasses and rubs them on her shirt, which sticks out from beneath her coat.

Before retiring, she worked as a middle school teacher in Vingåker. In her old age she's become involved with the local heritage association, which consists of three old people from Ormberg. I don't really know what they do, but from what I understand they're very committed to preserving the ironworks—they want to renovate it and open a museum there, and they're constantly battling the county to get more money for the project.

"Malin. *Dear girl*. It's been ages."

"It's been two years," I clarify.

"You should come home more often," she mutters, and puts on her glasses again. "Seems like the old place needs some repairs."

Do I look like a fucking carpenter? I want to ask her. But of course I don't, because it's not the house she's talking about, it's my mother. What she's trying to say is that *Mom* needs me. And maybe she's right, but the last thing *I* need is to rot away in Ormberg.

"What can we help you with?" Andreas asks, his feet still on the table.

"I'm here to report a robbery," Ragnhild says, stiffening her back a little.

"I'm sorry," I say, "but we're working on an investigation into the murder of the Ormberg Girl. You'll have to go to Vingåker to report that. If they're open—"

"I've never heard such nonsense," Ragnhild interrupts me. "Why in the world would you dig up that old story? It won't lead to anything. But here *I* am, a person in need of real help, and *I* have to go to Vingåker. Does that sound fair to you?"

"I'm sorry," I say, doing my best to sound understanding though I really just want her to leave.

Ragnhild doesn't answer, just gets a thoughtful, almost sneaky, look on her face, as if trying to figure out how to neutralize my arguments.

"What happened?" Andreas asks, and I want to give him a hard kick on the thigh, but I'm too far away.

"It's one of those immigrants staying at refugee housing. A young man. *A Muslim*. I saw him riding a stolen bike. One of those racing bikes, like they use in the Tour de France."

The idea of Ragnhild watching the Tour de France is so absurd I can't help but smile.

"So you saw this guy steal a bike?" Andreas asks, still not seeming to understand that Ragnhild will never let go of us if we entertain her complaints. She is a force of nature—much stronger and more persistent than superglue. We'll end up spending the rest of our time here running after lost cats and graffiti artists.

Ragnhild takes off her giant glasses again, rubs her eyes, and shifts her weight nervously from one foot to the other. Small puddles of snow spread beneath her boots.

"No, I said I saw him *with* a stolen bike," she says.

"And who owned the bike?" Andreas says, and reaches for his notepad.

"How should I know that?"

Ragnhild's throat is becoming red and splotchy.

Andreas pauses and looks confused.

"Then how do you know it was stolen?" he asks. "If you didn't recognize the bike and didn't see him steal it."

Ragnhild squeezes her glasses hard in her hand and clears her throat.

"It goes without saying. Those people couldn't afford racing bikes. He must have stolen it. And if the county paid for that fancy bike, then I plan to sue them—that's *my* money they stole. I've paid taxes my whole life. Do you know what a bike like that costs? *I* know, because Siv's daughter has one and it cost twenty thousand kronor."

Andreas and I exchange a look.

"Like I said, Ragnhild," I say. "I'm very sorry, but we have a lot to do. You'll have to talk to the police in Vingåker if you want to make a report."

It takes another ten minutes to get rid of Ragnhild. As she leaves, she slams the door behind her so hard that something falls to the floor in the old store area.

Neither of us goes to investigate what it is.

"*What a bitch!*" Andreas says, emphasizing every word.

I shrug.

"Ragnhild is . . . Ragnhild."

"I'm not saying she's not right," he continues, drumming his pen on the table.

"Sure. Even Ragnhild is capable of being right. Sometimes."

"We have quite a lot of problems with one of the refugee residencies outside Örebro," Andreas says. "But mostly threats and fights. Nobody gets along, that sort of thing."

"You'd think they'd try a little harder," I say. "Since we let them come here. Even if they went through tough stuff and all that. Because they did, of course. I know that."

I think about what I've seen on the news. Images of bombs falling on Aleppo and children washing up dead on Mediterranean beaches. It makes me feel so bad I turn it off. No one should have to leave their home because of war and starvation, especially not little children. But at the same time we can't take in everyone. We're just a small country, and we're a hell of a long way from those conflicts.

Besides, they'd probably feel better in a place with a culture more like their own. Sweden is a developed and equitable country. Women have the same rights as men. Just the thought of somebody trying to force me into a burka pisses me off.

And if our country has to take them: Why Ormberg, why this small, remote town, with so many problems of its own? Why not a bigger city, with good infrastructure and jobs?

Some *other* place.

"What are you thinking about?" Andreas asks.

I shake my head.

"Nothing. Any news on Peter?"

Andreas shakes his head sadly.

"No. I just talked to Svante. It's as if he's gone up in smoke. Two-day search and the only thing they found is a . . . *fucking sequin*."

We both fall silent, and Peter's face appears before me again.

They're an odd couple, Peter and Hanne. Not just because she's older. Hanne seems to be the one in charge, even though she doesn't say much. Peter follows her around like an obedient dog.

He seems very attached to her. Nothing he says exactly, but it's still obvious. The way he puts his jacket over her shoulders when it's cold in the office. How he goes to Vingåker to buy that tea she likes. How his eyes follow her when she moves around the room.

Yes, I'm sure he loves her.

"What do you think of what she had written on her hand?" Andreas asks.

I shrug and try to sort my thoughts. Concentrate on the ink numbers on Hanne's injured hand.

"Maybe it's part of a phone number. Or a code of some kind. Something she didn't want to forget, but couldn't or didn't want to write in her book."

"GPS coordinates?" Andreas suggests.

"No, that doesn't make sense. Not for anywhere in Söderman-land anyway. I checked."

Andreas flips through his notebook.

"Svante finally got the information from the cell phone opera-tors," he says. "Neither Peter nor Hanne went to Katrineholm on Friday night, despite what they told you. Or at least their phones stayed here in Ormberg. Hanne's phone made contact with the tower next to the highway Friday night, around seven o'clock. It's been quiet since then. And Peter's phone made contact with the same tower around eight. I don't know how to interpret that, but I don't think they left Ormberg. And I've gone through their call records and text messages over the last few days. You can check, too, but I couldn't find anything strange. And Peter's bank card hasn't been used since Friday."

"So what were they doing in the woods?" I ask.

"Yes, what the hell were they doing in the woods? I also talked to the technicians. There was actually some kind of print in the field near where Hanne was found. Someone had tramped around through the mud in high heels. Right where they found that se-quin."

"So she was right, the woman who found Hanne," I say. "There was another woman there, in a sequin dress and high heels."

"Seems likely. But it doesn't help us now. There are too many unanswered questions. Where did Hanne and Peter go? Where is Peter now? *Who* was the woman in the dress? What was *she* doing in the woods? And where in the *hell* is Peter's car?"

We fall silent for a while, united in almost palpable frustration.

Then Andreas looks at me, leans back a little on his chair and smiles.

"Malin," he says, as if he's just thought of something important.

"Yes?"

"How about we go to Vingåker and get a beer tonight?"

My temples burn, and I can feel my annoyance spring to life again, just when I was almost starting to like him.

"I can't tonight."

I hesitate for a moment, but then go on:

"Besides, I'm engaged, and I'm moving to Stockholm in five months."

*"And?"*

Andreas's smile grows wider. He drops the pen on the table and slowly runs a hand over his stubble, then takes the tobacco out of his mouth with his thumb and index finger and puts it into its container.

He disgusts me.

Everything about him disgusts me: his self-satisfied smile, the tobacco, and his arrogant way of ignoring my refusal. As if our conversation were just a game, just studied and elaborate foreplay.

"You think you're irresistible, huh?"

Andreas doesn't look away while he answers:

"No, but I think you are."

That stumps me.

Before I'm able to formulate a devastating comeback, I hear the door open and heavy steps approaching from the other room.

Andreas doesn't react. Instead, he continues smiling at me, as if I were some kind of animal on display. A cat with five legs or a calf with two heads.

It infuriates me.

Manfred enters, and I force myself to push down my rage. I've seen his sharp look when Andreas and I squabbled in the past. That look made it clear he wouldn't put up with any fights.

Manfred stands in the middle of the floor, slowly unbuttoning his coat, and observing us in silence. His pants are dripping. Then he sits down on one of the chairs, leans forward and looks at Andreas and then at me a second later.

"Our colleagues have found a body at the cairn," he says.

*"Peter?"* I whisper, and feel my stomach cramp up.

Manfred shakes his head and looks at me with an empty, somber expression.

"No. A woman."

"But . . . ?"

I have no words when I realized the significance of what he's saying.

*"But?"* I say again.

"We're headed there now," Manfred says.

# Jake

The school bus drops us off near downtown Ormberg.

Saga and I stop outside the old grocery store, and the other kids head off in various directions.

Dad says the best thing about Ormberg is the nature around here. It's the most beautiful place in Sweden. And hunting, of course; there's plenty of deer, moose, and wild boar. I don't agree—I think the best thing about this place is all the empty old houses you can hang out in. Until just a few months ago, Saga and I used to hang out in the grocery store after school, but then somebody put a huge padlock on the door.

And now the building is full of cops.

Saga pokes her foot at the snow, pushes her pink hair out of her face, and stares in through the big, dirty shop windows.

There are some lamps on in the back—warm light spills out over the floor of the shop room and I can just make out a portable heater on the floor. Somebody cleaned up inside as well: All the old beer cans and newspapers are gone.

"Do you think they'll find him?" Saga asks.

I stare at the cars parked outside and think of P, Hanne's boyfriend, who disappeared in the woods. And I think of all those people looking for him: the national guard and those weird organizations who search for missing people.

Dad says it's only a matter of time before they find him frozen to death. He says nobody could survive that many nights in the forest at this time of year, especially not some city slicker with no equipment or experience.

"What if somebody murdered him," Saga says, leaning toward the window, holding her hands on either side of her face while peeking in.

Then she seems to lose interest in the store, pushes her hands into her coat pockets, and turns to me again.

"What if a murderer lives in Ormberg?" she continues quietly, as if she's afraid someone might hear her. "What if it's the same guy who killed that little girl by the cairn?"

"A murderer? *Here?* Are you kidding me? Besides, it's been forever since that little girl died."

Saga seems a bit self-conscious, shrugs.

"Why not? Mom says Gunnar would kill a person without blinking."

"Gunnar Sten? Isn't he, like, a hundred?"

"That's what I mean. He's old enough to have killed that girl twenty-odd years ago. And he's a mean bastard. Apparently, he almost beat a boy to death by the lake when he was young. Whacked him on the head with a stone until he was unconscious."

"Really?"

Saga nods earnestly, and her gaze meets mine. In the dusk her eyes are almost green.

"Well?" she asks. "Who do you think it could have been?"

I ponder the question for a moment. I can't think of anybody in Ormberg who could kill someone. All the people who live around here are so incredibly normal and boring. Sure there are a few crazy old ladies and men. But most are just regular people.

Except for the refugees, of course. I don't know them, the ones who live in the old TrikåKungen factory. We never go there.

"The Skog family?" she suggests.

I nod slowly.

The Skog family lives in the old manor house by the lake. They're from Stockholm, raise horses, and never hang out with people from the village. Dad says they're "too fancy" for that. I don't really know what that means—I don't get what's fancy about spending your time in horse stalls mucking up shit all day.

Obviously, they're nuts.

But are they murderers?

I shake my head.

"I know," Saga says. *"Ragnhild Sahlén!"*

"Oh, come on. That old shrew?"

But Saga tugs on my sleeve enthusiastically and continues:

"You know she killed her brother."

"Didn't he cut his own leg off with a chain saw?"

Saga's grip on my arm tightens, and she drags me closer, then whispers:

"Well, that's because Ragnhild was standing next to him nagging his head off. And apparently she used his ashes as fertilizer for her raspberry bushes. Then she made jam from the berries and gave it to his girlfriend."

"You must be kidding?"

Saga shakes her head.

"I swear to God. Or, it could be René Stillman," she says, smiling conspiratorially and narrowing her eyes a bit.

"And why would *she* kill a cop?"

"She's earned a lot of money on those dog clothes. Millions. She's even gonna build a pool this spring."

"Yes, but why would that mean she's a murderer?"

Saga shrugs, a bit offended. Wraps her coat tighter around her body and stands with her back to the ice-cold wind.

"I don't know. Do you have any better suggestions?"

I don't.

Ormberg is the opposite of exciting. I can't imagine a murderer hiding in one of those red cottages scattered around in the woods. Or that anyone I've known forever could be capable of taking a person's life.

"One of the refugees, maybe?" I suggest.

Saga shakes her head.

"They just got here. The little girl died a looong time ago."

She's right. It's unlikely it would be one of the refugees.

The door to the old grocery store swings open with a creak, and a man around Dad's age comes out. He's large and stout and dressed like the stockbrokers in the TV show I started watching yesterday. His brown coat stretches across his stomach as he turns to us.

Behind him come a younger, dark-haired man and Malin, who's a cop now and thinks she's *so damn special* just because she works in Katrineholm.

Or that's what Dad says.

They jog over to a large black SUV parked nearby.

"*Shit,* why are *they* in such a hurry," Saga says.

"Maybe something happened."

We turn around and start walking.

Saga tosses her schoolbag onto her shoulder.

"I can go over to your house for a while," she says. "Mom's not home yet—she's meeting Björn."

Björn Falk is Saga's mother's new boyfriend. He's a jerk, wears a baseball cap year-round, and drives a fancy car he bought with his inheritance, which won't last long.

"Should I?" Saga says. "Hang out at your house, I mean."

I think about Dad, the stacks of beer cans and the mountain of trash in the kitchen. Or the couch in the living room, which he's turned into a bed, and the checkered blanket he always has around his shoulders.

"Maybe. I have to talk to Dad first. I'll text you."

Saga nods and hunches over against the wind.

"Talk later?"

"Sure."

She disappears in the direction of the church. Her shoulders bob up and down as she hurries home.


Dad is indeed asleep on the couch when I get home. I can hear him snoring from the front hall. It sounds like there's a big cat lying in the darkness, growling as I enter the room. The scent of sweat, warm beer, and old food permeate the air. The checkered blanket has slid down onto the floor and lies in a heap near his feet.

When I bend down to pick it up, I see something peeking out from under the couch. I sink down, stretch my hand, and my fingers meet a cold cylindrical metal object.

It takes a moment for me to realize it's the barrel of a hunting rifle.

Why is there a rifle under the couch?

Dad doesn't have a gun license, but now and then he borrows a rifle from Olle and goes hunting anyway. But surely he hasn't been out hunting lately?

As I gently push the rifle back under the sofa until the barrel is no longer visible, it scrapes against the wood floor. Dad moves a little and mumbles something in his sleep.

Melinda enters the room with her hand raised, as if she wants to signal to me to be quiet.

"Don't wake him up," she whispers. "He was in a really shitty mood, but I made him some food, and he finally went to sleep."

When she says this it occurs to me that we talk about Dad like he's a little kid. As if Melinda and I were his parents.

We go back to the hall again.

"Did something happen?"

"What do you mean?" Melinda asks.

"I mean since he was in such a bad mood."

"Oh. I don't really know. He didn't want to talk about it. But he did that thing, you know, that he does when he doesn't feel good. Where he paces around the living room."

Something cold spreads through my chest. I don't want Dad to feel bad, especially not when he has a rifle under the couch. But I convince myself there must be a perfectly natural explanation for why a gun is lying there. Maybe he was planning to go hunting with Olle.

"He ate all the food, by the way," Melinda says, and heads up the stairs. "But check the fridge. I think there are coconut balls."

I enter the kitchen and open the refrigerator. Reach for a pack of coconut balls, take out three, and pour myself a glass of Coke. Then I pound on the built-in ice machine until a few pieces come out.

I hurry up to my room—all day I've been wondering how things were going to turn out for Hanne. I almost couldn't wait to get home so I could keep reading her story.

I take out the diary and sit down in bed. Flip to the page I dog-eared, and push a coconut ball into my mouth.

Morning.

The worst has happened!

I was so terribly tired when the clock rang. Didn't wake up. When I finally opened my eyes, P was sitting naked in the small chair by the window.

He was reading the diary!

I screamed. Jumped out of bed. Ran over to P and tore the diary out of his hands.

P didn't try to stop me, he just looked at me with a mixture of astonishment and fear. It took me a moment to realize he truly was afraid. Terrified. Perhaps that's not so strange—I've always been the emotionally stronger one of the two of us. Calm & reliable.

What will happen when I'm not strong anymore? How will P manage? Who will be his rock when I'm not here anymore?

We just had breakfast. P squeezed my hand tight. Told me he loved me, and nothing would ever change that.

That made me happy, of course, but at the same time I felt caught in the act, and so humiliated. As if I'd stolen money from his wallet, even though he was the one who read MY diary.

Isn't it strange that illness comes with such shame!

At the office.

We just had a meeting. We continued reviewing the case: the medical examiner's reports, the forensic investigation, the interviews.

Manfred spoke with the former head of the investigation, a retired prosecutor. He said he'd "never bought the traffic accident theory." He believed it was a pedophile.

I'm a bit skeptical of that hypothesis. Either way: Our important task at the moment is to identify the girl.

We have a meeting booked with the medical examiner to learn more about the Ormberg Girl. Manfred is especially interested in an old injury on her wrist. He thinks it might help us identify her. Apparently, it wasn't looked into during the original investigation. Manfred was upset about that. Called the old investigative group a "an aggravating collection of incompetent sluggards."

Maybe he's right.

I HOPE he's right. Otherwise, we don't have much to go on.

# Malin

We park at the back of a line of cars on the side of a country road.

It's almost completely dark now. It must be colder, too, because the chill hurts my cheeks. The snow crunches beneath our feet as we make our way toward the edge of the woods.

Manfred points his big flashlight at the trees and steps over the small ditch that separates the country road from the woods.

The cairn.

I think of all the times we came out here as teenagers. Not just that fateful evening when we found the Ormberg Girl, but all the other times. Foggy spring days when the frost still held the ground captive in its cold jaws. Warm, starry August nights when my friends and I tried to conjure up the spirits we thought lived out here. I remember how we moved a drinking glass from one letter to another on a wrinkled sheet of paper with the help of a single finger, under the light of candle, while the mosquitoes ate us alive.

Where did the story of the Ghost Child come from anyway? And *when* did it start? I have to ask Mom about it.

"What do we know about the dead woman?" Andreas asks. "Could it be the woman in the sequin dress?"

"We don't know shit," Manfred says, trudging through the snow in his shiny dress shoes.

He really doesn't fit in here—you can't lumber around in the snow wearing hand-sewn Italian shoes without looking like a complete ass. Besides, you'll freeze your toes off.

Even a Stockholmer should know that.

The spruce branches bend under the weight of the snow. It's as beautiful as a postcard and completely silent, as if the forest itself were asleep.

Manfred makes his way with surprising ease over the terrain. His long legs stride smoothly over the snowy stumps and stones.

Andreas turns back toward me.

I meet his eyes. My foot sinks through the snow, down into a small hole.

Andreas stops and offers me a hand.

I nod a thank-you, just as a branch snaps into my face and powdery new snow falls down the back of my neck. I push my hands deep into my pockets, trying my best to warm them up. I forgot my gloves in the car.

Then the woods thin out, and I see some lights shining between the spruces. Soon we're at the edge of a clearing that's bathed in light. The silhouette of Orm Mountain rises in front of us, its peak towering up into the night sky. It's impossible to say where the mountain ends and the darkness begins.

As if Orm Mountain were connected to the sky.

The cairn stands in front of us under a layer of snow. Large portable floodlights have been placed at the edge of the clearing, and three people in white coveralls and surgical masks are hunched down near them. One of them is holding a large camera, and I see a big bag in the snow a few meters away.

Forensic technicians.

Our colleagues from the local police are already in place and blue-and-white barricade tape flutters in the wind. The flash of the camera blinks again and again.

Manfred turns to me and Andreas. His face reveals nothing of what he feels, but I can see him clenching and unclenching his fists as if he's squeezing a ball.

Of course, we're infinitely grateful it's not Peter who's been found dead in the snow. But at the same time the situation feels absurd: Hundreds of people have searched through these woods for him for two days. And when they finally find a body, it's somebody else.

We head toward Svante.

He raises his hand when he sees us.

Svante is wearing the same colorful homemade stocking cap as before. His beard is frosted, and I'm reminded once again of Santa. A real, old-fashioned Santa Claus who arrives with sacks full of gifts, who lets all the children sit in his lap.

I notice Svante glancing at Manfred's expensive coat. At the pocket handkerchief sticking out of the breast pocket like a thirsty exotic plant.

"What the hell is going on?" Manfred asks, nodding at the body at the edge of the woods, running a hand over his beard, which makes a scraping sound against his glove.

He continues:

"We're searching for a missing colleague, and find a woman who's been shot instead."

Svante nods. "Yep. And all I can do is agree. It's damn weird. I'll brief you on it in a moment. But there's something else. We found something after I called you."

Manfred wrinkles his forehead and arches his back so that his coat stretches across his stomach.

"What?"

Svante waves for us to follow and heads for something that looks like a big suitcase in black plastic. It stands in the snow, next to one of the floodlights.

He bends forward and takes out a transparent plastic bag. Then he hands it to Manfred and turns the flashlight toward the bag so we can see.

Manfred examines the contents. Inside is a blue sneaker, covered with big brown stains. Clumps of partially melted snow lie next to the shoe.

I gasp.

"That's Hanne's shoe," I say.

Manfred nods.

"Hanne?" Svante says. "The one who lost her memory?"

"Yes," Manfred says. "Where did you find it?"

"About twenty meters from the body. Just inside the woods. We never would have found it under the snow if it hadn't been for Rocky. Our dog."

Manfred meets my eyes, then shakes his head in disbelief as if he's having a hard time accepting it's actually Hanne's shoe.

"How the hell did it get here?" Manfred says, and hands it back to Svante.

And then:

"We're gonna go talk to Hanne again when we're done here. It's worth a try."

Manfred is quiet for a moment, as if working through something, his eyes turned toward Orm Mountain. A lonely snowflake sticks to his beard. He brushes it away and continues:

"Can you sum up what we know so far?"

"A K9 unit found her at two-oh-five in the afternoon," Svante says, and nods toward the dead woman under the bright shine of the floodlights. "The medical examiner believes she's been dead for at least three days, maybe four. The temperatures dropped on Sunday, so if she'd been out here longer the body would be in worse shape. And if she'd been here for a shorter time, the snow cover on her would have been thinner. Only one of her feet stuck out from under the tree, but it was covered in snow."

Manfred looks thoughtful.

"Didn't they search this area yesterday?"

"Yes," Svante says. "But they must have missed her. Probably because she was hidden."

Manfred falls silent. He eyes sweep across the scene, and he nods curtly.

"You say she's been here three to four days? That means she must have died on Friday or Saturday."

Andreas clears his throat.

"That's exactly when . . ."

His words trail off, and he looks over at the floodlight-bathed bundle in the snow.

"When Peter disappeared," Manfred says quietly. "It can't be a coincidence that Hanne's shoe was here. What do we know about the victim?"

"Not much," Svante says. "Female. Around fifty years old. Barefoot, thinly dressed. Shot in the chest and blunt force trauma to the head."

"Shot *and* beaten?"

Manfred seems surprised.

"Correct," Svante says. "Shall we go take a look at her, and I'll tell you more?"

There's a flash as the technician takes another photo. Manfred's face looks swollen and tired in that intense light.

Andreas stares down at the snow-covered stones and then turns his eyes up toward the sky.

"What is it about this fucking place?" he says, and nods to the mound of stones.

Nobody answers, because what is there to say? The feeling that Ormberg's evil is centered in this cairn is hard to shake.

I think of the Ormberg Girl, and memories flood over me with surprising force. When I close my eyes, I can almost feel Kenny's warm hand in mine, hear the quiet clink of the beer cans in his plastic bag. I remember the ferns' small, divided leaves tickling my thigh as I squatted down to pee, and how my fingers brushed against something white and smooth between the stones.

And now this.

It all seems to be centered here, at an ancient cairn in a clearing in the woods.

It has to mean something, but what?

Svante takes off his gloves and puts his hands on his bright red cheeks, trying to warm them.

"Let's go," Manfred says, and walks ahead of us toward the woods.

We take turns approaching the body, because there isn't enough room on the plastic disks the technicians have placed on the snow. Svante goes first, stands next to the body and waves to me and Manfred.

The plastic bends under our weight.

When we get there we each stand on our own plastic disk and crouch down.

Branches have been cut from the bottom of the tree in order to get to the body. They lie in a pile just a few meters away, next to a tarp with sawdust on it, which I suppose they used to protect the body when they were sawing off the branches.

There she lies, beneath what's left of the tree, with her face turned away from us. Her hands are folded across her chest.

Ice crystals cover her clothes and the very pale skin of her throat, hands, and feet, making it shimmer under the bright lights.

The woman is wearing a pair of black sweatpants and a jean shirt that's way too big for her. A large, dark spot spreads out across her chest. She's barefoot, and her thin gray hair is long, probably waist-length.

When I see the bloody, formless flesh that was once her face, I feel my knees start to buckle.

*Just like Kenny.*

Near her head lies a rock, also bloody.

I turn away, a wave of nausea washing over me.

"You said the medical examiner's been here?" Manfred says, apparently unaffected.

"Right," Svante says.

"And?"

"Shot and killed, and then received blunt force trauma to the head."

"In *that* order?" Manfred asks.

"Yes. Otherwise, there would have been significantly more bleeding from the wounds on the head. But we'll see what the autopsy shows."

"Hmmm," Manfred says. "And we have no idea who she is?"

"Not the faintest."

Manfred turns to me.

"Anyone you recognize from Ormberg?"

I force myself to look at the woman again. At the hair flowing out into the snow. Push away the memory of Kenny.

The woman doesn't look the least bit familiar.

Even though her face is destroyed beyond recognition, I'm sure she's not from Ormberg. I would have recognized her.

"She's not from here," I say, considering the unimaginable co-incidence of two murder victims found in the same place, eight years apart.

"Any ballistic findings?" Manfred asks, turning to Svante again.

"The gunshot wound in the chest comes from a rifle, that much we know. But we haven't found any cartridges or cases."

"Could the shooting be hunting-related?" Manfred asks.

"It's not very likely that somebody would accidentally shoot a woman wandering around barefoot in the woods, is it?"

Svante laughs a little at his own comment, but Manfred doesn't seem to be amused.

"Are there a lot of guns around here? Do a lot of people hunt?"

Svante laughs even louder now, and I know why. Manfred's comment reveals just how little he knows about Ormberg.

"Lord. If I had a penny for every rifle hidden in a house out here . . ."

Manfred nods. Then he cocks his head and leans in toward the body on the ground.

"The face is pretty badly damaged."

I force myself to look at the woman's face again. It's a formless red mass of crushed tissue. Her eyes are two wells of frozen blood.

I sway and almost fall off the plastic disk. The forest spins around me, and my mouth goes dry.

Manfred grabs my shoulders.

"If you're going to puke, please do it elsewhere," he says drily.

"No, I'm okay."

I'm not okay, but I can't exactly say that to Manfred. This is exactly what I wanted: hunting down real criminals, working on the worst crimes.

And now I've gotten far more than I wished for.

It's one thing to see dead people in a picture, or even on an autopsy table—the clinical environment takes the edge off of the horror.

But this.

I glance at the woman's face again. At the fleshy, bloody hollows in her face. A tiny piece of bark sticks out of one cavity.

The thought of Kenny pops into my head again and the nausea returns.

"A horrible way to die," Svante mutters.

Neither Manfred nor I answer, but I think he's absolutely right.

It's so wrong, so unfair, so against nature.

The woman on the ground isn't old. She could have lived for many more years if someone hadn't believed they had the right to take her life.

She was someone's daughter, maybe even someone's mother or sister.

Now she's nothing, just a pile of frozen meat under a mutilated spruce.

The snow has started to fall again. The wind catches the flakes, and they dance around us where we squat.

The flash of a camera lights up the scene.

"Can you walk me through what we know about what happened?" Manfred asks, rising with some effort.

For a moment, I think the plastic disk might break under his weight.

Svante and I rise, too.

"Probably shot first and then placed here, under the tree. Then the face was beaten. We believe that stone was used."

We look over at the bloody stone—the size of a grapefruit—lying next to the head of the woman.

Another flash lights up the glade.

"Interesting," Manfred says, looking at the body in the snow and cocking his head to the side.

I squeeze my eyes shut, but the outlines of the dead woman are burned into my retina by the flash. The holes that were once her eyes stare back at me.

"Any footprints? Can we see which direction the victim or perpetrator came from?"

Svante shakes his head, making the tassel on his stocking cap bounce from side to side.

"There was no snow this weekend, so . . ."

Manfred nods.

"Of course. Damn, I didn't think of that."

The forest starts to spin again, and I grab Manfred's shoulder. Another flash.

I close my eyes, feel the nausea coming. Sob and turn around. Make my way over the plastic disks as fast as I can, jogging toward Andreas, who's still standing next to the floodlights.

"You okay?" he asks as I squeeze by him.

"Fine," I say.

"Are you sure?"

I take one more step. Heaving again.

More flashes.

Even though my eyes are closed, I can't turn off the image of that scene.

"I told you I'm fine."

"Malin. The technicians need to swab us."

"Why?"

"It's routine. We may have contaminated the crime scene. They save our DNA in the elimination register."

"Whatever," I say, and open my mouth as the young woman in white clothes comes over.

She puts the Q-tip into my mouth and rubs it against the inside of my cheek.

Andreas is approaching behind me. The snow crunches under his steps.

"Are you done?" I ask the technician.

"Yes, thank you," she says, sticking the Q-tip into a small bag.

I nod, turn around, and vomit into the snow.


I don't stop shaking until I'm in bed in my childhood bedroom with a down-filled blanket pulled up to my nose.

Mom's hand rests heavily on my shoulder as she scrutinizes me worriedly.

"Are you sure you don't want a cup of tea?"

"Yes. I just want to sleep. But thanks anyway."

Mom nods. Bends down, gives me a light kiss on my cheek, and strokes my nose with her finger, just like she always used to when I was little.

I feel the warmth of her hand radiating against my cheek and inhale the familiar, comforting smell of soap and cooking that is her. Part of me wants to reach for her and keep her here, as if I were still a little child and she were my only real security.

But instead I lie still, watch her leave the room and close the door gently behind her.

Outside, the darkness presses against the window like a big black animal, and for a moment I'm afraid that the panes might break under its weight, and the winter night might flow like cold water into a sinking ship.

I knew it would be like this—that this investigation would drag up so much shit I've spent years trying to forget.

I squeeze my eyes shut, and moments later I see him in front of me.

*Kenny.*

The sandy, somewhat stringy hair. The slanted green eyes and high cheekbones. Hands that were hard and lips that were soft. Arms pocked with mosquito bites, and his back slick with sweat as we made love.

That night, when we found the skeleton, we'd just started dating. I don't even remember if we'd had sex yet.

We were together for two years—a long time for anyone but an eternity at that age. We weren't that compatible, and yet I was so in love with him I almost peed my pants every time I saw him.

I don't want to, but no matter how hard I struggle to suppress it, I can't help thinking about that autumn evening when it all went to hell.

We'd been partying at the old mill. Me, Kenny, Anders, and two other girls. Kenny had brought along two bottles of moonshine he'd nicked from his dad, and everyone was trashed.

Everyone except Anders, who was taking some kind of antibiotics for tonsillitis, which absolutely couldn't be mixed with alcohol.

As I remember it, we had quite a bit of fun, at least until one of the girls vomited into Kenny's hair and he had to wash it out in the ice-cold water of the creek.

After that, the party was over.

Anders, who'd just gotten a driver's license, was assigned to drive Kenny's dad's old Renault home.

I remember the mood started getting better as soon as we got into the car, as if the warmth of that cramped compartment reawakened our desire to party.

Kenny, who sat in the passenger seat in the front, turned the radio up all the way, rolled down the windows to blast the music out, and shouted that he wanted a beer.

I found some beer cans on the floor, picked one up and handed it to him from my place right behind him, and then . . .

It was just some stupid whim. A terrible and bizarre event that would have a huge impact on the next few years of my life.

For some reason, Kenny got the idea that we should lean out the front and back passenger-side windows and I should hand the beer to him that way. So he unbuckled his seatbelt, got up on his wobbly legs, and hunched over so as not to hit the ceiling. Then he stuck his head and his upper body out the window.

I did the same from the back, then opened a beer can and stretched it toward Kenny.

I remember we both shouted loudly and toasted, our hair flapping in the wind, rain whipping against our faces.

We were just some drunk kids in the middle of nowhere who had no idea our youth was about to end in less than a minute.

The road in front of us was a blur of darkness and rain that autumn evening. Kenny's upper body was still sticking outside the window when I sensed something next to the road, maybe a hundred meters in front of us. I shouted at Kenny to watch out and got back down into my seat. But instead of doing the same, Kenny turned and stared forward, in the direction we were driving.

That was it.

A bunch of overgrown children. An idiotic game.

Then came the thud.

Maybe the weather made it impossible for Anders to see, or

maybe he was distracted by what was happening inside the car. Whatever it was, he didn't notice the timber trailer that someone had parked next to the road while we were partying.

We didn't crash into the trailer, we just passed very close by it. Close enough for Kenny to be hit in the face by one of the logs.

Afterward he looked like the woman at the cairn.

Afterward his face was gone.

# Jake

S o freakin' cool!"
Saga leans over the Eiffel Tower, examining the middle section and smiling widely. Her pink hair is almost luminous in the light of the desk lamp. Outside it's dark. Neither the forest nor the creek is visible, only a blackness that turns the window into a mirror.

I never texted Saga—I forgot after I found Dad's rifle under the couch. But she came anyway; she just showed up.

Because Saga doesn't ask for permission.

She does what she wants, and if you want to hang out with her, you have to accept that.

"Thank you," I say, looking at the Eiffel Tower.

"And you only used beer cans?"

"And some glue and wire."

"So cool. You are a genius! You know that, right?"

She gives me a quick hug, and then our eyes meet.

Something knots inside my stomach. I don't know what to say. That happens pretty often with Saga: that I sort of lose my train of thought. Either because what she says is so crazy, or because she stands close to me and looks at me. It's not uncomfortable, but it feels like I've got a mouthful of rocks and my legs get warm and soft, like cooked spaghetti.

Saga bounds across the room, jumps onto the bed, and sits cross-legged. Then she says:

"You're definitely gonna get an A for that. *Sweet!*"

I go over to the bed and gently sit down at the other end, as far away from her as I can.

"Do you think I should paint it?"

She grimaces.

"Why?"

"The real Eiffel Tower is painted. It was dark red in the beginning, and now it's brown."

She moves closer to me, and my stomach flips again.

"Of course you shouldn't paint it. Then you wouldn't be able to see what it's made of. That's the whole point—it's made of beer cans. We're supposed to recycle something. That's the assignment."

My body feels stiff, and I try to force it to relax. I lean back, but I end up askew and have to put my hand on the wall to support myself. But that position feels weird, too: unnatural, uncomfortable, and above all embarrassing.

"What did you build?" I ask.

"Oh, well, I haven't come up with anything good yet. First, I wanted to build something out of tampons. They're terrible for the environment. Do you know how many tampons are sold every year?"

"No."

"Exactly. *Nobody* thinks about it. But you can't recycle used tampons."

Saga makes a disgusted expression and twirls the ring in her nose.

"Anyway," she continues, "I thought I'd make a dress of those empty pillboxes. You know, from medicines. Mom has fibromyalgia and takes a lot of drugs, so I collected the empty boxes.

Have a whole bag at home. They are pretty nice, actually. Silver—shiny, sort of."

"Good idea."

I move farther up in the bed and lean against the wall. Saga feels dangerously close, but I can't sit bent over like a cheese doodle.

"But guess what? It's not enough! You can't even make a skirt out of them. Imagine, a whole bag isn't enough."

"Maybe you can build something else from them?"

Saga sighs and leans against the wall next to me. She's so close I can feel the warmth of her body against my cheek and hear her breath.

It's as if there are two dueling voices in my head. One wants me to move away from her, and one wants me to stay: next to her breath and warmth and the slight scent of her citrus perfume.

"Fuck. I'm not gonna have time," she mumbles.

"I'll help you."

She turns her face toward mine. We're so close now that our noses almost touch. I look straight into her bright eyes, see the freckles under her makeup and the thick black eyeliner that turns up like bird wings.

And then she does it.

Slowly, she leans forward and kisses me. When her lips touch mine, it's as if something inside my body explodes. The only thing that exists is Saga's soft mouth against mine. This kiss is so light you can barely feel it. A kiss I might have thought I'd imagined if my lips didn't burn like I just drank something hot.

I don't want to move away anymore.

The voice in my head that thought I was too close is silent. It's given way to something else. I want to grab her, drag her close to me, and kiss her again. But I don't dare, of course. Instead, I sit as still as I can, as if my life depended on it.

"You're the best," she says, and she sounds like she means it.

. . .

After Saga leaves, I sit for a long time in bed with my fingers on my lips. They feel just like before, and yet everything is different.

I wonder if we're together now, or if everything will be the same as before when we meet again.

I wonder if I'm in love.

How can I tell? All I know is that it felt good everywhere, and that it changed me. Like I became someone else. As if the cells in my body exchanged places, though I look the same on the outside.

But what I wonder most is if Saga is in love with me. I think so, but would she still like me if she knew about *The Sickness*?

Probably not.

I put it out of my mind—it's too confusing—and take out Hanne's diary again. I almost feel bad that I haven't finished reading it yet, because in some mysterious way I feel like I know her now. Almost as if she's my friend for real, just because I've read her notes.

And you don't leave a good friend in the lurch.

You show up if something terrible happens.

ORMBERG, NOVEMBER 24

We just had a Skype meeting with the medical examiner (Samira Khan) in Solna.

She summarized her conclusions: The Ormberg Girl was found in the autumn of 2009 after lying in the forest for about fifteen years. Thus she was murdered in 1994.

She was about five years old when she died, so she was probably born in 1989 (plus or minus a few years).

The cause of death was blunt force trauma. There was a cross fracture on the back of her head, resulting in multiple bone fragments. Several ribs were also broken.

The medical examiner didn't want to speculate on what had happened, but suggested the damage could have occurred either as the result of an accident or abuse.

There were metal plates in the girl's right radial bone, just above the wrist. They'd been inserted there after a broken wrist (a common operation, which seemed professionally performed). There were also traces on the skeleton near the plates, indicating an infection (which may help us identify her).

The doctor believed the wrist surgery had been performed sometime in the early nineties, based on the technique and type of screws that held the titanium plate in place (which were only used for a limited time in Sweden. Apparently, such things go out of fashion, too). The bone had just begun to heal when the girl died. She was probably murdered within three months of the surgery.

Andreas and Malin are going to contact the hospitals to find out if any patient matches the description. (This was never done during the original investigation.)

We also looked at what was left of the girl's clothes. Most of them were completely rotted, but a blue synthetic shirt was still in a relatively good condition. There was even a tag left with the letters "H&M" on it.

This detail stung.

Who hasn't gone shopping at H&M? I thought of the mother or father who bought that shirt. They never could have imagined it sitting here today, so many years later, while we looked at pictures of the girl's skeleton.

The thought made me dizzy.

No remnant of shoes had been found, which was noteworthy. (Shoes often contain plastic or rubber, which don't break down as quickly in nature.)

Finally, the medical examiner told us that the girl had been buried outside Katrineholm.

The gravestone has no name engraved on it, only a heart and a small bird.

After the Skype meeting, Malin asked if the perpetrator could have taken the girl's shoes as a trophy.

I said it was possible, but not likely. Of course, some murderers do take trophies, but shoes . . . ? I have never heard of any criminal that saves their victim's shoes. They usually take smaller things: jewelry, locks of hair, or, sometimes, body parts.

I promised to look into it anyway.

Then we went through the interviews that were conducted when the girl's body was found (especially with residents in the area).

There are three properties near the cairn. We're going to talk to all the owners again.

The closest: a small cottage that belongs to an elderly couple—Rut & Gunnar Sten. Andreas and Malin are going to talk to them tomorrow.

A little bit farther away, on the other side of Orm Mountain: Margareta & Magnus Brundin. (That situation is a bit "delicate." Margareta is police officer Malin's aunt, and Magnus is her adult son, i.e., Malin's cousin).

P and I will talk to them.

Finally, the Birgersson family. They live a few hundred meters south. The father, Stefan, a carpenter, is according to Malin an unemployed alcoholic. The mother died a year ago (cancer). Their two children, Jake and Melinda, also live there.

P and I will talk to them, too.

I put the diary on my lap. It suddenly feels very heavy and unwieldy.

They talked about us, about *our* family. And they called Dad an *alcoholic*.

Something cold spreads inside me, as if the black water of the creek were flowing through my veins instead of blood. Sure, Dad likes to drink beer, but an alcoholic? Wouldn't you be sick and drunk all the time?

I glance over at the Eiffel Tower on the desk. How many beer cans did I use? And maybe more important: How many cans of beer does Dad drink a day?

I haven't thought about it before, but the garage is actually filled with paper bags of empty beer cans. They cover almost a whole wall.

There's a knock.

I quickly put the diary on the bed and pull the blanket over it.

The door opens, and Melinda comes in. She has on a short red skirt and a tight black sweater that clings to her breasts. Her lips are raspberry red, and she smells like hairspray.

She stops in the middle of the floor, looks at me, smiles, and does a little pirouette.

"Do I look okay?"

"You look really pretty," I say, and mean it.

What I can't say is that I too would love to wear such beautiful clothes one day.

A closet filled with short shiny skirts and tight tops, long sweeping dresses and high-heeled boots with rivets. I love the feeling of fabric under my fingertips: baby-soft velvet, slippery silks, and rustling tulle. Sharp sequins, tight wool, and soft, thin cashmere.

Everything you don't find in Ormberg.

All the things that exist only on the Internet and in Melinda's magazines.

I think she notices my eyes. She can probably smell my longing, smell *The Sickness,* because she suddenly seems a bit confused. As if I asked her a trick question, even though I was quiet the whole time.

"What?" she asks.

"Nothing."

I hesitate for a moment, but then gather my courage.

"Is Dad an *alcoholic*?"

Melinda freezes. Seems surprised, as if this was the last question she expected, then shrugs her shoulders.

"Why do you ask that?"

"Just wondering."

Melinda walks over to my mirror, pulls at her top a little and readjusts her skirt. Then she runs her hand through her thick brown hair, purses her lips, and makes that face she always does when she takes selfies.

"I don't know," she says. "He definitely loves his beer. A lot."

She looks at the clock and continues:

"Shit. Have to go. Markus is picking me up in five minutes. I made food for you and Dad. He's asleep. Don't wake him up, okay?"

"Okay," I say, following her with my eyes as she walks out of the room.

A whiff of her perfume lingers like an invisible memento of her visit. It feels like it's teasing me, reminding me of who I am in my innermost being, but can never really become.

# Malin

Berit Sund's little red cottage is idyllically situated between the woods and a snowy field.

I haven't seen Hanne since Manfred and I visited her at the hospital on Sunday, though he's talked to her on the phone.

Berit, who must be at least seventy by now, meets Manfred and me at the front stairs. She's short and square. A childish barrette holds her sparse gray bangs in place above one ear. Her old white and brown shaggy dog noses around our feet.

"Holy moly," she says, and squeezes my hands so hard it hurts. "*Malin!* You're all grown up. And a cop, too. Who would have believed it."

She hesitates for a moment, smiles wide so I see all the fillings in her yellow teeth, and then gives me a quick, tight hug.

"Well, come in! Can't stand out here freezing," she continues, and herds us into the hall.

Then she stops, pulls at her shirt a little, and nods in the direction of the woods.

"Is it true? Did you find a dead woman at the cairn?"

I nod. "Yes. Unfortunately."

Berit shakes her head.

"Jesus, Mary, and Joseph. Do you know who she is?"

"No," Manfred says, without offering to expound.

That seems to work, because Berit doesn't ask any more questions. But she gives me a long worried look.

The hall is tiny and cramped, and I recognize the scent of coffee and wood smoke. In the window some yellow rickety geraniums are wintering, and on the floor, shoes stand in a neat row.

We enter the kitchen, which has a real woodstove. Orange flames lick at the gaps in the cast-iron door. The small table is already set with coffee and gingerbread.

"I'll get Hanne," Berit says. "Sit down and have some coffee."

We take our seat on Windsor chairs and stare out through the window. A snowy yard spreads out in front of us. Leafless bushes stand at the edge of the property, and behind them a field stretches out until it reaches the forest.

A cat passes by under the table, and its soft fur brushes against my legs. Berit appears in the doorway. After a couple of steps she stops, sighs, and turns toward us.

"It's the hip."

She grimaces and disappears into the room next door.

I meet Manfred's eyes. He looks at me without saying a word, and then pours coffee into a chipped cup. Steam is still rising from the piping-hot liquid when he hands it to me.

Voices can be heard in the room next door, and then Berit and Hanne enter the kitchen.

Hanne looks much more alert now than at the hospital. Her gaze is steady, and her curly hair is newly brushed. Most of the scratches appear to have healed, though I glimpse a few scabs on her hands and face.

When Hanne sees us, she stops, seems to hesitate. Then her face breaks into a cautious smile, and I'm reminded again just how beautiful she is.

*"Manfred!"*

Hanne takes a few quick steps toward the table. Manfred rises, and they hug for a long time in silence. Then Hanne turns her gaze to me, her head tilted to the side, and blinks a few times.

Just like at the hospital, I think, as she stretches a hand in greeting to me.

I take it gently and smile.

"Hello, Hanne. It's me, Malin, your colleague."

Her eyes narrow and she opens her mouth a little as if intending to say something, but hesitates.

*"Malin?"*

She lingers a little on the word, as if tasting the syllables.

I do my best not to look disappointed or shocked. Don't want to throw her off balance now that so much depends on her remembering something that happened last Friday.

We sit down around the table, and Manfred serves Hanne some coffee as Berit puts a couple of logs into the stove.

"Don't you want some coffee, Berit?" I ask.

Berit limps over to the table.

At this close range she looks very old. A web of deep wrinkles spreads around her eyes and the skin on the back of her hands is thin and transparent, like wax paper. Blue veins wind beneath it, like snakes trying to make their way out of her skin.

"No thank you, my dear," Berit says. "Just had some coffee. You probably need your privacy. I'll take Joppe out for a walk."

As she turns around, I see three long lacerations on Berit's left forearm. It looks like somebody scratched her.

Berit notices my eyes on her. Blushes and moves her hand toward the sores. Pulls down her sleeve to cover them and wanders out of the room with her dog in tow. As they disappear into the hall, I notice that the dog limps, too.

It's quiet for a moment.

Hanne, who sat down next to Manfred, fiddles with her coffee cup, seeming a little self-conscious.

"Sorry," she says, and meets my eyes. "For not recognizing you."

I wave her concerns away. "It's no problem."

Hanne nods, looks at Manfred, and smiles again.

"The beard suits you."

Manfred runs his hand over his chin and smiles.

"You think so? Afsaneh disagrees. She thinks I look like a motorcycle thug. Claims I'm scaring Nadja."

"Motorcycle thug?" Hanne laughs. "Come on! That's the last thing you look like."

"Afsaneh?" I say.

Manfred turns his eyes from Hanne to me.

"My wife. And Nadja is our daughter. She's almost two."

"Oh, okay," I say.

"How is Nadja?" Hanne asks. "Have you figured out her ear problems?"

"She's doing well now. They put in tubes. Since then, knock on wood, we haven't had a single ear infection. It's a fucking miracle, if you ask me."

Hanne leans over to Manfred and readjusts his pocket square. The gesture is so intimate, so full of care, that it shocks me.

"When we worked on the investigation of the decapitated woman," Hanne begins, "you were a *wreck*, Manfred. Quite literally. Nadja's ears were bothering her the whole time."

Manfred laughs a little and sips his coffee.

"I don't know if that was because of Nadja's ear infections or the investigation."

I almost feel like an intruder here.

It's so obvious that they share a past I have no access to. They haven't just worked together, they know each other's families and children and have been through ear infections and diaper changes and God-knows-what-else.

Manfred glances at me, perhaps sensing what I'm thinking,

because he takes out his notebook and clears his throat. Hanne also seems to pick up on it; she straightens a little and says:

"I know why you're here, and I'll do my best to help you, but I'm not sure I can. It's so odd. I remember so much. My childhood, for example. How to get to school—every tree, house, and step are burned into my memory. And I remember my job. The murders, the rapes. But since we came back from Greenland, it's as if nothing really stuck, if you know what I mean. Everything is a blur in my head. And the more I try to remember, the blurrier it gets."

"That's okay," Manfred says, putting his large hand on Hanne's. "We'll help you."

"Berit told me you haven't found any trace of Peter yet."

Hanne's voice is brittle.

"That's right," Manfred says. "We're still looking. And we *will* find him, I promise."

Hanne stares out through the window, at the snow-covered field and the evergreens beyond it.

"It's so cold now," she says. "So cold. Imagine if he's somewhere in those woods in this cold."

Manfred squeezes her hand.

"We found a dead woman in the forest yesterday," he continues, and looks at Hanne. "At the cairn. She'd been murdered. And one of your shoes was found nearby."

"What are you saying?"

She twists her hands together and blinks several times.

"Hanne. I think you were there, in the woods, when this woman was murdered."

Manfred pauses as if to give Hanne time to take in what he's saying. Then he continues:

"I know it's difficult to remember, but anything at all will help. A sound, a scent, an image with no context that seems uninteresting."

Hanne nods and closes her eyes.

"Greenland," she says. "That's the last thing I remember clearly. Then it's all a blur. Though I do have a few fragments, which I think might be from the day Peter disappeared. I remember being in the woods. I was running, as if I were fleeing from something, or someone. Yes, at least that's the feeling I have. That I was afraid and out of breath. My whole body hurt, but I kept running. And I was freezing, of course. It was so unbelievably cold."

"Very good," Manfred says, and squeezes Hanne's hand. "Do you remember what time of day it was?"

Hanne closes her eyes and takes a deep breath. The corner of one of her eyes twitches.

"It was dark."

"Good. And the weather?"

Hanne squirms in her chair and wrinkles her forehead.

"I remember rain against my face. And . . . a branch falling from a tree. Yes, a storm. It was stormy."

Manfred turns to me and mouths: "Friday."

Hanne must have been in the woods on Friday night during the storm.

That means that she must have wandered for a full day before she was found.

"Okay," Manfred says. "Very good. You've been saying 'I' this whole time. Was Peter with you in the woods?"

Hanne opens her eyes and sits very still. She looks out through the window at a snowy field bathed in morning sun.

"I don't remember. I think . . . *No.* I don't know."

"Okay," Manfred says. "Can we back up a little? Do you remember why you were in the woods?"

"We . . . No. *I'm sorry!*"

Hanne slowly shakes her head and then goes on:

"I'm really sorry. It's all so blurry. But it *must* have been connected to the investigation. Why else would we go out in those woods? Bird-watching? Making out behind some trees?"

Manfred smiles crookedly.

"What do you remember from the investigation?" I ask.

Hanne doesn't answer right away, and when she does, her expression is troubled.

"To be honest?" she says slowly. "Nothing."

Manfred's eyes meet mine, and I can see the disappointment there.

"Okay," he says. "Don't worry. What else do you remember?"

Hanne nods and closes her eyes again. A few rays of sunshine make their way through the window, and a lock of her coppery hair begins to glow.

"We were in a dark, cramped room."

"Wait a minute—what kind of room?"

Manfred stares intensely at Hanne.

"Well, a room. Or a space, I guess. Maybe a garage or a small cottage. I don't know if that was before or after the forest. Then I remember . . ."

Hanne looks up toward the ceiling. She wrings her hands.

"Boards. Or at least that's how they felt under my palms. Sort of prickly."

"What kind of boards?" I ask.

"No clue. Just . . . boards. And . . ."

"What?"

Manfred looks eager.

"Books," she says emphatically.

"Books? What kind of books?"

"I don't know. Regular books. Just . . ."

Hanne is quiet, her eyes closed. She puts her hands to her temples.

"English books. In stacks on the floor. On that disgusting, dirty floor."

Manfred throws me a quick glance. There's a crackling sound from the fire, and Hanne opens her eyes.

"*Where?*" Manfred whispers.

"I don't know."

Hanne bends her head, and for a moment I think she might start to weep.

"Speaking of books," I say. "You don't happen to remember where your diary is, do you?"

Hanne shakes her head.

"My diary? No. And believe me. If I knew where it was I'd have grabbed it, because I wrote down everything in there."

We talk a bit longer, but she doesn't remember more, so we decide to head back to the office.

Just as Hanne rises to give Manfred a farewell hug, I see a necklace glimmer inside the old, washed-out men's shirt she has on. When she turns to me, I can't help asking about it.

"What a beautiful necklace, Hanne. Is it new?"

Once again her face goes blank, which I've come to realize means she doesn't remember.

"I don't know," she says hesitantly, her face troubled, moving a hand to her throat. Then she pulls the necklace out so I can see it.

A gold medallion hangs on a thin gold chain. The medallion has a green border that appears to be made of enamel, and there are what might be small diamonds set in the middle. Around the stones, a wreath is engraved.

"It looks old," I say, bending forward to get a better look.

Hanne nods and blushes.

"Maybe you got it from Peter," I suggest.

"Maybe," Hanne says, and blushes even more deeply, as if ashamed she can't help us.

# Jake

They found a woman murdered at the cairn.

Dad told me this morning before I left for school. He also said he'd bet a month's salary that the victim and murderer came from the "Arab colony" in the old TrikåKungen factory.

Everyone was talking about it at school, too, but no one knew what happened.

Saga and I talked about going out to the cairn and checking it out, but she had to babysit her little sister after school so I went home instead.

I'm at my desk now, with Hanne's diary in front of me.

I've placed it inside my history textbook, so I can hide it if Dad or Melinda walks in. The Eiffel Tower stands next to me. It's done, or as done as it'll ever be.

On Thursday I have to hand it in.

Something's happened to me, but I don't really know what. Maybe it's because Saga kissed me, or Hanne's story, which has crept into my head and made a place for itself among all my other thoughts. Anyway, everything feels different, as if the Coke tastes more like Coke and the trees and the creek outside are more beautiful than I remember. Each evergreen tree is a perfect white-powdered cone, and the creek runs by like an infinite, shining snake through the hills and stones.

And it's as if Hanne has her own voice, which speaks directly to me through the tightly written pages of the book. As if every word, every syllable, was meant just for me.

It's exciting, but at the same time scary, because the further into the story I get, the more responsibility I feel for her and P, even though I don't really know how I feel about him. I am after all the only one who knows what they did those last days before disappearing into the woods.

When I think about it, my stomach goes cold, like someone forced me to swallow a big piece of ice. I feel guilty that I've spent the last few days building the Eiffel Tower and hanging out with Saga instead of finishing the diary.

I run my hand over its pages.

The paper is a bit dented and feels rough. When I see that familiar spindly handwriting, my heart jumps in my chest.

"Hello, Hanne," I whisper.

Saturday & free.

I worked a bit in the hotel room in the morning. Searched online for violent criminals who kept shoes as trophies. Found a serial killer in the United States who stole his victims' shoes. He was a fetishist & schizophrenic, who wore the shoes after the murder and masturbated. He also cut a foot off one of his victims, brought it home and put shoes on that as well.

Odd: I'm able to put on my analytical glasses and state that this murderer's tendencies had deep-seated psychological causes. I can sift through his childhood to find mitigating circumstances.

But I still can't UNDERSTAND.

It troubles me, because it clarifies that invisible but undeniable boundary that separates individuals from each other. You can never fully understand another human being. Or trust them, for that matter.

I'm thinking about P.

We went for a long walk in the woods after lunch. Went to the cairn. Climbed up Orm Mountain. The sun was shining, the air was cold & clear.

P was in a terrific mood, talked about the investigation. I asked who Malin was. It just popped out of me. I should have checked the diary instead.

It was as though a light extinguished in his eyes, to be replaced by watery emptiness. He let go of my hand.

I tried to explain away my faux pas, but he didn't fall for it.

P is many things (unreliable, insensitive at times), but he's not stupid. After thirty years as a cop he knows a lie.

He made me promise to call the doctor on Monday.

(I lied, of course. I never want to see that doctor at the Memory Clinic again. The one who likes to tell me about all the WONDERFUL group homes available to dementia patients—as if she were selling me a charter trip, not health care facilities where you sit in a chair in front of a television and pee into a diaper.)

I'm not there yet, but I will be.

Unless . . .

I've started thinking: I don't have to let it happen. I can choose to end my life before I become a vegetable.

The difficulty is, of course, knowing when. I do fine for now. And I really have no wish to die. Still: I'll have to do it before I completely lose myself. There will be a point-of-no-return: a time when a plan can no longer be implemented. After that, I'll be forced to sit compliantly in front of a TV at a nursing home & eat my purees.

I close the book and look out the window. It's dark, but I can still make out the glitter of the black creek winding through the trees.

A lump has grown in my throat.

I don't want Hanne to die.

I don't want anyone to die, but especially not Hanne. I think of that thin figure in a wet blouse with bare feet in the woods. Of her hair lying in wet strings on her shoulders.

I thought she was dangerous, a murderer.

I grab my phone and google "fetishist" and "schizophrenic" to stop thinking about Hanne, but she won't let go of me. It feels like she's whispering to me from the book, as if she's asking me for help.

What is she doing at this very moment?

Dad told me she's staying with Berit in the house behind the church. He said it's crazy that they let that "old fool" take care of Hanne. Still, he admitted there's so much crazy shit happening these days it's only logical.

It made me wonder if it was different before. If things were better then, less nuts. But I didn't have time to ask before Melinda came in wearing a very short skirt, and she and Dad started shouting at each other.

That's what they do, Dad and Melinda—argue about things that aren't important to avoid talking about what does matter.

Like Mom.

We never talk about her even though it's been less than a year since she died, even though all her clothes are still hanging in the closet and her side of the bed lies untouched.

I look at the clock and then out into the darkness again.

Half past four.

There's nothing preventing me from going to Berit's to check how Hanne is doing. Not to visit, but just to get a glimpse of her, make sure she's okay.

The more I think about it, the more convinced I am that that's the best course of action. Not just that I could, but that I *should* go look in on her.

I carefully place the diary into the desk drawer, turn off the desk lamp, and get up.

· · ·

Berit's little house is lit up like a Christmas tree. Warm light streams out through the windows, turning the snow outside gold.

I've hid my moped in the woods and walked the last bit on foot. Even though there's nothing forbidden about coming here, I don't want to be discovered—how would I explain why I'm here, why I'm so desperate for a glimpse of Hanne?

It's really, really cold tonight.

My breath turns to smoke, and my cheeks are numb. Even though I have my thickest gloves on, my fingers are frozen.

I make my way slowly toward the cottage, trying to figure out which window is the best to peek in through. The window to the right of the front door is low, so low I could easily stand in the flower bed and look in.

Everything is calm. No movement, no sound. It's just me, the cottage, and the silence of a scentless winter evening.

The bushes under the window stick to my pants. I take a step toward the window and realize too late it's a rosebush. The thorns tear me at my thighs, sting and bite.

But I can see inside.

The room is empty.

On the right, two sofa beds stand along the wall, and to the left sits a small table with stools around it. At the far end there's a door. It's slightly ajar, and I can just make out some movement in there, as if someone walked by.

I back away from the rosebushes, think for a few seconds, and then walk around the corner of the house, over to the next window.

It's too high up, impossible to look in if you don't have anything to stand on.

A snowflake lands on my face, and then another.

I look around, but can't find anything to climb on, no box or bucket or ladder sticking up from the snow. Instead, I grab ahold of a wooden panel and climb up from the ground, wedging my feet into the small gap between the façade and the stone foundation, hold on to the batten. I peek in through the bottom edge of the window, where a potted plant conveniently sits.

They're by the table in the kitchen.

Berit has her back to me. The short, thick nape of her neck sticks over her shirt, like risen dough. Hanne sits opposite her, facing me. On the floor in front of the woodstove, Berit's old dog lies stretched out on its side.

My first impulse is to jump down, but then I realize they can't see me. It's dark outside, and I must be hidden by the potted plant.

I almost don't recognize Hanne.

Her hair is long, curly, and fluffy. She's holding a cup of tea in her hand and laughing at something. She has a shawl draped around her shoulders and a big necklace peeks out from her neckline.

She looks so strong, so happy, and filled with energy. Not at all like someone who wrote that she might want to die. But that's just how it is: These terrible thoughts are invisible from outside; they exist only internally, in a dark box with a very thick lock. Inside there's room to long for death, or for *The Sickness* to hide out.

I guess that's where Dad put his memories of Mom.

Berit rises, walks over to the stove, and reaches for the teapot. She limps a bit, as if she's in pain. Hanne holds out her teacup and lets Berit fill it with hot liquid.

The kitchen table stands near a window on the opposite side of the house, the church side. A straw Christmas Star hangs from a hook in front of the window. On the windowsill there's a sad, sickly potted plant. The leaves are yellow and hang from the stem. A few lonely pink flowers stare into the darkness of the windowpanes.

My arms burn from the exertion, but I hold on to the wood paneling, enchanted by the scene in that little kitchen. It's almost impossible to believe Hanne's sitting there. In a way, I know her better than any other adult, but still she's a stranger.

A sound echoes through the night: a muffled thud, but I can't tell if it came from inside or out.

Berit sits down again. I can hear their muted voices, but can't make out what they're saying.

Then that sound comes again, sort of like a scratching, as if someone were slowly dragging their nails over a metal sheet. I stiffen, because now I'm sure the sound is coming from outside. Someone or something is moving around out here in the garden.

But Hanne and Berit don't seem to notice; they keep talking and laughing and drinking tea.

Then I see it.

Beneath the Christmas Star in the other window—a pale, expressionless face surrounded by night. The eyes are holes of darkness. The mouth is a thin line.

I lose my grip on the wood panel and fall back into the snow. As my back hits the ground, I realize the person standing outside that other window must be around the corner, less than ten meters from me.

My back hurts, and I gasp for air. I get up and start running over the thin layer of snow toward my moped.

My chest burns from the effort. My nose is running, but I don't dare slow down or glance behind me. I'm too scared that the person standing outside that window might catch up with me.

But no one is coming.

Nobody puts a bony hand on my shoulder just at the moment I think I got away. Nobody breathes on my neck as I climb onto my moped. No one pulls me down as I start the engine.

It's just me and the darkness and the snow falling silently onto Berit's little cottage.

# Malin

I stare out the windshield. Realize I've almost forgotten how perfectly black the night is here.

Almost like a grave.

Plus it's still snowing, making the visibility even worse, and forcing me to slow down to a crawl.

When I arrive home, I notice that the outdoor light is broken. I remind myself to buy new bulbs for it tomorrow. Ragnhild wasn't so far off when she pointed out that Mom's property needs some attention. And even I can screw in some lightbulbs, though I'm probably the least handy person in Ormberg.

When you live in the country, you're supposed to be handy and strong.

This isn't a place for people who are all thumbs. Trees fall, roads get snowed in, cars break down in the middle of the forest, and the power goes out during autumn storms.

It's a demanding way of life.

Nor are you supposed to be a wuss or a whiner in Ormberg, or find life better anywhere else, for example in Stockholm— *especially not* in Stockholm. And if you do, you better keep it to yourself. Or you'll end up frozen out as quickly and surely as the summer vacationers disappear in August.

Mom is standing by the stove when I come in. Her short, square figure is so different from my own. We used to joke about it when I was a little, how I didn't look like her at all, how she must have picked me up from a troll in the woods.

The elk stew simmering on the stove smells like juniper, and she's holding a glass of wine in her hand.

"Hello!" she says, putting down her glass to give me a quick, tight hug that almost squeezes the breath out of me.

Yes, Mom is made for life out here.

Strong, tough, and for the most part satisfied with life. Or at least with *her* life—she worries herself to bits over me. Mostly because I'm a cop. I don't think she understands that my work in Katrineholm consists primarily of dealing with drunks, interviewing shoplifters, and filling out paperwork. Maybe that's why I was so pleased to be asked to take part in this investigation.

Finally, some excitement—a serious crime, a murder investigation, a chance to make a difference.

And in the most unexpected of all places: Ormberg.

I don't think any other serious crime had been committed here since that German tourist was knifed at the campsite down by the lake during a fight three years ago. But he needed only three stitches at the doctor's office in Vingåker before going back to slurping beers under the awning of his RV.

Otherwise, not much happens here: some petty theft, some vandalism and graffiti at the building that used to be Brogrens Mechanical, but which now seems to exert an almost hypnotic force on the teenagers of Ormberg. There's also some drunken domestic abuse calls and some arrests for drug possession— people do a lot more drugs in the countryside than you'd think.

But that's it.

Until a few days ago, anyway.

I sit down at the kitchen table and turn to Mom.

"Do you need help?"

Mom shakes her head, wipes the sweat off her forehead with the back of her hand, and takes a sip of wine.

"No, no. Sit, you've been working all day."

And I reflect that that's exactly what I've been doing all day. Sitting: at the office, at Berit's, and then at the office again.

"It's just terrible," Mom says. "About the dead woman at the cairn."

"Yep."

"Was she from here?"

"No. I've never seen her before."

Mom takes a sip from her wooden ladle. Reaches for the mortar, takes a pinch of something inside, and sprinkles it into the pot.

"And that cop from Stockholm. Have you found him?"

I think about Peter. For the first time since his disappearance, I admit to myself that the likelihood that something terrible happened to him is much greater than that we'll find him nursing a broken foot in one of the summerhouses.

"No, we haven't found him."

"How long has he been gone now?"

"Five days."

Mom tilts her head to the side as if trying to calculate how likely surviving five nights in the woods would be.

I think she too finds the probability microscopic, because she says nothing more about it. Instead, she puts the ladle into the stew and stirs it.

I notice that the table is set with four faded flowery plates. And with the good silverware, which is usually kept in a wine red felt case in the top drawer of the china cabinet.

"Are we four tonight?" I ask. "I thought it was only you, me, and Margareta."

Margareta is my father's sister, but we don't meet very often nowadays. Like Mom, she's spent her whole adult life in Ormberg. And also like Mom, she's made for the countryside—physically strong and the opposite of wussy. Nor have I ever heard her express the slightest desire to live anywhere else.

This is either the center of the earth or the end of it, depending on how you look at it.

"Magnus is coming, too."

I nod. I haven't told Mom how I saved Magnus from a beating by a bunch of brats in the woods on Monday. In part because I promised to keep it quiet, in part because just thinking about it upsets me.

"Did you talk to the priest about the wedding?" I ask.

Mom stiffens. Then she walks over to the table, wipes her hands on her apron, and sits down across from me.

"Malin. Sweetheart. Have you two really thought this through?"

"What do you mean?"

She wrings her hands and looks down at the table.

"It's just that . . . sometimes I get the feeling or, I wonder . . . do you really *love* him?"

"Are you crazy? Of course I love him."

Mom sighs.

"Marriage is a big step. Do you have to move so fast? Why don't you live together for a while first?"

Mom's right that we haven't lived together for very long. We met when I was studying at the Police Academy, and only lived together a month before I got the job at Katrineholm and moved. Now we commute back and forth and, of course, that's not an ideal situation. But I still don't understand why Mom is saying this. Why she doesn't respect my choices like I respect hers.

I mean, the fact that she chooses to live in this backwater, for example.

But Mom continues:

"Sometimes I wonder if . . . I mean, you know after what happened with Kenny . . ."

"Please! *Stop!*"

"Okay, okay," Mom mumbles.

"Why are you even saying this? Don't you *like* Max?"

Mom takes a deep breath and looks straight at me. Her pale blue eyes are red-rimmed. The wrinkles around her mouth and her heavy eyelids make her seem tired and sad.

"Yes, I do. But I'm not the one marrying him, Malin. Tell me why you love him, *what* you love about him."

"What is this? A goddamn test? I love him because . . . We have it good together, okay? He's a good guy. He's fun and smart and makes good money and we'll have a good life."

"In Stockholm?"

"What does that matter?"

"It doesn't matter where you live. But sometimes I get the feeling you want to run away from here. And that's not a good basis for a marriage. If you run from something, make sure it's not yourself you're running from."

Mom's right, of course: I do want to escape this place. Any sane person would if you ended up here. You don't put down roots in Ormberg unless you're crazy, or born here, or both.

But what I have with Max has nothing to do with wanting to leave.

Max is perfect for me. I can't explain it any other way. He's everything I've ever wanted: ambitious, urban, and financially secure.

And besides: What is love anyway, other than friendship spiced up with a little sex? I fuck my best friend, and I'm fine with that, thank you very much.

But that's hardly something I can say to Mom.

Why do people talk about love all the time, as if it were some sort of supernatural force? Almost like a religion. I don't believe in love, and I don't believe in God.

I believe in hard work, determination, and persistence, things that give results.

I believe in facts and science, not superstition and emotions.

Especially not emotions—you should be damn careful about those. Otherwise, you don't know what might happen. You might end up knocked up and stuck in a place like Ormberg. Tied for an eternity to some snot-nosed kids and some guy that seemed exciting for one summer evening down by the lake when you were young and dumb and had five or six beers in you.

Something blinks outside the window—headlights approaching in the dark. An old, rusty Saab drives up in front of the house.

Magnus and Margareta.

Mom looks at the clock.

"Right on time. I told Margareta seven."

As soon as Mom opens the front door, Zorro, a huge German shepherd, comes bounding in. He barks, jumps around our legs like a pinball, and licks my hands. Then he runs into the kitchen to investigate if there's anything edible on the floor.

My aunt's old dog is much more good-natured than he seems. She's had him for as long as I can remember.

Magnus comes inside, stamps off the snow on the doormat, and hangs up his jacket. Margareta follows behind him, wearing a dirty old coat and a big pink scarf. Her short brown hair stands on end when she takes off her knitted heart-patterned stocking cap.

Mom takes off her apron, runs a hand over her sweater, and walks toward them.

"Hello!" she says. "How are you two?"

Magnus stares down at the floor while pulling off his boots. When he bends forward, I can see that the hair on top of his head has thinned out. The bare spots shine under the warm light of the ceiling lamp. His big body is more hunched than it used to be, his face more wrinkled. You can tell he's passed forty-five.

"Yes," he drawls. "Fine."

I give him a tight hug, and, for once, he hugs back. Maybe he's still grateful I saved him in the woods.

"Things are *great*," Margareta says in her husky, cigarette-soaked voice, and gives me a hug that smells like smoke and old dog.

"Malin. *Jesus,* I forgot how tall you were. You should have been a basketball player instead of a cop."

Margareta laughs at her own comment and smiles widely. Her teeth are crooked and dotted by ugly fillings. The hands resting on my shoulders are strong and sinewy.

Magnus's washed-out fleece sweater is stretched tight over his heavy belly, and he's wearing the kind of jeans you buy at the gas station halfway between here and Katrineholm.

"Come in," Mom says. "The food is ready."

We go into the kitchen and sit at the table. Mom and Margareta complain loudly about snow removal, and Margareta says she may call the county office to complain again this year, otherwise they won't do shit.

Margareta is good at making things like that happen. She has a finger in most pots here in the village. In fact, she's probably the most influential person in Ormberg, which is impressive considering she's a retired midwife and a single mother to her village-idiot son.

Before Kenny died, I'd do anything I could to avoid spending time with Margareta. Mom used to remind me how tough Margareta had it, and how she needed us. Her first child died from pneumonia, at six months old. And her husband, whose name we were never supposed to say within earshot of Margareta, left her for a hairdresser from Flen while Margareta was pregnant with Magnus.

I guess that's why they're so close.

"Magnus got a job," Margareta chirps.

"Congratulations!" Mom says with a smile. "What are you going to do?"

Magnus stares down at his lap.

"He's gonna help Ragnhild Sahlén clear brush by the creek," Margareta answers. "In the spring, of course."

"That's a wonderful job," Mom says, smiling encouragingly at Magnus.

"Congratulations," I say, and think there are actually some advantages to living in a small town like Ormberg. The people here take care of each other. It's a kind of solidarity I've never seen in Katrineholm or Stockholm. And even though the kids throw stones at Magnus, he has a place here. He can be part of the community.

He's allowed to be needed.

We talk about snow removal a little while longer, then Margareta turns to me and puts a bony hand on mine.

"It's just awful, Malin. Absolutely awful. Running into that corpse. And by the cairn of all places. Isn't it odd?"

I nod.

"What exactly happened?" she asks.

"I can't really talk about that."

"Of course," Margareta agrees, but then she pats my hand a little and continues:

"And what about that cop from Stockholm? Has he turned up yet?"

"No."

She shakes her head slowly and purses her mouth into the shape of a pale raisin.

"So terrible!" she says. "Imagine if he's out there in the woods. Frozen like a fish stick."

"Oh, *Margareta*," Mom says, and slams down her glass.

"I'm sorry! But surely that's what you're all afraid of?"

Margareta's eyes meet mine.

"Yes," I say, trying not to picture Peter as a fish stick.

"No disrespect to the Stockholmers," Margareta says, and coughs, "but it's easy to get lost in the woods around here if you don't know your way. Easy to underestimate the danger. And as for the cairn. I find it hard to believe in things that you can't see, but I'd bet my life there's ghosts there. I remember that German family who—"

"*Please*, Margareta," Mom says.

Margareta shrugs her shoulders slightly and looks insulted. Magnus continues mechanically shoveling elk stew into his mouth during the silence.

"Do you think his disappearance has anything to do with the woman by the cairn?" Mom says.

"No clue," I say. "Maybe. There must be a reason why Peter and Hanne—the one we found in the forest—went out into the storm. But we don't know. Although . . ."

"*What?*" Margareta asks, her eyes wide.

It's very typical of Margareta: the unbridled curiosity, the shameless digging into other people's business.

"We'll find him," I say, trying to sound sure. "As soon as Hanne starts to remember what happened."

"Then let's hope she does," Margareta says. "He can't lie out there in the snow all winter."

Mom throws her a look of warning, but says nothing.

"I'm just saying it would be terrible if one of the children found him," Margareta says.

Magnus stops with his fork halfway to his mouth.

"Who's dead?" he asks, and suddenly looks afraid.

"Nobody we know is dead," I say, leaning forward and patting his hand. He pulls it away.

"But what does she say then, the woman who lost her memory?" Mom asks, reaching for her wine.

"Hanne? I can't tell you that. The details of the investigation are confidential."

Margareta turns to Mom and holds up a pack of cigarettes.

"May I?"

"Sure," Mom says, pushing the old ashtray with the Cinzano logo on it, the one we've had as long as I can remember, toward her.

Margareta lights a cigarette and takes a deep, satisfied drag. Then she coughs.

"Why in the world they would leave that poor, confused woman with Berit is beyond me."

"Is she staying with *Berit Sund*?" Mom asks in astonishment.

Margareta nods, and her eyes shine.

"Insanity," she says emphatically. "That old biddy can barely take care of herself and her limping dog."

She takes another drag. The cigarette crackles and turns red.

"I've heard Berit is having money problems," Mom says. "She probably needs the extra cash."

"Berit *always* has money problems." Margareta chuckles. "I remember the winter of '85. I was on my way to attend a delivery in Berga. A critical situation—breech—and they couldn't get to the hospital because of the storm and . . ."

I wish I were somewhere else. I can't stand listening to Mom and Margareta's never-ending gossip.

Magnus is still staring down at the table. Not once during the meal has he met my eyes. He's looked everywhere else: at Mom, Zorro, the stew, and the kitchen ceiling.

Just as Margareta is launching into a very detailed story about how Berit borrowed money to replace a car that she then managed to set on fire, my phone rings. Usually I wouldn't answer in the middle of dinner, but at the moment it's a welcome break. I've heard the story of Berit's car at least a hundred times.

"Excuse me," I say, stand up, and go to the hall. "Have to take this, it's work."


It's Manfred calling.

I can hear the drone of the portable heater in the background and realize that he hasn't left the office, even though it's past nine.

But, of course, his wife and daughter are at home in Stockholm. There's not much else to do besides work.

Ormberg is full of things you *can't* do.

Can't go to the gym, can't have a beer at the pub, can't order a pizza. Can't stop by a cafe and grab a latte or pick up the evening paper. Can't go to the post office or buy milk or a carton of eggs to make some pancakes, if you happened to forget to buy them earlier.

Nevertheless, Manfred has gone back to Stockholm only once since we got here two weeks ago, even though it takes just a couple of hours to drive there.

I wonder what Afsaneh thinks about that.

Manfred doesn't apologize for calling late. He's not the type to apologize for anything. Instead, he says:

"The technicians called."

"And?"

"The blood on Hanne's sneakers . . ."

"Yes?"

"It wasn't hers. The DNA test isn't ready yet, but they checked the blood type to see if it matched Hanne's. Which the technicians and medical examiners do before the DNA test comes. The blood on Hanne's shoes was type O positive. Hanne has B negative."

"Could it be Peter's blood?"

"No. He has AB−, a very unusual blood type. Only one percent of Sweden's population has it."

"So what you're saying is . . ."

My voice dies away as I think of that thin woman in the snow. Of the face, which is no longer a face, and the long, thin gray hair.

"It just so happens that the murdered woman's blood type is O+, like thirty-two percent of the population, so I'd bet the blood on Hanne's shoes comes from the murder victim. There's no other logical explanation. Hanne must have been there when she died, Malin. I can't prove it yet, but I know it's true."

# Jake

The class had a half-day field trip to the indoor pool in Vingåker, but I decided to skip it. I hate sports, probably because I'm so small and always come in last when we compete. Melinda says I'll grow, that I'll run faster and swim faster than all the others as soon as I get a little bigger. But I measured myself yesterday, and I'm still at the same blue line on the doorway to the kitchen that we drew last summer.

And when we change clothes for gym, I'm still the smallest. Even if I get up on my toes, I can barely reach Vincent's shoulder.

Not that I'm standing next to him, and definitely not in the locker room—if I did I'd end up with my head in the toilet.

Anyway. Swimming: To be honest, it's not the only reason I skipped the field trip. I barely slept last night. I couldn't stop thinking about that pale face with its empty eyes outside Berit's window.

I should have found out who it was, but I was too scared.

By the time the sun rose, I'd convinced myself that it was all my imagination. I mean, who would spy on Berit and Hanne in the dark?

And why?

Anyhow. I've thought a lot about Hanne.

She's super old, but also strong and smart.

And she only does interesting things, like traveling to Greenland and hunting down a murderer. She never lies around on a couch drinking beer or watching TV or does things like check in at the unemployment office.

I wish my life were that exciting, but nothing happens in Ormberg. There aren't even any murderers. Except for whoever killed the woman by the cairn, of course, but surely he's not from here.

I heard Dad and Melinda talking about it. Dad said it must have been an immigrant, a Muslim. They have a different view on the "value" of human life and on women.

"They'll kill you if they don't get what they want."

I wondered what he meant by "what they want," even though I suspected he meant sex. I wrote it on my hand to remind myself to ask Melinda later, but I forgot.

Men and women seem to want different things.

Men always want something from women. Their bodies, for example. It's as if men have dangerous urges inside them, which women have to be careful about.

It makes me feel sad and confused.

Don't women want anything from men, or do only men *get what they want*?

Does that mean when I grow up I'll become the kind of person who's willing to do anything to *get what I want*? The kind of person girls have to watch out for? Will I lose control of myself when I grow up? Is that what it means to become a man?

If so, I don't want to be a man.

I think of Saga, how soft her lips were when they touched mine. Of the scent of her pink hair and the warmth of her body. That explosion in my chest when she kissed me, how that moment felt more important than anything else that had ever happened to me before. As if somehow it divided my life cleanly into a before and after, and nothing would ever be the same again.

Like when Mom died, but in a good way.

Saga didn't seem scared of me. Saga actually seemed like she *wanted* to kiss me.

It doesn't make sense.

Maybe only Muslims are dangerous to girls. Maybe because of the book they read, the Quran, where it says you have to make war and be unfaithful. I've seen the pictures on TV of masked men and black flags with Arabic text. They blow things up, drive trucks into people, cut the throats of their prisoners, and are trying to create a worldwide caliphate. Sometimes I'm afraid they'll come here to Ormberg, but I don't really think they want a caliphate here.

Fucking Ormberg is too boring, even for those crazy ISIS fighters.

The Bible says you should love your neighbor like yourself. Our teacher says that means you're not supposed to hurt or kill another person. But Saga says the Christians have killed more people in the name of God than the Muslims. She claims it's religion itself that's dangerous—that religion turns you into a slave.

I don't know what I believe in.

Not God, because if he exists he let my mother die of cancer, and I don't want anything to do with him after that.


I've packed my Eiffel Tower into a cardboard box and put it on the back of Melinda's moped. We have to turn in our assignments this afternoon. The diary lies in my backpack as I drive to Brogrens Mechanical.

I'm not supposed to be driving—I'm not fifteen yet. But everyone in Ormberg does it anyway, because it's the only way to get around. Dad doesn't want us to use the moped when there's snow, but he's still asleep, and besides, I drive very carefully.

The wheels skid as I turn toward a big red building of corrugated sheet metal. The sky is dark gray with streaks of purple, ominous in some way. Crows are circling above the building as I park. I remove the box with the Eiffel Tower inside, and enter the broken door with a yellow sign on it: "Access Prohibited for Unauthorized Persons."

The huge machine hall is quiet and empty.

Concrete pillars of different colors hold up a high ceiling and a pale light filters in through the dirty skylights. Enormous machines made of gears and knobs still stand along the walls. There are rollers and lathes and other machines for sheet metal processing, which I don't know the names of. Chains with hooks extend from the beams, and a huge crane the length of the hall is held in place by gigantic bolted steel construction. Large folded hoses hang down from the machines, like giant vacuum cleaners. There are shelves along the walls as well, with many empty compartments. The whole place smells vaguely of oil.

Dad's the one who told me about the machines.

He worked here, until production was moved to Asia and the factory was shut down.

I pass by the monstrous machine that once squeezed enormous sheets of metal into tiny cubes, and try to imagine what it was like working here. Dad says it wasn't so bad, that it was full of light and clean back then, that the pay was good and his colleagues were nice. He says the politicians betrayed Ormberg, that his life would have been so different if they hadn't moved production abroad.

I wonder what exactly would have been different. Wouldn't Mom still have got cancer? But maybe Dad wouldn't drink so much beer if he didn't have to check in with that bitch at the unemployment office.

When Dad talks about Brogrens he always looks sad, and I do my best to make him feel better. Try to explain that there are positive things about not having a job there anymore, like all the time he has to work on the house. He never would have built that huge deck if he worked, for example.

Then he laughs, grabs me around the waist, lifts me, and says

I'm damn right. To hell with those idiots at the unemployment office, and Brogrens, too.

I like when he does that.

At the far end of the machine hall sits the foreman's desk. It's empty, of course, but on the floor next to it are old phone books. It was very complicated in the old days: If you wanted to talk to someone you had to look up their number in these encyclopedia-size books.

Sometimes I flip through them. All the names and numbers of all the people who lived here and all the companies are still in there. The paper is thin and puckered from moisture and it rips if you touch it too roughly.

On the floor next to the desk there's an old dirty mattress and next to it some candles. Beer cans and cigarette butts cover the floor—I'm not the only one who comes here.

I carefully place the Eiffel Tower's box onto the concrete floor, sit down on the damp mattress, and open my backpack. Take out the diary and a Coke that I brought from home, go to the page I dog-eared, and start reading.

Something strange just happened: P went into the bathroom. A moment later I went in to get some hand cream.

P was standing in the corner with his pants around his knees texting someone when I entered.

I asked him why he was texting in the bathroom. P got angry and told me to stop spying on him.

Why would you text in the bathroom?

Why?

ORMBERG, NOVEMBER 27

We just had a meeting.

Major progress!

Andreas got a bite from our inquiries at the hospitals. Kullbergska

Hospital in Katrineholm operated on the wrist of a 5-year-old girl in November 1993. The girl suffered a serious infection afterward and was treated with intravenous antibiotics for three days before being sent home. The medical examiner has compared the X-rays and the hospital records to the autopsy report, and they're "99 percent" sure it's her!

The girl's name was Nermina Malkoc. She was born in Sarajevo on New Year's Eve 1988. Arrived as a refugee in the summer of 1993 with her mother, Azra Malkoc, born in 1967 in Sarajevo.

Bingo! Malin said when Manfred told her. She sounded so happy, so sure. Victorious.

I looked at the pictures of the dead girl's skeleton. At the skull and its long wisps of hair. It felt so surreal, so shameful. Here we sat, eating buns, cheering about having identified her.

Her death. Our happiness. The cinnamon buns.

All of us snug in our filthy little office.

Nermina and her mother Azra lived at the refugee camp in Ormberg—in the old TrikåKungen factory. It was used as housing for asylum seekers in the early nineties, when there were a lot of refugees coming from the former Yugoslavia.

Apparently, Azra and Nermina were denied a residency permit in early December 1993. After that there's no more information about them.

But: Azra's big sister, Esma Hadzic, also lived in the refugee camp here. And she still lives in Sweden.

In Gnesta of all places.

It's only an hour drive from here. Apparently, she's on vacation in Gran Canaria right now, but Manfred talked to her on the phone. She said she hadn't heard from Azra or Nermina since they disappeared from the refugee camp. She also said Azra was pregnant at the time.

Andreas & Malin will interview Esma and gather a DNA sample as soon as she gets home.

We started working right away with the new information.

Manfred contacted the Swedish Migration Agency. Malin and
Andreas started researching the asylum seekers' housing: Who was
employed there in the early nineties? Did anything happen that could
be linked to Azra & Nermina?

P reviewed the list of convicted criminals in the area and contacted
the prosecutor.

We also discussed the possibility that Azra killed her own daughter.
When a child is murdered, the perpetrator is often a parent or steppar-
ent. The fact that Azra disappeared after Nermina's death certainly
points to that. Maybe she went underground.

We'll dig into Azra's past, try to find out if she had any psychological
problems or a history of violence.


A sound interrupts my reading. A bang from the other side of
the machine hall, like the slamming of a door.

I quickly put the diary into my backpack and focus on listening.

Steps echo in the silence.

I look up from behind the desk and can just make out the silhouette of someone approaching in the dim light. A second or
two later I realize it's Saga. My stomach flips, and I start to feel
warm inside.

She's wearing striped tights, heavy boots, and a puffy jacket,
and she's swinging her backpack back and forth in her right hand.
Her pink hair is in a knot on top of her head.

I raise my hand in greeting, and she starts jogging toward me.

"Hi," she says, sounding breathless. "I knew you'd be here."

"Hi," I say. "You didn't go swimming?"

"No. I hate pools. Do you know how many chemicals they use?
To kill the bacteria in the water?"

"No idea."

"Exactly. It's not something anyone wants to think about."

"Why do they have to kill the bacteria?"

Saga drops her backpack near the mattress and sits down next to me. The shoulders of her coat are wet, and I realize I must have been sitting here a long time, and it's probably started snowing again.

"People piss in the water. It's disgusting!"

"And then they have to pour in chemicals?"

"Exactly. Though I think the chemicals are more dangerous than a little piss."

Saga glances up at the ceiling, as if pondering something. Then she says:

"But still. You don't want to drink too much of that water. It's probably more poisonous than, like, radioactive waste. And *much* more disgusting."

I can't help laughing.

Saga falls silent for a moment, pulls a feather from a small hole in her coat, then another. And another. They fall on the floor like the snowflakes outside.

"Jake," she says slowly.

"Yes?"

"Are we together now?"

"Yes," I answer.

We sit for a while on the old seedy mattress. It feels good and not at all strange, like it's the most natural thing in the world that we're together now.

As if it doesn't change anything, even though everything *is* different.

Then Saga grabs her backpack and takes out a bag. She takes something out of the bag that's around half the size of a milk carton.

"What is it?" I ask.

"My special assignment. It's a pyramid made of used matches."

"Very nice."

Saga smiles indulgently.

"Not particularly. But anyway. It's the Pyramid of Giza."

She strokes her hand over the matches, gently. Her chipped black nail polish gleams under the dim light of the skylights. Somewhere, water drips onto the concrete floor.

"They're not glued? How do they stay together?"

"I tied them together with used dental floss. I wanted everything to be recycled."

*"Wow!"*

"I don't think I've ever used so much floss as I have this week. My gums bleed if you barely touch them now. But if I'd used new floss it would be cheating. Right?"

I nod.

A muffled bang interrupts us, and I hear voices rising and falling in the distance. Laughter, then a shrill howl, and then steps approaching.

We instinctively duck behind the old desktop, but it's too late. They've seen us.

Vincent, Muhammad, and Albin set their sights on us, like bloodhounds on the scent. Vincent goes first. He always goes first—he's the undisputed leader.

Ormberg's King of Assholes.

When he gets to us he spits out his tobacco with surprising power—it's like a brown projectile—and crosses his arms over his chest. He clears his throat, leans his head back, and stares down on us.

"Well, what do you know, *Jaaakey*, did you get yourself a girl?"

Muhammad and Albin laugh loudly, and Albin lights a cigarette. Takes a drag, holds it in his mouth for a few seconds, and then blows it toward the ceiling.

They come closer, and Saga presses against me. I suddenly feel hyperaware of everything: the raw cold pressing in under my coat, the smell of mold, the sound of Saga's breath, the faint scent of Albin's cigarette as he takes a drag.

"Are you together with the retard?" Vincent asks, and nods

toward Saga. "If so, I'd like to thank you. None of us would fuck her if she begged us to. So you're doing us all a favor."

Vincent smiles widely and then goes on without pausing:

"Fuck. What a couple. The retard and the faggot. It's like a fairy tale."

Loud laughter. Muhammad grins widely. Albin takes another drag and looks uncertain.

"We're leaving," Saga says, gathering her things.

Her puffy coat rustles as she stands up. There are red spots on her cheeks, and her hands are trembling.

"Why?" Vincent says. "We just got here."

He reaches for Saga's pyramid, which is standing on the desk, holds it in front of him and wrinkles his forehead as if trying to solve a difficult math problem.

Like two plus two.

"What the hell is this?"

He twists and turns the little match building. Holds it up to the light and peers at it. Then he shakes it as if to see if there's anything inside.

"Give it to me!" Saga says, and reaches for the pyramid.

"Only if you tell me what it is."

Then Vincent notices the box with the Eiffel Tower standing on the floor next to the mattress and drops the pyramid. It lands with a crash, and matches spread out over the damp concrete.

Muhammad and Albin look uncertain, glance at Vincent as if waiting for orders, and Vincent takes a step forward and picks up the Eiffel Tower.

It shines dully in the dim light and creaks a little as Vincent holds it by the top and swings it back and forth.

"Don't tell me you've been sitting at home building this shit? Don't you have anything better to do? Do you miss your mommy? Can't you hang out with that horny sister of yours?"

"It's the Eiffel Tower," I say quietly.

Vincent drops the Eiffel Tower on the concrete. It lands with a screech, on its side, slightly bent, but still intact.

Vincent turns around and nods to Albin. He steps forward and stands uncertainly beside Vincent, flicks his cigarette at an old machine, and clears his throat.

I feel sorry for Albin.

Everyone feels sorry for Albin. Not just because he's an idiot who fails all of his classes, but also because his dad is handicapped. His grandmother took some dangerous medicine when she was pregnant, which caused Albin's dad to be born without legs.

I feel sorry for Vincent, too.

Or Melinda does, anyway. His dad works on an oil rig in the North Sea and almost never comes home.

I try to think about all of that as Albin stands next to the Eiffel Tower staring vacantly at me. I really try to envision the stumps of his father's legs and how the wheelchair gets stuck when he tries to drive it over a high threshold.

But it's impossible.

No matter how hard I try I can't feel sorry for him now. And the fear remains; it's getting harder and harder to breathe, as if somebody wrapped a rope tightly around me and my lungs are filled with green slime.

Albin looks questioningly at Vincent.

Vincent nods, says:

"Crush that piece of shit!"

"No," I scream, and jump up. "No. *Nooo!*"

Albin looks at me with a dull expression on his face. Then he shrugs his shoulders, as if it's just one more of the weird things that Vincent tells him to do every day. Just another order he doesn't have the energy or will to question.

Then he lifts his foot and stomps on the Eiffel Tower with his big wet sneakers, like it's just a spider on the floor of a basement.

# Malin

The medical examiner, Samira Khan, is so short she barely reaches my chest.

She greets us all with a handshake.

Her long, dark hair hangs in a thick braid down her back. She has a plastic apron over her green scrubs, which rustles when she moves. There are gloves and protective glasses on a counter next to her.

It's been almost two weeks since our Skype meeting about the skeleton in the cairn.

Little did we know then that we'd be visiting Samira to discuss another murder. Or that Peter would disappear without a trace.

Manfred, Svante, and I have driven the 180 kilometers to Solna to meet Samira in person. Andreas is still in Ormberg. He has a meeting with Svante's colleagues to discuss how best to coordinate our investigations.

Even if we're not one hundred percent sure yet that the blood on Hanne's shoe comes from the murder victim at the cairn, we will move forward on the assumption that it does. This means that Hanne, and perhaps Peter as well, witnessed a woman's murder, or at least were in the vicinity when the crime was committed.

Of course, this will have an impact on the investigation into

Peter's disappearance. First, we can assume that he and Hanne disappeared on Friday—on the day the woman was murdered—and that these events are connected.

Second, we must now assume that he may have been the victim of a crime. The fact that he's been gone without a trace for six days points toward something other than an accident. If he'd been helpless in the woods with a broken leg, or slipped and drowned in the creek, we would have found him by now.

Samira pulls on a pair of gloves.

"How is the search for your colleague going?" she asks, as if reading my thoughts. "Have you found him?"

"Not yet," Manfred says.

Samira snaps her glove in place and wrinkles her forehead.

"And you think his disappearance might be linked to the murder of this woman?" she asks, and nods at the body lying on the stainless steel autopsy table at the other end of the room.

"We can place our other colleague, Hanne, at the scene of the murder," Svante says.

"Hanne? The woman with memory loss?"

"Correct," Svante says.

Samira readjusts the plastic apron and straightens up a bit.

"Okay. Shall we begin?"

We walk toward the stainless steel tables. The female body on the autopsy table is pale and skinny. Long gray hair hangs in locks from her head.

The body has been neatly sewn up after the autopsy.

Samira starts rattling off facts. Her voice is quiet and matter-of-fact, committed, but lacking any emotion.

She must have done this a hundred times.

"Unknown woman, approximately fifty years old. Height, one hundred and seventy-five centimeters. Weight, fifty-eight kilos . . ."

Svante interrupts her:

"Isn't that underweight?"

"No, she has a BMI of just under nineteen. It's considered normal, though near the bottom of normal range."

Svante nods and buries one hand in his big beard, as if he's searching for something inside.

I glance at the woman on the autopsy table, but avoid looking at her destroyed face.

"She was healthy and in good physical condition," Samira continues. "All internal organs were in good condition. But there is one thing . . ."

She glances at her paper and then goes on:

"You can see a certain amount of muscle hypotrophy—that is, a weakening of the skeletal muscles. It may indicate she had a disease I haven't been able to detect, or it could mean she was physically inactive. We can say with certainty that she didn't work out. And there's another thing."

Samira takes a step toward the woman's head, extends her hand, and parts the woman's lips.

It makes a smacking sound, and I squeeze my eyes shut.

"The teeth are in very poor condition. She had widespread periodontitis, many cavities, and has lost several teeth. There are a couple of old fillings on the premolars—that is, the front molars in the lower jaw. They appear to be made of gold alloy. The forensic odontologist hasn't looked at them yet, but I don't think they were made in Sweden. Look at this."

Samira's voice is calm, her words exact and her approach deliberately pedagogical—yet I find it difficult to take in what she's saying. And I'm even less capable of looking at the woman's face.

"Interesting," Manfred says, and it sounds like he means it.

Svante makes an affirmative sound next to him.

"Is it common for people to have these kinds of problems with their teeth?" Manfred asks.

Samira nods.

"It's not uncommon. The most common cause is odontophobia—

that is, when you're afraid to go to the dentist. We also see teeth decay like this among addicts and the mentally ill."

Manfred and Svante mumble something, both bent over the autopsy table.

"But there's nothing to indicate she was an addict," Samira continues. "She has no visible scars or wounds from injection needles. Also, I've received some of the tox screen back. Blood and urine were negative for . . . Wait a second."

Samira glances at some papers lying on a counter next to the autopsy table and continues:

"No trace of antipsychotics, zolpidem, benzodiazepines, or γ-Hydroxybutyric acid, also known as GHB. But I'm still waiting on the results of a few more tests."

Samira falls silent, takes a step to the side, and meets my eyes. Then wrinkles her forehead.

"Are you okay over there? Do you need to sit down?"

Manfred and Svante turn around and examine me without a word.

"It's fine," I lie, and force a smile.

Samira nods briefly, bends over the body on the table, and continues.

"She's given birth to at least one child—you can see that in the pelvis."

"Only one?" Svante says.

Samira smiles coolly.

"It's impossible to see that. All I can say is that she has given birth *at least* once."

An idea occurs to me, and I step over next to Manfred, near the woman's head.

"You mentioned that the fillings in the woman's teeth could have been done abroad," I say, and meet Samira's dark eyes.

"That could be the case, yes. And, of course, her dental problems could be because she had no access to modern dental care.

She might be a refugee, for example. For instance, I don't think that dental care works particularly well in Syria."

Samira makes a sad grimace, tilts her head slightly, and places her fingers gently on the woman's arms. The gesture contains a tenderness that surprises me.

"But she appears to be European," Samira says. "The current armed conflict lies outside Europe."

The room is silent. Manfred clears his throat.

"Should we look a little closer at her injuries?" he asks, and points to the bullet hole in her chest.

I share a car with Manfred on my way back to Ormberg. Svante, who's headed to Örebro, had taken his own car.

"Do you think she's an immigrant?" Manfred asks as he exits off the E4 highway.

I stare out the window and think.

"The girl in the cairn, Nermina Malkoc, lived at the refugee camp in Ormberg. Both were found in the same place. Both shot. Both missing shoes. And just like in the early nineties, when Nermina was murdered, the TrikåKungen is being used as housing for asylum seekers. I'm just wondering if it's a coincidence."

"You mean someone's running around killing refugees? You think we may be dealing with a racist?"

I shrug my shoulders and look out at the outlines of high-rise buildings set against a darkening sky.

"Who knows."

Manfred nods.

"You and Andreas should go talk to the person in charge of the refugee camp tomorrow. Surely they'll know if someone went missing."

• • •

Andreas raises his hand in greeting when we get back to the office. Then starts to complain about the journalists who've been camped outside in their cars all day.

I look at him sitting there alone at the table.

Hanne's and Peter's chairs stand gapingly empty.

Even though the table's far from roomy, we haven't removed any of their papers or other things. Instead, they sit like a silent, but stubborn, reminder of what happened—Peter's tobacco, his notebook of scribbled notes; Hanne's tube of hand cream.

Manfred gives a brief report on our meeting with the medical examiner. I hang up my jacket and sit down opposite Andreas without meeting his gaze. Then I start going through my emails.

Max calls a few minutes later. Andreas looks at me searchingly as I answer my phone. I go out into the old store area for some privacy.

I stand staring out the dirty window behind what used to be the checkout counter, scrape my foot a little in the dust on the floor. It leaves deep marks, and I get a glimpse of the mustard-colored tiles beneath the dust. Outside, it's already dark and large snowflakes wind down from a black sky.

In less than a month it'll be Christmas.

I hope we find Peter safe and sound and solve these murders by then. And I hope I'm far away from Ormberg.

Max is doing well.

Really well, actually. He was praised by his boss for his contribution to the settlement of a complicated personal injury case. A fifty-year-old woman with an alleged whiplash injury has been suing the insurance company Max works at and, thanks to his efforts, the company won't have to pay anything for her injury.

"It's amazing—she won't get a single krona," he says with barely concealed pride.

Yes, he uses those precise words.

Something bothers me vaguely about his lengthy monologue. I

don't think it's the fact that the poor injured woman didn't get any money, but more that he's so long-winded and tedious about it. I've never found listening to him talk about his job very interesting. And besides, he doesn't ask me a single question about myself.

Mom's words pop into my head out of nowhere:

*Do you really love him?*

It makes me even more annoyed, though, with Mom now. She thinks she knows what's best for me, even though she never managed to escape this backwater. Even though she still lives in the house she grew up in, socializes with the same people she did as a child.

Max finishes up by saying he can't see me this weekend, he has to work, and I tell him that's fine, I have to stay in Ormberg because of the investigation.

"Oh, okay" is all he says, still not asking me how I am.

When I hang up, I feel inexplicably uneasy. As if I just had an insight, but can't quite formulate it for myself.

Then I realize what it is.

I don't *want* to go to Stockholm this weekend. I don't feel like sitting in front of Max's new flat screen listening to him talk about his job. I have no desire to eat entrecote or drink two and a half glasses of red wine. I don't want to sleep with him in his big, expensive bed with its double mattresses stuffed with horsehair and its linen backrest that perfectly matches the bedspread.

What's wrong with me?

I have everything I've ever wanted, and now it's as if it's no longer important to me.


"Everything all right?" Andreas asks, and raises his eyebrows slightly when I sit down.

"Why wouldn't it be?" I say, and hear how curt I sound.

Manfred clears his throat.

"Shall we review the tips our colleagues received about Peter's disappearance or do you have anything else you need to do first?"

He meets my eyes. He looks tired. His eyes are red and his large frame is hunched over in the chair like an old sack of potatoes.

"Sounds good," I say.

Manfred flips through the papers on the table.

"A total of four tips, three of which were anonymous. The first is from one Ragnhild Sahlén, who lives next to the old TrikåKungen factory, where they house the asylum seekers."

Andreas lifts his eyes and looks straight at me.

"Isn't she the one who . . ."

"Yes," I say. "The old biddy who reported the stolen bicycle."

Manfred looks confused.

"Did I miss something?" he asks, and grabs a pen as if intending to take notes.

"Absolutely not," I say. "Ragnhild Sahlén came here one day trying to report a theft. She was convinced that one of the men from the refugee camp had nicked a bicycle."

"Then she has to go to Vingåker," Manfred says. "We don't have time for that kind of thing."

"That's what I told her," I say. "What did she say when she called?"

Manfred moves the pen along the paper as he reads.

"She said she heard one of the refugees scream 'Allahu Akbar' the night Peter and Hanne disappeared. According to her . . ."

Manfred pauses and rubs his eyes before continuing:

"She thinks he was somehow involved in Peter's disappearance and that's why he screamed like that."

"You're kidding?" Andreas says, picking up his tobacco container and putting a wad in his mouth.

"Unfortunately not," Manfred says. "Can we ignore this tip?"

"Absolutely," I say.

Manfred continues:

"In fact, all three of our anonymous tips are about the refugee camp. One person claims he saw two dark-skinned men carrying a rolled-up rug into the factory building the night Peter disappeared and the unknown woman was murdered. A rug big enough to hold a human body."

Manfred makes air quotes when he says "human body" and then continues:

"And one woman says she saw three young dark-skinned men heading into the forest that day near the church. Three men who, according to her, looked threatening."

"How did she draw that conclusion?" Andreas says. "That they were threatening, I mean."

"She didn't say." Manfred sighs. "Finally, one man called to report that something was burning on the grounds of the camp on Saturday. He believes they were perhaps burning a body."

"Jesus Christ," Andreas says. "Burning a *body*? Because he saw some smoke? What is it with this fucking place?"

We all fall silent for a moment, and I feel my irritation return. I feel a sudden need to defend the people of Ormberg, who Andreas apparently thinks so little of, even though he himself was born and raised not so far from here.

"The fact is," I say, "that if you go out to the cottages and actually talk to people—I mean, really take the time to sit down and *listen* to them—you'd understand why they call in with tips like this."

"Is that so?" Andreas sounds doubtful.

"Ormberg is a small community," I continue as calmly as I can, though my cheeks feel hot. "For some reason, the county government has decided to place a hundred Arabs in the middle of the forest, in the middle of the people who live here. A hundred people who come from countries with completely different values. Who have gone through war and torture and misery. And here they get all the help they need: a roof over their heads, food, money, and education. You have to understand that people around here haven't had it easy. The population numbers have dropped. All the factories have shut down and moved to Asia. The post office closed; the daycare closed. Even this fucking grocery store went bust."

"It's like that in many places," Manfred says curtly.

"Yes. But in Ormberg it's been like that for generations. Before the textile crisis and the Brogrens bankruptcy there used to be an ironworks here, and a sawmill. Now there's nothing. Absolutely nothing. People feel betrayed. So of course when the refugees come here and get everything served to them on silver platters people feel provoked. Plus they demand a lot of special treatment. Arabic-speaking staff at the health center in Vingåker, special times for women at the pool . . ."

I fall silent when I see Andreas's eyes. They're full of both disbelief and fear, as if he's run across some rare and dangerous animal, or maybe a child playing with a loaded gun.

"What are you getting at?" he asks.

"I'm just saying I understand how they think. Even if I don't agree with everything they say. Because I don't. I'm *not* racist, if that's what you're thinking."

"Do you hear yourself?" Andreas asks. "Do you really hear how you sound . . . Malin, it could have been you."

"Excuse me? What do you mean by that?"

"I mean it could have been you who had to flee from war and starvation."

"Oh, come on. That's exactly my point. I *am* from Ormberg, and nobody helps us. You have to clean up your own messes before you help the rest of the world."

Manfred slams a large hand so hard against the table the papers lift up and flutter down onto the floor. Coffee splashes out of his paper mug.

"Jesus Christ! What is it with you two? Whatever your problem is, save it for your free time."

Then he stands up and starts pacing the room.

"But," I say, turning to Manfred, "I'm just trying to explain what motivates people around here. They're disappointed because they never got any help. Because *Ormberg* never received a tenth of the resources the refugees get. What do you think? Haven't you thought about it before?"

Manfred stops and turns with ominous slowness toward me. He's as still as a stone.

"It doesn't matter one whit what I think about the refugee camp. It's fucking irrelevant what my opinion is about special pool times for Muslim women. We are here to investigate a murder. And now it's *two* murders. *At least* two murders, because if Peter's dead, then it's three."

I turn to the picture on the wall. Of the Ormberg Girl's skeleton and the body of the faceless woman in the snow.

Manfred doesn't seem to notice. Instead, he continues:

"If you two can't put your political disagreements aside, I'll send you home. In addition, I'll contact both of your superiors and tell them how unprofessional you've been. Is that clear?"

He sinks down into one of the chairs, sighs deeply, and stares up at the ceiling.

"No fucking way I'm going to keep pampering you two like this," he says with exaggerated slowness. "Get it the *fuck* together."

He sighs again, rubs his temples with his thumb and index finger. Then he continues:

"Go to the refugee camp tomorrow and talk to the staff, find out if the woman from the cairn came from there. And then go visit Nermina's aunt, Esma, in Gnesta. She came home from Gran Canaria today. We need to find out more about Nermina Malkoc. And we have to find her mother."

# Jake

Saga and I are sitting in her bed watching a horror film on her computer. The movie is about a girl who's become possessed after having sex with a guy who had a demon inside him. And now she has to have sex with a new guy to get rid of the demon.

"I think they're afraid of sex in the US," Saga says emphatically, as though she knows everything about sex, and also the United States.

"Mmmm," I say, while digging around in a bag of sugary candy.

Saga bought it for me after what happened with the Eiffel Tower. She felt sorry for me. I know that's why, but it still makes me happy.

I think about Vincent, Muhammad, and Albin. Remember Albin's bored expression when he shrugged his shoulders and stomped on the Eiffel Tower. Destroying weeks of work in just a few seconds.

The two of us gathered up the remains of the Eiffel Tower afterward, me and Saga. Saga's pyramid made it through relatively okay. She was able to put back the matches that had come loose, and it almost didn't look like it had been broken.

But the Eiffel Tower couldn't be saved. It was flat as a pancake and so slanted that you couldn't see what it was supposed to be.

I brought it to school anyway. Turned it in and explained what happened. Our teacher Eva's throat turned red as Saga told her what Albin did. She was going to talk to the principal right after class, she said.

Maybe she did, but it doesn't change anything.

The Eiffel Tower is destroyed, and Vincent and Albin and Muhammad will always be twisted assholes.

That last is something Saga says; she loves calling Vincent a "mental asshole" when he can't hear.

Dad says Vincent and his friends will settle down, that they'll be fine when they grow up. He says he feels sorry for Vincent, that puberty's tough, that the body and head don't really cooperate with each other.

He says it's just a "guy thing."

Vincent has been taken hostage by his own body, I think. By the muscles and the pimples and everything else.

Yet another reason not to become a man.

Saga's eyes meet mine.

"On a scale?" she asks, and nods to the laptop.

I look at the demon girl shuffling through the woods with her mouth hanging open.

"Eight, maybe. I think it's pretty good. You?"

"A definite nine," Saga says emphatically, and scoots a little closer to me.

The heat spreads through my chest, and my heart starts to race when I feel her arm against mine. I sense more than feel the fine hair on her forearm against my skin.

Of course I've thought about it a thousand times: that it might happen again. That we might kiss again.

That's what you do when you're together.

The idea is both exciting and intimidating. A little like standing at the top of the diving tower by the lake, staring down at the mirror-blue surface of the water, hesitating—even though you know it's not dangerous, you're still afraid something might go wrong.

Saga pauses the movie with the touch of a button. Blinks and stares at me seriously. The mascara has left a dark shadow under her eyes. The blush on her cheeks glitters in the dim light of the screen.

"Do you think there are ghosts in the cairn?" she asks.

"You mean do I believe in the Ghost Child?"

She nods and licks her lips, and her eyes widen a little.

"I don't believe in ghosts," I say. The moment the words leave my mouth, I remember the bony, pale face outside Berit's window. The black holes where eyes should be and the thin line of a mouth.

"Neither do I. But it *is* weird."

Saga runs a fingertip over the keyboard.

"What's weird?"

She hesitates, then seems to decide she can trust me.

"That they keep finding corpses there. I mean, it can't just be a coincidence. Two people were found dead there. Even if there was twenty years between the murders."

I think of Nermina, who fled to Sweden only to die. About all the things I can't tell Saga.

Everything is *The Sickness*'s fault.

If I hadn't gone out in Mom's dress that night, I could have taken the diary to the police immediately. Then I wouldn't need to lie.

Saga looks at me, hesitating. Then she says:

"The woman they found on Tuesday. She'd been shot. And she was barefoot."

"What? Barefoot in the snow?"

Saga nods seriously.

"How do you know all this?" I ask.

"Mom's sister's ex-husband, who lives in Brevens Bruk, has a son who is together with a girl from Kumla. She works at the front desk at the police in Örebro. But you can't tell anyone. *Promise!*"

"I promise. What else did she say?"

Saga plays with the ring in her nose.

"That she looked like a ghost. With long scary gray hair."

"Dad says she probably came from the refugee camp. The murderer, too."

"How could he know that?"

Saga lifts her perfectly drawn eyebrows a bit.

"Who else would have killed her?" I ask. "Gunnar Sten? The Skog family? *The Ghost Child*?"

"Nathalie says she's heard the Ghost Child wailing at the cairn," Saga says. "Two times. One time it even talked to her, whispered for her to come closer."

"Nathalie's full of shit."

Saga looks embarrassed.

"Yeah, but . . ."

Her voice dies away, and she leans toward me. Her eyes are big and black in the dim light, and her face is serious.

I sit there, petrified: don't dare to move.

Don't want to move.

Then she kisses me again, and I kiss her back. It's easier this time, as if our lips know what to do.

She tastes like chewing gum, and I close my eyes without knowing why. It's as if there are too many impressions otherwise, as if I'm not capable of taking in everything that's happening.

Steps approach outside, and we immediately pull back from each other.

"Your mom?" I ask.

"Oh. She's on tranquilizers. She won't bother us."

But just as she says that there's a gentle knock on the door.

"Saga, you have to come clean up after yourself in the kitchen."

"Later," Saga shouts, and rolls her eyes.

"No, *now*! And I want to talk to you about something."

Saga sighs and stands up. Runs a hand through her pink hair.

"I'll be right back," she says as she leaves.

But Saga doesn't come right back. Instead, minutes tick by and nothing happens. I hear raised voices coming from the kitchen, but can't make out the words.

I glance at the laptop, but I decide I have to wait to watch the movie until Saga gets back. Finally, I take my history textbook out of my backpack, the one that has Hanne's diary hidden inside, and start reading.

The first few pages are about various interrogations conducted by Hanne and P. It's super boring, so I flip forward a few pages.

ORMBERG, NOVEMBER 28

P's changed the code to his cell phone. I discovered it while he was showering. I was just planning to check the weather. I punched in the old code, the one he's had forever, and couldn't unlock the phone!

He's never changed it before. The only person who uses P's phone, besides him, is me.

There must be something on there he doesn't want me to see. I remember when he was texting from the bathroom with his pants around his knees.

He's hiding something.

I have to find out what it is!

Early afternoon at the office.

Malin and Andreas just visited Rut Sten, who was the director at the refugee camp in Ormberg in the early nineties.

She remembers Azra and Nermina, but can't recall that there was anything of note about them. They left the camp voluntarily on December 5, 1993. Rut thought it had something to do with their residence permits.

Manfred's eating buns.

I don't begrudge him that. P asked him if he really SHOULD be eating them. I felt so sorry for Manfred. (He's overweight, but he's also a grown man, capable of deciding what to put in his mouth.)

If P had been sitting next to me I would have given him a poke, but he was near the door looking at his phone.

That phone.

I've decided not to say anything. If I accuse him of secrecy, he'll turn it against me. You're the one keeping secrets, he'll say.

And he'd be right.

So: I say nothing. I don't ask why he changed the code. It could be just a coincidence, mere chance, and nothing to do with me, THE CENTER OF THE UNIVERSE.

No, that was ironic. I'm not the center of the universe. Not for P, nor anyone else. Barely even to myself—it feels like I'm slowly crumbling into tiny pieces that float off in every direction, bobbing away like autumn leaves on the cold, black waters of the Ormberg Creek.

This is the diary of my disappearance.

Not physically but figuratively—because I slide further into the fog as each day progresses.

What will I do when I'm no longer Hanne? When what makes me, me—my memories, my stories—fades, ground to dust by this disease? What will I be then? A body with no soul? A soul without a functioning body? A piece of meat, with blood pulsing through its veins?

I think about it all the time.

I'm not afraid of death, but I am afraid of losing myself.

That's why this diary is so important. As a document, but also as a tool to remind me who I am.

I exist! For a little while anyway.

P has checked the police records. There aren't many criminals in Ormberg and the surrounding areas. Mostly people who got in fights when they were drunk & did drugs.

However, there are two of interest:

Björn Falk: born and raised in Ormberg, but lived in Örebro from 2009 to 2016. Recently moved back to Ormberg after inheriting his parents' house. Convicted of battery, assault, and criminal harassment. Beat his former partner almost to death on two occasions—once by throwing the woman into a hot sauna and then blocking the door. The woman needed three skin transplants to repair burns to her upper body. Björn Falk has had two restraining orders filed against him by former girlfriends whom he's harassed.

My stomach cramps up when I read about Björn.

That's Saga's mom's new boyfriend, and I'm pretty sure she doesn't know he's an abusive piece of shit. I really should tell Saga, so she can warn her mom.

But I can't.

I can't tell anyone about the contents of the diary.

The back of my neck tingles, and I realize once again that there are things in Hanne's diary I shouldn't, and maybe don't want to, know. Things that should remain secret.

Maybe it would be better if I stopped reading. But just as that thought occurs to me, my eyes catch something in the next paragraph and my heart starts to pound in my chest.

The other one is Henrik Hahn: a pedophile who's assaulted children in Örebro (at the school where he worked). Hahn was sentenced to criminal psychiatric care in 2014 and is at Karsudden Hospital outside Katrineholm. His wife Kristina and son Vincent live in Ormberg.

I drop the book on the floor in shock.

Vincent's father is a pedophile?

Vincent says he works on an oil rig in the North Sea.

Says he's responsible for all the computers and IT systems, and almost never makes it home to visit.

Is he in Karsudden with all the lunatics?

Is he a *perv*? A way bigger perv than even I am. Last I checked it wasn't illegal to like girls' clothes and makeup.

Vincent Hahn.

*Ormberg's King of Assholes.*

Maybe Dad was right after all—I really *should* feel sorry for Vincent.

# Malin

The century-old brick buildings are rather magnificent: The main building is huge, with a row of high vaulted windows running down its long side. Warm light streams out into the blue-gray December gloom and paints the nearby snow gold.

Light also shines from the manager's villa, which lies fifty meters from the main building. A lonely Christmas Star hangs in one window.

The snow crunches under our feet as we walk the short distance from the parking lot to the main entrance.

"*Goddamn* it's cold," Andreas mutters.

I nod.

The thermometer read minus nine this morning when Mom and I were eating breakfast.

I stop for a moment to take in the palatial building. More than two hundred people worked here until TrikåKungen went bankrupt in the early sixties.

I think about what it must have been like during its glory days, in the late fifties. At that time the factory supported entire families. Parents worked in shifts and relieved each other here in the courtyard. The children waited at home, probably occupied by the newfangled technologies made possible by their parents' double income: a television, an Ericofon, and a record player. And far above these endless forests, in the quiet blackness of space, the Sputnik satellite flew by.

Progress, a belief in the future.

Then the darkness fell over Ormberg like a wet blanket.

We knock on the small brown door located to the right of the large main entrance.

A woman opens the door. She has short gray hair, and she's wearing a poncho knitted from natural-colored wool. Her blue eyes are framed by thick eyeliner, and her mouth, which is painted a dark red, looks like a bloody wound in the middle of her face. Around her neck hangs a large piece of jewelry. It looks like a beetle, maybe a dung beetle, made out of enamel.

The woman smiles and the wound on her face cracks open, and she introduces herself as Gunnel Engsäll, social worker and director of the refugee housing facility.

Her handshake is surprisingly firm, and her laughter when Andreas stumbles over the threshold arrives with an unexpected rumble—like a thunderstorm on a sleepy summer day.

"Giddyup!" she says. "You're not the first to fall on your nose there. Come in!"

We walk down a corridor, pass an open door. Catch a glimpse of a large room, maybe a dining hall or a meeting room. A few children are playing on the floor. One boy runs by with a hockey stick in his hand. Two teenage girls are giggling together on the sofa.

We continue through the corridor into a small office, and each sit down in an armchair.

The decorations are sparse, but it still feels cozy. Perhaps because of the colorful pillows in the armchairs.

Gunnel explains she has only twenty minutes for us, then a representative is coming from the county. They have to discuss fire safety routines and "other bureaucratic bullshit."

Her laughter rumbles through the room as she says the last bit.

Andreas takes out his notebook and explains why we're here.

"On Tuesday, a woman was found dead in the forest, less than two kilometers from here," he says, flipping through his notebook. "She was—"

Gunnel raises her hand. Her bracelets clatter.

"She's not from here."

Andreas opens his mouth as if to say something, but no words come.

"How do you know?" I ask. "We haven't even—"

"I've already heard about her," Gunnel says. "In her fifties. Long gray hair?"

Andreas catches my eyes, his expression uncertain.

"Where did you hear that?" I ask.

Her face doesn't change.

"Ormberg is a very small town. And I keep an eye on all of our residents. No one is missing. If someone had disappeared, I'd know about it."

"Okay," Andreas says. "Very well. Then I have just a few more questions before we go. If we go back a week, to last Friday . . . December first."

Andreas glances down at his notebook.

"Was that when she was murdered?" Gunnel asks.

An awkward silence sets in.

Andreas clears his throat.

"I can't discuss that. The preliminary investigation is confidential. But I'd like to know if anything unusual happened that evening."

Gunnel's eyes wander over to the window. Then she slowly shakes her head.

"I don't believe so."

"We received a tip that you were burning something here."

Gunnel blinks and looks uncomprehendingly at Andreas.

"Burning something? Well, perhaps we did. Yes, a few of the

guys tried to, anyway. Until the fire got out of hand. Why? Is that not allowed?"

"Absolutely. I just wanted to verify that information. We also have a witness who claims that a rolled rug was carried into the refugee camp that evening. A rug that was big enough to hold a body."

Gunnel crosses her arms over her chest and looks at us sternly.

"Is this some kind of joke?"

Andreas clears his throat and looks down at his shoes.

"We have to follow up on every tip," I explain.

Gunnel shakes her head.

"If someone had brought a corpse in here we would have noticed it. And we usually grill lamb sausages and marshmallows, not body parts."

Gunnel stands up and starts to pace around the little room. She stops in front of the window. Stares out at the gray day.

"What's wrong with people?" she says, more to herself. "There's so much hate. So many project their anger onto the refugees. Why attack the weakest, people who are already down? Explain that to me?"

Neither of us says anything. Andreas looks like he'd like to sink into the ground. I'm torn. Of course hatred and violence are terrible, but there's something annoyingly priggish about Gunnel and her politically correct comments on xenophobia.

Gunnel continues:

"And yesterday, that lunatic was here. *Ragnhild* . . ."

"Ragnhild Sahlén?" I say.

"That's the one. She was rambling on about a bike she thought one of our residents had stolen. And she threatened to have us shut down."

Gunnel walks back to her chair. Sits down again. Andreas meets my eyes.

"She said that?" he asks.

Gunnel nods.

"Did you work here in the early nineties?" I ask in an attempt to change the subject, because even though Ragnhild's behavior is noteworthy, I find it hard to imagine she had anything to do with the woman in the cairn.

Gunnel nods and straightens up a bit.

"Yes, I worked here for a while during the Yugoslavian war. It was the same thing then. People were so freaking upset that the refugees were here. I remember we literally had to sleep in the garden holding a fire extinguisher some nights. Somebody kept setting fire to the bushes in the courtyard. We reported it to the police; they came here several times, but never found out who did it."

"Do you remember a five-year-old girl named Nermina Malkoc?" I ask. "She lived here with her mother, Azra Malkoc. They left in December 1993."

Gunnel wrinkles her eyebrows and absently fingers the large pendant hanging from her necklace.

"No. Unfortunately. But I'm not good with names."

Andreas takes out a picture of Nermina and hands it to Gunnel. She examines the photo in silence, and then shakes her head.

"I'm sorry. You should talk to Rut Sten, who was the director here back then. She's retired now. Or you can try Tony; he was the caretaker."

"We talked to Rut," Andreas says. "She remembered Azra and Nermina, but didn't know where they went after they left Ormberg."

There's a knock on the door and a young man with a ponytail sticks his head inside.

"They're here," he says. "We're sitting in the manager's villa. You coming?"

Gunnel nods.

. . .

"*Well?*" Andreas says once we're settled in the car on our way to Gnesta to meet Esma, Azra Malkoc's sister.

We're hoping for some clue that might help us find Nermina's mother.

"Well, *what?*" I ask.

"That wasn't so bad, was it."

"You need to fucking drop this," I say. "How many times do I have to tell you I'm not a racist?"

I think of our argument in front of Manfred yesterday. About what Andreas said, that it could have been *me* who had to flee from war and starvation. Such a cheap shot. Andreas isn't just an egocentric male chauvinist pig, he obviously wants to prove he's morally superior at my expense.

Manfred must think I'm the worst kind of racist at this point, thanks to Andreas's bullshit.

We sit in silence for the rest of the drive to Gnesta. Dusk falls outside. The snow starts to fall just as we reach Gnesta's central square.

Andreas parks the car outside the gray three-story apartment building Esma Hadzic lives in.

I wrap my coat tighter around my body as we jog the last bit from the parking lot to the entrance. The snow that swirls around us in the darkness absorbs all sound, so the only thing we can hear is the crunch of our boots on the thin crust of the snow.

Esma opens the door after two buzzes. She's tall and dark, with finely drawn features. Her hair is cut in a short bob. She looks to be around fifty, but her face has something childish, almost doll-like about it, as if the wrinkles were just a mask that could be pulled off to reveal a girl's face.

Only when I take her hand do I notice she's leaning on a crutch, and that her fingers are gnarled like old tree branches.

She notices my look.

"Rheumatism," she says curtly. "I've been on disability for more than twenty years."

Then she heads toward the kitchen, leaning on her crutch and gesturing to us to follow.

We take off our boots and coats and head after her.

The apartment is small, clinically clean, and painted in bright colors. The floors in the hall and the living room are covered with drab oriental rugs, but the walls are as bare as a monastery. The kitchen feels Spartan, too. A table and four chairs stand in the middle of the linoleum floor. There are no curtains, flowers, or decorations.

We sit down and Esma serves us coffee and gingerbread cookies. I immediately feel guilty seeing her struggle to hand us cups with her stiff hands.

"Can I help?" I ask.

"No," she says firmly, and sets a cup in front of me.

She pours a coffee for herself, and then sits down very slowly next to Andreas.

"Is it Nermina?" she asks in a steady, but weak voice.

Her Swedish is perfect, but I detect a slight accent. Andreas clears his throat, and I can see his look wander to Esma's disfigured hands.

"As our colleague explained when he called, we're not completely sure yet. We need to confirm her identity with a DNA sample from a relative. But there are several things that indicate it *could* be Nermina who was found near Ormberg in 2009. There were metal plates in the radial bone of one of her forearms, probably put there during a wrist operation. And if we understand correctly, Nermina broke her wrist in the winter of 1993."

Esma's eyes move up to the kitchen light. Her eyes are shiny, and she blinks fast a few times.

"It was in the middle of November. She fell down from a tree at the refugee camp and landed on her hand when she fell. They operated on her in Katrineholm. She came home that same day, but had to go back three days later because of a high fever. She was in hospital for several days before coming home again. Azra was so worried. This . . . *skeleton* they found. The girl in the cairn. Do you know when she died?"

"The medical examiner believes she died just a few months after the wrist surgery, because the injury hadn't completely healed. If it is Nermina, that means that she died sometime in early 1994. But the body was only found eight years ago. They failed to make an identification at the time, so the case was abandoned until we started working on it at the end of November."

Esma nods.

"And how did this girl . . . who might be Nermina . . . die?"

"Blunt force trauma," Andreas says. "It could have been either an accident or an assault. Would you like to know the details?"

Esma takes a deep breath, then nods so that some of her dark hair falls onto her face. She pushes it away with her bent fingers.

"Yes. I *want* to know. Virtually my whole family died in the war, and I had to identify almost every single one. I've held pieces of my husband's leg in Tuzla. I buried my brothers in Srebrenica. I visited the mass graves in Kamenica and the football field in Nova Kasaba where thousands of boys and men were held before execution. You just need to know; that's how it works. After everything else has been taken away, knowledge is the one thing that helps you move on. Do you understand?"

Andreas nods silently. Fumbles with the papers in his bag, takes out a map of Ormberg and some postcards of the cairn. He lays them carefully in front of Esma. Then he tells her about the cairn and the skeleton found there in 2009. Explains how the investigation hit a dead end, but that the police are now making an investment in cold cases. He concludes by explaining how the medical examiner was able to identify the body.

I sigh with relief that he doesn't mention I was the one who found Nermina.

Esma stiffens when Andreas shows her the picture of the cairn.

She sits immobile for a few seconds, then whimpers loudly, and puts her hands on the paper. Strokes her swollen, gnarled hands over the trees and rocks.

"Nermina," she says. "Nermina, my love. *Were you lying under those stones?*"

Then she buries her face in her hands and sobs.

Andreas reaches for a roll of paper towels with hearts on it and tears off a piece. Hands it to Esma, who thanks him and wipes her nose.

She sits immobile for a few seconds, then seems to collect herself. Crumples up the paper towel with difficulty and lays it on the table.

"It's not certain it's Nermina," I say quietly, though I know the likelihood that it's anyone else is quite small.

"Of course it's her," Esma says brusquely. "Besides. I already knew they were dead. But still, it hurts."

"What do you mean?" Andreas asks. "How could you know they were dead?"

Esma raises an eyebrow.

"Azra was my little sister. It's been almost twenty-five years since she and Nermina disappeared from the refugee camp in Ormberg. The only reasonable explanation for why she hasn't contacted me is that she's dead."

"You say she disappeared. But the former director at the camp said that she and Nermina left," I point out.

Esma smiles sadly, brings her cup to her mouth and takes a sip of hot coffee.

"Disappeared, left. Azra believed their applications for a residence permit were going to be rejected. She was going to try to get to Stockholm."

"I thought all Bosnians were allowed to stay during the war," Andreas says.

Esma shakes her head.

"In the summer of 1993, the parliament issued permanent residence permits to fifty thousand Bosnians in Sweden. But at the
same time, a visa requirement was introduced for Bosnia. Not
because the situation had stabilized, but because they wanted to
reduce the flow of refugees."

Esma snorts a bit when she says the last bit. Then she continues:

"Azra and Nermina were in Croatia at that time. They managed to get Croatian passports and were able to enter Sweden
despite the visa requirement. But that meant they had problems
getting the residence permit. Even though they could prove they
were actually Bosnians."

"So they went underground?" Andreas asked.

Esma nods.

"Azra didn't think they'd be allowed to stay. And there was no
future for them there, not in Croatia or in Bosnia."

"Do you remember the day they disappeared?" Andreas asks.

Esma nods.

"The fifth of December."

Andreas records the date in his notebook.

"Do you know where in Stockholm they were planning to go?"
he asks.

"No. I'm sorry. I have no idea. I just know they knew someone
who was going to help them get to Stockholm, but I don't know
where they were planning to go or who that person was. I do think
Azra had friends in Stockholm. Other Bosnians, who'd arrived
earlier."

"You mentioned to our colleague that Azra was pregnant when
she disappeared," I say. "Is that right?"

Esma blinks a few times.

"Yes. She told me that."

"How far along was she?" I ask.

"I don't know. But she wasn't showing yet. I think she got pregnant in the summer, just before going to Sweden. But, of course, Azra was skinny as a rail for most of her first pregnancy, so I can't be sure."

"How did she feel?"

Esma shrugs. "She felt good."

"Psychologically as well?"

Esma looks at me. There's a subtle caution in her eyes.

"Yes. *Why?*"

"We need to know," I say without any further explanation.

"Psychologically she was doing great," Esma says sharply.

Andreas clears his throat.

"Her husband?" he asks.

"Dead," Esma says matter-of-factly. "They never found him. He returned to Bosnia from Croatia, and nobody knows what happened after that. He's probably buried in one of the mass graves. They'll never find everyone who disappeared."

Andreas carefully gathers up the pictures, puts them into the folder, and returns them to his bag.

"Nermina's body was found in 2009," he said. "Did you know about that? A little girl was found dead in Ormberg? It was covered pretty extensively in the newspapers."

Esma shakes her head and pokes the little ball of paper towel.

"No. Or, I don't know. Not that I remember anyway. If I heard about it on the news, I certainly didn't connect it to Nermina. And why would I? It had been so long. And I thought she was with Azra."

Her voice dies out.

"You said you knew that Azra and Nermina were dead," I say. "You don't think Azra could be in hiding? That someone killed Nermina, but Azra survived? She might live in Stockholm or—"

Esma interrupts me.

"Are you serious?"

Esma's beautiful, lined face turns hard, and she stretches a bit.

Catches my eye, and squeezes her cup so hard her knuckles turn white.

"She would have contacted me if she could," she says quietly. "It wasn't that important to her to be in Sweden. She wouldn't stay in hiding for over twenty years. Sweden's not exactly worth it."

Esma stares out the black window. A few snowflakes swirl by, almost hovering in the light of the kitchen lamp.

Her comment provokes something in me, irritation perhaps. I guess I'm surprised she's not more grateful that she found a refuge here. Or that she was allowed to stay, despite the end of the war. Some might argue there's no logical reason why Esma should be allowed to live on a Swedish disability pension year after year when she could just as well return to her own country. And I can see their point.

"Could she have returned to Bosnia?" Andreas asks.

Esma shrugs.

"You mean would she have returned after the war? Yes, I suppose it's possible. I actually thought she and Nermina had gone to Bosnia when I didn't hear from them. But even if she had, she would have contacted me. We were very close, Azra and I, even though I'm seven years older. I was almost like a mother to her. No. I don't believe she's alive."


We stay just a little longer at Esma's. Andreas swabs the inside of her cheek so the technicians can compare her DNA to what we think belongs to Nermina. He puts the swab in a small plastic bag and stuffs it into a brown envelope.

Then Esma brews another pot of coffee and shows us pictures from Bosnia. The photo album is bound in green leather and embossed in gold. It's so old the pages stick together. Even though the Polaroids are faded, I'm struck by the dazzling green of the Bosnian hills.

I tell her that—how beautiful it is—and she agrees.

Azra is beautiful, too, and very similar to her sister. Same narrow face, high cheekbones, and dark eyes. Just younger. Young and happy, with no knowledge of the future, standing in the sun in front of a small stone house, wearing a flowery blouse.

The image is unusually sharp and the details are quite clear: her plain earrings, the sun playing in the strands of her dark hair, her slightly crooked front tooth, and the beautiful necklace she wears—a gold medallion with a green border. It looks familiar in some way, as if I've seen it before, but I can't place where.

Esma flips through a few pages.

"It's hard to understand," she says, showing a picture of Nermina as a baby.

She wrinkles her forehead a little and continues:

"How can people do such things? And I don't just mean what happened to Nermina. I mean the war. How neighbor turned against neighbor, robbing and killing. Eight thousand men and boys were killed in the massacre of Srebrenica. They were separated from their families, detained, and executed like cattle. And the world just watched. Eight thousand! What is wrong with humanity? And it never ends. Evil feeds on evil. There's a Bosnian proverb: *Ko seje vjetar, žanje oluju.* It means: Those who sow the wind, harvest the storm."

"Those who sow the wind, harvest the storm," Andreas echoes. "It's almost biblical."

Esma shrugs. "Perhaps it is."

I look down at the picture of Nermina again.

Chubby baby cheeks, pink rompers, and a pacifier with a flower on it.

And suddenly I remember why Azra's necklace looked so familiar. My stomach knots up, and my mouth goes dry.

"Can you show me that picture of Azra again?" I ask.

"Of course," Esma says, and flips back a few pages.

I lean forward and study Azra's necklace closely.

"Beautiful necklace," I say.

"The medallion was our mother's. Azra always wore it. You could open it up. She kept a picture of Nermina inside."

"Was she wearing the necklace when she disappeared?"

"She never took it off."

"Can we borrow this picture?" I ask. "We'll be very careful with it, and you'll get it back."

She raises her eyebrows a little.

"Yes, that's fine," she says slowly, loosens the old photo and hands it to me.

"We have to go now," I say, pulling Andreas by the arm a little. He seems to take the hint.

We say our goodbyes to Esma, promising to return as soon as we know more.

As soon as Esma closes the door Andreas turns to me and whispers:

"*What is it?*"

"The medallion," I whisper. "Azra's medallion. Hanne was wearing it when Manfred and I met with her."

# Jake

Dad's sleeping, even though it's not even six yet.

I sneak by him as quietly as I can, past the living room and into the laundry room. I'm carrying a plastic bag full of dirty laundry.

Before, when Mom was alive, we had a wicker hamper with blue stripes on it. A bag of dried lavender hung from the edge. But the hamper broke during a party of Melinda's, and Dad never bought a new one.

It doesn't matter—a plastic bag works just as well. Though I miss the smell of lavender. Saga's mother has soap that smells like that, and every time I use it I think of our old hamper and Mom.

I turn on the light. The floor is covered in dirty clothes.

I kick a few dirty shirts aside to get to the washing machine. Then I stuff it full with my clothes, pour the detergent into the small compartment, and turn on the machine.

The washing machine starts to gurgle, and takes a small leap.

I remember what Saga said earlier today. How Nathalie heard the Ghost Child at the cairn twice, that it talked to her, whispered for her to come closer.

Ghosts aren't real, are they? And even if they were, they wouldn't be able to kill two people.

*Right?*

And that woman who was murdered, who was barefoot in the middle of winter? Who was she, and what was she doing at the cairn?

Just as I'm about to turn off the light, I notice one of Dad's checkered shirts crumpled up near the wall. I don't really know why, but I bend down and reach for it. It's not logical—the floor is full of clothes, so why this shirt—but something feels off about it in some vague way. Partly, I don't understand how the shirt ended up there, and also I see long threads hanging from it, like it's ripped.

I've seen that brown checkered shirt a thousand times—it's one of Dad's favorites. One sleeve is torn off, hanging by just a thread. And there's a big brown stain. It feels stiff when I poke it.

I wonder what happened, and why Dad put the shirt there instead of throwing it away. But above all, I wonder what to do with it. In the end, I put it back where it was and go up to my room.

Maybe I should talk to Melinda about Dad when she gets home. I haven't told her about the rifle under the couch: Somehow that would feel like a betrayal. As for this shirt—there must be some simple explanation. But still.

The stain looked like dried blood.

I imagine that Dad must have caught his arm on something, cut himself, and torn his shirt. When I close my eyes I can see his blood on his freckled skin.

Tears burn behind my eyelids, and it's hard to breathe.

Ever since Mom died, I've been afraid something bad would happen to Dad—that he'd drive off the road, that the creek would flood and drown him, that he'd be infected by some flesh-eating bacteria.

I take out Hanne's diary, feel the weight of it in my hands, and breathe in the smell of old, damp paper.

The pages stick together, and I have to pull them apart carefully so they won't rip.

If Hanne were here now I could ask her what to do about Dad. I'm sure she'd know.

I start to read, but end up in the middle of a long and boring summary of a meeting with someone called the prosecutor. Just as I'm about to put away the book my eyes catch a sentence farther down the page: "*. . . just visited the Birgersson family.*"

The Birgersson Family—that's us. Me, Dad, and Melinda.

Was Hanne *here*?

I keep reading.

ORMBERG, NOVEMBER 29

P and I just visited the Birgersson family.

The road to the house was terrible, got progressively more narrow. Large, deep potholes covered the roadway. I thought we were going to get stuck.

P said we needed a "damn tank" to get out there.

We still had no idea what to expect.

Far into the forest, next to the creek, stood a house that reminded me of Villa Villekulla. It must be from the turn of the last century, and it had been built onto in every possible direction. Strange additions that grew like cancerous tumors out of that poor house. A giant deck encircled it. Piles of wood lay under tarps in several places on the lawn.

I concluded that someone must still be building onto the house.

The yard was full of trash & discarded odds and ends: bikes, tires, grills, and broken tools. But the deck was neat, and seemingly new: The wood was green from waterproofing.

There was a garage, too. Black trash bags were stacked along one wall.

P went over and looked inside: They were full of empty beer cans.

Stefan Birgersson opened the door.

He stank of stale sweat & old alcohol. Probably hadn't showered in a week. He was wearing an old tracksuit and had only one sock on.

He showed us into the kitchen. Explained he was alone (the children

were in school). He apologized: hadn't had time to clean. We told him
it didn't matter.

I tried not to be affected by my surroundings, but still I was shocked.
Such misery!

But it wasn't poverty, it was neglect. There was no shortage of
gadgets (a huge fridge, an espresso machine, a SodaStream, a bread
machine, etc.). Old food and garbage lay everywhere: in the sink, on
the floor. Empty beer cans lined the walls.

Stefan is 48. His wife, Suzanne, died a year ago (leukemia).

Stefan spoke for a long time about his wife and children. Got tears
in the eyes. Blew his nose. Apologized again for the mess. Whispered: I
don't know what I'd do without my kids.

I thought: It should be the exact OPPOSITE. The kids shouldn't be
able to get by without you. But I didn't say anything, because he
looked so miserable.

P asked if he had any help. Stefan replied that both his and Suzanne's parents were dead. But, he said: I've got unemployment
benefits. We won't starve. And I do odd jobs for the summer visitors now
and then.

Stefan talked for a long time about his children: Jake & Melinda.
Said they were good kids. Thoughtful and smart. Took care of him when
he couldn't. But he was worried about Jake, called him "frail."

P started the interrogation. Asked if Stefan & Suzanne had lived here
in the nineties (yes), and if they remembered the Ormberg Girl (of
course; it was all people talked about for months). Did he remember
that the TrikåKungen buildings were used as refugee housing during
that period (absolutely; everyone hated it, they didn't want "trouble").

P told him about Nermina Malkoc. Explained it was probably her
body found in the cairn in 2009. He asked if Stefan recognized the
name, or had ever been to the refugee camp.

Stefan had never heard of her. Nor had he been to the refugee
camp, not in the nineties and not now, he said. Said he did his best to
keep himself & his children "away from there" now that the refugees
from Syria had arrived.

I asked why, and he replied that they didn't want any "trouble."

There it was again: that word "trouble." (As IF the refugee camp, and NOT unemployment, depopulation, and the inverted demographic pyramid, weren't Ormberg's real problems.)

I wanted to understand, so I asked again: What KIND of trouble?

Stefan didn't answer the question. Instead, he went to the fridge, grabbed a beer, opened it, and sank down on his chair.

(I felt almost nauseated by his smell, but still liked him in some way. Maybe it was the softness in his voice when he talked about his children. Maybe the fear in his eyes when he called the son "frail.")

P asked again if he was absolutely sure he'd never visited the refugee camp in the early nineties.

Stefan fell right into the trap. Said he'd NEVER been there.

P took out some old documents Andreas had found, which proved that Stefan did carpentry work at the facility a total of five times in 1993. Stefan was clearly embarrassed, but apologized by saying he must have forgotten.

After that we didn't get any further. Stefan's daughter Melinda came home: a pudgy teenage girl wearing too much makeup and clothes that made her look cheap.

Stefan didn't say goodbye as we left. Instead, he opened another beer.

Even though I felt a great deal of sympathy for him, I have to agree with Peter, who found his behavior suspect. Why lie about working at the refugee camp?

There's something off about it. Stefan Birgersson is hiding something.


The book slips out of my hands. My chest collapses; it feels like I'm caught in a vice, breathing through a straw.

It can't be true.

It's not *allowed* to be true.

Could they seriously believe Dad had something to do with the murder?

# Malin

It's almost nine in the evening when Andreas and I park the car in front of Berit Sund's red cottage. The windows are lit, and smoke curls up slowly from the chimney before scattering into the viciously cold air.

We've talked all the way from Gnesta: about Esma, the war in Bosnia, and Nermina. And we tried to figure out how her mother's medallion could have ended up with Hanne—if it even is the medallion.

When I saw the picture at Esma's, I was so sure, but now I no longer know.

Snow crunches beneath our boots as we walk the short distance to Berit's front door.

Andreas knocks, and we wait, but nothing happens. Then the dog barks.

"I think Berit's hard of hearing," I say. "You may have to—"

Andreas nods and before I finish the sentence he makes a fist and pounds hard on the front door. After a few seconds, steps approach, and Berit opens up. She has curlers in her hair and a kerchief wrapped around to hold them in place. The dog's stopped barking, but sticks his nose out the door and sniffs the air.

"Malin?" she says, looking confused. Then she looks at Andreas. She blinks a few times and opens her mouth as if intending to say something.

"I apologize for coming so late," I say. "This is my colleague Andreas, from Örebro. We need to talk to Hanne a bit."

*"Have you found him?"* Her voice is a whisper.

"No, this is concerning another matter."

Berit shrugs slightly.

"Well then, you'd best come in."

She limps down the hall.

"We're drinking tea," Berit says with her back to us.

We take off our coats and shoes. The faded geraniums on the windowsill look even more miserable than I remember. Yellow, semidry leaves litter their pots.

The kitchen is pleasantly warm. The woodstove crackles and a kerosene lamp is lit on the table. A straw Christmas Star hangs in the window facing west. Hanne sits with a cup of tea in her hand. She has a shawl wrapped around her shoulders. She stands up expectantly when we enter.

"Hello," I say.

Hanne looks at me curiously. As she stretches her hand to greet me, I realize she still doesn't remember me. I should have been prepared for that, but for some reason, I thought she would now, since she was getting better.

"Hello, Hanne. My name is Malin. I'm a colleague of Manfred's."

Hanne's face breaks into a gentle smile.

"Oh. How is Manfred?"

"He's good."

Hanne wrinkles her eyebrows and looks troubled.

*"Peter?"* she whispers.

I put my hand on hers.

"We haven't found Peter. That's not why we're here. We just need to talk to you about something."

Berit clears away her teacup and turns toward us.

"I'm going out with Joppe. Could you put another log on the fire soon?"

I nod and look at Berit in her curlers. The wounds on her left forearm are an angry red today. They look infected.

"That doesn't look good," I say.

Berit puts her hand on the sores.

"It'll be fine," she says, turning around and heading out into the hall.

The dog limps after her.

Andreas and I sit down at the table opposite Hanne.

"How are you?" I ask.

Hanne shrugs. "Good. My scratches have almost healed. Though I still don't remember what happened in the woods, so if that's why you came here I can't help you."

"We want to talk to you about something else. Your necklace."

"My *necklace*?"

Hanne looks confused, lets her shawl slip down on her shoulders and moves a hand to her neck. Something glitters between her fingers.

"Could we have a look at it?" Andreas asks.

"Yes, of course."

She takes off the chain and hands me the necklace.

The medallion feels warm and heavy in my hand. I examine it closely. An enameled green border runs around the edge, and there are stones set in the middle. They glitter in the warm light of the kerosene lamp.

"This *must* be it," Andreas says.

I don't say anything, just nod, because he's right. The medallion looks exactly like the one Azra Malkoc was wearing in the picture from Esma's album.

"*What?*" Hanne says, her eyes darting back and forth between me and Andreas.

I turn toward her.

"You and Peter were working on an investigation here in Ormberg. Do you remember?"

Hanne lowers her eyes.

"Yes. No. There's just so much I don't remember. It's all so blurry."

"A little girl was murdered here in the early nineties. This piece of jewelry belonged to her mother," Andreas says. "Her name is Azra Malkoc."

Hanne looks horrified.

"I had no idea."

"Do you remember how you got this necklace?"

Hanne shakes her head.

"No. *I'm so sorry!*"

For a second, I think she might start crying, but then she takes a deep breath and seems to relax a little.

Andreas roots around in his pocket and takes out his notebook. Opens it and plucks out the photo of Azra that we borrowed from Esma.

"Do you recognize her?" he asks.

Hanne takes the photograph and lays it on the table in front of her. Then reaches for the reading glasses sitting next to the tea, puts them on, and stares for a long time at the picture of the young woman in the flowery blouse, squinting against the sun.

"No. I don't recognize her. But I see she's wearing the necklace."

"Hanne," I say. "Can we borrow the necklace?"

"It's not even mine," she states quietly. "Of course you should take it."

I pick up her hand. It is thin and cold, despite the warmth of the room.

"If you remember something, anything, write it down. Can you do that? And you know you can call us whenever you want."

Hanne nods without answering.

· · ·

We sit in the dark car outside Berit's house.

"You were right," Andreas says, looking down at the medallion resting in his hand.

"I wish I'd been wrong. We can probably rule out that Peter suffered some accident now."

"Hanne and Peter must have been on the trail. They must have gone somewhere on Friday and then . . ."

He leaves the sentence unfinished.

"But why didn't they tell anyone else?"

Neither of us says anything. Even though we just made a crucial discovery, I feel no joy. There is so much that feels hopeless: the realization that something terrible probably happened to Peter, Hanne's tangible confusion in Berit's kitchen, and the memory of Nermina Malkoc's skull between the heavy, moss-covered stones of the cairn.

And then the woman without a face; she looked just like . . .

Before I even think his name, my temples start to sweat and my pulse races.

Why did I say yes to this fucking assignment anyway? I should have stayed in Katrineholm, continued with the bicycle thefts, the drunken fights, and the never-ending paperwork.

Andreas drums his fingers on the medallion, as if lost in thought. A moment later it clicks open in his hand, like a clam. And I suddenly remember what Esma said, that the medallion could be opened and that Azra kept a photo of Nermina inside.

"Turn on the light!" Andreas says, and I do. Fumble for the ceiling lamp, which floods the car with a light so bright I have to squint.

Andreas looks disgusted.

"What in the *hell* is that?"

I look down at the medallion and see a photo, but I see something else, too. At first I think it's just a dark piece of fluff on top

of the picture. I run a trembling finger over its downy, silk softness.

I catch my breath.

"Hair," I say. "It's hair."


It's ten o'clock by the time we pull up outside our temporary
headquarters, having decided to drive by and drop off the medallion. Tomorrow, we'll send it to the forensic technicians. I need to
pick up my car, too. It's parked, or rather snowed in, outside the
old store.

The cold wind sneaks in under my coat as we push our way
toward the door through a new layer of snow.

It whines and whistles around the corner of the building.

A man comes running out of a red Audi parked not far away.
Seconds later, another car door opens.

"The fourth estate is in place," Andreas says, and starts to
hurry.

I too increase my pace to escape the journalists.

And I glance into the store window.

To my surprise I see a light coming from the back office, which
casts a ghostly shine across the floor of the old store.

"Why's the light on?" I ask.

It's Friday night, and even if Andreas and I are planning to
work the whole weekend, Manfred had decided to go home to his
family in Stockholm. He should have left several hours ago.

"Maybe he forgot to turn it off," Andreas suggests as he pulls
open the door.

We enter without paying any heed to the journalist shouting
behind us. Then stomp the snow off our boots.

The heater is running, too. Its dull drone fills the room—like
hundreds of insects flying around in the half-darkness.

Manfred is sitting at the table when we enter the office.

His laptop is closed and his papers stand in a neat pile next to his briefcase, as if he were about to leave. His phone lies on top of the papers.

"You're still here?" I ask.

Manfred doesn't answer. In fact, he doesn't even look at us where we stand with snow melting off of our coats.

"We met with Esma," Andreas begins. "Hanne has a piece of jewelry in her possession that we think belonged to Azra Malkoc."

Manfred nods quickly, as if his thoughts are elsewhere. His eyes are focused on an invisible point on the wall next to me.

"A lot has happened," he says.

We wait for him to continue, but he just shakes his head slowly. In the end he clears his throat and continues:

"First of all, we got a tip from some seventeen-year-olds from Vingåker. They claim they saw a dark Volvo station wagon, an older model, parked on the road between the cairn and the old mill, the night Peter disappeared and the woman was murdered."

"Is it credible?" Andreas asks. "Why didn't they inform us earlier?"

Manfred looks down at his large chapped hands. Pokes at a cuticle with one thumb.

"They claimed they were driving mopeds from Vingåker."

Andreas shakes his head uncomprehendingly.

"And?"

I give Andreas a discreet poke in the side.

"They were driving a car," I say. "But they don't have a license. That's why they didn't tell us earlier, isn't it?"

Manfred nods, and continues.

"Seems likely. They saw a dark Volvo. There was a bald man sitting in the car."

I catch my breath.

"Stefan Birgersson," I say. "The description fits. And he has a dark blue Volvo."

"We'll pick him up tomorrow," Manfred says. "I'm calling the prosecutor soon, but I'm pretty sure we have enough for an arrest."

Manfred rises slowly. Goes to the wall and stands in front of the image of the faceless woman in the snow. Lifts his hand, pushes his index finger against the glossy paper, and says:

"But there's something else. The medical examiner called. The DNA analysis of the murdered woman is complete."

"Already?" Andreas says. "It usually takes—"

"It's a high-priority case," Manfred interrupts him. "They put everything else aside."

"And?" I say.

Manfred shakes his head slowly.

"Her DNA profile is suspiciously similar to Nermina Malkoc's."

"What does that mean?" Andreas says.

It takes a few seconds before I make the connection.

The room starts to spin, and the dull buzz of the heater gets louder, as if those insects had multiplied, had become a gigantic black swarm of blowflies with shiny green bodies and compound eyes and were about to attack us in our little office.

I slide down into one of the chairs and grab the edge of the table, suddenly afraid I might fall over; it feels like the floor is heading up toward me.

"Oh my God," I whisper. "It's her mother, isn't it? The woman in the cairn is Azra Malkoc, isn't she?"

"Very closely related," Manfred says. "That's all they can say with certainty right now. But yes. The guy I talked to admitted it's most likely Azra Malkoc."

# Jake

Saturday morning is silent and gray.

Cold leaks in through the window, and I crawl farther down under the covers in search of a warmth that isn't there.

I am so angry with Hanne. Maybe I'm disappointed, too, I don't really know.

Can you even be angry and disappointed with a person you've never met?

Hanne doesn't like Ormberg. Or my family, or our house. And she thinks Melinda is pudgy and cheap.

As if Hanne is so freaking great.

I think Hanne's being unfair—I don't agree that Dad smells bad or that the extensions on our house look like cancerous tumors.

Cancer makes me think of Mom: of her soft hands and long, narrow nose. Of her hair, which was light on top and dark underneath, and of her voice, which was almost always kind. Of the English romances about love "against all odds," which she read when she was at the hospital in Örebro.

Her scent changed when she got sick.

Before, she always smelled good, as if she'd just showered. But then, after she started taking all those medications, her smell turned chemical in some way, as if they were pumping something poisonous into her. And that was exactly what they did. Chemo-therapy is poison, explained the doctor, who came from Iran and whose name was Hadiya, and who had nice breasts and good makeup.

The poisons made Mom tired.

She lost her hair and nails and vomited into a plastic bucket. And still she was always happy. Happy and so interested in what I was doing in school.

She promised she'd get better, but she lied.

Adults do that.

I know it's to protect their children, but I wish she had been honest, because I was so unprepared for the day her body decided it couldn't go on. I was even angry, though of course she couldn't help getting cancer and dying.

It was nobody's fault, Dad said, but I blamed God, because He seemed to make mistakes about as often as He did the right thing.

Everything changed after Mom was gone.

Dad seemed to deflate, like a popped balloon. As if he got smaller for real, and he didn't have the energy to do anything. Melinda, on the other hand, seemed to get bigger and stronger. Instead of sitting in her bedroom listening to music or making out with her boyfriend, she started doing the cooking and shop-ping and everything else that Mom used to do.

I guess I changed, too, I just don't know how. Something inside me must have been rearranged, even if I looked the same on the outside. Just like when I kissed Saga.

Dad never talks about how he changed. He only talks about other things, like Arabs or Melinda's skirts, which are way too short.

Dad and Olle have begun talking about starting some kind of citizens guard. Dad says the murder of the woman in the forest was "the straw" and that it's their duty to protect the women of Ormberg, even if it means "giving a few Arabs hell."

I asked how he could be sure the Arabs were dangerous, but he didn't answer. Instead, he hit the door of the fridge so hard ice cubes rolled out of the icemaker and onto the floor.

I can't imagine Olle and Dad standing guard here in Ormberg. Where would they even go—there's just woods. Would they tramp around randomly through the snow hunting Arabs?

And where would they keep their beers while they were on duty?

I pick up the diary from the floor and weigh it in my hand.

Last night, I actually considered throwing it away, but the more I think about it, the more I'm sure I have to finish reading it. Especially now, when Dad's involved.

We felt quite low when we left the Birgersson family.

The misery isn't isolated to them.

Ormberg breathes decay and dejection: abandoned factories, closed stores, crumbling houses.

The suspicion toward the refugees isn't so strange in that context.

That's how it works, isn't it?

The brain looks for causal relationships. It's easy to blame the refugees for your misfortunes. To believe that unemployment, depopulation, and decline of public resources are their fault.

And when you stand there, deprived of your livelihood and dignity, it's very tempting to point the finger at someone else.

Immigrants, for example.

I think of Nermina. Her bones in the photos: white, weathered. Long dead.

She's resting now under a headstone that bears no name.

I have to help her!

Afternoon.

P & I met with Margareta Brundin (Malin's aunt). She lives with her adult son Magnus south of Orm Mountain.

Magnus & Margareta's relationship seems symbiotic, on the verge of unhealthy. I was immediately curious and wanted to find out more. (I'm going to ask Malin at the earliest opportunity.)

Margareta said she hadn't had any contact with anyone at the refugee camp—not in the nineties and not now—and that she and Magnus steer clear of that place.

I asked why.

She explained that she had no "business" there and neither did her son. Then she said she didn't believe the killer had come from Ormberg.

I asked how she could know that.

Her answer was what I expected: Everyone knows each other in Ormberg. It had to be an outsider.

Very strange—everyone says the same thing: There are no murderers in Ormberg. The perpetrator must come from the refugee camp / Katrineholm / Stockholm / Germany.

It's almost like they had a public meeting in the village to go through their talking points!

We went back to the office without learning a thing.

Evening again.

P's out and jogging (in the dark, with a headlamp—why would anyone do such a thing?). I think he's having a midlife crisis. He's become so silent and withdrawn. He's started running more than usual. Examines his body critically in the mirror.

Poor P: It's not enough that he has to deal with my aging, he must be wrestling with his own mortality, too.

No! I don't feel sorry for him at all!

He's never had to take care of me, not until now. I've just loved him. Never made any demands. Never extracted any promises about our future.

I have been so damn accommodating, like a worn-out, shapeless bra.

I'll admit one thing: I'm extremely angry. Bitter about the life that gave me this disease. And yes, I'm angry at P sometimes, too, because

I know he'll leave me when I get worse. I think I'm taking my anger out in advance. Because I KNOW it will happen!

P is like a bent little tree on the side of a mountain: He bends with the wind, adapts, follows the path of least resistance.

You might even call him spineless.

He said it didn't matter that I was sick when we got together, he'd love me no matter what happened.

I don't know if it was a conscious lie or wishful thinking on his part, but I knew even then it wasn't true.

Maybe I'm the real villain in this drama: cold, egocentric, and driven by urges. Because I knew all this, but wanted him anyway.

It was like eating pastries even after you know you should stop. I wanted to have that wonderful, indulgent time: the trip to Greenland, the passion. The slight sense of irresponsibility & closeness in the middle of all that was bad.

A drug.

P has been a drug for me. A wonderful drug I absolutely do not want to quit.

So who am I to blame him now?

I look out the window. Get a glimpse of a light. It bobs up and down, approaching slowly.

P is on his way back.


The doorbell rings—I hear it clearly, even though my bedroom door is closed.

At first, I think it's Saga—we didn't make any plans today, but she pops in when she wants to—but then I realize it's way too early for that. Saga sleeps in late on weekends.

I sneak out of bed, open the door a bit, and hear unknown voices in the hall.

A man and a woman are talking to Dad. It is impossible to make out everything they're saying, but I hear the man introduce himself as Manfred. After a minute, they come inside and go to the kitchen with Dad.

I go down the stairs, at first hesitantly, but then my curiosity gets the better of me, and I hurry to the kitchen door.

It's cold, and I'm in a T-shirt and underwear. My skin is covered in gooseflesh, and I shiver as I peek in through the crack in the door.

Dad is sitting with his back to me. He has the checkered blanket around his shoulders, and his neck is shiny, as if from sweat.

Opposite Dad sits Malin Brundin and the fat cop who dresses like a stockbroker—the one Saga and I saw come out of the old grocery store. That must be Manfred.

I suppose that's the same one Hanne writes about in the book. The man who likes to eat buns.

Malin leans forward and stares at Dad. There's something about her body language that makes me uneasy. It almost looks like she wants to jump onto Dad and eat him up.

"And so that's why we'd like to ask you where you were on Friday."

Dad runs his hand over his head as if trying to fix the hair that's no longer there.

"Friday? Hmmm, well. It's been a few days. So, nope. Don't really remember."

"It's only been a week," the fat cop says, and crosses his arms over his suit jacket.

"Yes, yes," Dad says, then falls silent for a while.

Then he stretches a bit and continues:

"Oh right. I was with my buddy Olle. In Högsjö."

"Are you sure about that?" Malin asks.

Her voice is sharp, and I don't like it. I'm afraid of what they're going to do to Dad. He's not at all sharp and, besides, he seems totally unaware of the danger. I want to scream at him not to trust her, but I can't. Instead, I stand there stiff and silent behind the door, with the lump in my throat growing ever larger.

"Yes, goddamnit," Dad says. "I'm sure of it."

"Because he says you *weren't* with him on Friday," Malin says.

"He says you were together on Saturday, which you already told us. Apparently . . ."

Malin looks down at her notebook and then goes on:

"Apparently you were playing *Counter-Strike*."

Malin smiles a bit when she says the last bit, but it's not a nice smile.

"That may be right," Dad says. "Maybe that was Saturday. Yes, we played *Counter-Strike*."

"So what did you do *Friday*?" Manfred asks.

"No fucking clue," Dad says, throwing his arms wide.

"So why did you say you visited Olle on Friday?" Malin asks.

I turn cold inside. They're trying to set Dad up, that much is obvious. Just like in the police shows on TV. They're two and Dad is one, and they're trying to lure him into a trap. Even though he's just confused and mixing up the days.

"I remembered wrong. Is that illegal?"

Dad's voice is shrill now.

Neither Malin nor Manfred answer immediately. Then Malin stands up.

"Can I use your toilet?"

"Sure," Dad says, pointing to the door on the other side of the kitchen.

I see Malin disappear in the direction of the bathroom and living room.

Manfred and Dad sit in silence, as if each is waiting for the other to start talking. Then Manfred mumbles something, but I can't make out what.

Dad mumbles back.

Steps approach down the hall, and Malin appears in the door. She's wearing light blue gloves and carries the rifle in her hand.

"I didn't know you had a gun license," she says, nodding to Dad.

Dad shakes his head.

"It's not mine," he says, slumping into his chair. "I don't hunt."

"I thought every bastard hunted around here," Manfred says.

"Yes," Dad says.

"Possession of a weapon without a license," Manfred says quietly, "is illegal according to the ninth chapter, first paragraph of the weapons act."

Then he says something that I can't make out. Dad shakes his head violently.

"Yes," Malin says, and lets her eyes slide over Dad. "You're coming with us to the station. We'll talk more there. About the rifle and other things."

Malin looks up, and her eyes meet mine.

She freezes.

"It's *not* my rifle," Dad repeats tonelessly.

Malin doesn't answer. Her eyes are fixed on me.

"Hi, Jake," she says. "Come in."

I open the door, but stay in the hall. Suddenly I feel very naked in my T-shirt and underwear.

Dad turns around and looks at me. His eyes are red and watery and wide. His mouth trembles.

"Your dad is coming with us to Örebro," Malin says.

# Malin

Svante stands in front of the whiteboard with his legs wide. He nods to me and Manfred as we enter. He's wearing a Norwegian folk sweater, and he's stuffed his jeans into his socks. There's something on his beard that looks a little like scrambled eggs.

I sit down next to Andreas. He moves his chair closer to me, and I immediately move away. It happens automatically, I don't even think about it. But as usual he gets too close, and I feel a sting of irritation.

"Did you get anything?" Svante says.

We're in a conference room in the Örebro Police Station. It feels strange to be in a real office again, after freezing in a shack that stinks of mold for more than two weeks.

Even though it's Saturday, it's bustling with activity here.

The information that the woman at the cairn is Azra Malkoc has led to completely new theories and questions. And finding the rifle at Stefan Birgersson's has awakened hopes that we may have identified the perpetrator.

I look around.

Malik sits opposite me. I haven't spoken to him yet, but I know that he's been working with Svante for a few years, and that he recently completed a one-year forensic technician course at the National Forensic Centre.

Malik, who appears to be in his thirties, has green eyes, a face like an angel, and the long, narrow fingers of a pianist, the nails shiny and well-kept. His androgynous look is reinforced by the fact that his dark hair is put up in a bun. Around his wrists sit braided leather bands of various colors, and on his left hand a gold ring with an amber stone glitters.

The door flies open and one of the detectives comes in.

Suzette is a muscular woman in her forties with short blond hair, heavy makeup, and long, intensely blue nails. She has a notebook and a pen in hand and walks a little bent over, as if she has a stomachache.

"Damn, you all look serious," she drawls. "Did somebody die?"

It's the oldest joke on the force, yet I can't help smiling.

Rumor has it that Suzette works at her sister's beauty salon in Örebro in her free time, and that her specialty is Brazilian waxing.

Andreas calls her the Queen of the Brazilian and says she's damn tough, whether she's hunting down hooligans or doing that "other thing" at the beauty salon.

Suzette settles down next to Malik, smiles at me, and puts a hand on her notepad.

I wish Andreas hadn't told me about the intimate waxing, because now that's all I can think of as her long blue nails drum against the notepad.

I meet Svante's eyes.

He clears his throat.

"Manfred, you might want to start?"

The pretrial leaders have decided to coordinate the investigations of Peter's disappearance and the murders of Nermina and Azra Malkoc—and they have good reason to: No one believes these are isolated events.

The new, merged investigative team will be based here, but

we'll keep our small field office in Ormberg. In addition, we're getting reinforcements from NOD in Stockholm at the beginning of next week.

The purpose of this meeting is to brief Malik and Suzette on the case. And we'll do so as soon as we've related to the group what came out of the interrogation of Stefan Birgersson.

That's what everyone wants to know, right away.

The news that we have caught him spread like wildfire around here.

Manfred nods quickly, stands up, and goes over to Svante.

"We've just done our initial questioning. Stefan Birgersson maintains his story. He says he mixed up the days. That he visited his friend Olle in Högsjö on Saturday. What he did on the night of the murder—that is, on Friday—he doesn't remember. But he thinks he may have 'driven around' in his car."

Manfred makes air quotes around the last.

"There was a hell of a storm that night," Svante says, crossing his arms over his chest and balancing them against his large stomach. "Why would he have 'driven around' in his car?"

"He couldn't answer that," Manfred says. "He also says he may well have been parked for a while between the cairn and the ironworks. But he claims he was never in the woods."

"And the fact that he worked at the refugee camp in the early nineties—what did he have to say about that?" Svante asks.

"He maintains he forgot that, too," Manfred says. "And as for the rifle, he claims—"

"He doesn't remember?" Svante finishes, and chuckles at his own comment.

Manfred nods, without even the slightest hint of a smile.

"I was *joking*," Svante says. "You mean he said that? For real?"

"Yep. He did."

Svante seems confused. As if he can't decide if Stefan Birgersson is incredibly stupid or a straight-up genius in some sophisticated way that he can't yet perceive.

Manfred rubs his knee, heads for a chair, and sits down with a quiet thud next to the whiteboard. Then he continues:

"I'm going to call the prosecutor. The plan is to search his house tomorrow. It's Saturday today, which means the prosecutor has to apply for a warrant from the judge by Tuesday. We'll try to tie up all the loose ends by then. Sound good?"

Everyone nods, but nobody says anything. The only sound is Suzette's nails tapping on the table. As I watch her hand move, I remember something.

"Wood," I say.

Manfred looks confused.

"*Wood*. Hanne said she remembers boards," I explain. "And Stefan Birgersson has a hell of a lot of boards in his yard, under tarps."

Manfred nods in appreciation.

"Well done! We'll look into that when we search the house. Best case, we might be able to find traces of Hanne at Stefan Birgersson's house."

Suzette wets her dark red lips with the tip of her tongue and says:

"So. What happens to his children if we keep him here?"

"I talked to social services," I say. "They're sending someone over there tonight."

Manfred nods.

"And the gun?" he asks.

"On its way to NFC," I say. "But we don't have any cartridges or empty sleeves to compare it to, so I don't know how much we'll find out."

The room falls silent.

"Do we really believe it was him?"

It's Malik's question. Although his tone is tactful, I hear doubt in his voice; it rubs like a small but annoying rock in one's shoe.

"I don't believe shit," Manfred says. "But we'll have to figure it out."

He massages his knees, grimaces, and closes his eyes. Then he continues:

"He seems like a very broken individual. I can believe he may have mixed up which day he was in Högsjö. Fuck, I can't even keep track of the days anymore. And it's possible he parked his car on the highway that night without being involved in the murder. Honestly, there's not much else to do in Ormberg other than watch TV or drive around in your car. But I have a much harder time buying the bit about the refugee camp. You forget working at a place on five separate occasions? And he knows sure as shit where that rifle came from. So. He's hiding something. We just have to find out what."

"Or maybe he just doesn't want to tell us," I say.

"Doesn't *want* to?"

Manfred raises his bushy red eyebrows and his forehead wrinkles like an accordion.

I try to figure out the best way to put this.

"People don't really trust cops in Ormberg. Don't trust any authorities, actually."

"He's only making it harder for himself," Manfred says.

I observe my colleague from Stockholm—his expensive suit, his large Swiss watch, his perfectly trimmed beard.

How can I explain to him what I mean? Is it even worthwhile to try?

"I know," I say. "I'm just trying to explain how people think in the village. They don't trust us."

For a moment, I think he might start tearing into me again, like when I tried to explain why the people of Ormberg didn't like having the asylum seekers housed there.

But he doesn't say anything, just nods.

"Let's move on from Stefan Birgersson for a while," Svante suggests. "We need to bring Suzette and Malik up to speed on everything."

Manfred nods to our new colleagues. Then he stands up,

brushes something from his jacket, and walks over to the white-board. He picks up a marker and draws a long time line and writes down a number of years.

"Azra and her five-year-old daughter, Nermina, arrive here from Bosnia in the summer of 1993. The fifth of December of the same year, they leave the refugee camp in Ormberg. Everyone assumed they left the residence of their own free will, and no one reported them missing to the police. Azra's sister, Esma, has stated that she believed they returned to Bosnia, but over the years she became increasingly convinced they were dead because she never heard from them."

Manfred reaches for a bottle of mineral water standing on the table, takes a gulp, and then continues:

"Nermina Malkoc was probably murdered at the beginning of 1994. We can determine this because she was operated on in mid-November 1993, and the wrist fracture had not completely healed when she died. The cause of death was probably blunt force trauma. The body was hidden under a cairn and first found by a group of teenagers in 2009."

Manfred nods toward me.

Everyone's eyes turn in my direction, and I can feel my cheeks burning. I feel uneasy every time that story is brought up.

Manfred turns back, looks at his time line, and puts a cross in the middle.

He continues:

"We came to Ormberg on November twenty-second to investigate the murder of the then still unknown girl in the cairn. On the twenty-seventh of November we made a preliminary identification of her as Nermina Malkoc. Four days later, Friday, December first, Peter and Hanne disappeared. Hanne was found in the forest on Saturday evening, December second, confused and suffering from hypothermia. Peter is still missing. Azra Malkoc was shot to death, probably on Friday, December first. No one saw anything

or heard the shot. The body was found on December fifth—
a Tuesday. The medical examiner has confirmed that she was shot
from the front, in the chest, with a rifle, from about twenty meters
away. She was barefoot. And yesterday, we were told she's most
likely Azra Malkoc, Nermina's mother. One of Hanne's shoes
was found near the scene of the murder. There were traces of
Azra Malkoc's blood on the shoe, which allows us to place Hanne
at the scene. Hanne also wore a piece of jewelry that probably
belonged to Azra Malkoc."

"Has it been confirmed that it was Azra's blood on Hanne's
shoes?" I ask. "Last I heard they only knew the blood type."

Manfred nods, and sinks down onto his chair with a deep
breath.

"Yes."

"And the medallion," Malik asks. "Have the technicians looked
at it?"

"Hastily, yes," Manfred says. "They said it probably wasn't
manufactured in Sweden, which makes sense. They also confirmed that it contained human hair. They're doing a DNA analysis. Apparently the hair did include some roots, which means
they're hopeful that they can make a normal DNA analysis. But if
that doesn't work then they can analyze the mitochondrial DNA.
Don't ask me to explain, but it takes longer and isn't as precise."

Andreas shakes his head slowly.

"How in the *hell* did Hanne end up with that necklace?"

"She had no idea," I say. "She didn't remember anything when
we asked her."

Manfred rubs his temples. Then he turns around and looks at
the time line, which stretches from 1993 to 2017. There are a lot of
notes at the beginning and end of it, but the middle is empty other
than a cross at 2009, the year Nermina was found.

"Nermina died in 1994," he says slowly. "Azra was murdered
twenty-three years later. They were found in the same place. It

*must* be the same perp. Stefan Birgersson was twenty-five when Nermina was murdered. And he lived in Ormberg. He could have committed both murders."

"Yes, but . . ." Andreas says, and falls silent.

"Peter and Hanne may have been on the trail," Svante continues.

"Yes, *but*," Andreas says again. "Where was Azra Malkoc for over twenty years? Neither the Swedish nor the Bosnian authorities have any information about her."

"Maybe she went underground," I say. "But she couldn't have lived nearby, because then we'd know about it."

Manfred nods. "Ormberg is too small. Too hard to hide in. But in Stockholm . . . Well, maybe. Or in the Balkans, definitely. In any case, if no one is looking for you."

He shrugs.

"But," Andreas says. "Her daughter was murdered. Why didn't she go to the police?"

"She may have been afraid of being deported," says Suzette, who has put her notebook aside and is leaning forward so her breasts rest on the table.

"She surely was," I say. "But when your child is murdered, wouldn't you do anything you could? Isn't it more important that the perpetrator is arrested than that you're granted asylum?"

"It was already too late," Malik says carefully. "Her child was gone. Nothing could change that. So she maybe fled. And then she returned to Ormberg to say goodbye. Like visiting a mass grave."

"It's possible," Manfred says. "It even sounds probable."

"There's another possibility," I say. "Suppose Stefan Birgersson *isn't* guilty. The most likely perpetrator when a child is killed is a parent. *If* Azra for some reason killed her daughter, that might explain why she went underground."

Manfred nods.

"Makes sense," he says. "But then who killed Azra?"

"Maybe someone was seeking revenge?" Suzette suggests.

"Someone who knew she killed her daughter and murdered her seeking some kind of justice."

"Stefan Birgersson," Andreas says. "Perhaps he . . ."

Manfred rolls his eyes, and I sense he's starting to find our reasoning far-fetched.

I clear my throat.

"The sister said she was pregnant. I counted. She would have been in about the fifth month when she disappeared. If her pregnancy was successful, that would mean that she gave birth in the spring of 1994. We should check out the hospitals."

"Good, Malin!" Manfred says. "*Very good!*"

His overenthusiastic comment makes me feel like a schoolgirl who just got an A+ on her test.

"Why was she running barefoot through the woods?" asks Svante, who seems to have sunk into his own thoughts.

"Could she have come from a nearby car?" Suzette suggests. "There's a road nearby."

"She may have lost her shoes if she was being followed," Malik says.

Manfred nods and says:

"Doesn't sound likely, but I guess it's possible."

The room is silent for a moment. Svante squirms a little.

"Do we have any other suspects?" Suzette asks.

"Just a few," Manfred says. "We have a pedophile, Henrik Hahn, who's currently interned at Karsudden. Hahn was sentenced to criminal psychiatric care in 2014. He had leave on Saturday, but not Friday, so if we think our timetable is right then we have to rule him out. And, ironically, at the beginning of 1994 he was serving in Bosnia as a UN soldier, so he couldn't have had anything to do with Nermina's death. Svante, your group had a good talk with his wife?"

Svante nods.

"She gives him an alibi for Saturday and Sunday. I've actually visited him on an earlier occasion as well."

"How was he?" I ask, mostly out of curiosity.

"Nice, social. Convicted pedophiles often are. They need good social skills to get close to their victims."

"Fucking hell," Andreas says with a grimace.

"Any other suspects?" Malik asks.

"There's Björn Falk," Manfred says. "Convicted of battery, assault, and criminal harassment. He's had several restraining orders placed against him. We took him in for questioning. We shouldn't forget that the murderers could have racist or xenophobic motives. I'll call the Swedish Security Service and see what they have to say."

"So what do we do now?" Suzette says to her nails.

"We need to address four main questions," Manfred says. "First of all, I want to know everything I can about Stefan Birgersson. Background, what he was up to on Friday, which boards he nailed together at the refugee camp, who he's fucking, and how the hell he likes his eggs cooked."

Manfred writes "Stefan Birgersson" on the board.

"I think he mostly drinks beer," Andreas says.

Suzette suppresses a laugh.

Manfred continues as if he didn't hear:

"And if Hanne dropped a single hair on his property I want it found during that search, understood? Then we need to map out exactly who worked and lived at the refugee camp in the beginning of the nineties. Azra and Nermina didn't have much contact with the people outside. The probability that the perpetrator lived there, or visited it at some point, is high. In addition, Esma said someone was helping them get to Stockholm. Who was it? Could it have been Stefan Birgersson? And be sure to look up that old caretaker the director mentioned, Tony."

Manfred writes "the refugee camp" on the whiteboard in big red letters.

"Thirdly," he continues. "Thirdly, we need to find out where Azra Malkoc went after her daughter's death. Nobody disappears for twenty years without leaving a trace. We have to double-check with the Swedish and Bosnian authorities, make sure we haven't missed anything. And we have to contact all of Azra's relatives. There has to be somebody left, even if they bombed the shit out of each other during the war. Contact all the delivery clinics as well. Check if Azra, or any anonymous woman who may have been Azra, gave birth to a child in 1994."

Manfred writes "Azra" on the board.

"And the fourth?" Andreas asks.

"And fourthly," Manfred says, and puts his marker to the board again.

It squeaks as he writes the words "Peter & Hanne."

"We have to find Peter, figure out what happened that night," he says quietly. "They knew something. There are several threads we can pull on here: We can continue knocking on doors, say we have to find Peter's car. And it would be a damn good thing if we could get ahold of Hanne's diary, too, because I'm convinced she wrote down every step they took."

I bend forward and meet Manfred's eyes.

"We've searched everywhere for that book. It's not in their hotel and not in our office. I think she had it with her when she disappeared, so it could be in Peter's car or in—"

"Just find the damn book," Manfred growls.

I nod without a word.

"I thought of something else," Andreas says. "The cairn. Why were both Azra and Nermina found there?"

"It may be a coincidence," I suggest.

Manfred stands up, readjusts his jacket, and goes over to the map of Ormberg that hangs on the wall. The contour lines around the Orm Mountain make it look like a huge, open eye, staring at us from the wall.

Manfred stands there with his back to us, swaying a little. Then he takes a pen from his jacket pocket and says quietly:

*"Nermina. Azra. Hanne's bloody shoe."*

He draws a ring around the cairn.

A thick red ring.

And then one more and one more. The pen scratches against the paper as the blood red circles grow.

Someone knocks on the door, but nobody moves or says anything—everyone is hypnotized, their eyes glued to the map.

Manfred turns around and meets my eyes. Slowly puts the pen back into his pocket.

"Does this look like a coincidence?" he asks rhetorically.

And at that very moment there's another knock on the door, and it opens gently and a young, dark-haired woman, whom I recognize vaguely, enters.

"Gunnel Engsäll called from the refugee camp in Ormberg," she says. "She wants to talk to one of you."

Manfred crosses his arms over his chest.

"Tell her we'll be in touch Monday."

The woman in the doorway hesitates. Switching her weight from one foot to another.

"It was apparently important."

"Did you hear me," Manfred says with exaggerated slowness. "We'll take it on Monday."

"But," says the woman in the doorway, whose cheeks are now blossoming red. "Apparently, they found a huge pool of blood behind the residency."


Gunnel Engsäll meets us at the door when we arrive. In the windows I catch a glimpse of worried faces, and I see children pushing their curious faces against the glass. A woman pulls a little girl from the window and holds her protectively close.

Manfred, Andreas, Malik, and I have driven here to investigate the discovery.

The others went home.

It is after all Saturday night, and the likelihood that the blood-stain found here has anything to do with the murders is unlikely.

Gunnel is wearing a thick puffy coat with reflective stripes on it. Underneath it, I notice the big beetle pendant of her necklace.

She starts to walk in front of us along the side of the building. She's holding a flashlight in her hand.

"It was one of the children, a little girl named Nabila, who found the blood. But I have no idea how long it's been there. At least since . . ."

Gunnel seems to hesitate a little.

She steps over a fallen branch, clears her throat, and goes on:

"Yes, in view of everything that's been happening, I figured it was best if I contacted you right away."

"It was very good that you called," I say.

We walk around the corner of the building.

I sense the silhouettes of trees against a black sky.

Gunnel stops and directs the flashlight at the ground, maybe one and a half meters from the trunk of the nearest tree.

A big reddish black spot can be seen in the snow. It's probably fifty centimeters in diameter and seems frozen.

Malik puts down his large bag and takes out a flashlight. Directs it toward the stain and takes a few steps closer.

Then he squats down.

"Looks like blood," he states matter-of-factly. "And there are traces of drops around the larger spot."

Malik points to a few smaller spots surrounding the large puddle of frozen blood.

"And there's a long trail of drops running from the tree trunk to this stain."

Malik makes a sweeping gesture with his hand.

"As if an injured person walked from the tree to here," Andreas says, pointing to the spot.

"Hmmm," Malik says.

"What?" I ask.

"There are just two problems," Malik says, and cocks his head to the side so that his long hair rests against his shoulder. "First of all, the blood is lying on top of the snow, like . . . *a glaze*. Fresh blood is warm. It should have melted holes in the snow."

Gunnel turns her head away, but I can see her disgusted expression.

Malik continues:

"And secondly . . ."

"There are no footsteps," Manfred fills in, and nods to the spot in the snow. "If an injured person had walked by here, there would have been tracks in the snow."

"Precisely," Malik says. "There are no footprints between the tree and the bloodstain. But there are many tracks around the tree itself."

"Maybe it spattered or gushed over here," Andreas suggests.

Malik shakes his head.

"No. Gushing looks quite different. These are classic drops. The only force that has affected the blood here is the gravity, which has dropped straight into the snow from . . ."

Malik stands up, leans his head back, and directs his flashlight upward, toward the branches of the tree.

And there, maybe four meters above our heads, hangs a bloody, shapeless lump, attached to a rope that's wrapped around a mighty branch and then goes all the way down the tree trunk.

Malik follows the rope with the beam of the flashlight. It's tied to a branch maybe one and a half meters off the ground.

Then he points the light to the object hanging from the tree again. I see something that looks like pale skin under all that blood.

"*What the fuck,*" Manfred mutters.

# Jake

've been lying in bed almost all day, trying to understand what happened, that the police were actually here this morning, and that they took Dad.

I keep telling myself everything will be okay.

Of course the police won't hurt him, I know that; we don't live in, well, Africa. But what if they don't believe him, and decide to keep him in jail in Örebro.

There's another fear, too, a fear that's much deeper and almost impossible to open the door to. It's so awful I won't even let myself think it, let alone speak it. It's like every monster and beast and natural catastrophe combined.

What if Dad *is* involved.

What if they put him in prison, and he disappears, just like Mom.

When I think about it, I get a sinking feeling in my stomach and something burns behind my eyelids.

I can't imagine Dad killing somebody. That's truly impossible. He's far too kind and confused. He can't even cook pancakes or go to parent-teacher conferences—how could he *kill* somebody? But I can't stop thinking about the rifle and the bloody, torn shirt behind the basket in the laundry room.

Plus he's been acting strange lately. More tired than usual, and surly.

When I think of all that, I feel like my head might explode, like it might burst into a thousand little pieces, crushed just like my Eiffel Tower.

I sit up in bed and rock slowly back and forth.

It's dark outside again.

A whole day has gone by without me doing anything.

I slowly get up and go into Melinda's room. It's dark and smells like cigarette smoke. She texted and said she'd be home around six, and she'd bring some food with her.

I go to the closet and grab the handle—a glittery plastic shell.

As soon as I open the door, I feel calmer, as if all the clothes inside whisper to me that everything will be fine. That Dad will come home soon, and it will all be normal again.

I take off my T-shirt and pull on a tight black dress.

In the dim red light of the bedside lamp, my skin looks like baked ham.

Melinda's clothes fit better than Mom's. They're smaller and more formfitting, though they still hang a little loose.

I grab a lipstick from the desk and paint my mouth red. It's hard to make it look good. I suppose girls have to practice a long time before they get good at it. That it takes years of single-minded practice to get it perfect.

But I plan to get good at it.

I'm going to practice and practice until the eyeliner is straight and evenly applied and the red on my mouth is symmetrical. Until the rouge sits *on top* of my cheekbones and the mascara doesn't clump under my eyes.

I'm going to practice until I'm as beautiful as Melinda.

I put the lipstick back and examine my face in the magnifying mirror on her desk. Two disgusting thick strands of hair protrude from the skin of my upper lip.

I root around in Melinda's makeup bag, find the tweezers she uses to pluck her eyebrows, and pull out the hairs by the root. It hurts so much I want to cry, but afterward it feels better. I stand in front of the full-length mirror. Tuck my hair behind my ears and stretch my back up.

I smile provocatively and the girl in the mirror smiles back, as if we share a secret.

One day, I think, one day I'll be you for real.

It's a wonderful thought, as liberating as sunshine on bare skin after a long winter, and as exciting as Saga's soft lips against mine.

Still, I know it's wrong.

I'm a guy, and I can never, ever let anyone see me like this. It's sick, disgusting, and wrong. It's against God and nature and all of the unwritten rules of Ormberg.

Like pissing on a Bible.

Aberrant: a word I learned yesterday and realized it fits me perfectly. When I googled I found it meant: *against nature, abnormal, filthy, distorted, perverted, morbid, unhealthy, and corrupt.*

I am *aberrant.*

*So why does this feel so good?*

I will become a man one day and no matter what I do, I can't change that.

It's in the genes, in the Y chromosome. And one day, when my body decides it's time, the fucking Y chromosome will send out his orders to my body to produce the human hormones that will turn me into a monster. A hairy, disgusting monster with swelling muscles and a mind that thinks only about getting *what it wants.*

Like the Muslims at the refugee camp. Like Vincent, Albin, and Muhammad. Like every man who ever lived.

Like Dad.

We read about it in biology class. I know how it works, and I know it's inevitable.

When I think about it, I just want to cry.

I leave Melinda's room and go to mine, still wearing the dress. I climb into bed and take out Hanne's diary. Weigh it in my hands and turn to the page I dog-eared last. The spindly, forward-slanted handwriting is no longer difficult to read; it almost feels like I've written it myself.

A thought occurs to me, a pretty crazy thought, but still. The more I consider it, the more sure I become.

I'm still angry at Hanne, but still, I think she'd understand me. I don't think Hanne would think I'm *aberrant*.

Back to the office. A short briefing.

Our only suspect right now is Stefan Birgersson, and all we have against him is lying.

We survey him in detail now.

He has no criminal past, except he was a suspect in a fire at the old sawmill next to the creek when he was fourteen years old; but he was never proven guilty. He seems to have lived a relatively normal life: wife, two children, worked at Brogrens Mechanical until he was fired for showing up drunk on several occasions. Then things seem to have gone downhill fast: His wife died, his alcohol problems increased.

I bite my lip so hard I can feel the taste of blood mix with lipstick in my mouth.

The old sawmill—skinheads from Katrineholm burned that down, that's what Dad told me so many times. Of course he didn't burn it down.

Why would he?

And he lost his job at Brogrens because the factory shut down. *Right?*

My stomach feels queasy, as if I'm standing on a precipice staring down into the abyss. But at the same time I'm angry. Mostly I'm angry with Hanne, who accuses Dad of a bunch of things that she doesn't know shit about. Just when I was starting to forgive her she goes and writes all that bullshit about our family.

That sinking feeling in my stomach again, and suddenly I know what it is.

It's the feeling of not being able to trust anyone.

It's the feeling of being completely alone in the world.

I squeeze the diary tight and keep reading.

Evening and DARKNESS. In both senses of the word.

P is out running again. I take the opportunity to write down a few lines.

A moment ago, I made P sit on the bed so we could talk.

(There's only one chair in the room, we have to sit in bed to talk.)

He seemed surprised and maybe a bit hesitant, but still sat at the edge of the bed, his arms crossed.

I explained that he seems angry and grumpy. That he doesn't look at me anymore and treats me like a ghost at work.

P said I was overreacting. Said he loved me. He leaned over and gave me an awkward hug.

And then. BANG!

I slapped him! I don't know how it happened—I'm not the violent type. I don't think I've ever hit anyone, not even when I was a child—I was shy, overweight, wore glasses, and was obsessed with Eskimos.

I became very upset. I apologized over and over again.

P said it wasn't me, it was the "disease." Then he went out running.

I'm sitting alone writing now. The north wind has started to howl outside our window. It's really not the weather for a run. I would have worried about him if we hadn't fought. Been afraid he'd fall down in the dark, get hit by a car.

But I have no room for any more emotions. I'm filled with emptiness, a horrific and infinite darkness.

Perhaps Ormberg has finally moved inside me.

I am interrupted in my reading when Melinda enters my room. When she sees me on the bed she freezes and the smile disappears from her face. And I'm so absorbed by Hanne's story that I don't understand why. For a second, I think it's because the police picked up Dad.

Then it hits me as hard as one of Vincent's icy snowballs.

*I'm wearing Melinda's dress.*

I'm sitting in bed, in a tight black dress, my mouth painted red.

This must be what dying feels like, I think, just before Melinda rushes out and slams my door behind her.

# Malin

W ill you ever be ready?"

Manfred is impatiently watching Malik, who's spent the last half hour photographing, measuring, and collecting samples.

"Yep. You can loosen the rope now."

Manfred unties the rough rope from the branch and starts to cautiously lower the object from high up in the tree. The branch it's looped around creaks ominously.

Andreas points a flashlight at the shapeless, bloody bundle as it approaches.

It looks like organic matter, yet not quite human. A bit like an unidentifiable, mutilated body part.

*"Jesus!"*

Manfred stumbles, shouts, and loses his grip on the rope, which flies through his bare hands with a whoosh. The object falls into the snow with a muted thump. The snow swirls up around it where it landed.

Manfred runs over, rubbing his palms against each other and grimacing with pain. Andreas takes a step forward, but stops short in front of me.

*"Jesus Christ!"*

I lean forward to get a better look.

A bloody hog's head is lying in the snow, attached to a heavy, rusted butcher's hook.


Mom's hand trembles a little as she pours coffee into the small, beautiful gold-edged cups Grandma and Grandpa saved for special occasions, like graduations, birthdays, and Midsummer.

I took a very long shower when I got back from the refugee camp. As if the hot water could rinse away the memory of the bloody hog's head, and something far worse: a hate so strong that someone would go to the effort of hoisting that hog's head up into a tree outside a place where Muslim refugees live.

Malik gave us a detailed explanation of why exactly pigs and pork are considered unclean and therefore *haram*—forbidden—within Islam.

The violation, or threat, that gray head was meant to represent was surely directed at the refugees. But as for whether or not it has any connection to our investigation . . . well, that remains to be seen.

I look at Margareta.

She raises her wrinkled and sun-spotted arm. She cradles the cup in her palm like a piece of jewelry.

"Just a sip," she says, and coughs. "Have to head off soon. Rut and Gunnar want a few kilos, too."

Margareta has come by to drop off some frozen elk meat. The hunters who hunt on her land took down too many elk this year, and she has more meat than she knows what to do with.

Mom sits down, shakes her head, and turns to me. Her eyes are filled with distrust and fear.

"It's just so *terrible,* Malin. Do you mean someone *smashed* that poor woman's face off?"

I regret telling her about Azra's injuries. But it can hardly be news to Margareta. She knows everything that happens in Ormberg, sometimes almost before it happens.

"Yes, it's terrible."

Mom puts the coffeepot on the table.

"Who would do such a thing? It can't be anyone from around here."

"Of course it's nobody from the village," Margareta sniffs. "But there are so many random people in the area nowadays, who even knows where to start looking."

I bring the cup to my mouth, take a sip of hot, weak coffee, and wonder what they'd say if they knew Stefan Birgersson was sitting in jail in Örebro. A man who is neither an Arab nor a Stockholmer, who's just as deeply rooted in the Ormberg mud as we are.

"And you still haven't found that cop from Stockholm yet?" Margareta continues.

"No, but we will."

"You can't be sure about that. I once attended to a woman whose husband got lost outside Marsjö, and they never found him."

"Please, Margareta," Mom says. *"Must you?"*

"I just mean that the woods are large around here," Margareta says, looking offended. "And the lakes are deep. It's possible to disappear. Forever."

"We *will* find him," I say again. "Somebody has to have seen something. And Hanne, who was with him in the woods, remembers a few things."

"What kind of things?" Mom asks.

I shrug.

"Nothing I can discuss."

Mom shakes her head and puts a hand to her chest, as if she's having a heart attack.

"What if he's dead," she whispers.

"Of course he's dead," Margareta says drily. "Coldest winter in living memory. Minus ten degrees and thirty centimeters of snow. Nobody could survive that. You'll find him when the snow melts, mark my words."

Mom sniffs loudly.

"What in the world is going on these days? Ormberg has always been such a peaceful, safe place. Things like this don't happen here. I just don't understand it."

The warm light of the lamp falls on my mom's plump, rosy cheeks.

I think of what Hanne told us. The memory fragments could be real memories—or just a bunch of dreams and fantasies.

I get an idea. Ormberg isn't big, and if anyone would know about the people living here, it's Margareta and Mom.

"Do you know anyone who likes to read English books in Ormberg?" I ask.

"English books?"

Mom shakes her head and puckers her mouth, but Margareta looks thoughtful.

"Maybe Ragnhild," she says. "Yes, I'm not sure, but she's so conceited about how she used to work as a language teacher. I wouldn't be surprised if she has English books."

And then:

"Or Berit. She had an Irish boyfriend in the eighties. A gardener. He was fond of reading thick books, as I remember it. But not so fond of working. Unfortunately. But Berit always did have terrible taste in men."

Margareta sighs and shakes her head.

I ponder a bit more. Decide I might as well ask the second question, too.

"You've lived here for a long time—do you remember when that story of the Ghost Child at the cairn started being told?"

Mom and Margareta look at each other.

"Honey," Mom says, shaking her head. "That's just foolishness."

"Of course," I say. "But *when* did the rumor get started?"

Mom's gaze turns upward, toward the ceiling.

"I don't rightly know. Sometime when you were little, maybe."

"Sump-Ivar saw that child," Margareta inserts helpfully. "He saw a naked infant in the grass at the cairn. Pale as death with blue lips. But when he went to pick up the baby, well, poof, it turned to smoke."

Sump-Ivar was Gunnar Sten's brother.

He lived on the other side of the church, next to the marsh, until he died eight, maybe nine years ago. He was psychotic and thought his neighbors were spying on him and had placed radio transmitters in his teeth. One winter he wrapped his entire cottage in Bubble Wrap to stop the radio waves from penetrating it.

Me and my friends had a lot of fun with that. We climbed all over his house, and plunged a knife into the ridge of the roof.

I feel ashamed when I remember it.

"Sump-Ivar was mentally ill," I say.

"But he *saw* the baby," Margareta says, nodding seriously.

"He saw all sorts of things," Mom says. "I wouldn't trust a word he said."

"When was this?" I ask.

Margareta purses her thin, wrinkled mouth.

"Must have been after Berit burned up her old jalopy. Yes, that's when it was. But it was before Rut and Gunnar built that flashy sunporch."

"And when was that?"

Margareta shrugs.

"I don't know. But I can ask Ragnhild. She may remember."

Then she stretches, pushes her thin hair aside with a wrinkled hand, and takes a deep breath as if preparing to tell another one of her stories.

"Listen, you two," I say. "I need to head to bed soon. I have to get up early tomorrow."

"Tomorrow?" Mom says. "Are you going to work on a Sunday?"

"We're investigating a murder, Mom."

"Well, I won't keep you any longer," Margareta says, deflating a bit as if disappointed that I don't want to listen to her anymore.

She empties the coffee cup and places it back on its dish with a tiny bang. Then she stands up. Turns to me and meets my eyes. Her expression is very serious.

"Promise me you'll be careful, Malin."

I nod.

Margareta squeezes Mom's shoulder lightly and thanks her for the coffee. Heads out toward the hall.

Mom stands and follows after her.

I look around the room.

Sitting here on Grandma and Grandpa's old sofa drinking coffee from their cups evokes a wave of vague anxiety. Everything in the room—the drab wallpaper, the sagging old sofa, the clumsy paintings of Norwegian mountain motifs—transports me back to growing up. To nocturnal swims in the creek, drunken parties, make-out sessions in rumpus rooms with cork floors, and unbelievably boring dinners with Margareta and Ballsack-Magnus that never seemed to end.

This was my childhood, I think as I grasp hold of the delicate porcelain cup, carry it to my mouth, and feel the steam rise from the hot coffee to my lips.

This is me, but not for long.

Soon I'll be gone, in Stockholm.

My boring condo in Katrineholm with its handicap-accessible bathroom and kitchen is just one step on the path away from here.

It's sad, but it still feels right. I've always known I would leave Ormberg. Not because I had a bad childhood—I had tons of friends and my parents were neither better nor worse than any others. No, there's something about Ormberg itself that I can't stand. It's as if the air here is heavy and hard to breathe, as if the woods are watching me, as if all the miserable lives that never managed to escape are trying to hold me here.

Maybe I'm afraid of Ormberg—or maybe I'm afraid of what would happen to *me* if I stayed. I'm convinced I'd drown in the hopelessness that hovers over everything here and end up like everyone else in those cottages.

Gray, narrow-minded, devoid of dreams.

And then there's Dad. And Kenny. And the skeleton in the cairn that was no mushroom but instead a murdered little girl.

They're all here in Ormberg: the dead who won't leave me alone.

And now they've been joined by a faceless woman.


When Mom comes back, I'm sitting on the sofa with a framed picture of Dad in my hands.

She gives me a long look, but says nothing.

Even though Dad's death wasn't as shocking as Kenny's, of course I loved him.

We were close. In many ways closer than Mom and me. Maybe because we were more alike: impulsive, emotional, but at the same time pragmatic and unsentimental.

When Dad was younger he was quite outdoorsy. We used to ski in the winters and camp at Långsjön Lake in the summer. Mom never came along. I think she thought it was silly to sleep in a tent when there's a perfectly good house to live in instead.

Later, when Dad started having heart problems, we stopped going out on excursions. Instead, we used to sit in front of the woodstove and plan trips we both knew would never happen: Rome, Paris, Krakow, and Prague.

Dad liked big cities.

Mom gently takes the photo from my hands and puts it back in its place on the shelf. Then sinks down next to me.

The sofa creaks under her weight.

She cocks her head and looks at me.

"I talked to the priest today," she says, stroking my cheek gently. "Midsummer's Eve will work."

"Thank you. That was kind."

"And then I mentioned to Margareta that we might want to borrow her barn."

"I told you I don't want to have the party there."

"But *Malin . . .*"

Mom has that slightly reproachful tone, the one she gets when she's done something for me and I'm not appreciative.

"I don't want to be at their place."

"There's not enough room here; not everyone will fit," Mom says.

"Yes they will. If we set up a tent in the garden."

Mom shakes her head and sets down her small coffee cup so hard I'm surprised it doesn't break. The pale flesh on her throat wobbles as she jerks her head back.

"A tent? I have never heard anything so stupid in my life! When you could have a roof over your head."

"Stop! I don't want to be at Margareta's. She always inserts herself into everything."

"We owe a lot to Margareta."

"I know. But this is different. This is about *my* wedding. Okay?"

Mom snorts, but I can see that she's resigned.

Margareta has always ruled the roost here in Ormberg. She's one of the biggest landowners and better off financially than most, which is hard to believe when you visit her and Magnus in their ugly house in the woods. There's not a family in Ormberg who hasn't borrowed money from her at some time. That's what's given Margareta her influence. People listen to her and usually do as she says.

But it's not just about her power over people. She's resourceful and has done a lot of good things, too, like ensuring that when the road was rebuilt the bus line from Vingåker was redrawn almost all the way to the church. And she forced the county to improve snow clearance as recently as last winter.

Mom sighs heavily, but seems to have decided not to argue anymore on that matter.

"Have you found a dress yet?" she asks, her voice soft and conciliatory.

"No."

"You could take mine. We'd have to take it in a great deal, of course."

Mom laughs a little.

She's fat, always has been.

It's not something we talk about much, and nobody cares about that in Ormberg anyway. I have vague memories of her doing various diets when I was younger—for a while she ate only eggs and iceberg lettuce. Another time, it must have been in the late nineties, she lived on clear soups and grapes. After Dad, I think she just gave up on diets and indulged her love for fatty foods and pastries.

"Wait a minute," Mom says, getting up and going over to the bookshelf.

She returns with an old photo album under her arm.

"Mom," I say. "Surely we can look at this tomorrow?"

"I just want to show you one thing," she says, flipping purposefully through the album.

Pictures from my childhood flit by: a thin girl with two long, dark braids, my unimaginably pale childish body in a small inflatable pool on the lawn, Ballsack-Magnus looking at me with thick lips shaped like an O while Margareta pushes me in front of her on the gravel road in his old red soapbox car.

I yawn.

Mom doesn't seem to notice my reaction. She keeps flipping toward the beginning of the album.

"Here!" she says.

I examine the faded Polaroid of Mom and Dad in front of the church. They look so stiff and uncomfortable I have to smile. I'm overcome by an unexpected tenderness, consisting in part of love, and in part of a stinging sadness at what once was, but will never be again.

Dad is wearing a dark suit and has a red flower in his button-hole, maybe a carnation. Mom is wearing a lace dress stretched tight across her bust and around her chubby arms. The fabric is beautiful and could certainly be used again.

"Yes," I say. "Very nice."

"There's a good seamstress in Vingåker," Mom begins.

"Please. I want my *own* dress."

Mom falls silent and runs her thick fingers over the thin plastic film that covers the photo.

"I just thought that . . ."

Her voice dies away, and I immediately feel guilty.

"I'll think about it," I say, stretching for the photo album and flipping through a few pages.

"Your first summer," Mom says, and smiles introspectively.

I look at the pictures of myself as a baby, trying to find any familiar features in that round face. It's me and yet not: the dark eyes, the slightly plump upper lip, and the eyebrows like arches on the thin, snowy white skin.

Another thought sneaks in—maybe because we were just browsing through a photo album of old baby pictures. I think of Andreas and my meeting with Esma Hadzic in Gnesta. Of the photos of Azra and Nermina and of Esma's bent fingers stroking the pictures in the same way Mom just did.

I wonder if Azra ever had another child and where it could be. I actually called the medical examiner and asked how likely it was that she gave birth to the child. The doctor couldn't say for sure, but explained that if Azra had made it through her first trimester without complications, the probability was "quite high" that she went on to give birth to a healthy child.

I'm convinced it's just a matter of time before we find that child's remains buried. And I plan to make sure of it, even if I have to turn that forest upside down. The child has to be given a grave, and Esma deserves to know what happened, even though she annoys me in some vague way.

I can understand fleeing from war and misery. But why should I, and every other taxpayer, fund her disability pension when she could have returned to Bosnia a long time ago? Mom has never received any subsidies, though God knows she's needed it. Instead, she's had to borrow from Margareta, like everyone else in the village.

The phone rings just as Mom, apparently lost in memories, is about to show me a photo where I'm pulling a slimy pike out of the pond next to the old sawmill.

I apologize and answer.

It's Max.

I ask him to wait a few seconds and then leave the living room and go toward the stairs.

Mom looks a little disappointed as I disappear, and it makes me feel guilty again.

Staying with Mom was not a good idea—adults shouldn't live with their parents. I don't understand how Margareta and Magnus can stand it. He should have moved away from home twenty-five years ago.

But Margareta doesn't have anybody else, and neither does Magnus.

Loneliness is apparently a far more powerful adhesive than love.


I stand in front of the window in my old childhood room and talk to Max. He's in a really bad mood today. A cyclist who was hit by a local bus won a trial against his insurance company and was awarded the maximum sum the law allows.

"What kind of injuries did you say he suffered?" I ask while absently using a finger to draw in the moisture on the window.

Outside, snowflakes swirl by.

Max tells me about a twenty-five-year-old man who's confined to a wheelchair, who uses a catheter to empty his bladder and bowels. I can feel the cold sneaking in—the cold and something else: an uneasiness and irritation I can't quite define.

Perhaps it's because Max sounds so harsh, or because all that talk of car crashes makes me think of Kenny again.

"So you don't think he should have got anything?" I ask, still running my finger over the cold, steamy windowpane.

He explains that that wasn't what he meant, but that he works for an insurance company, not some sob-story TV show. And besides, do I have any idea how many of these so-called invalids fake their symptoms? How many people receive compensation every month and then tear off their neck braces and go home to jump on their trampoline with the kids?

I draw a heart on the window. And then another.

"What a shitty job you have," I say.

"Pardon?"

Yes, he says "Pardon?" Max had a *fancy* upbringing and would never say "What?" when he doesn't catch what you said. It's one of the many small things that divide us, and probably something that attracted me in the beginning.

"I said you have a shitty job. You sit behind your posh desk with all your legs and arms intact and wheedle money out of people who can't even pee by themselves."

An awkward silence sets in.

"*What the hell,*" he says finally. "When did *you* turn into a socialist?"

"Maybe when I met you."

I hang up and look down at the phone without really understanding what just happened. I regret it immediately. I insulted and hurt Max for no real reason, and he's absolutely right that he's just doing his job.

I know I need to call back and apologize. Explain how tired I am and how much pressure we're all under. Tell him about Azra and Nermina and Peter. About my fear of finding my colleague dead or the equally terrifying option: not finding him at all.

And then about all the rest, everything I've never really tried to tell him: about how little he truly knows and understands my family and the people who live here. It doesn't matter how well he and Mom get along when they meet. Max will always return to his pedantically clean turn-of-the-century Stockholm apartment, with its expensive Italian furniture and brass bathroom fixtures. To his horsehair bed that cost a month's salary—a month's salary for him, not me; mine would never suffice.

Could he ever understand what it's like to have your legs crushed by a bus or lose your job at TrikåKungen and never get a new one because every company's gone under and the county doesn't have the money to support the ones who are left behind, even though the refugees get food and housing and education without doing a goddamn thing?

What does he know about the darkness of Ormberg?

And maybe more important: How could he ever understand me?

But I don't have it in me to call him. Not now.

Instead, I look at the hearts on the window. Wipe them away with my hand.

Love just isn't my thing.

# Jake

Snowflakes whip against my face as I ride away from home. The moped struggles forward down the unplowed country road. The darkness and falling snow make it difficult to see, and I drive so slowly I'm afraid I'll roll at the turn. I try not to think of what might happen, because if I roll over out here, nobody can help me.

But today it feels like that doesn't matter.

Nothing matters anymore.

I think of Dad sitting in the police station in Örebro. And then I think of Melinda, of the expression on her face when she saw me in bed wearing a dress and lipstick. The surprise and the fear in her eyes was a painful reminder of who I am, or rather *what* I am.

*Aberrant.*

As soon as Melinda disappeared, I changed clothes and left.

I have my backpack balled up in the moped's seat. Inside it I stuffed Hanne's diary, my phone, a frozen loaf of bread, and two cans of Coke.

When I get to the main road, I turn off toward what everyone around here insists on calling downtown, even though it's just a few ramshackle houses in a field.

Or that's what Hanne thinks, anyway.

I drive onto the small road that leads to Saga's house. Park my moped outside, run up the small staircase to her door, and ring the bell. I can hear shouting coming from inside.

Saga's mother opens the door wearing pink sweatpants. Her long dark hair sits in a ponytail on top of her head. In her hand she holds a damp dishrag.

"Jake? What are you doing out in this weather? Come in!"

She opens the door, and I step into warmth, pull off my boots, and hang my winter coat on one of the hooks in the hall.

Saga's mom keeps her house very clean. It's basically her main hobby. Everyone in the family has a hook with their name on it, and a spot on the shoe rack. There's even a special spot for guests, too, so I put my boots there.

I can hear the TV blaring from the living room.

Bea, Saga's little sister, who's twelve, wanders out of the kitchen carrying an iPad. I notice right away that she's angry, and I realize I must have interrupted some kind of argument.

"*He* was the one who hit *me*!" she yells.

Saga's mom turns to Bea and crosses her arms over her chest.

"You're still not allowed to hit back. I don't want to have any more conversations with your teacher about this. Do you understand? It's embarrassing. You're a *girl,* Bea, you should know better."

"But he hit *me*. Really hard!"

"He probably hit you because he likes you—boys do that. They're incapable of saying it when they like you. When you grow up you'll understand."

Saga appears in the doorway of the kitchen.

Her hair is now a darker shade of pink, almost cerise. Long threads hang from her ripped black jeans and her soft, pale skin peeks out through the holes on her thighs and knees.

Her face breaks into a smile when she sees me, and she takes a few quick steps toward me.

"Hey!"

"Hi," I say, suddenly very aware that I don't have a good reason to be here.

But Saga just smiles, takes my hand, and pulls me into the living room. Pushes me down onto the couch next to their cat, Mouser.

"How's it going?" she asks, and places herself next to me cross-legged.

"Good," I lie. "What are they fighting about?"

"Eh. Bea hit somebody in the face again."

I think of what Saga's mom told Bea, that boys hit you when they like you, because they don't have any other way to say it. As if all guys are, like, mentally disturbed monsters who talk with their fists. *Bang*—a fist to the face: You're cute. *Pow*—a fist to my stomach: I like you. *Poof*—a kick in the back: Do you wanna be my girlfriend?

Saga smiles crookedly and runs a hand over her hair.

"I dyed it darker. What do you think?"

"Really cute!"

"Thank you. Mom thinks I look like a whore."

There's a scrape in the hall, and Saga's mom appears in the doorway.

"Young lady! I absolutely did not say that! We don't use that word in our home. And where are my black jeans, by the way?"

"Don't know. Why?" Saga rolls her eyes.

"First of all, they're mine. And secondly, I'm going over to Björn's this evening, and I wanted to wear them. So you better go find them," her mom says, then stalks off, away from us and back to the argument with Bea.

Saga sighs, and my cheeks suddenly feel hot.

*Björn Falk.*

Saga's mom's new boyfriend. Who's been convicted of assault. Who threw his girlfriend into a burning-hot sauna for so long she had to have a skin transplant. And I can't tell anyone, even though I know I should.

"Your hair is really pretty," I say instead, and mean it.

The color reminds me of the flowers that grow next to the ditches in the summer, the ones Mom liked so much.

"It has more *attitude*," I add.

"Exactly!" Saga says, looking pleased.

I shiver.

Saga places a hand hesitantly on my sleeve.

"Oh. It's wet. Wait, I'll get you another shirt."

"It's fine," I say, but Saga's already disappeared into the hall.

A few minutes later, she returns with a T-shirt and a thick, warm, pink wool sweater. It's almost the same color as her hair. A long loop of yarn hangs down from one sleeve.

Saga puts her finger through the loop, raises her eyebrows, and smiles.

"It gets caught on *everything*."

I take the sweater. Hesitate a few seconds, but then, because I don't want to disappoint her, I pull it on.

The pink sweater is long, reaches halfway down my thighs.

"Really cute. You look good in pink."

I don't respond.

I've always liked pink, but I can't say that.

An awkward silence ensues. The argument seems to be over, and the only sound is the drone of a newscaster coming from the TV. Outside the black windows, large flakes swirl around in a dance that never seems to cease.

Mouser stretches a bit, and when Saga pets the soft fur on his belly, her bracelets jingle.

"So, do you wanna watch a horror film?"

"Sure."

Saga puts on an old movie about some young people who go out into the woods searching for "the Blair Witch," and end up lost. It looks homemade, but Saga says that was just a marketing trick.

"The whole point is you're supposed to think they filmed it

themselves. Some people totally bought it. Back when the movie came out. Mom said she thought it was, like, 'terrifying' when it came out."

"Seriously?"

"I know, right?" Saga says, and we both giggle.

Her hand sneaks into mine; it's warm and damp, and even though I'd like to readjust my arm a little, I don't for fear of ruining this perfect moment. I want to float on the warmth spreading inside me, and keep those addictive butterflies in my stomach for as long as I can.

"What if Ormberg's become a super-dangerous place, even though it's the most boring place in the world," Saga says. "Mom told me some TV reporters wanted to interview her yesterday. But she didn't have any makeup on so she said no. And now there are murder tourists here."

" 'Murder tourists'?"

"Yeah, you know. People who are curious about crime scenes. She met a whole bunch of them downtown asking how to get to the cairn."

I shudder and think of Hanne's diary, sitting in my backpack, waiting to be read.

"Damn, that's disturbed," I say. "I mean, a woman died—she was a real person who lived and breathed. And walked around just like we do. Maybe she liked watching movies or had a family . . . And now she's a tourist attraction. Like the outlet stores in Vingåker."

My voice fades away.

"Mhmmm," Saga says. "It *is* disturbed. Not that anyone thinks about that fact. Except for us, since we're *morally superior*."

More giggles.

"Do you remember the girl I was telling you about, who works as a clerk at the police in Örebro?" Saga asks.

"Your cousin?"

Saga rolls her eyes. "*No*. She's together with Mom's sister's ex's son, and she's from Kumla. Anyway. She says the murder will soon be solved. The police have *a suspect*."

My skin crawls when I realize she must mean Dad.

Saga examines her nails and continues:

"She says she hopes they put him away forever, where the sun don't shine."

Something inside me breaks when she says that. My stomach twists in knots, and my mouth goes dry.

*Dad. Locked in a dark room forever.*

"Wonder if that old lady they found in the forest will recognize him," Saga continues without noticing my reaction. "The one who lost her memory. Anyway. It's so crazy that she's living with Berit behind the church now. A super-old lady taking care of another super-old lady. Mom says it will all go to hell in the end. Even though Berit used to work with that kind of stuff. Taking care of the disabled and retarded people."

"I didn't use those words!"

Saga's mom is in the doorway again. But she doesn't look angry, just amused. She's swinging the dishrag back and forth in her hand.

"Jake," she says. "Maybe you better start heading home?"

I look down at the carpet, panic washing over me when she says those words.

Saga's mom observes me silently, wrinkles her forehead. Then she says:

"Or you can sleep on the couch if you want. That's fine by me."

Saga smiles, but says nothing. She just pulls on one of the long threads hanging from her jeans until it breaks, and then sits there with it in her hand like it's a worm.

I'm lying on the couch under an old musty blanket Saga's mom took out of storage.

Saga's mom is nice—she didn't have to let me sleep here.

I think of what Dad always says: People around here take care of each other; it's one of the advantages of living in a small town. And maybe he's right.

I take out the diary. Hesitate, but then turn on the floor lamp and start to read.

We're not friends at the moment, Hanne and me, but I still have to find out what happened. If only so I can find the real killer and save Dad.

Maybe I'm the only one who can.

ORMBERG, NOVEMBER 30

At the office.

The weather is terrible, almost a storm.

The rain is pouring, the wind lashing against the building. It's ice cold in here and the ceiling is leaking, even with the floor heater on full blast.

We just had our morning meeting. Summarized the state of the investigation, reviewed time lines, hypotheses, technical evidence, & witness statements. We've received more pictures of Nermina from the Bosnian police as well.

We enlarged them and taped them up.

Death stared at me from the wall. I stared back.

Manfred was frustrated. Asked me what kind of perp we're dealing with here.

I told him I saw three options: (1) Someone killed Nermina by mistake (e.g., a traffic accident) and hid her body in the cairn. (2) Azra killed her daughter, which would also explain why Azra disappeared afterward. (3) An unknown person killed Nermina. The motive could have been sexual.

After that we went through the personnel at the refugee camp in the early nineties. Most had nothing suspicious in their backgrounds. One person had been convicted of assault. Only two of the employees lived in Ormberg: Rut Sten, the former director, and Berit Sund, an old woman who lives between the church and the old mill.

According to Malin, Berit is completely harmless.

She wouldn't hurt a fly.

I wake up because I'm freezing.

The blanket has slipped onto the floor. Dim light from the kitchen has made its way into the living room. Something crunches under me on the couch as I reach for the floor—maybe an old chip.

That's the sort of thing Saga's mom detests—chips in the couch. If she knew it was here, she'd definitely come down with her vacuum cleaner, even in the middle of the night.

I pull up the blanket, then stop, turn and look at the floor again.

*The diary is gone.*

I get off the couch and down onto my knees, look under the couch, but the diary isn't there. Nor has it slid between the cushions.

She's sitting in bed with the diary on her lap, her cheeks streaked with tears. Her pink hair falls over one eye.

"Hi," I try.

Saga shakes her head as if she wants me to go.

*"Please, Saga."*

"It's her book, right? The woman who got lost in the woods?"

I nod.

"You *should* have told me," she says quietly.

I stand as if stuck frozen to the cold floor, and feel a cold breeze at my ankles. The glass panes rattle as the wind starts to press against the window.

Yes, I should have told her. But I didn't. And now I can't even tell her why.

"You should have told me that you found it, you should have told me Björn Falk is a fucking disturbed piece of shit. What if he tries to kill Mom, too? What if he throws her into a sauna? Maybe you didn't even think of that?"

"*I . . .*"

"Why didn't you tell me? I thought we trusted each other."

Her voice is a whisper.

"Cuz. Cuz . . ."

Saga shakes her head again and wipes away a tear.

"Because your dad might have killed someone?"

"No. *No!*"

"Because you wouldn't have a mother or a father if they locked him up?"

"Dad would never . . ."

"You don't know that," Saga says with a dry laugh. "You can't know that kind of thing. And besides, what would you do about it? You surely weren't going to go there by yourself?"

"Go where?"

Saga snorts.

"You haven't even read it all, have you?"

Then silence. Saga rocks back and forth in bed with her eyes turned to the wall.

"Saga," I say. "Don't tell anyone. Please!"

Saga turns to me. Her eyes look like black metal balls. She squeezes the diary so hard her knuckles turn white.

"Is that all you care about? Me keeping my mouth shut?"

"No, I . . ."

"Leave now," she screams, and throws the diary at me.

The pages flutter and rustle as the diary flies through the air. It lands on my left foot with a thud, but I feel no pain, just a horrible emptiness as I realize I've probably lost Saga.

"Go," she continues. "And never come back."

She turns around and buries her head in her pillow.

# Malin

I don't know what wakes me up, maybe the noise outside. I can hear the wind whistling around the corner of the house and a lone branch tapping against the window—it sounds like Suzette is sitting out there in the dark, slowly tapping one of her long blue nails against the window.

The moon casts a pale shine on the rug, and a few lonely snowflakes float by.

I think about Max and Kenny and what Mom said a few days ago about how you can't escape yourself.

Maybe she's right.

Maybe Max is my escape from Ormberg, or from Kenny, and ultimately also from myself.

Something broke inside me when Kenny died.

Not because it was a terrible accident, not because we were drunk, but because I learned how much it hurts to lose somebody you love.

I never wanted to feel that pain again.

I hear a scraping noise coming from downstairs, almost like a chair being pulled out.

I glance at the clock: five past five in the morning. Maybe Mom is going to the bathroom.

After Kenny died, I didn't want to get out of bed, and I didn't want to eat. It felt like food expanded in my mouth, and it made me nauseous. All I could think of was Kenny's face, which was no longer a face—just a deformed, fleshy mass.

Mom and Margareta stayed by my side, day and night. Sure, Dad was around, too, but he had to work. And taking care of depressed teenagers is women's work.

Then when Mom and Dad came down with the flu a few weeks later, and got very sick, Margareta moved in. Made breakfast, lunch, and dinner for all of us. Cleaned the attic, boiled winter apples and made applesauce, washed and pressed all the linen, and scrubbed the floor.

That's when I realized how much Margareta means to me, to our entire family. She's no soft, sensitive person, but she's there when it counts. She's the hub around which we all turn, what unites our small, fragmented family. The help she offers can be harsh and wordless, but she'll never desert you.

And in the end, isn't that what matters?

A thud sounds from downstairs, and then a bang as the front door slams.

I sit up. My heart pounding, sweat starting at my temples.

Would Mom being going out *now*, at five in the morning?

I get up, wrap the blanket from the foot of the bed around my shoulders, and sneak toward the stairs.

Everything's quiet. The moon shines a ghostly light over the room. The floor is cold, and I wrap the blanket tighter around me.

Dad used to walk in his sleep. Usually he ate. Mom would catch him at the fridge with his hand literally in the jam jar and blueberry marmalade all over his pajamas.

I creep down the stairs and check the hall and the kitchen.

Empty.

The bushes outside the kitchen window bend under the heavy wind and cold air nips at my ankles.

I move on to Mom's room, open the door slightly, and listen.

Her breathing is heavy and even, and her scent hangs in the air. I carefully pull the door closed behind me and go back to the hall, and my eyes are drawn down the snowy driveway toward the trees in the distance. And there, between two of the biggest, I sense movement.

Someone or something is moving between the tree trunks. It could be a human, or could just as well be an animal.

At that very moment, something dings in the living room.

I turn around.

Something is glowing on the coffee table, bathing its surroundings in a cold, artificial shine.

*My laptop.*

Didn't I turn off my computer yesterday?

I enter the living room and bend over the laptop. Various colors dance around each other on the screen. Next to my computer my notebook lies open, just as I left it yesterday. My notes about Hanne and what little she remembers from the night Peter disappeared fill two whole pages.

I push a key and the log-in page replaces the screen saver.

The computer is locked.

I let out a deep sigh, but at the same time my glance falls onto the floor next to me. A damp spot spreads out on the fake hardwood floor, shining dully in the light of the computer screen.

My heart starts to race and my ears throb.

I go out into the hall, unlock the door, and stare out into the darkness. The cold wind catches hold of my hair, and I shiver.

At first I don't notice anything strange, but then I detect something in the snowdrift right next to the door.

It's a footprint.

I sink down and examine it. The contours of a five-pointed star sit in the middle of the sole.

. . .

Hanne is sitting at Berit's kitchen table with a teacup in her hand. Two candles are lit on the table.

It's the second Sunday of Advent.

My head aches from fatigue—after hearing those sounds downstairs and finding my computer turned on early this morning, I couldn't fall back asleep. Instead, I lay awake, tossing and turning until my alarm rang.

On my drive to the office this morning, I thought about telling Manfred what happened, but in the pale light of morning it felt so silly: a thud, a footprint in the snow that might be fresh but could just as well be old. A movement between the trees, which could have been conjured up by my own fears rather than by the trespasser I dreaded.

I stare at the table in front of me.

Next to the candlesticks lie pictures of Azra and Nermina Malkoc's dead bodies, the map of Ormberg, the interrogation reports, and the notes Manfred has taken.

We've been sitting here for more than an hour while Manfred reviewed every single detail of the entire investigation, explaining to Hanne all we know about Nermina and Azra, Peter's disappearance, and the medallion. He hasn't mentioned Stefan Birgersson, a conscious choice—he doesn't want Hanne to have any preconceived notions about a possible perpetrator.

Hanne has been reading, making small notes in her notebook, and asking questions. Berit's brewed more tea, walked the dog, and, finally, sat down in the next room to knit.

It's quite obvious Hanne doesn't remember anything from the investigation. Both Andreas and I have a hard time understanding the point of this visit. If Manfred was hoping Hanne would remember something, he was way off. And we have a lot to do—the prosecutor needs all the help he can get before issuing a search warrant.

Outside Berit's window, the morning sun shines over Ormberg.

A thin strip of pink hovers above the treetops, and the fog is lifting at the edge of the forest.

It's lovely, but the meteorologists have warned of heavy snow-fall and traffic problems later this morning.

Hanne lays her glasses on the table and rubs her eyes. There's a crackle from the woodstove.

"You know I don't remember, right?" she says, meeting Man-fred's eyes.

Manfred nods and lays a big hand over Hanne's.

She smiles. He smiles.

Everything between Hanne and Manfred seems to happen with an unspoken understanding.

"What would you like to know?" Hanne asks.

"I want to know if the same person who killed Nermina also killed Azra Malkoc. And then I want you to tell us who it is."

Hanne laughs and squeezes Manfred's hand.

"I'm not psychic."

"Yes, you are," Manfred says, smiling widely.

Hanne lets go of Manfred's hand and runs her hand through her long hair, twisting a lock between her fingers.

"I'll do it for you, Manfred. But you have to understand that what I say is nothing but hypotheses based on a *very* superficial review of the material."

"Of course."

Hanne sighs and slowly shakes her head. She almost looks worried.

"I don't like to draw hasty conclusions."

"But if you were to do so?"

She nods.

"Then I would say that the murders are definitely connected. It's unlikely that a girl and her mother would be found murdered in the same place by sheer chance, even if these events are sepa-rated by many years. So, yes, I think we could be dealing with the same perpetrator. Secondly, there are certain aspects of the perpe-trator's conduct that lead me to believe that he or she had a per-sonal relationship with the victims."

"Please enlarge on that," Manfred says.

Hanne nods.

"The perpetrator displayed a certain . . . care. He or she—but let's say 'he' for the sake of simplicity—placed the little girl on her back, with her hands clasped over her chest, before covering her with stones. Almost like a funeral. It feels like he . . . *respected* her. The same is true with Azra. The perpetrator placed her under the tree and clasped her hands together just as he did Nermina's. I think he knew them. Maybe even liked them."

Hanne puts on her glasses again, looks at her notes, and con-tinues:

"But then we have the business of Azra's battered face."

Her forehead wrinkles and she falls silent. Stays quiet for a long while.

We watch her without saying anything. Berit coughs in the other room.

"At first glance, it makes no sense," Hanne says. "Not if he respected the victim. You wouldn't crush someone's face with a rock. You do that when you detest someone, or when the crime is driven by rage. But there may be some other reason he did so. Of a more instrumental nature."

Manfred looks up from his notebook.

"Yes," she continues, sounding surer. "That could be the case. He may not have had time to hide the body and so crushed her face in the hopes of making it difficult to identify her."

"But you can identify a person anyway," I say. "With DNA, for example."

Hanne shrugs slightly.

"Sure. But it's more difficult. Then you need something to compare it to. Same thing with fingerprints."

"And the fact that both victims were barefoot?" I ask.

"Hmmm," Hanne says, tapping her pen against the table. "*If* we're certain the girl was barefoot. Her shoes may have decomposed. She was lying in the cairn for fifteen years before she was found. But her mother . . ."

Hanne falls silent and stares out at the snowy field.

"Can the technicians ascertain if the shoes were removed before or after the murder?" she asks.

"They can't be completely sure," Manfred says. "But she had scratches on her feet, so they think she probably walked barefoot through the woods."

"She may not have been psychologically healthy," Hanne says. "Or . . ."

"*Or?*" Manfred says.

"Or she made a hasty exit from somewhere, a nearby house or car."

"There are no houses nearby," I say.

"But there's a road," Hanne says, pointing to the map. Manfred nods.

"So?" he says slowly. "Who is he?"

Hanne smiles ruefully.

"I wish I could say. But I think he's lived around here for a long time because of where both murders took place, and because such a long period of time passed between them. I'm pretty sure it's a man, simply because most killers who shoot or beat up their victims are men. He's physically strong and knows the area well. I'd say he should be somewhere between forty and sixty-five . . ."

"Wait a minute," Andreas says. "How can you know that?"

Hanne nods, and appears almost energetic.

"Murder is a serious crime. Most murderers have some kind of criminal record, or at least what we would call a *pathological development curve*. So if we assume that the killer was at least eighteen years old when he killed Nermina, he's at least forty-one today. Then we have the murder of . . . what was her mother's name again?"

"Azra Malkoc," I say.

"Thank you. The terrain was rugged and the body had been moved and placed under a spruce. It must have required a certain amount of physical strength. That excludes the elderly and handicapped. I don't believe the perpetrator is older than sixty-five."

Everyone is quiet.

Hanne seems pleased. Her eyes twinkle.

"Any more?" Manfred asks.

"Well. One could speculate on the type of person the perpetrator is. If one wanted to. But I would rather not."

Hanne's voice is teasing, and she stares hard at Manfred.

"Come on!" Manfred says.

"Okay. I would say that he's impulsive and disorganized. At least the murder of the woman indicates that. It was . . . *sloppy*. Rash and not particularly smart."

"Could the perpetrator be an addict, or maybe an alcoholic?" Manfred asks.

Hanne shrugs.

"It's possible. Or, maybe it was sloppy because it was unplanned. And as I said earlier, I think he had some kind of relationship to the victims. Start there, and maybe you'll find him."

Manfred bends forward, his eyes on Hanne. Then he reaches for the map. Places it on the table between him and Hanne and points to the cairn.

"Why here, Hanne? Why the cairn?"

Hanne shakes her head, and seems troubled.

"My first thought was that the place might have some meaning for the perpetrator. But I'm not so sure. It could be that . . ."

"What?" I ask.

Hanne's eyes meet mine; she closes them and seems to be concentrating. The dog, who until now was lying still on the kitchen floor, lifts his head and looks at us, as if sensing something important is taking place here, at the kitchen table in Berit's little cottage.

"Imagine a crossroads that you have to pass by to get out of or into a city," Hanne says. "A place that everyone drives by, not because they want to, but because they have to. Perhaps the girl and her mother passed by this place on their way to or from another place. A car. A house. The cairn lies in a clearing, so a person who passes by will stop and look around, as if to orient themselves. And if someone's following you, they'd have a clear view of you in that clearing."

Hanne lifts her arms and cocks her head as if she were holding a rifle and taking aim at something.

Manfred nods and makes notes.

"So, we'll look at the nearby properties again?"

"I think so," Hanne says, pushing the papers aside. "The properties and vehicles that drive the road near . . . in the vicinity of . . ."

Hanne bangs her hand on the table in frustration and squeezes her eyes shut.

"Close to that . . . *the pile of stones* . . ." she says finally.

"The cairn," Manfred adds, gently.

Hanne meets Manfred's eyes. Blinks several times and clasps her hands together.

Then she sighs audibly.

"This doesn't feel good. I had that woman's . . . What was her name again?"

"Azra," Manfred says.

Hanne nods.

"I was wearing Azra's necklace. And her blood was on my shoes. I don't think Peter is in any of the summer cottages out there. I think something terrible happened to him."

No one answers her, but Manfred squeezes Hanne's hand hard.


We're back in the office. Andreas hangs up his winter coat and sits down in the chair across from me.

"How could she know all that?"

I shrug. I'm as surprised as he is. Hanne, who was so quiet and reserved throughout the investigation. Who listened in on all our meetings, took notes, nodded, and barely asked a question.

I never really understood her abilities, even though Manfred said she was good, maybe even the best. It's almost as though she was holding back for Peter's sake.

"There's a reason they call her the witch," I say.

Andreas nods.

He looks good today, has done something with his hair. Maybe he cut it, maybe it's wax, because it lies close to his head, and for once he's wearing a nice sweater and a pair of jeans that aren't too short for him.

I think he notices me looking at him, because he glances up from his computer and meets my eyes. I look away, but a moment too late—he's already fired off one of those self-satisfied smiles, as if I've just confirmed how hot I think he is.

Manfred enters. Hangs up his coat and sits down. Flips through a stack of papers and then says:

"We should take it for what it is. Hanne's damn sharp, but she's also confused and doesn't remember anything from the investigation. Still, I'd bet my tweed cap that there's quite a bit that's right in what she says."

"Stefan Birgersson certainly fits her description," I say. "He's forty-eight years old, lives close to the cairn, knows these woods, and seems quite . . . How was it that Hanne described the murder? 'Disorganized'? 'Sloppy'?"

Manfred nods and picks up his notebook. At that very moment his phone rings. He glances at it and notes drily:

"NFC. I'm glad they work weekends nowadays."

Then he holds five fingers in the air.

"Five minutes."

He gets up and disappears into the store area to talk on the phone undisturbed.

Andreas's expression is inscrutable.

"I think we should look for the child," I say. "The one Azra gave birth to."

"Did you check with the delivery clinics?"

I nod. "No Azra Malkoc gave birth to a child in the spring of 1994. No unknown women, either. But she may have used a false identity. In any case, the child is surely buried in those woods somewhere."

"Yes. The question is where to start looking. The forests are huge around here. And now everything's snowed under. We won't be able to search the ground until this spring."

"But if we *know* where to start looking—"

"And where is that?" Andreas interrupts, looking skeptical.

"The cairn," I say. "There's too much pointing to that place to ignore it."

I pause for a moment, before adding in a lighter tone of voice:

"And then there's the Ghost Child to consider."

Andreas's face is impossible to read.

"What?" I ask.

"Seriously. You don't believe in ghosts, do you?"

"Of course not. They're just a form of mass hysteria. What I'm wondering is if there might be some real event at the base of that rumor. I mean, what if someone actually heard an infant crying there at some point. What if there was a child. And then the story was retold again and again until it turned into legend. I think the rumor started about twenty years ago. The timing fits."

I don't say anything about Sump-Ivar, who claimed to have seen a dead infant at the cairn. I don't want to acknowledge that I'm taking the ravings of a schizophrenic seriously.

Andreas meets my eyes, seems to be weighing my words.

"I guess we could search the cairn thoroughly. Considering everything that's happened there."

He pauses for a moment and then continues:

"In the spring. After the snow melts."

"There *must* be some way to do it sooner. We could shovel the snow, or maybe use some kind of heaters to melt it. Take the cadaver dogs there."

Andreas looks doubtful.

"Can they even find a body after so many years?"

"Yes. Some dogs can. I've looked into it. Cadaver dogs have found parts of skeletons that are over thirty years old."

"Okay," he says.

"Okay, what?"

"We can suggest that to Manfred."

I'm surprised.

I thought I'd have to work a lot harder to convince him. Wheedle more. Persuade and explain and maybe even put up with some humiliation.

Andreas smiles provocatively.

"Wanna get a beer after work today?"

In just a fraction of a second, the satisfaction I felt over convincing him of my point is transformed to anger.

He doesn't give a shit about what happened to that child. The only thing he cares about is getting in my pants, which is never going to happen, not if he's the last man on earth.

When I look up, I see his self-satisfied grin. His tobacco peeks out from under his lip, looking like rat shit, and his eyes shine puckishly. And there he goes again: leaning back, his legs wide.

As if he's quite pleased with himself.

"Are you a complete fucking idiot? Haven't you noticed that I'm not interested in you?"

"Well, well, well," he says, still smiling.

If I were ten years younger I would have slapped him. I would have marched right over and slapped the grin off his face. But I don't do things like that anymore. I don't live in Ormberg anymore, and I don't slap people just because they're idiots.

Andreas stands up and looks me over slowly.

"Gotta piss," he says, nods at his statement, and disappears from the room.

I stare at the computer screen, my cheeks turning hot. Take a deep breath, trying to get a handle on my feelings.

This thing with Andreas is so weird.

As soon as I start thinking he's nice, he does something to sabotage it.

My glance falls on the printout next to Andreas's computer, the one with the results of the research he did: the names of every inhabitant in Ormberg with a police record.

And there, somewhere in the middle of the list, I see it.

*Mom.*

Why is she there? She's surely never done anything illegal, never even stolen fallen fruit.

I log in to the system and search for the list. Input the data and press *Enter*.

The computer starts to buzz as if I've just asked it to do something very strenuous. Blinks.

And there it is.

I click on it and open the report. Read through it, and then just sit there, unable to move.

On a November evening three years ago, right after the death of my father, Mom was found injured and inebriated on the slopes of Orm Mountain. The officer who first arrived on the scene described her as "very depressed after the recent death of her husband." She was transported to Katrineholm for "medical attention and suicide watch." The officer also wrote that she absolutely did not want them to contact her closest relative, her daughter, Malin Brundin, who had recently begun studying at the Police Academy in Stockholm, saying that she shouldn't "lose focus."

My stomach knots up and tears burn behind my eyelids. Poor little Mom.

Was she so devastated by Dad's death? And still, she didn't want to bother me.

It's heartbreaking.

I keep reading. Apparently, Mom asked the police to contact Margareta instead. It turned out Mom had fractured her ankle, and Margareta promised to help out during the time she was laid up.

I think back.

Of course, Mom must have mentioned Margareta visiting quite a bit when I was first at the academy.

I didn't think about it at the time, but now I understand.

In Ormberg we take care of our own.

I can imagine that Margareta must have cooked all the food. She probably cleaned and swept until the whole place smelled like soap and the windows sparkled.

Because that's what she does. That's what she did after Kenny died.

I just wish Mom had told me. I would have helped as well. And then we could have talked about what happened. Because now, I can't even bring this up with her—it's a privacy issue.

I bury my face in my hands, sadness and frustration expanding inside me.

I never should have come back to Ormberg.

I should have stayed in Katrineholm. Steered clear of all this old bullshit, been nice to Max.

Steps approach, and I stretch and fix my hair.

Andreas returns to the room and sits down at his place. Manfred is a few steps behind him. His cheeks are rosy, and there's a new spring in his step.

Luckily, he doesn't seem to notice how upset I am, because this is not something I want to discuss with him.

"I spoke to the woman coordinating our forensic analyses at NFC," Manfred says, sitting down. The chair totters for a moment.

He continues:

"They've examined the clothing Hanne was picked up in. They found soil and plant residue, as expected, since she'd been wandering through the forest for twenty-four hours. But they did a chemical analysis as well and found traces of . . ."

Manfred puts on his reading glasses, flips through his notepad, wipes some stray crumbs from his mouth, and continues:

"Silicon dioxide, magnetite, and carbon."

"Chemistry isn't my strong suit," Andreas says.

Manfred bends his head forward and looks at me over his glasses.

I shake my head. "Sorry. Not mine, either."

"Magnetite, also called black ore—it's an iron oxide," Manfred says quietly, and leans forward. "It's used in the production of iron, if I understood correctly. Silicon dioxide is a waste product from the production of iron. And carbon . . . Well, carbon is coal. Pyrolyzed biological material, to be exact."

The room falls silent. The only sound is the drone of the heater.

"Well, I'll be damned," Andreas drawls.

"The ironworks," I say. "Hanne must have been there."

# Jake

The snow's at my knees as I drag the moped in under the small tin overhang on the short side of the large red building, then press my way through the opening in the wall.

It's dark and cold inside. I sense, more than see, the large concrete pillars and the crane that runs the length of the ceiling. My phone is warm from being in my pocket. I scroll through my messages and see that Melinda has texted me twice. Apparently, some old lady from social services has been by, and she's going to take care of us until Dad comes home.

She doesn't mention finding me dressed up in women's clothes.

I know I have to go home sooner or later. But I just can't be around Melinda right now. Can't stand to see my shame in her eyes. So I send her a short text, write that I'm sleeping over at a friend's.

Where I'll actually sleep I have no idea. I can't go back to Saga's, because she hates me now.

The machine hall is dim; shadows hover behind the large steel beasts that stand scattered across the concrete floor. My steps echo through the silence, and one of the chains that hangs from the ceiling rattles, as if an invisible hand were pulling on it lightly.

Brogrens Mechanical was the only place I could think of. I have nowhere else to go.

I head for the foreman's desk and sit down on the old stained mattress on the floor. Light one of the candles there, open my backpack, and take out a Coke and Hanne's diary.

Lunch.

Andreas & Manfred have gone to Stockholm. They're meeting with someone at immigration and some officials at the Bosnia and Herzegovina Embassy. They'll be back tomorrow evening. Malin is at her mother's, eating lunch.

Just before Malin left, I asked her about Margareta and Magnus Brundin, why they lived together, even though Magnus is past forty. She said that Magnus is all that Margareta has left. Her husband, Lill-Leffe, left her for a hairdresser from Flen when she was pregnant with Magnus. It's apparently a very sensitive subject, and no one in the family is allowed to mention Lill-Leffe by name, even after more than forty years.

It's not easy being human.

A few things have happened.

First: I went to the bathroom and didn't recognize myself in the mirror.

I was terrified! It took me several minutes to calm down.

How is that even possible? How could you not recognize your own mirror image? The face you've stared at year after year. The wrinkles you saw coming, the hair that turned gray before your very eyes.

I know that the disease affects my face memory. I have difficulty recognizing people.

But MYSELF?

Second: P dug up an old police report from November 1993. The staff at the refugee camp saw a brown van on the road outside on several occasions. They were having problems with vandalism (someone kept lighting the bushes on fire), and they suspected the van could be connected to the fires.

We're interested for completely different reasons.

The report was made in November, not long before Nermina and her mother disappeared.

There may be a connection between the van and their disappearance.

P's checking to see if someone in Ormberg owned a vehicle matching that description at the time. (There was no information about license plate number or make, but there aren't so many people here, so it's surely possible to go through the lists.)

Evening.

I'm lying in bed at the hotel. P's in the bathroom.

It's raining and howling outside, and I feel down.

I despise Ormberg. I just want to leave here and never come back.

Besides: P is so silent and cold again.

I felt so furious with him that I had the impulse to grab onto the handbrake and jerk it as we were driving home.

Imagine if I were to hurt P! Imagine if I made us drive off the road or pushed him into a creek!

I don't want to, but it feels like I'm no longer in control of my feelings.

It feels like life is running out of my hands.

It feels like everything is coming to an end.

I'm awakened by the sound of steps echoing in the machine hall, and then a dull bang, as if somebody kicked one of the old metal plates that are lying around here and there.

It's darker now—I've slept for several hours. My body feels stiff and sore as I put the diary back into my backpack and peer out into the gloom.

The steps get closer, stop, then start again. A shadow expands from out of the darkness.

My stomach knots up when I realize who it is.

How could I be so stupid? I knew he hung out around here. And still I came back.

As if I was begging for a beating.

"Well, fuck, it's *Ya-ke*. I didn't know you were here!"

Vincent stands with his legs wide, a plastic bag from the gas station in his hand. His downy upper lip curls, like he's about to start laughing at something.

He walks toward me slowly, until he's standing just a few meters away.

I sit on the mattress and stare up at him. Maybe it's the fluttering light of the candle, but for some reason he looks even more insane than usual. His jeans are wet, and his old winter coat is dripping. He reminds me of a ghost from the sea that was in one of the horror films Saga and I watched a week ago. The ghost had been killed by his own pet—a dog that was really a werewolf—and fell off a cliff.

After watching that movie, Saga said she never wanted a pet, even if it was the cutest thing in the world, because you'd never know when it might turn into a monster.

"Ya-keee. Where did your emo girl go? Did the retard get tired of you already?"

He leans his head back and spits his tobacco over my head. It lands somewhere in the darkness behind me. Then he squats down so his face is in front of mine.

He's so close I can smell the snuff on his warm, damp breath and see the sparsely placed strands of hair that are growing on his pale, pimply chin.

"You know you're named after a *fag*, right?"

I swallow hard.

"I'm named after an actor," I say, looking down at the fraying edges of the mattress, stains from beer and wine and other disgusting God-knows-what on the fabric.

Vincent pushes me so hard I fall onto my back.

"Bullshit. That actor, Jake *Gyllen-something,* he was a fag in the faggiest movie ever made. About two cowboys who fucked each other and really liked it. Didn't you know that? Didn't your mother tell you that before she up and died?"

I roll aside and stand, a few meters from Vincent.

"His name is Jake Gyllenhaal," I say quietly.

Vincent takes a step toward me.

"And he's a fag. Just like you, *Ya-ka.* Love the pink sweater, by the way. Did you get a new boyfriend?"

Something cold drips from the ceiling into my hair. A chain rustles somewhere in the distance. I wish I'd gone home. Anything would have been better than this. Even Melinda's disgusted look as though she thought I was sick and mentally disturbed.

Vincent takes another step closer.

"Blow me, faggot!"

"I'm not . . ."

*Pow.*

The punch hits my stomach, and I fold over in pain. Sink down and have to brace my hands against the cold, damp concrete to keep from falling over. It feels as if all the blood has run from my head and gathered near the glowing ball of pain in my abdomen. I gasp, struggling to keep my balance.

What would Hanne do? Hanne who's so cool and strong: She'd never let anyone treat her the way Vincent treats me.

"Admit you're a fag!"

Something happens inside me. I can't explain exactly what, but it's like something falls apart.

Images of everything he's done to me flicker through my mind. I see him rubbing yellow snow into my face, see him pushing my head into the seat of the school bus, and I see the Eiffel Tower lying on its side on the concrete floor just seconds before Vincent ordered Albin, *"Crush that piece of shit!"*

I see all of it, and something inside me breaks and makes room for another feeling, one so strong I'm afraid to lose control of it. As if Vincent's blow released a wild animal inside me.

I rise slowly, bend my knees, take a deep breath, and fling myself at him.

Totally surprised, Vincent falls back onto the concrete floor with me on top. We land with a thud.

"You fucker!" I scream, and I can hear how strange my voice sounds. I don't recognize it, it's so husky and hateful.

I grab his blond hair and slam his head against the floor over and over again with a strength I didn't know I possessed.

"You fucker. You fucker. *You fucking twisted fucker.*"

"What the hell," he whimpers. "It was just . . . a . . . joke."

I let go of his head and pull my hands back, as if I've burned them on his pale skin.

"If you ever touch me again, if you even get anywhere close to me, I'll tell every single fucking person in Ormberg what your dad did. Tell them he's a disgusting pedophile who went to prison for groping little boys in Örebro. Do you understand me?"

Vincent's eyes are wide, and his face is stiff with fear. A thin string of saliva runs down his cheek from the corner of his mouth.

And it feels as if I'm watching all of this happen from above, still trying to make sense of one simple fact: Vincent is afraid of *me.*

How could that be possible?

Vincent is afraid of *Ya-ka*, his *favorite person to hate.* The guy he loves to punch and kick and spit at.

We're both completely still for a moment, I don't know exactly how long, until I become aware of both our breathing. Of the cold in the machine hall, the wind howling outside, and the slight rustling of chains near the ceiling.

I stand up. Staying in front of him without backing down. My eyes pinned to him.

Vincent shuffles backward, away from me. His expression is

like a hunted animal; it reminds me of Hanne's eyes that night in the woods.

"You're completely *cra . . . cra . . . zy*," he stammers quietly. "*Totally fucking . . .*"

His voice fades away.

At that moment, I know I will never have to run from Vincent again. I just know it.

He shuffles back a few more meters, and I take another step toward him.

Vincent stands up and runs, all hunched over, into the darkness.


After he's gone, I sit on the mattress for a long time, trying to make sense of what just happened. How did I do it? How could I, Jake, scare away Vincent—Ormberg's King of Assholes?

My satisfaction is mixed with something darker and sharper, which rubs at my chest.

If I'm capable of this, does that mean I've become like him? That some part of me is as evil and twisted as Vincent?

I throw my bag over my shoulder, grab a candle in one hand and the mattress by the other, and drag it with me across the room.

Behind the machine called "Innocenti" there's a small area that's almost invisible, maybe two meters wide and one meter deep.

I'm safe in here.

I push the mattress inside, put the candle on the floor, and sit down on the bed. Lean against the cold wall and open up the diary again.

Night. I can't sleep. I can't stop thinking about P.

I had another outburst at him today. Lost control completely, threw his computer at him and screamed.

P wrestled me to the ground. Said he'd call an ambulance if I didn't settle down. Slapped me hard.

What's happening to me?

What's happening to us?

I set the diary aside.

Is Hanne going crazy for real? Or was she just very tired when she wrote that?

What if she had something to do with Peter's disappearance; what if she really did push him into a creek, like she was afraid of?

*What if I'm reading the diary of a murderer?*

I rub my eyes. There aren't many pages left now, but I'm hungry. My stomach grumbles, and I'm trembling from the cold.

I open my backpack and dig out the bread. Open the package and take a bite. The loaf is still frozen in the middle, but I eat all of the soft, doughy bread around the hard core. Then I open the second Coke I brought and drink it down in one gulp. Burp and throw it aside.

It rolls away into the dark.

I think about Hanne, and decide I feel sorry for her after all. Even though I'm mad at her, and she seems crazy, I feel sorry for her.

And I'm getting pretty pissed off at P.

I don't understand why she's together with him. She could have stayed in Greenland, with the Inuits, and never even come here, to Ormberg.

Before I read Hanne's book, I never thought that there were any disadvantages to living here, but she doesn't seem to like Ormberg, and maybe she's right that it's just an ugly little backwater.

I don't know.

I don't know anything anymore, except that I have to read the rest of Hanne's story.

The diary sits on my lap. There's not much left of the candle. I have to hurry.

ORMBERG, DECEMBER 1

I woke up early. Heard P breathing next to me: regular, peaceful, completely unaware of my agony.

I tried to hold him.

He woke up and pushed me away. Mumbled he was too warm.

Too WARM!

I NEEDED his closeness! It felt like I might break apart otherwise.

But apparently what P needs is to never be subjected to any of my needs.

I got up instead. Read yesterday's notes and remembered everything: the fight, the slap.

I flipped back and read the entire diary, from the first page to the last. It was an awful reminder of how much worse I've gotten lately. We were so happy and in love in Greenland. And now everything is awful.

Is it over? Not with a bang but a whimper, as T. S. Eliot wrote.

We ate breakfast in silence.

P read the newspaper thoroughly. Every article, every ad received his full attention.

I sat opposite him. Ate my toast, drank my coffee. Watched him.

P looked up at me now and then. Smiled. Seemed a little self-conscious; maybe he thought that I was staring.

We've been in Ormberg for one and a half weeks now.

It feels like an eternity.

We've driven around the village, tramped through the woods, and interviewed the locals. I still don't understand this place. It's as if a thick membrane covers everything. As if something's hiding just below the surface.

Evil, under a façade of melancholic normality.

I tried to explain it to P.

He didn't understand what I meant. Said I was being dramatic. That we were "investigating a crime in a small town, not trapped in a horror film."

I didn't tell him that was EXACTLY what it feels like! As if we were the naive cops who strolled into a house where a whole family's been murdered, lured into a trap by a maniac with a chain saw under his arm.

We arrived at the office around nine. The storm was raging outside.

Malin was already at her desk. Manfred and Andreas were still in Stockholm. They're coming back late this evening.

Malin just left; she's going to her mother's place to eat lunch. P's out buying something.

The storm is roaring, rain falling down in sheets. It's only noon, but it's dark outside.

It never really gets light here.

For me Ormberg has become synonymous with darkness. Perhaps metaphorically as well, because I still maintain that something evil lured us here, no matter what P says.

P found somebody who owned a brown van in the early nineties, the one the staff at the refugee camp saw standing outside.

A person living in Ormberg had a brown Nissan King.

BUT he didn't want to tell me who it was. All he said was that it was "very sensitive."

It made me terribly sad and upset. Yes, I am more confused, but I would never share such a thing.

Who does he think I am these days? I'm forgetful, not lacking in judgment!

Oh, dear, it sounds as if something has blown down outside the store.

Have to stop.

# Malin

We're at the old ironworks. The snow is up to my knees, but it's soft and light as I make my way back toward Andreas. Every step creates a flurry around my legs.

It's blowing more than before, and I hunch over against the wind.

I put my phone in my pocket, pull on my thick gloves. Turn on my flashlight and try to take in what Max just said.

Take a *break*.

What the hell does he mean by that? We're getting married this summer. I need his help planning the wedding. We can't take a break.

Not now.

Or does he mean he wants to break up? Was that it, but he couldn't or wouldn't put it into words?

I know I should have called him and apologized for what I said the last time we spoke. I was really unpleasant. Not just that, I was unfair, too. He can't help the fact that he has the job he has. That he spends his days ensuring that people injured in accidents get as little compensation as possible.

Or can he?

I try to push that thought away, but still it comes, like an uninvited guest who won't leave even after you've offered him wine, coffee, cognac, and a late supper.

He *could* get another job. He's a lawyer—there are plenty of jobs for lawyers in Stockholm. Nobody forced him to take that job.

Doesn't the fact that he chose it say something about him, about his character?

The various buildings stand around me in the dark: the blast furnace, the roasting furnace, the coal house, and the old smithy. Some of them have collapsed, but others—those made of bricks—stand like a silent reminder of all that Ormberg once was.

Next to them, the creek flows silently by. Large sheets of ice have grown along the shoreline.

Andreas looks up at me as I arrive.

"I thought you knew your way around here?"

I sense a bit of annoyance in his voice. He stamps his feet in the snow and pulls his hat farther down over his ears.

It's cold, we're all freezing, but that's hardly my fault.

"It's never easy to find your way in the dark," I answer.

Manfred, Andreas, and I have spent the last hour out here searching for any trace of Peter and Hanne—something to confirm they were here during the night of that fateful storm just over a week ago. We've searched through the buildings and wandered rather aimlessly through the deep snow.

We haven't found anything.

We know Hanne was here, because traces of iron were found on her clothes, specifically on the back of her jeans, as though she'd been sitting on the ground.

A large figure approaches through the snow: soundlessly lumbering our way, like a bear.

Manfred.

I aim the flashlight downward so as not to blind him.

"Let's forget about this," he says. "The technicians and the dogs will search this place tomorrow."

I think for a moment.

"Soon," I say, and look around. "I want to check one more thing." I head toward the roasting furnace.

"Goddamnit, Malin." Manfred sighs, apparently tired of freezing his butt off.

I hear Andreas behind me, panting as he approaches.

"What are you checking?" he asks.

"One thing."

The roasting furnace's beautiful brick silhouette rises in front of us in the darkness. The chimney stretches up toward the sky. The windows are broken and covered with graffiti, but the crooked old door is slightly open.

"What kind of *thing*?"

I sigh and wait for him.

"There was a storm that night," I say. "It's likely she would have sought shelter in one of the buildings if she came here. And this building is the only one with doors and windows."

The old wooden door whines as I pull it open.

"I've already checked in there," Andreas says.

"Just one minute," I say, entering.

I shine my flashlight into the darkness.

In the middle of the room stands the impressively huge, round roasting furnace. Cast-iron hatches are built into it just above the floor. The floor is littered with old beer cans and empty wine bottles. There are piles of cigarette butts along the walls.

"Where would you sit if you came in here seeking shelter from a storm?"

Andreas looks around. His breath turns to white clouds in the shine of the flashlight.

"There," he says, pointing to a pile of old wood that sits at the farthest corner of the building.

"Exactly," I say, making my way around the enormous furnace and heading for the wood.

Old rusty nails stick up here and there out of the floorboards.

I sit down on the top plank, take my hand out of its glove, and feel the board beneath me. The sticky, frosty wood reminds me of something else.

"Hanne said something about boards," I say. "She remembered boards."

"Boards and a dark room," Andreas adds.

"Could it have been this she was referring to?"

We look around. Andreas sweeps his flashlight over the angular room.

"She said the room was cramped," he says. "It's not particularly cramped in here. But perhaps she mixed it up."

I nod and put my glove on again and look around one final time.

"Maybe we should go," I say, rising up.

At that very moment something gleams near my feet, something beneath the boards.

*"Shine right here!"*

Andreas does as I say.

I bend forward and pick up the gleaming item.

*"Fucking hell,"* Andreas murmurs when he sees what it is.


The blowing of the heater and the purr of the engine fill the car.

Manfred weighs the phone in his hand.

"It *is* Peter's," he says, and presses the *Home* button with a gloved thumb.

Nothing happens. The screen is black.

He connects the phone to a cord hanging under the dashboard.

"Shouldn't we call the technicians?" Andreas asks.

"Absolutely," Manfred says. "But I'm not gonna wait for them to get here. It's a Sunday evening. And we don't even have a newly murdered corpse to tempt them. If there's anything important on this phone, I want to know it now."

It's warm in the car; the fan is set to *Max* and the fog has started to dissipate from the windows. The smell of damp wool and wet fabric fills the air. I take off my hat and unbutton my thick coat.

Andreas does the same.

The phone buzzes and blinks to life.

Manfred puts it on his knee. Takes off his gloves, opens the glove compartment, and roots around for something inside. Takes out a blue latex glove and puts it on his left hand. Grabs the phone with his left hand and presses the display with his right index finger. Then he turns to us.

"Your guess is as good as mine. What do you think the code could be?"

Half an hour later we haven't gotten anywhere.

We've tried the most common codes, the unimaginative combinations most of us use, like 0000 or 1234. And of course, Peter's and his son's birthdays.

"There are tens of thousands of possible combinations," Andreas says quietly, scratching at his chin. "Maybe we better hand it over to the IT guys."

Manfred sighs and puts the phone on his knee.

"Wait," I say. "Try 3631."

Manfred shrugs his shoulders and enters the code. The phone buzzes.

"Wrong," he says.

"Try 3632 or 3633."

Manfred does as I say.

"Wrong. And wrong. What's this about? It's locked again, by the way. It says that we have to wait five minutes."

We wait in silence. The only thing we hear is the engine's hum and Manfred's labored breathing, though I know that outside the wind and snow are rattling through the trees.

"Keep going," I say when the phone flashes. "Try 3634 and 3635."

"Nope. Wrong."

Manfred turns to me and Andreas.

"Can we go home now?" he asks.

"Wait," I say.

"Let me guess," Manfred says. "3636?"

He puts in the code, takes a breath—probably so he can say something surly—but then freezes.

The phone dings.

*"What the hell?"* he whispers. "How could you know that?"

"Those were the numbers on Hanne's hand," Andreas says. "She'd written 363, and then something unreadable."

Manfred shakes his head like he can't believe his eyes. He clicks through text and email.

We both fall silent.

"Nothing we don't already know," Manfred says after a while.

"Check the photos," I say.

Manfred opens the camera roll.

Hanne stands in front of a bay—turquoise glaciers float on the water, and sunshine dances on the waves.

He scrolls forward: Hanne sitting on a bed in an unknown hotel room, smiling and holding a sandwich in her hand.

"Keep going," I say. "These must be from Greenland."

Manfred scrolls on and pictures of Ormberg start to pop up: our office, the cairn, the steep slope of Orm Mountain, the spruce trees with blueberry bushes growing at their base.

"Keep going," I say. "This was all before the snow arrived."

The pictures replace each other, their character slowly changing. The first snow appears: a powdery dusting on the field in front of the church, like a delicate warning of winter arriving. Then the snow deepens. And, I note, the pictures of Hanne become more rare.

But one of the last photographs is a close-up of Hanne. I guess she must be lying in bed, because she's holding something that looks like a cover against her chin. She smiles widely and her hair is messy. Her eyes shine and I can almost hear her laughter bubbling up. The love between her and Peter rings out so clearly—like a note being played, a vibration through time and space—in that one picture alone.

It's hard to breathe as I realize they'll probably never meet again, that this might have been one of the last times they were happy together.

The last two photos are taken indoors.

The first shows a staircase down to something that might be a basement. The concrete walls have large moisture stains and the plaster has chipped away here and there. At the bottom, clothes hang on hooks, or maybe there's some sort of coat rack.

"Where's this taken? Malin, do you recognize that staircase?"

Manfred holds the phone in front of me, and I look very carefully.

"No," I say. "But it looks like a basement staircase. Check out the next picture."

Manfred scrolls forward. It's blurry, as if the person holding the phone were moving. You can just make out a person's head at the left edge.

It's Peter—you can't mistake that slightly crooked nose and the disheveled gray-blond hair.

On the right-hand side of the picture you can see something in the distance. It looks like a human being curled up on the floor.

"*Fucking hell,*" Andreas says again.

# Jake

The candle goes out with a hiss, and everything goes black. The dim daylight has been replaced by a darkness so compact that I can't see my own hand in front of me. My back hurts and my fingers are stiff from cold. The wind howls outside, whistling by in gusts and whispering to me to keep reading. The rustle of the chains hanging from the ceiling is constant, as if the building itself were writhing anxiously.

I wonder what Hanne is doing right now, there in Berit's little cottage behind the church. And Dad: Have the police let him go?

Melinda and Saga I don't even want to think about.

I take out my phone, put on the flashlight, and balance it on a huge screw that sticks out from the body of the machine.

Just a few pages left now.

I saw P enter his code into his phone: 3636.

I had no paper nearby, so I wrote it down on my hand so I wouldn't forget.

I'm gathering my courage now: I intend to check his phone at the soonest opportunity. I suppose I shouldn't, it's not what you're supposed to do: sneak into other people's phones or diaries. But I need to know.

Half past four.

We told Malin we were making an early night of it. Might go to Katrineholm. Eat something good, something that didn't taste like cardboard.

She said she was going to work a while longer.

But P didn't drive to Katrineholm. Instead, he drove far out into the woods to a house I've never been to before. Parked behind a tree. Told me to wait in the car and asked me to call him if anybody showed up.

Then he left.

I was prepared to keep watch, but soon discovered that P had forgotten his phone on the driver's seat, so now I'm sitting here, and I don't know if I should stay or not.

It's stormy outside, and the rain lashes against the windshield.

I'm freezing but don't want to start the car, even though the keys are in the ignition. I don't dare bother Peter inside the house.


A quarter to five. P has been inside for fifteen minutes now.

My guess is that the owner of the brown van lives here. From here I can just make out part of the house and the garden behind the trees. On the lawn stand some sort of weird wooden figures—two gnomes, a giant mushroom with a red cap, a lamb, and a pair of hugging bears.

Strange: The windows are dark, but I just saw a cone of light moving inside the house.

It must be P!

Why use a flashlight?

Was no one at home? Did P go inside to snoop anyway?

Sounds like him.


Ten 'til five. I'll wait a little longer. Then go get P if he doesn't come back.


I'm not going to sit here freezing forever! My toes have turned to ice cubes.

P's phone is lying on the passenger seat. The code is written on my palm.

Do I dare?

I can't stand it anymore.

I don't want to. Life hurts too much.

I checked P's phone and found a text message to my doctor.

P wrote that I'm worse and doing everything I can to hide it. Said I have terrible, angry outbursts and that he's afraid I might hurt him or myself. He loves me very much, but doesn't know if he can take care of me anymore. He asked if it sounded like I was still able to live at home or if there was "another solution."

The doctor replied that she couldn't decide anything without seeing me.

I started to cry.

Haven't I suffered through ENOUGH!

But I feel so ashamed too: I accused him of being cold and distant when really he's worried about me.

I understood something else when I read their conversation: P is afraid. He's afraid of being alone. And he's afraid of not being able to handle the fear.

I'm so embarrassed! And I feel so helpless.

Like when I was nine years old and saw my puppy Ajax fall through the ice.

I stood there watching him struggle. Saw his paws trying to grab onto the ice. Heard his whimpering, until finally he disappeared beneath the water.

This feels the same.

Except now I'm the one who's drowning.

I'm going to burn this diary when this is all over. Erase the last two weeks of my life. Forget Ormberg and all that happened here. Until we got here life was perfect, despite the disease.

Dear God, I ask of you only this: Help me forget!


P was just here.

He didn't notice I'd been crying.

He was excited. Said the person he wanted to talk to wasn't home, but that he'd "nosed around a little in the house" and discovered something important.

He'd measured the kitchen and the room next to it. They should be the same length (sitting wall to wall with the hallway, facing the short side of the house), but the kitchen was missing a meter.

In front of the "missing" space in the kitchen, he found a hidden door, covered by the shelves at the room's short end with a small lock at the bottom.

Why build a hidden door?

P plans to open it. He wants his phone with him to take pictures. I gave it to him.

He didn't notice it was unlocked.

I told him to call for reinforcements before going back in. P doesn't want to.

He also gave me a necklace, a gold chain with a medallion on it. It was apparently firmly wedged on the floor below the hidden door. P asked me to take care of it, said it might be important.

I had no idea where to put it. Was so afraid to forget it somewhere so I put it around my neck.

P is inside again.

I'm waiting in the car.

Shivering from the cold.

The storm is raging outside: leaves, branches—everything is flying around.

It feels like I'm sitting in a tumble dryer.

Something must have happened. Something is very wrong.

P hasn't come back.

Should I wait or stay?

I'll g

The words stop.

I flip to the next page, but it's empty. I flip farther. Freeze when I see big, brown, stiff spots on the paper.

*Blood—it has to be blood.*

In a few places, there are bloody thumbprints.

Cautiously, I brush my own fingers over the prints. It almost feels like I'm touching her. As if I've opened a hole through time, and I'm there with Hanne, can feel her despair and sadness.

Something must have happened in that house with the wooden gnomes outside. A house I've been to many times.

Yes, that's it.

The solution must be there—the answer to what happened to that cop. And to who killed the girl and the woman in the cairn.

*The answer that will save Dad.*

# Malin

It's as dark as a grave in Ormberg, and the tiny cluster of houses so misleadingly called the downtown lies silent and deserted. Even the journalists who hounded us earlier this week are gone.

Everyone's at home on this Sunday evening, eating buns and watching TV.

Manfred's gaze is almost frantic, the corner of his eye twitching as he takes off his coat and sits down at the table. He takes out the little plastic bag with Peter's phone inside it, gently places it on the table, and opens his laptop.

"The technicians are coming by to retrieve it soon," he says, nodding to the phone.

His big hands move rapidly across the keyboard, clicking as he writes.

"Have you transferred it over?" Andreas asks.

Manfred slowly turns the computer so we can all see the screen.

And there it is—the picture from Peter's phone. Manfred emailed it to himself so we could look at it on the computer screen and enlarge it.

We examine the blurry image silently—the forms are distorted, difficult to interpret, the color scale going from sepia to a dark graphite gray.

"Definitely Peter," I say, pointing to the face seen in the profile on the left.

Manfred zooms in farther and focuses on the person squatting in the right-hand corner. The contours of a skinny arm become visible. The head is bent forward, but the hair is gray and very long.

"It's her," I say. "It's *Azra Malkoc*."

Something shines in her hand.

"What's that?" I ask, pointing to the object.

"A knife?" Andreas suggests.

"It could be anything reflective," Manfred says. "A mirror, a metal object."

"But what if it *is* a knife," I say. "What if Azra *was* dangerous. What if she *was* the one who murdered Nermina, and maybe even hurt Peter."

No one says anything.

"And what's that over there," I say, pointing to the right of Peter.

*It looks like . . .*

"It could be books piled up," I say.

And as soon as I say it, I know I'm right, the pieces fall into place, my brain interprets the picture correctly, and I'm able to distinguish the objects stacked on top of each other.

"Yes," Manfred says. "*Yes!* Hanne said she remembered English books lying on a dirty floor."

"She must have been there," I say. "But *where* are they?"

"Impossible to say," Andreas says. "We'll have to see what the image analysts say, but I doubt they'll find much more."

"Look at the other picture," I say. "Of the stairs."

Manfred clicks forward to that image. It's much sharper and shows a staircase, which seems to lead into a basement. At the bottom you can see clothes hung neatly on the wall. Dishware sits on a tray on the floor.

No people in sight.

"This *must* be a basement," Manfred says. "We'll check out which nearby properties have basements. The land survey may contain that data, or the city architectural office. I'll call Svante as soon as we're done. They can help us. I have to catch a few hours' sleep tonight."

"Who took the picture of Peter and Azra?" Andreas asks. "Peter is in the picture, so someone else must have taken it."

"Hanne," I say. "Maybe she had Peter's phone. Maybe that's why she had the code written on her hand. She may have been the one who left it at the ironworks, too. We can't know if Peter was ever there."

Manfred rubs his temples.

"Suppose they were on the trail and ran into Azra Malkoc. We know their phones were in Ormberg. So they found Azra somewhere in the area. I'd guess something went to hell after that. Azra was murdered. Hanne fled or got lost. And Peter . . ."

He leaves the sentence unfinished. The picture of Peter appears in my mind once more. I glance at the shelf where we put his and Hanne's things. It took a week before we moved them off the table. It felt so final to clear them away completely, so we placed them on the shelf instead.

Manfred continues:

"Peter may be alive, Peter may be dead. He's like Schrödinger's fucking cat. And it's driving me mad."

He pauses, his eyes wandering toward the old store, where the floor heater stands humming. Then he shakes his head and continues:

"Why didn't Peter and Hanne tell me they'd found something new? Why did they keep the rest of us in the dark?"

"Maybe there was no new trail," I say. "They might have gone to meet someone who was already a suspect and stumbled into Azra Malkoc."

"*Like who?*" Manfred leans forward and fastens his eyes on me. I feel how, against my will, my cheeks get hot.

"Stefan Birgersson?" I suggest. "Björn Falk? Or the pedophile, Henrik Hahn? Or maybe they met a witness who turned out to be more than just an innocent messenger. One of the employees at the refugee camp, for example."

Manfred leans back in his chair. He doesn't seem entirely convinced.

"Hmmm," he says.

The door slams and steps approach.

Malik appears in the doorway. He has snow on his shoulders and hat.

"Knock, knock," he says.

"Howdy," Andreas says, and raises a hand in greeting. "Are you visiting Ormberg?"

"I'm headed to the ironworks with the technicians. Thought I'd pick up that phone as well."

Manfred nods to Peter's phone, in the plastic bag on the table.

Malik stamps the snow off his boots, doffs his hat, runs a hand through his black hair, and gathers it into a bun on top of his head. He fastens it with a black hair tie from around his wrist.

"How did the search go at Stefan Birgersson's?" Manfred asks him.

"Good. Other than that the daughter was hysterical. We found a torn, bloody shirt in the laundry room. Otherwise, we didn't find anything remarkable. We'll see what the technicians say when they're done. Oh, one thing: There was a sequined dress hanging in the dead mother's closet. Gold, size thirty-six. I don't know if it's important—Stefan Birgersson could hardly have worn it—but we brought it in anyway."

"Hmmm," Manfred says again. "Anything else?"

Malik shakes his head.

"Not from the search. However, we did get ahold of Tony."

"*Tony?*" Manfred asks.

"I thought Svante had called you," Malik says, with surprise in his voice. "Suzette talked to a guy named Tony. He worked as a caretaker at the refugee camp in the early nineties. Stefan Birgersson got the boot. He wasn't employed really, but he was booted after they caught him sneaking around in the garden late one night. He was spying on a resident. And guess what? This was autumn 1993."

"Azra and Nermina," I whisper.

Malik reaches for Peter's phone.

"Exactly. We're interrogating Stefan Birgersson at eight o'clock tomorrow morning, if you want to join."

Manfred nods.

"We wouldn't miss it. And as for these pictures, we probably can't do much more tonight. Shall we meet at seven-thirty tomorrow morning instead?"

Ten minutes later, Andreas and I are alone—Malik and Manfred have gone.

I go out to the store, turn off the heater, and make sure the bucket is positioned right under the ceiling leak.

Andreas looks at me when I come back. Then he smiles a little. It's not one of his usual self-confident grins, but more a friendly, almost considerate smile.

"Do you want to come home with me?" he asks.

I stop in mid-movement. I almost deliver one of the caustic remarks I have prepared for these sorts of occasions. But then I look at him, meet his serious expression, and think of everything that's gone to hell—that bloody pig head, Nermina's bones, Azra's faceless body on the autopsy table, and Peter, who's apparently become Schrödinger's cat. I think of Kenny who never made it home, of Max who may never come back, and of Mom who lies awake—probably unnecessarily—puzzling over how the wedding can be held as cheaply as possible.

I think of all of it, but more than anything I think of how desperately short life is. A mouse turd in eternity before the darkness comes and extinguishes us all.

I think of something else too: the picture of Hanne in bed with the cover up to her chin. The laughter in her eyes and the love that vibrated off the photo.

Why has it never been like that between Max and me? Have I deliberately chosen to keep love out of my life? Is it because of Kenny?

"Okay," I say.

Andrea's face is expressionless, but his eyes widen a bit in surprise.

He hadn't expected that answer.

"You mean . . . ?"

"Shall we leave before I change my mind?" I say.

We drive through the woods in silence. The spruces have a thick layer of new snow on their branches. A few flakes swirl by in the headlights.

Ormberg is particularly beautiful in the winter. As beautiful as it is dark and deserted.

I don't know how far we drive—twenty kilometers, maybe thirty. Andreas doesn't say a word and neither do I. Soon the forest ends and is replaced by wide, snow-covered fields. He turns off onto a smaller road, drives past a gas station still lit up. After a bit we come to a small neighborhood of row houses built in the seventies.

We park the car in front of one of the identical, miserably ugly boxy houses and get out. Andreas wrestles a key out of his pocket and unlocks the door. Turns on the light and leads me into the warmth.

"Well, this is where I live."

The house could have been in Ormberg.

It looks like the houses of my childhood: furnished with a mix of old and new that don't go together. Ugly leather sofas and imitation oriental rugs in front of a big TV with oversized speakers. A bookshelf with no books. Dumbbells on the floor and a pile of car magazines next to the sofa.

Next to the TV there stand a couple of empty Coke cans and a bowl with a few chips. Exercise clothing hangs over an armchair.

This is exactly what I've been running from, I think.

Ormberg, the countryside, the dreary predictability of the future, the vast fields and the quiet forests. Nights in front of the TV with chips and wine and trips to the nearest superstore to stock up.

The bitter darkness of the winter nights and summer's ruthless clarity.

The feeling that everything's over when it's hardly even begun.

I remember what it said in the police report about Mom. That she was found on Orm Mountain, drunk, sad, and injured three years ago.

*Poor little Mom.*

I think of everything she could have done if she hadn't stayed in Ormberg. Of the jobs she could have had, the people she could have met, and the places she could have seen.

But for her Ormberg was the beginning and end of it all: a completely satisfactory existence. A universe that contained all she needed and wished for and didn't feel at all limiting to her.

Why isn't it like that for me?

What was it that Mom said, exactly?

*If you run from something, make sure it's not yourself you're running from.*

"Do you want something to eat?" Andreas asks. "I'm not sure I have much around here, but . . ."

"No, thanks."

"A cup of tea?"

I shake my head and wander in his direction.

His dark hair is wet, and his shirt smells slightly of sweat. His eyes are serious and a little slanted, just like Kenny's.

I've never thought about it before, but Andreas has Kenny's eyes.

On his cheek I see a small, fresh wound—maybe he scratched himself when we were at the ironworks.

A small drop of blood glitters at the edge of the wound.

He looks like he doesn't really know what to do with me now that he's finally taken me home.

"Well," he says.

"Well," I say, suddenly very aware of his proximity.

I take a step closer; he doesn't move an inch.

His breath is warm and damp against my cheek, like the summer wind on a muggy day down by the creek. I feel the heat of his body radiating against mine.

When I kiss him, he retreats a step.

"Is this a good idea?" he whispers.

But his doubts last only a moment. Then he pulls me close and kisses me back.

# Jake

The moped struggles to move forward as I rev on the gas. The snow sprays around my legs. I don't care anymore about driving slow, but I keep my feet near the ground in case I wobble.

It's half past two on a Monday morning.

I slept a few hours after finishing the diary. Not just because I was tired, but I'd decided that the best time to head here was in the middle of the night. Surely no one's crazy enough to be up now?

When I woke, I saw that Saga had sent me seven text messages— the first four were angry, but the last three were more worried. I decided I'd call her in a few hours. I don't want to wake her up.

I think of Hanne and P. Wonder if he "deserved her" or if she was "too good for him," which are questions Mom used to ask about her girlfriends' relationships.

Women are usually too good for men. Maybe all men are so bad that they really deserve to be alone.

And what about Dad? I don't think he's bad, or at least he wasn't before Mom died.

A gust of wind envelops me and for a moment I think I might roll over, but then the moped steadies, and I keep plowing through the snow.

Around me is only darkness. Tall spruces line the road on either side, their snowy branches stretching over the road as if
they're trying to reach each other.

It's strange that I'm even doing this. But so many strange things
have happened lately I'm no longer sure what's normal. Not even
sure who I am. I think of Dad's eyes as the cops took him away. Of
Saga's soft lips against mine, of my hands ramming Vincent's
head against the concrete floor, of the words I said to him, my
threat to tell everyone who his father really is.

*What's happening to me?*

I don't know, but whatever it is, I don't think I can stop it. I just
have to go with the flow and hope for the best.

The buildings are dark and silent when I arrive. The larger
house is maybe fifty meters away, next to the edge of the woods. It
has a big satellite dish on its roof and three windows facing the
driveway.

I stand in front of the smaller house—it reminds of the big
house, except for the satellite dish. And it has only two windows
in the front.

The wind is stronger, and small, light snowflakes whip against
my cheek as I walk toward the front door.

The wooden figurines on the lawn are buried beneath a thick
blanket of snow.

I've been here many times before. I know every bush, every
tree, but I've never been inside either house.

A plastic wreath hangs on the door, swaying a little in the wind.
Snow lies in drifts up to the front door.

I gently try the handle.

Locked.

I peek in through the kitchen window. Everything is dark and
quiet, with only a tiny light shining like an unblinking yellow eye
on something that looks like a refrigerator. Dim light comes from
the room next door, which must be the hall.

There are geranium pots lining the steps to the front door. My guess is that they're plastic, because the flowers look unnaturally healthy and colorful, even with a thick layer of snow on top of them. I take my gloves off, put them in my pocket, and grope around in the snow near the bottom of the flowerpots. Lift them one by one until *bingo,* I find an old rusty key.

No one in Ormberg is particularly concerned about safety.

That's a big mistake, Dad says. Most people hide an extra key somewhere near the door, but the refugees aren't trustworthy like the locals. They could break in and rape you or raise the caliphate's black flags or steal everything of value.

Whatever that means. I don't know anyone who has anything particularly valuable, except maybe a computer or flat screen.

The key slides into the lock easily. I turn it, and the door opens silently.

I stand at the threshold.

Obviously, I know I should call the police instead of entering this dark house by myself.

But the cops think Dad's a mentally disturbed drunk. They actually believe he could have murdered that woman. They might lock him up for life.

The lump in my throat—the one I'd almost forgotten—comes back again.

No, I have to find out who killed the woman at the cairn so they'll let Dad go. I step over the threshold and gently pull the door closed behind me.

The hallway smells like pizza and sour dishrags. A single bare bulb hanging from the living room ceiling throws a pale, yellow light across the floor. Bags of garbage stand next to the front door and a pair of boots sit next to them. Coats hang from nails on the wall.

I wipe my shoes as much as I can on the doormat and then sneak into the kitchen. The floor creaks and I stop several times to make sure nobody's coming. The only thing I hear is the faint buzz of the fridge and the radiator clicking a bit. At the far end of the room, I see some shelves.

I go over to them and hunch down. Run my hand along the baseboard.

It takes a few minutes before I find it: a small metal hinge a couple of centimeters above the floor. I have to fiddle with it for a while, and then the secret door slides open with a slight click.

It's no ordinary door; it's thick and has metal on the inside.

A puff of moist air hits me: It's just like Saga's storeroom, which she says has mold in it that they'll have to clean when they can afford it.

I stand up, step into the dark space, and pull the door behind me so that only a narrow streak is visible.

It's cooler in here. Cool and damp.

I shiver. Take out my phone, whose batteries will soon be drained, and turn on the flashlight.

I have to be stingy with the batteries from now on.

The stairs are steep and wet with moisture. The walls are stained, and spiderwebs hang from the ceiling; they flutter in the draft of the open door.

In the middle of the stairs there's a tobacco container and a glove still in the shape of a fist—it almost looks like it's reaching for the tobacco.

I climb down step-by-step. Slowly and cautiously, trying not to make any sound. The air feels thicker as I descend, harder to breathe, and the stench of the humid basement is more intense. Clothes are spread out on the floor near a coat hanger. I look at the wall: Three gaping holes reveal where the hanger used to be attached. Next to the clothes lie a broken plate and a broken glass.

There are two doors: one on the right and one on the left. The right door has a big bend in the middle, as if someone kicked it, and the lock looks broken.

I hesitate before I push on the door. Anything could be on the other side of that door: a ghost, a zombie, a . . .

The thought fades quickly when I suddenly realize ghosts or zombies can't scare me anymore. Everything I once imagined and feared has lost its power over me: slimy corpses, demons, and flesh-eating undead. Ax murderers, chainsaw hooligans, and aliens waiting to take over the world and eat human brains like popcorn.

Reality is so much worse.

I nudge the door, and it glides open. Silently. It's heavier than I thought and has metal on the inside, just like the secret door to the kitchen.

The room is small, windowless, and cold, but above all it's empty.

No human or rotting body can be seen. Just a lonely bed standing along one wall. In the bed are some pillows and a blanket with a flower pattern on it. Next to the bed stands a floor lamp and a small bedside table. On the bedside table sits a water glass and a ChapStick. On the floor next to the bed: a pile of clothes—all neatly folded. Next to the wall are piles of books. There must be at least a hundred. I walk over to them and shine the flashlight over their spines.

All in English.

At the far end of the room is another door.

I walk to the door and open it, shine my phone inside.

A toilet and a sink.

On the edge of the sink lies a fringed pink towel. A roll of toilet paper stands on the floor, warped by moisture. On the wall opposite the toilet: a shelf with a toothbrush, a deodorant, a small cracked soap, and a pink hairbrush.

I reach for the hairbrush.

It is full of long gray hairs.

Saga's words appear in my head.

*She looked like a ghost. With long scary gray hair.*

Did the murdered woman at the cairn live here in the basement?

The pipes that run along the ceiling start to rumble, and it shakes me out of my thoughts. I back out of the bathroom and look around the room again, trying to find some detail I may have missed.

Above the bed I see a pattern in the concrete wall, like a weak grid. I go closer and direct the light at the wall. Small stripes appear; they look like someone carved them into the concrete.

I bend forward, see something that looks like a fence: four vertical lines, and then a fifth crossed over the other four.

I back up and see more fences next to it. Take a few more steps back, sweep the light across the concrete, and realize to my horror that the entire wall is filled with stripes.

*The whole damn wall is filled with stripes!*

And at that very moment, when I understand what those lines mean, panic overtakes me. Not from the dirty little room, the disgusting toilet with stains on the floor, or the spiderwebs hanging from the ceiling.

It's the insight that someone must have spent years here. Not days, weeks, or months, but *years*. A human being carved those lines into that damp concrete to keep track of the days and nights as they passed by.

Was it her, the woman with the long gray hair?

I stagger, have to take a few steps in order not to lose my balance and fall.

How could someone survive here? Wouldn't you die, from lack of light and fresh air? Wouldn't you rot like a vegetable that's forgotten in a cold, damp refrigerator?

The air grows thick again, and my chest feels bound by an invisible rope. The walls creep closer, bend over me, and my heart turns over in my chest.

*So many days, so many nights.*

I back out of the room with my heart still pumping in my

chest. The realization that someone lived here, held captive be-hind that thick door, makes me sick and dizzy.

My hands shake as I walk out into the small hall. I stumble on the tray and the porcelain clinks.

My heart stops in my chest, and I hold my breath.

It's quiet.

The only sound is the pipes and a quiet buzzing behind the other door.

I turn around and shine my phone toward it.

It looks like a regular door, and when I try the handle it's not locked.

I open it, shine my phone into the room.

Another cold, windowless basement space, even smaller than the other one.

The only thing in the room is a giant freezer standing against one wall—the kind with a door on top, just like the one we have in our basement at home that Dad usually keeps elk and deer meat inside.

You can fit almost a whole deer inside this one.

The floor is covered by large dark brown spots—I don't even want to think about what they might be.

A line of dark drops runs from the largest of the spots to the freezer.

I go over to it and put my hand on the door handle. At that very moment it starts to hum, almost as if it's trying to tell me something.

I carefully open the door.

The freezer sighs as the cold air streams out. I lean forward and shine my phone inside.

Inside, next to a big tub of ice cream, there's a human being. A man, curled into a fetal position.

He's covered by a thin layer of sparkling frost, but I can still make out his gray-blond hair, his blue coat, and the checkered shirt he's wearing beneath it.

I try not to look at him, focusing instead on the smiling clown on the lid of the ice cream.

It doesn't work.

The nausea rolls over me. I drop my phone on the floor and let go of the door; it slides out of my hands, and I can't stop it from falling with an ominous dull thud.

Though my body is unable to move, and even with the room spinning and vomit trying to come up, my brain keeps churning out hypotheses, testing theories.

I remember what it said about P in the article in the local newspaper:

*. . . At the time of his disappearance he was wearing a red-and-white-checked flannel shirt and a blue coat.*

The man in the freezer is P.

I pick up the phone from the floor and slip it into my pocket. Then I stumble back out of the room into the tiny hall. Lean against the concrete wall, sink down to the floor, and start to crawl on all fours up the stairs, like a dog.

All I can think about is getting away from here. Something far worse than I ever could have imagined took place here, beneath the floorboards of a boring house in the world's most boring town, where every day is exactly the same and nothing dangerous ever happens.

The steps seem to transform into mountains and I have to climb them one by one. They hit my knees and my nails split against the concrete, but I feel no pain anymore. All I feel is paralyzing terror.

When I'm almost halfway up, I stand. The floor is damp and slippery and the thought of the man in the freezer makes my legs unsteady. Just as I think that I absolutely must not fall, I stumble on something.

As I fall, I realize it must be the tobacco and the glove.

The back of my head hits the floor with a thud.

The pain is sharp, but fades away as fast as it arrived. It's re-placed by a feathery lightness, a feeling like floating.

The darkness around me dissolves and turns white, like snow.


When I wake up, my whole body hurts. I don't know how long I've been lying on the concrete floor, but my body is stiff with cold as I stand and feel the back of my head. The bump is sore and the size of a Ping-Pong ball, but no skin is broken.

I check my phone—it's cracked and dead.

Slowly I go up the stairs, careful not to trip on the glove and tobacco again. The narrow strip of light above me grows. Just as I'm about to push the secret door open, I notice that the light is turned on in the kitchen. I peek through the gap and hold my breath. Put my hand against the rough concrete wall and lean forward to get a better look.

The ceiling light is on, and just a few meters in front of me I see a pair of powerful legs.

# Malin

The moment I wake up, I know my life has changed forever. I've crossed a boundary, stepped into a foreign land I'll never leave again. Everything I thought I knew about my life and my future was wrong: a lie I constructed, woven from my conviction that happiness must reside elsewhere, far, far away from Ormberg.

I lie on my side and peer into the dark toward Andreas.

He's asleep on his back, his arms stretched above his head, like a child. His breathing is deep and almost soundless.

*Fucking Andreas.*

If it hadn't been for him, I could have managed it.

I would have married Max and moved to Stockholm. Left Ormberg behind and stopped thinking about this wasteland, until even the memory faded like one of those old Polaroid images in Mom's album. It would have become a picturesque story I told at one of those dinner parties Max and I always go to.

*No, I grew up in Ormberg. You've never heard of it? Well, that's not so strange: It's very small, and not very exciting, but quite beautiful and . . .*

I stretch a hand toward him, touch his shoulder lightly and feel the tiny strands of hair on my palm.

He's ruined everything.

So why does it feel so good? Why does it feel like I've found something I didn't know I was looking for?

Andreas grunts, turns on his side. And his scent . . . It's strangely familiar and yet so new—irresistibly attractive and at the same time so forbidden.

It's Kenny's scent.

It's the scent of everything I denied and fled from: desire, a loss of control, dark forests, TrikåKungen's brick buildings and the ruins of ironworks.

It's Mom's stocky figure in front of the stove, and Magnus's blank expression when he jerks on Zorro's collar and lowers his eyes to the ground.

Actually it's kind of hilarious—even if everything's gone to hell, I must admit that.

I'm lying in bed with a country bumpkin who likes to read car magazines on the couch in front of the TV, and who doesn't want more from his future than some new furniture now and then, time to work on his biceps, and a trip to Thailand once a year.

Or, that's what I imagine I know about him. The truth is, I don't really know him that well, and this picture I have of him has been stitched together by my own conception of the world.

I look at the gold ring gleaming on my finger. Take it off and lay it on the nightstand.

It makes a tiny click.

Andreas opens his eyes and looks at me without saying a word. Then he takes my wrist and pulls me closer. Hard.

I lie on his arm and rub the hairline under his navel.

I don't know how long we stay like that—maybe a few minutes—but then the alarm rings.


We arrive in Örebro around seven in the morning. The snow's just starting to fall over the still dark city as we park the car outside the police station.

Manfred is already here. He looks hollow-eyed, and I suspect he hasn't slept. His face is pale and his hair is plastered to his head, as if he just took off his hat.

"Hello," I say.

He nods without answering.

Only then do I think of the pictures in Peter's phone. I feel a twinge of guilt that I was able to forget about the investigation for so long, and that I spent the night in Andreas's bed instead of keeping Manfred company.

The others arrive ten minutes later, and we head down to the interrogation room.

Svante and *Suzette-who's-damn-tough* will conduct the interrogation. Suzette's nails are vomit green today and have small sparkling stones on their tips.

Manfred, Andreas, and I will sit in an adjacent room and watch through a one-way window. To everyone's surprise, Stefan, after being informed of our suspicions, has declared he won't need a lawyer present at his interrogation because he's "one hundred percent innocent."

The atmosphere is tense but expectant—today's the day it's going to happen: Today we'll find Azra and Nermina's murderer.

Stefan Birgersson looks confused as he enters the room. He glances around, his eyes fastening on the one-way window, and even though I know he can't see us, it makes me uneasy.

He's wearing black track pants with white stripes and a jean shirt that's buttoned wrong; one side hangs down over his groin. He holds his hands in front of his eyes when Svante turns on the light.

Svante and Suzette enter soon after. Suzette walks hunched over, and I wonder if maybe she has a problem with her back, or maybe her stomach.

They sit down. Svante starts recording and rattles off the formalities.

Stefan sits with his head bent forward and his hands clasped on his lap. His eyes are focused on the tabletop.

"And that's why we want to talk to you today," Svante says. "To get to the bottom of what happened at the refugee camp in 1993 and 1994."

"Oh," Stefan says, and rubs his eyes. "So you put me in prison so you can talk to me about a contracting job?"

Svante ignores Stefan's comment, but Suzette smiles softly and says:

"Jail, not prison."

"Whatever. I told you I forgot I worked for them. I already explained that. Damn. This is fucking crazy. Don't you understand what you're doing to me and my family? Don't you get . . ."

Stefan's voice dies away mid-sentence.

Svante leans back, clasps his hands on his chest, and examines Stefan. Then he says, slowly:

"Why did you stop working there?"

Stefan stiffens and looks up. Then shrugs his shoulders.

"Didn't need me anymore."

Suzette leans forward and cocks her head a little.

"Listen, Stefan. It'll be much easier if you work *with* us. We don't want to hurt you or your family, we just want to find out what happened that winter."

"Nothing. Happened. I worked there for a while, and then I stopped."

"What did you think about the refugees?" Svante asks.

"What do you mean, *think*? I didn't think anything much."

"Did you think it was a good thing that the refugees were in Ormberg?" Svante asks, leaning forward.

Stefan shakes his head.

"I see you shaking your head," Suzette says. "But we're going to need you to put your answer into words."

She nods to the microphone hanging from a cord in the ceiling.

"Nah. Not really," Stefan says. "Obviously I didn't *like* it. But I had nothing against any of them. Not personally, that is. It was

more, well, you know. I don't know. I thought they should probably live somewhere else."

Svante scratches his big beard.

"Weren't you actually a little fond of two of them—Azra and
Nermina Malkoc, for example?"

Stefan shakes his head vehemently.

"Answer the question with words," Suzette reminds him.

"No, damn it. I didn't know anyone at that place."

"Why were you spying on the refugees?" Svante asks.

His tone is delicate, and the question comes casually, as if in
passing, like it's not particularly important, just something
Svante's a bit curious about, in general.

"I didn't."

Stefan buries his face in his hands and sniffles again.

"Fuck," he mumbles. "You're ruining my life. Do you understand that?"

Suzette leans forward again and puts a steady hand on Stefan's
arm, as if trying to see how much of the good-cop act she can get
away with.

But Stefan doesn't react.

"Stefan," she says soothingly, as if she were speaking to a puppy.
"We talked to the people who worked there that winter. They told
us you were found in the garden one evening, in the autumn of
1993. You have a rifle at home even though you don't have a gun
license. You and your car were seen near the murder site. And we
found a bloody garment in your basement yesterday, a torn shirt.
You have to understand that all of this makes you a suspect."

Stefan buries his head in his hands and starts to shake.

Manfred bounds out of his chair. Nods at the window and
whispers:

"We got him!"

Stefan is sobbing uncontrollably. His whole body shakes, and
he lets out a low-pitched howl like an injured animal.

Suzette pushes a box of Kleenex toward him, but Stefan doesn't seem to notice it.

"Stefan," Suzette says. "Help us understand. Tell us what happened!"

Stefan seems to pull himself together a little. He sits up a bit straighter, nods, and blows his nose into a tissue.

"It was me," he says, and starts sobbing again.

Suzette freezes, and Svante straightens up. They exchange a quick glance.

The moment is here—what everyone has been waiting for.

I hold my breath and look at Manfred, who is sitting completely still next to me.

"It was *meee*," Stefan howls.

Suzette leans forward and puts her hand on his arm. The green nails look almost luminous.

Stefan sniffs. Sobs again and then meets Suzette's gaze. She nods to him to continue.

"I burned those bushes outside the refugee housing," Stefan continues, and sobs again. "That's why I was there in the garden in the autumn of 1993. And the blood on the shirt you found. It . . . it was from a pig's head that Olle and I strung up in a tree outside the residency. But we weren't trying to hurt anyone, we just wanted to, you know. *Make an impression*."

He falls silent, but continues after a few seconds:

"And we were pretty drunk, too. I don't really remember. But I don't want my kids to know. I don't want them to think I'm a bad person. I really don't. Please, please don't tell Jake and Melinda."

Stefan's voice cracks.

"I'm really, really sorry," he finishes, then sobs again.

Suzette and Svante look at each other. I see the shock and confusion on their faces.

"*What the hell*," Manfred mumbles, and sinks back in his chair.

Suzette is the first to regain her composure. She throws an un-sure look in our direction and clears her throat.

"Stefan, you lied to us before. How do we know that this isn't a lie, too?"

"Ask Olle," Stefan sobs. "He was with me; he burned those bushes, too."

"Olle Eriksson, your friend in Högsjö?"

"Yes. And the rifle is his. I borrowed it. We were gonna start patrolling Ormberg in the evenings. Protect the young people. The women, that is. You never know what the hell those Arabs will do."

Manfred holds his hands in front of his face, as if trying to close the whole scene out. Mumbles:

*"Damn, damn, damn . . ."*

The door opens, and Malik sticks his head inside.

Manfred sits up.

"Track that fucking Olle down as fast as you can," Manfred hisses.

"Already on it," Malik says. "But there's something else. We checked which properties near the cairn have a basement, and ac-cording to the information we got, it's the following: Berit Sund's, Rut and Gunnar Sten's, and Margareta Brundin's."

*"Berit,"* I whisper.

"What?" Manfred asks.

"Berit worked at the refugee camp in the early nineties. And she had some unexplained lacerations on her arm when we visited her. Why didn't we think of that before?"

"Hmmm," Manfred says. "Berit doesn't fit Hanne's descrip-tion of the perpetrator."

"What about the others?" Malik asks.

"Rut Sten was the director of the refugee camp in the early nineties," I say. "So there's that connection. And her husband was supposedly violent when he was young. In addition, they have no alibi for the night of the murder."

"Hmmm," Manfred says again.

"And Margareta Brundin?" Malik says.

"She doesn't have a basement," I say. "I've been there a hundred times, and she and Magnus don't have a basement. Plus they have an alibi for the evening of Azra's murder. They were in Katrineholm, right?"

"*Margareta* has an alibi," Manfred corrects me. "She was able to show some receipts from a couple of stores and a restaurant. That doesn't necessarily mean that Magnus was with her."

"Either way," I say. "He wouldn't hurt a fly. Magnus Brundin is completely harmless."

# Jake

I peer out through the narrow gap. It's no more than a centimeter wide, but I see the kitchen clearly.

Ballsack-Magnus is standing next to the kitchen table with his legs wide.

He's holding a cell phone in one hand and scratching his crotch with the other. His dark, thin hair is messy. His sweatpants hang off his hips beneath a big, pale belly. His eyes are on the window.

A bluish light trickles in through the windows.

My head hurts so much I feel like it might explode. I close my eyes and try to concentrate on breathing silently, releasing air as slowly as I can and only through my mouth, but I still feel like panting. And my heart is pounding so hard it surely must be audible in the kitchen.

*Ballsack-Magnus. The fool. The village idiot.*

I think of those small lines on the wall down there, so painstakingly carved into the damp concrete. Of the long gray hair in the brush and of P lying in the freezer next to a tub of ice cream.

Everyone knows Ballsack-Magnus is a freak. When I was younger, my friends and I used to hide around the driveway here and throw stones at him when he arrived.

Dad used to call Ballsack-Magnus an "imbecile," but that

made Mom mad. She said he couldn't help it that he was "slow," and that she'd give me and Melinda a thrashing if she ever found out we were mistreating him.

Did he hold a woman prisoner in his basement?

Did he murder people?

It's hard to understand anyone doing something like that, least of all Magnus, who's never had a job, can't drive a car, and according to Melinda can't even read and write.

If he did it, someone must have helped him; he's so weak and dumb.

And yet: The basement speaks for itself. Plus there's something else that gnaws at me: the cairn.

I think I know why both Nermina and that woman with long gray hair were found there.

If you run straight into the woods from Margareta and Magnus's house, you end up with the creek on your left and Orm Mountain on your right. The path gets narrower and narrower, until you reach the clearing and the cairn. It's almost like a net you'd use to catch a fish.

It's possible to get to the cairn from a lot of different places, but it's only possible to get away from Margareta and Magnus's house through the cairn.

If you don't want to take the highway, that is. Which you wouldn't if you were running from a crazy murderer.

And, of course, Magnus knew that.

He must have waited for Nermina and that woman at the cairn, like a hunter waiting for his prey. Shooting that woman was probably the only way to stop her. Magnus is too slow and clumsy to run down an adult.

My thoughts grind on, and bit by bit the puzzle pieces fall into place.

Magnus kept that woman captive in the basement. When Hanne and Peter came, they opened the door and let her out.

Magnus discovered them and killed Peter. Maybe he planned to keep him in the freezer until spring, when the ground thawed and he could bury the body.

But the woman with the long hair managed to escape. That's why she didn't have any shoes on. She probably just rushed outside. Into the woods and straight for the cairn, where Magnus shot her.

And Hanne?

She must have escaped, but then got lost.

I look at Magnus again.

He's sauntering back and forth across the kitchen with the phone in his hand. His steps are careful, as if he's walking on thin, slippery ice. He hems and haws into the cell phone, listens for a while, and then says in a drawling voice:

"Did you read *that* in *Malin's* paperwork?"

Magnus sighs deeply.

"But Berit's there," he says, pulling out one of the chairs and sitting down with his back to me.

And a few seconds later:

"Because I don't *want to*."

He falls silent again, drums his free hand a little on the seat of his chair.

"I still don't want to."

Then he sighs again.

"But, Mom, she's gonna forget everything again. She's really old."

He falls silent for a long time.

I think for a moment.

Magnus is talking to Margareta, his mother. And they're talking about Hanne. My stomach knots up, and I clench my hands so hard my nails pierce my palms.

"Do I have to?"

Magnus's voice is pleading. He sounds like a child who's been told to clean his room, but doesn't feel like it. He sounds like Saga when her mom forces her to do her math homework, or like Melinda when Dad says she has to put on a real sweater, one that won't show "half her fucking belly to the Arabs."

The refrigerator starts to hum with a sigh.

Suddenly, I become very aware of the stifling stench of mold coming from the basement. I imagine how it must be oozing out through the door gap and spreading through the kitchen.

Can Magnus smell it? Can he sniff out the fact that the door is open, like a bloodhound?

"Can't we do it another day?" Magnus asks. "I'm *really, really tired.*"

And a few seconds later:

"But it's gonna snow more later this week. Do we have to do it *today?*"

Magnus is quiet for a long time. Scratches his neck with his huge hand.

"Okay," he says at last, but still he sounds doubtful. "But I have to get dressed and eat, so not right away, but . . ."

A short pause.

"Yes. That works. At the cairn. Should I bring the gun?"

Magnus sinks deeper into his chair and stares up at the ceiling. Turns his head a bit so that I see him in profile, and yawns.

"A *stone?* But. Why?"

My heart leaps in my chest when I realize what they're talking about. It never occurred to me that Hanne could be in danger, even though she works for the police, and even after I saw that pale, hollow-eyed face in the window outside Berit's house.

That must have been Margareta.

She must have stood out there in the dark spying on Hanne and Berit. It's clear Margareta is afraid Hanne will remember what happened to P.

Why didn't I think of that earlier?

This is all my fault.

If I could have resisted *The Sickness,* none of this would have happened.

"Okay, okay," Magnus says, sounding tired. "Love you."

Then he stands up. Groans a little. Puts his phone in the pocket of his sweatpants and stretches so that his T-shirt rises to reveal his big, hairy belly. He walks over to the fridge, opens it, and seems to root around for something inside. Moves things and rustles some papers.

My legs have fallen asleep, feel like logs.

I take a few steps in place trying to wake them up, but stumble a little. As I fumble for the wall, trying to regain my balance, I accidentally nudge the door. Not hard, but there's a slight knock and the door glides up a few centimeters.

I close my eyes and say a silent prayer, even though I don't like God, or even believe in Him.

*Dear God, help me! Don't let Magnus find me!*

When I open my eyes he's looking straight at me. Blinking and licking his thick red lips.

My body is as stiff as a statue. Just like people in horror movies when they meet zombies, aliens, or slimy ghosts. The only difference is that this monster is real. I'm not sitting on Saga's sofa eating chips. Not holding her sweaty hand in mine. There's no button to pause, and no adult to call for help.

I'm in an actual murderer's house, and he's looking straight at me.

But Ballsack-Magnus yawns again. Turns back to the fridge, takes out a yogurt, and drinks straight from the container.

I take a deep breath. And then another.

He hasn't seen me.

Even though I'm standing right in front of him, he hasn't seen me.

Maybe God exists after all, even if I have a hard time believing He'd have anything to do with me, an aberrant, when there's so much else that's wrong in the world.

Magnus puts back the yogurt, closes the refrigerator, and lumbers out toward the hall. His figure fades away in the dark. Seconds later I hear his heavy steps on the stairs to the second floor.

This is my chance—the only one I'll get.

This is the moment I've been waiting for.

Magnus is upstairs now. He's getting dressed to go meet Margareta at the cairn.

With a fucking stone.

I close my eyes and think of Hanne. Of Greenland, of the turquoise icebergs bobbing on the sea, and of P, whom she loved. P, who's frozen like a hamburger from the superstore that you're planning to grill in the summer.

I think about how terrible it must be to grow old and not be able to remember anything anymore, to have a whole life behind you, like a long tail. And then I think of how life can end at any moment, even if you're in the middle of something important, like growing up or writing a book or discovering the cure to cancer. Death can come whether you're old or young—like Nermina.

My whole body aches with longing for Saga, Melinda, and Dad, but most of all, for Mom. She would have known what I should do. She always knew what to do when things got bad. Like when Melinda fell from a tree and hit her head on a rock and bled a lot. Or when Dad got so drunk at Grandpa's on Christmas that he couldn't even walk.

Mom could get through anything.

Except cancer.

What do you do when you run across a crazy murderer, anyway? Would an adult even know?

I don't think so.

A part of me just wants to lie down on the floor and weep, give in to the fatigue and terror. But then I hear that voice in my head again—the one that whispers and coaxes, says nothing is impossible, that you can get through anything, can just let go of your thoughts and let them fly free, like birds. I think of Vincent, of his words: *Blow me, faggot!* And how then, through the chaos in my brain, that beast inside me woke up. How Vincent suddenly lay beneath me, terrified, because I'd done the inconceivable.

The unthinkable is unthinkable only until you've done it.

Then it's just a part of life, part of the tail you drag behind you.

I put my hand on the door to push it, and just as I feel that cool metal on my fingers I hear steps coming down the stairs.

I freeze and peer out.

Magnus passes by outside. He opens the fridge, and I can hear plastic rustling.

Then silence. An alarming silence.

I bend closer to see better.

Magnus faces me. His mouth is half open, and he looks surprised.

Then he walks toward me, raises his hand, and firmly pushes the door shut.

Everything goes black, and I hear a click as the door locks.

# Hanne

The snow falls heavily outside Berit's window, covering the ground and the trees. I can just make out a fresh set of animal tracks crossing the field and disappearing into distant snowfall.

I slept well, better than I have in ages.

I look down at my feet.

The bandages are gone, but the pale skin is still covered with scabs and small sores. The nails are blue and cracked and one small toe is taped up.

I get dressed and look at myself in the small mirror on the wall. Note that at least I recognize myself: the ruffled hair, which is now more gray than red, the red-rimmed eyes.

The freckles.

That's me, Hanne.

There's a photographer named Helene Schmitz. I think it was Owe, my ex-husband, who dragged me along to one of her exhibitions. He had a passion for culture—the more pretentious and difficult something was, the more he liked it. I doubt he was truly interested in art; rather, he saw it as a status symbol, something that made him feel like he was better than other people.

But Helene Schmitz's photographs were neither pretentious

nor difficult. Instead, they were stunningly beautiful and somewhat discomfiting, which may be the reason I still remember them.

The exhibition, which featured two series, depicted how nature takes over, or perhaps comes back, when humans retreat from what they've created.

One series consisted of pictures of beautiful old houses in a deserted mining town on the coast of Namibia that the winds are slowly but relentlessly filling with fine-grained sand. The other series of photos featured a fast-growing Japanese plant that has gained a foothold in the United States, choking out local flora, wrapping buildings in a deadly green quilt, and even crushing houses.

As I said, when I saw the exhibition I thought the pictures were beautiful and a little terrifying. But over time they've taken on a different meaning for me.

It feels like I'm a beautiful house on the coast of Namibia, and the sand is my disease, slowly but surely drowning me. I'm the flora and the buildings, and the kudzu is this accursed dementia.

I'm the narrator, I'm the story.

I'm the camera, I'm the houses.

I'm the object and the subject at the same time, because I can see it happening, but I can't do a thing about it.

And every day when I wake up, the sand has swallowed a little more of my reality. The kudzu has wrapped its branches around yet another of my abilities; another part of my life has been taken from me.

I run a comb through my hair, put some ChapStick on my lips, and go out into the kitchen. Trying not to think of all that I'm no longer capable of.

Berit is standing at the sink doing dishes.

She has an old apron tied around her waist. A radio plays dance band music at a low volume.

The fire crackles in the stove, and Joppe stands in the middle of the room, wagging his tail slowly, as if waiting for Berit's attention.

"Good morning!" Berit says, and smiles broadly. "Would you like some breakfast?"

She holds out a coffeepot.

"Gladly," I say, and sit down at the kitchen table.

Berit puts out bread, cheese, and butter. Then she limps over to me with the coffeepot.

I always feel so guilty when she waits on me like this, because in many ways I'm healthier than she is. Other than my memory. But that doesn't stop me from holding my coffee cup up.

Berit serves me, sinks down in the chair opposite, and smiles again. Her gray hair, which lies in neat curlers around her head, reminds me of my mother. In her bangs she has a hairpin with a flower on it.

I make myself a sandwich. Cut thick slices of cheese and place them on homemade bread.

We have it pretty good, Berit and me.

I like her—especially her undemanding, tranquil silence. She's one of those people who doesn't feel the need to fill in silence with talking. But more important: She's stuck fast. When I wake up in the morning, I remember her. I don't know if that means I'm getting back a part of my short-term memory or if it's just because we've spent so much time together and she's somehow become etched into my unruly brain.

We don't do much with our days.

Berit likes to bake and knit, and we go on long walks with Joppe when the weather permits.

Sometimes I wake up in the middle of the night and cry out for Peter. Then Berit gets up, lights the woodstove, and makes tea, which we drink in silence.

Sometimes she gives me a sleeping pill.

I'm beginning to doubt I'll ever see him again. And I've stopped hoping that Manfred will come. Instead, I've come to fear that visit, fear what he will say. Because I don't think Peter's alive anymore. For some reason, I've convinced myself that I would know it, from some inner vibration. A heat somewhere under my breast or a tingling somewhere near my heart.

At the same time, though, I know that's foolishness.

There's no way I can sense if he's alive or not.

It bothers me that I don't remember any of our time here in Ormberg. None of the investigation I participated in or the new colleagues I met.

The last clear memories I have are from Greenland. We had such a wonderful time there, Peter and me.

And there's no reason to believe it was any different here in Ormberg. Surely a couple of weeks in a backwater village in Södermanland wouldn't have changed anything.

So when Berit has asked me about Peter, I've told her that he's the man in my life, and that we have it very good together, that I'm very happy with him.

Berit grabs hold of the table and rises slowly. She stops at one point and grimaces.

"Are you okay?" I ask.

She smiles crookedly.

"Everything's gone to hell in this old body."

She walks over to Joppe, bends down, and scratches her shaggy dog behind one ear.

"I'm gonna take him out for a bit. I'll be home in a half hour."

"I'll clean up," I say, popping the last bit of my sandwich into my mouth.

"I'll take care of the dishes later," she says.

"No. I'll take care of that."

"You really shouldn't."

"It's no trouble."

I can see she'd like to protest, but stops herself.

"That's fine," she says, heading out into the hall with Joppe in tow.

As soon as she's gone, I stand up and start to clear away my late breakfast. When I'm done, I put a few more logs onto the fire.

It's cold today, even though it's snowing. Even with the fire blazing in the stove, the cold seeps in through cracks in this old house. And with the cold comes the dampness; it leaves its breath on the inside of the windows, and makes the bed linen limp.

I hear a weak knock in the hall.

At first I think I'm imagining it, but then there's another knock, harder this time. It's a knocking that knows what it wants, that won't give up.

I fold the linen towel, put it on the edge of the sink, and head out to open the door.

A slight uneasiness awakens inside me.

It couldn't be Berit—she just left. Besides, she wouldn't knock—she always comes straight in.

Maybe it's Manfred. Maybe they found Peter.

My chest aches, because I'm not sure I can handle news of his death.

Then another knock. Even harder this time. Urgent.

I head into the hall to open the door.

# Jake

I t's pitch black. Like a tomb.

I try not to think of P lying in the freezer in the room at the bottom of the staircase, because if this were one of the movies I watch with Saga, he'd be arriving right about now. His frozen legs and arms would have creaked and crunched as he slowly crept up the stairs.

I run my hands over the door, but all I feel is smooth, cold metal. There's no handle on the inside, and I know why.

You're not supposed to be able to leave.

I don't think Ballsack-Magnus saw me; I think he just noticed the door was open and closed it. But now I'm stuck here, in his murder basement, his twisted fucking torture prison, while he and Margareta prepare to kill Hanne.

And there's absolutely nothing I can do about it.

The basement has no windows or doors—the only way out is this huge, locked metal door. I can't even kick on the damn door, because then Magnus might discover me, and that's surely worse than being stuck here in the dark.

And my phone is fucked, so I can't call anyone.

I sit down on the top step, can feel tears coming and that familiar lump in my throat.

I miss Mom. I wish she were here so much that it almost feels like I'm going to explode.

I slam my fist against the door and start to cry. The bang is louder and heavier than I intended. Like a thunderstorm in the distance.

I freeze in fear.

What if Magnus heard me, what if he's on his way, what if he puts me in the freezer next to P?

I can hear a sound on the other side. A scraping sound and then a click as the door starts to open.

My heart stops.

It's over.

He's here.

But when the door glides open, Saga is standing outside, still wearing pajamas, but with a coat over them, and winter boots on her feet. She has snow in her hair, and her cheeks are red with cold.

"What are you doing here?" I whisper.

She takes me by the arm and pulls me into the kitchen. Then she looks around.

"He just left," she says, breathlessly. "We're alone."

I squint in the bright light. My head is pounding, and my mouth is dry.

"How did you know I was here?"

Saga looks at me seriously, and gently squeezes my arm.

"It was in the diary. I knew you'd come here after I read it yesterday morning. And when I couldn't get ahold of you last night, I called Melinda. She said she hadn't heard from you since yesterday. You sent her a text message and told her you were sleeping over at a friend's. But I knew that wasn't true . . ."

Saga falls silent, but I know what she's thinking.

I don't have any other friends besides Saga. So if I wasn't with her, she knew I was lying.

"Where did you sleep, anyway?" she asks curiously.

"Brogrens."

Saga nods and continues:

"Anyway. I decided to come here and check it out for myself. I waited for a super-long time in the woods outside, until Magnus left, and then I came in."

"You found the key?"

Saga nods and rolls her eyes.

"Under the flowerpot. People are so freaking predictable. Except for us, since we're so much smarter."

She smiles a little, but doesn't really seem happy.

"We have to hurry," I say. "They're going to kill Hanne."

"What? Who are 'they'?"

"Magnus and Margareta. They kept the woman at the cairn locked in the basement, and they killed that cop. He's in the freezer in the basement."

Saga wrinkles her nose, and her eyes widen.

"Seriously? In the basement? *Here?*"

I nod.

"You saw him?"

Her voice is a whisper. I nod again.

"Oh, fuck. What did it look like?"

I think for a moment.

"Do you remember that movie about zombies at the North Pole? He looked like one of them. Had, like, frost on his skin and . . ."

My voice dies away when I see Saga's terrified expression.

"We have to hurry," I say. "I have to warn Hanne. Can you call the police and tell them they're headed to the cairn?"

Saga nods seriously.

"My phone's dead," she says. "But I'll head home and call. I can be anonymous."

And then:

"And I won't say anything about you or the diary, either."

# Malin

We park outside Berit's little cottage. The snow is falling heavily as we make our way toward the front door.

The landscape is perfect and beautiful, a powdery, white lushness like I've only ever seen in Ormberg.

Andreas drove like a madman all the way here, and I sat with my heart in my throat. But the farther we got from Örebro, the more far-fetched it seemed to me that Berit would have had anything to do with the murders, even if there are circumstances I can't explain.

I just can't imagine that gentle, stubborn woman would be capable of killing someone. I lean toward Rut and Gunnar Sten instead.

Suzette and Malik are going over to check their basement.

Stefan Birgersson was telling the truth.

With just a little pressure, his friend Olle confessed that on several occasions in 1993, they'd set fire to the bushes outside the refugee camp. When they asked him why they did it, he just said they "were young and stupid." He also admitted they'd hung the pig head from a tree as well, but claimed that was "a joke."

Stefan was immediately released. Of course, he's probably guilty of several other crimes, but likely none so serious that he needs to be detained.

Just before we reach the house, Andreas stops.

"What's that?" he says, pointing to the forest on the other side of the field.

I look and see something moving between the trees, but the snow makes it hard to see what.

"Looks like somebody's walking in there," I say.

We peer into the woods, but whatever we saw is gone now, so we continue on to Berit's door.

We climb up a few front stairs and knock.

The door opens almost immediately.

Berit's cheeks are red, and she looks worried. A hairpin with a flower on it hangs loosely from her bangs, like a colorful artificial fly from a fishing pole.

"Hanne's gone!" she says before we even say hello. "I was just out with the dog, and when I came back she was gone."

Berit puts a hand over her mouth and pinches her eyes shut. For a moment, I think she might start crying, but then she takes a deep breath and meets my eyes again.

"Wait a moment," I say. "When did you get home?"

I look in the hall. A pair of boots stand in the middle of the floor and a coat is slung down beside them.

"Just a few minutes ago. But she's nowhere to be found. I've searched the whole house."

"May we come in?" Andreas asks.

Berit moves aside and we enter.

"Excuse me," she says. Then she puts away her shoes and hangs up her coat.

We search the little house together, but find no Hanne.

"Can we look in the basement?" I ask, grateful for an excuse to investigate it.

"Of course," Berit says, raising a brow. "But why would she be down there?"

She walks through the narrow hall and opens a low door. It slides up with a creak.

I go over to the door, turn on the light, and look down. Blue walls are lined with shelves of jars and seed packets. A sack of potatoes stands next to the stairs.

Otherwise, the room is empty.

I don't even need to take out the picture from Peter's phone to compare. That photo was not taken here; that's obvious.

Andreas walks into the kitchen and over to the window.

"Where do you end up if you walk straight over the meadow and into the woods?" he asks.

Berit shakes her head skeptically. "Do you think she's gone into the woods? Why in the world would she do that?"

"We saw someone in there when we arrived," I say. "Next to the fallen tree. And it looks like someone just walked across the field."

"I walk back and forth across that field all the time," Berit snorts, then leans toward the window and looks out.

She scratches at one of the sores on her left forearm. They look almost healed now. The angry red has subsided, and the scabs have fallen off to reveal thin pink skin.

Berit sees my gaze and nods.

"Rosebushes. I never learn."

Then she turns her eyes back to the woods again. Peers into the snow and wrinkles her eyebrows.

"Near the fallen tree, you said?"

"Yes," I say.

"If you go that way you'll get to the ironworks," Berit mutters. "Or to the cairn—depends a bit on which way you walk."

# Hanne

We trudge through the snow at the edge of the woods. As soon as we enter the shadows of the giant spruces, it becomes almost dark.

The forest is strangely quiet, as if the falling snow dampens all sounds.

The woman in front of me is small and bent forward, but she moves fast. Her thin legs stride through the deep snow as if she were strolling through a summer meadow.

I can't remember ever meeting her before, but of course I can't be sure.

I don't trust myself anymore.

She's wearing a long winter coat and snow pants. Thin brown wisps of hair stick out from under a knitted cap with hearts on it.

She told me her name was Margareta, explained that Peter had been injured, and said I had to come quick. We'll call Berit later, Margareta told me. She has a cell phone.

"Where is he?" I pant, trying to keep up with her.

Margareta stops and waits.

"Up on Orm Mountain," she says, then looks at me seriously. "We're meeting your colleagues there."

The forest grows thicker. The spruces seem to be crawling

closer to each other, as if they don't want to let us through. As if the forest itself were trying to prevent us from reaching our destination.

"How is he?"

Margareta stamps in place and seems impatient.

"Like I said. Don't really know. But there's not much time."

Then she looks around, peers up at the narrow strip of dark gray sky between the treetops.

"Better hurry."

She nods at the urgency of her own comment, turns around, and heads on.

It occurs to me that her behavior is a bit strange. Why did she pick me up, and not one of my colleagues? Why walk through the woods instead of going by car? And why couldn't we wait for Berit? It usually doesn't take her long to walk Joppe, even if he is old and lame.

"What did you say your name was?" I ask, and quicken my steps to catch up with her, but it's difficult, because the snow is up to my knees, and it's heavy. My legs burn from exertion.

"Margareta Brundin," she says without turning around.

"Are you from here? From Ormberg?"

She stops. Turns back toward me. Smiles a little, for the first time. A deep network of wrinkles spreads around her eyes, and I catch a glimpse of something that resembles affection or maybe even love on her face.

"Lived here my whole life. There's no better place in the world."

"And you work with the police?"

Margareta laughs loudly and takes off her mittens. Roots around in her pocket and takes out a pack of cigarettes. Lights one and takes a deep drag.

"Me, *a cop*?"

She laughs again, but it turns into a wheezing cough.

"Nope," she says, and clears her throat. "It's been a long time since I had a job. But when I did, I was a midwife. My niece, Malin, she's a cop. You know, she worked with you."

When I don't answer, she tilts her head and looks at me.

"Don't you remember her?"

"No," I say, feeling ashamed, as if I'd chosen this forgetfulness, when really it chose me.

Margareta shrugs her shoulders and glances up at the falling snow. Throws her cigarette down and puts on her mittens.

"We better go," she says.

We walk a few hundred meters in silence. The trees thin out. Here and there a stump rises up, testifying to the fact that the forest has been cleared. Then the terrain becomes hillier, and harder to navigate, so we're forced to walk around large stones and climb over fallen trees.

Soon we arrive at a country road.

"Almost there," Margareta says. "We just have to cross the road and head in by those trees."

She points to the spruces on the other side of the road.

"How much farther?"

"Not far," she says, stepping over a snowy ditch and making her way out onto the road.

I follow after her, but my uneasiness won't let go of me. Are we headed into the woods again?

The cold penetrates my thin hat, and my ears feel like ice cubes. My pants are stiff with snow and wet all the way up to the knees.

For a second, I consider staying here, in the light of a well-plowed road. But then I think of Peter. What if he's there in those woods, lying injured in some house? Alone, sick, and unable to move.

Margareta disappears between two spruces, and I follow.

Peter is alive, I think. It has to be true.

Why else would they have sent her to pick me up?

The terrain changes again. We start heading upward. At first there's only a slight incline, but it gets steeper and steeper. I have to grab branches and small trees in order not to trip. Big chunks of snow fall onto my face and down my collar. But Margareta just darts forward, like an inscrutable and tireless mountain goat.

When I glance over my shoulder, I'm surprised.

A seemingly endless snow-covered forest spreads out below us—we must have gone a lot farther and climbed much higher than I realized. I sense the church spire in the distance, but the snow turns the horizon into white mist.

"Wait!" I cry.

Margareta stops, turns around, and starts pushing back through the snow toward me.

"What?"

"I have to rest. I can't go farther."

"We'll be there soon," she says. "Come on!"

My feet are numb—they're rigid and stiff—but I do as she says and follow her up the mountain.

Here and there I see footprints cross the slope; maybe the police have searched the forest for Peter.

Then we arrive at a plateau, a piece of open, snow-covered ground surrounded by low trees and shrubs. To the right I see a grouping of snow-covered stones, placed in a circle.

Margareta stands on the edge of the clearing without saying a word. She looks over the forest with her hands hanging at her sides and her chin low. Then she slowly turns toward me. Her breath turns into small clouds that obscure her eyes.

"Look how beautiful," she says with unexpected softness, putting a hand on my arm.

# Jake

'm on my way up Orm Mountain. It's steep, and I have to hold on to bushes and branches to make my way forward. But every time I grab a branch, snow falls off and hits my face.

It feels like the forest is spitting on me, like it doesn't want me to be here. The headache comes back every time I look up, and along with it comes the nausea. For a while I was worried my brain might be bleeding, which is what killed Grandma, but I convince myself not to be afraid of that. Grandma was almost eighty and sick all the time.

Margareta and Hanne are maybe fifty meters above me. They look like two blurry stick figures in the heavy snowfall.

I've followed them all the way from Berit's cottage.

Just after I got there and parked my moped in the woods, Berit went out with her dog. And before I could warn Hanne, Margareta showed up and knocked on the door of Berit's cottage.

She must have been waiting for Berit to leave. Like a wolf lurking around after its prey.

I was hoping to get there before her, but instead I have to follow after them. For a moment, I considered taking the moped and driving straight to the cairn to wait for them, but I didn't dare.

Margareta might try to kill Hanne before they get there.

If I'm lucky, the police will be there already when Margareta and Hanne arrive. Saga said she'd call them as soon as she got home.

I look up at the stick figures, Margareta and Hanne.

I don't understand how they're able to move so fast, since both of them are really old.

Dad says everything goes to hell when you get old. You lose it all—your hearing, sight, memory—but in slow motion. So slow you almost don't notice it, like when you play an old movie frame by frame.

That's not what it was like for Mom.

She got sick and died quickly, even though she wasn't old. Even though Hadiya, the doctor with the nice tits, pumped her full of poison.

It's hard to understand, but above all it's unfair: Why are Berit and Margareta, who are so old, alive, and Mom is dead and buried?

Somewhere on the hill above me a branch cracks, and I hear a shout.

I stop, holding my breath. Peer upward, suddenly afraid Hanne might roll down the hill like a giant snowball.

But everything is calm.

No Hanne comes rolling down the slope.

I continue climbing. Put one leg in front of the other, again and again, though I'm so tired and hungry and dizzy that I'd rather just lie down in the snow and sleep.

But you can't do that. The cold is dangerous; it can make you tired and confused. Whisper to you that all you need is a few minutes of sleep—and then, *wham,* you're dead and frozen as a freaking snowman.

*Just like P.*

I try not to think of the body in the freezer. Climb over a snowy branch and look upward again.

Why did Margareta take Hanne up here? There must be so

many better places to kill somebody, so many places that are easier to get to.

Especially when you're old.

Orm Mountain is difficult to climb, even in the summer. Saga and I climbed up here a few times earlier this fall. Sat in the grass on Ättestupan, ate candy, and looked down from the cliff and out over the landscape.

The village looked pretty from above, almost like a postcard. Nothing looked ugly or run-down, all those things Hanne wrote in her diary, not from a distance. All the decrepit houses, graffiti-covered façades, and old cars faded away, as if Melinda had done a makeover on Ormberg with one of her fluffy brushes.

I look up again.

Hanne has stopped at the ledge in front of the Ättestupan, to the left of the ancient monument, but Margareta can't be seen; she must have gone farther.

*Farther ahead?* There's only a cliff there.

And suddenly I understand.

Suddenly, I know why Margareta brought Hanne up Orm Mountain. And why it was so important to do it today, when it's snowing.

I remember Magnus's words.

*But it's gonna snow more later this week. Do we have to do it today?*

I shudder and turn around.

Yes. The falling snow will cover Margareta's tracks. My own have already been covered by fluffy flakes.

I quicken my speed, almost running up the slope. But my feet slip, and I fall. Hit my head hard on the ground, and something sharp scratches my face. I tumble down the slope until I manage to grab on to a branch, then stand up and brush off the snow.

I take off my gloves, spit, and run my hands over my cold, numb cheeks. There's a gash there. Something hot and sticky is running down my face.

Blood.

But it's only a small cut, I tell myself. It's nothing next to what will happen to Hanne if Margareta succeeds in luring her all the way out on that cliff.

I continue up through deep snow until I reach the clearing. My heart is hammering in my chest, and I feel exhausted as I squat behind a snowy bush and peek ahead.

Hanne and Margareta gesture toward the bright sky. They're standing at the edge of Ättestupan, seem to be looking down over the village. It looks almost peaceful. Margareta's hand is resting lightly on Hanne's arm, almost as if she's protecting her, though the opposite is true.

Since she's an insane murderer.

Blood drips onto the snow in front of me, but I ignore it. All I can think of is Hanne. Nothing can happen to her—not just because it's my responsibility, but because she's my friend, even if she doesn't know it herself. What she wrote in the diary was more honest and more important than anything any other adult ever told me. And even though what she wrote about Dad made me angry, I don't regret reading the book.

*Please, back up,* I think. *Don't get so close to the edge.*

But Hanne remains standing next to Margareta, remembering nothing, understanding nothing. With no clue that the old hag is planning to push her off the cliff as soon as she gets the opportunity.

And the only thing that can stop her is me.

I stand up and start walking toward them. The snow dampens the sound of my steps, and they don't seem to notice me approaching from behind.

In the end I'm so close I see Ormberg spread out down below. I can just make out the church spire and the smoke rising from the cottages hidden between the trees.

I can almost touch them now, Hanne's shoulder or Margareta's stupid heart-covered hat.

Something inside me turns hard, or maybe it freezes. All the fear and despair I felt fades away. Begins turning into determination and strength.

I'm not going to let her kill Hanne.

"Hanne," I say.

# Hanne

Somebody says my name.

At first, I think it's my imagination, that my brain somehow conjured up a voice. Why would anyone call out my name here on the mountain?

But the woman who's with me, whose name I've already forgotten, turns instantly toward the voice. I do the same, but more slowly, because my legs and back hurt from exertion after the long climb up the mountain.

And in the snow in front of me, there stands a boy.

There's something vaguely familiar about him. Something about the gently curved arc of his upper lip and the intense, dark eyes. And then there's that voice; even though it's high, it sounds rich, almost like a singer's.

He's probably around fifteen, and he's wearing a dirty winter coat, a hat, and jeans that are icy up to the thighs. A long pink sweater sticks out from under the coat; a thread hangs from it and trails into the snow. There's a gaping wound across his cheek, and blood flows down his chin.

I look at the woman, at her wiry little body, her reddening cheeks, and her small black button eyes, which are wide with surprise.

"Jake Birgersson, what in *God's name* are you doing here?" she says. "Does your father know you're here?"

"Come with me, Hanne!" the boy says, his eyes locked on me. "We need to go."

"She's not going anywhere," the woman says. "But you're leaving *right now,* Jake Birgersson. March your butt home to your father! The Lord knows he needs all the help he can get from you and your sister."

The boy—"Jake"—takes a step forward and grabs my arm, while the woman's grip on my other arm tightens. His big dark eyes seemed determined, and unafraid of meeting my gaze.

"She's going to push you off this cliff," he says breathlessly, and nods at the woman.

"I've never in my life heard anything so stupid," she replies, and moves her free hand to her mouth, as if trying to prove how shocked she is.

"Yes. You're planning to push her off this cliff before she can remember again. You're afraid she'll remember that you and Magnus killed that cop, Peter. And that you had the woman with long hair locked in your basement."

When the boy says that about Peter, my legs start to fold. But his arm is steady, and I manage to keep upright.

*"Is Peter dead?"*

My words, a whisper that immediately fades away into the trees. As if even the forest doesn't want them said out loud.

The boy nods.

The woman looks at me sternly.

"You shouldn't believe . . . *that,*" she says slowly, nodding at the boy and then spitting in the snow. "He's been nothing but trouble since he was little. His mother worried herself to death over him. Come on, Hanne. We have to get to Peter. We don't have time for this."

"Don't listen to her," the boy says. "She's lying. She's a murderer."

The woman laughs out loud and then coughs.

"*Jesus Christ,* Jake. I will admit you've got quite the vivid imagination. Where'd that come from? Not from your drunk of a father, that's for sure."

I don't know who to believe. The situation is too absurd: I'm standing on a mountain in the middle of the forest, with snow up to my knees, with two people I don't know. The boy's story sounds incredible. But I have no idea what's happened to Peter. Anything at all could have befallen him, even a crime.

But *murdered*?

No, it's not possible. If that had happened, I would have remembered it. *Some* snippet would have stuck fast. Surely such a life-altering event wouldn't pass by me unnoticed?

I look at the woman, meet her small button eyes.

Why did she bring me up to the mountain anyway, to the edge of a cliff? Could there be something in what the boy says after all?

The woman nods slowly toward me.

"Hanne," she says softly, as if speaking to a child. "Surely you hear how crazy this all sounds?"

The boy pulls on one of my arms, and the woman pulls on the other.

I rock back and forth between them in the snow.

Slowly, we're getting closer to the edge of the cliff.

# Malin

We've been following the footsteps for almost an hour when we arrive at the cairn. We haven't walked that far, but the snow is deep, and the woods are littered with fallen branches and holes. Every meter was an ordeal; every step burns in your thighs.

The clearing is empty and quiet. Blue-and-white police tape still flutters in the breeze. The snow has been trampled in every direction.

"It's impossible to follow the tracks from here," Andreas says. "Too many people have been walking around. And now it's snowing again."

I look down at the snow-covered tracks of the police officers and technicians and curious onlookers. Then I brush the snow off one of the rocks of the cairn and sit down. My legs ache from the climb.

"Where do you think they went?"

I say "they" because Andreas and I had quickly realized Hanne wasn't alone in the woods—there were the tracks of at least two people, maybe three, in the snow.

Andreas trudges over to me, leans forward, and puts his hands on his knees.

He looks around. His breath is like a plume coming from his mouth, and his cheeks are red from the cold. Small clumps of ice have formed on his stubble.

"No idea," he says.

The cold sneaks into my thick coat. As long as I kept moving I was fine, but now I'm shivering. A layer of cold sweat sits under my coat, and the stone I'm sitting on feels cold as well.

Orm Mountain rises like a dark giant behind us. In the distance I hear the sound of a branch cracking, perhaps beneath the weight of a deer or moose.

As always when I visit the cairn, I think about the skeleton we found. About that and all the times I came here in the summer with my friends, sat around drinking beer waiting for the Ghost Child to appear—though it never did. I think of all my friends who left for Stockholm, Katrineholm, or Örebro.

And of Kenny, who went even farther than that.

Ormberg is full of things that never happened and people who didn't stay.

Mom's stocky figure flashes before my eyes.

What made her stay? Why didn't she move, like all the others? I can understand why Margareta and Magnus stayed here—they wouldn't fit in anywhere else; they're both so odd. But Mom could have made a good life for herself in Stockholm.

She didn't need to rot away in Ormberg.

There's a thud in the forest.

"What was that?" I ask, and peer between the snowy trunks of the trees.

Everything is quiet, and nothing moves among the trees. No humans, no animals.

Andreas shrugs.

"A deer, maybe."

I look at him out of the corner of my eye.

We haven't talked about what happened between us. I don't

know what he feels, and I definitely don't know what I feel. The only thing I'm sure of is that there will never be a wedding with Max, and strangely enough, I don't feel sad about that.

Returning to Ormberg had taken its toll.

There are so many memories here, so much to remind me of what I don't want to do with my life. And yet Ormberg has also given me some perspective on Max. And the more time I've spent here, the more strongly I feel I don't want to marry him.

I don't even know if I want to move to Stockholm anymore. It feels too far away from Mom. And if there's one thing I've realized these last few weeks, it's that I want to be closer to her.

As for studying to be a lawyer—why would I need to do that? I love being a cop.

Just as I stand up, my phone rings.

I stop, take off my mittens, and fumble in my pocket. My hands are so stiff from the cold I almost don't manage to answer.

It's Manfred.

"Have you found Hanne?"

"No. The tracks led to the cairn, just as we suspected. But there are so many tracks up here it's impossible to say where they lead. And now it's snowing again."

"Okay. Apparently someone called in a tip, claiming that there was going to be a murder at the cairn."

"What? Now?"

"Yes. Just a little while ago."

"Who called?" I ask.

"They didn't want to give their name, but according to our colleague who took the call, it sounded like a child, so it could be some kind of joke. In any case, we're headed out there now, but you'll keep your eyes peeled, too?"

"Absolutely. But it seems calm here."

"Okay. Well, well."

Manfred sounds distracted, as if his thoughts are elsewhere.

"Yes," he says. "One more thing. That piece of jewelry that Hanne was wearing, Azra's medallion. The one that contained hair."

"Yes?"

"Did you touch it? The hair, that is."

I try to remember when Andreas and I were sitting in the car outside Berit's house. How the medallion stood open like a golden clam in Andreas's hand, and how I put my fingertip on the dark hair.

"Yes," I say. "I think I did touch it. I wanted to know what it was."

I turn around and meet Andreas's eyes. He mimes a *"What?"* to me, and I raise my hand for him to wait a little.

"And when we found Azra at the cairn—was that when they swabbed you?"

"Yes. It was indeed. Why?"

"We can discuss it later," Manfred says. "I got a call from the technicians and they wondered, well . . . Eh. I'll explain when we meet. There's been a snafu."

"Okay," I say. "We're waiting at the cairn."

"Good. We'll see you soon."

We hang up, and I put my phone back in the warmth of my pocket. Put on my gloves and meet Andreas's eyes. They're black, and the frost glitters in his stubble.

"What was that?" he asks.

"Some kid called in claiming there was going to be a murder here. Backup's here in fifteen."

"Okay. And the other bit? You said something about how you touched it."

"Oh, that. Manfred wondered if I'd touched the hair in Azra's medallion."

"Why?"

"Don't know. The technicians must have called and asked."

Andreas wrinkles his forehead and adjusts his hat.

"Strange," he says.

I nod.

We hear a stifled bang, and turn around at the same time.

Voices are audible in the distance; it's so quiet it feels like you could have imagined them. It sounds as if they're coming from Orm Mountain. And at the same time, branches can be heard cracking from the other direction.

Andreas sinks down and whispers:

"Goddamn, there is somebody here."

He's right. Someone or some people are up on Orm Mountain. And someone else is headed straight for us from the road.

I hunch down next to Andreas and hope the small, snowy bushes will keep us hidden. I put my hand on his back for support.

The voices from Orm Mountain can be heard more clearly now. It sounds like two people talking to each other, arguing about something. And the steps coming from the road are getting closer.

I do my best not to move, hold Andreas's shoulder tight. A few seconds later, I see a person walking through the spruce trees.

It's a large man. He's walking hunched over, with slow, heavy steps, and he's holding something in his hand, but I can't see what it is.

I blink and hold my breath.

It's Magnus.

*Ballsack-Magnus. My cousin.*

# Hanne

The edge of the cliff is just a step or two from my feet.

I try not to look, but still catch a glimpse of the ground far below. The trees and bushes look so tiny, as if I were staring down at a miniature panorama, the kind you'd find around an old-fashioned toy railway.

"I read your diary," the boy pulling on my arm says.

"*What?*" I say.

"I found it in the woods."

"Bullshit," the woman hisses, and pulls on my arm even harder, so that I stagger and end up another step closer to the edge.

The boy doesn't give up:

"I know all about you and Peter. That you visited the Inuits in Greenland. And that you and Peter have a colleague named Man-fred who eats too many buns, and Peter thinks he needs to lose weight. I learned a lot of new words, too, like 'anomaly,' 'fetish-ist,' and 'schizophrenic.'"

I turn away from the woman and meet the boy's eyes. He wipes blood from his face with the back of his glove. Snow is stuck to the edge of the deep wound.

Is it possible? Could he have found my diary in the woods?

It would make sense. How else would he know about Peter and Manfred? He even knows about our trip to Greenland.

"And Ajax," the boy says. "Your puppy. Who fell through the ice and drowned. I read about him."

The ground rocks beneath me.

Ajax?

The boy *must* have read my diary.

"How do you know what happened to Peter?" I ask.

"Because in the diary you wrote about finding a hidden door in Magnus's kitchen. I went there. The secret door leads down to a basement. Peter was murdered there. I . . ."

The boy blinks several times and looks unhappy.

". . . *found him,*" he says quietly.

He's telling the truth.

I just know it, with devastating certainty. No fifteen-year-old would make that up.

I look at the boy again, and now I'm sure I've seen him before. I just don't remember where. Images of a dark forest and a glittery dress flicker through my mind.

The woman pulls my arm.

"He's lying," she hisses, and pulls me again. "Don't believe a word he says."

The boy pulls on my other arm.

"No, *she's* lying. She's a murderer."

They both pull on me.

I'm stuck in the middle and can't get free. The woman is small, but surprisingly strong. She's pulling us ever closer to the edge, slowly but surely. The boy and I do our best to pull the other way.

Below us, Ormberg spreads out.

I glimpse a figure moving through the clearing. It's a man, a large man making his way clumsily through the snow.

Something about the way he moves is familiar, something

about his shapeless and hunched-over body, and the way he puts his hands on his knees when he's trying to catch his breath.

And suddenly, I remember; a flood of memories washes over me. They're only fragments, but it's enough for me to understand.

That man chased me through the woods the night Peter disappeared, I remember that now. Me and the woman Peter and I found in the basement. Because . . . there was a woman?

Yes. *Yes!*

I remember her long gray hair and her terrified expression when Peter kicked down the door to her prison.

I don't know if she ran because she was free or because she was afraid of us, but she did flee. And I followed her. But just as we ran up the basement staircase, the man arrived.

He screamed something, grabbed the woman by her hair, and dragged her over the floor. But she got free, continued toward the front door. And the man stood in the kitchen with his hand full of long gray hair.

Then everything is blurry again, but I think the man and Peter fought, because I remember the sound of dishes breaking and muffled moans coming from the basement.

My next memory: the man chasing me and the woman up from the basement and through the woods. Rain whipping against my face. The storm roaring.

The man was clumsy and slow, but he had . . .

*A rifle!*

The man had a rifle!

I remember the loud crack of a shot, and then another. Then a bloody woman on the ground.

*The woman from the basement?*

A new image appears: I remember the woman on the ground grabbing the necklace. Wrapping her fingers around the medallion and trying to say something.

I shudder and blink.

Look again at the large man headed our way, suddenly very aware of the drama taking place here and now.

The boy looks at me. He seems completely terrified, but still determined.

He turns to the woman who's holding my arm.

"You know, Magnus is going to leave you?" he says.

And then:

"He wants to leave you, just like Lill-Leffe did. I read it in the diary. He thinks you're a mean old bitch who does nothing but nag."

For a second, the woman seems to lose control. She stares incredulously at the boy, her eyes wide. Her grip on my arm slackens a bit. I take the opportunity and wrench my arm free.

The woman totters, stumbles backward, but manages to grab the boy's coat. Takes a step toward the edge and pulls him toward it, bit by bit.

My stomach turns to ice as I realize what's happening.

I close my eyes and send a silent prayer to a God I don't really believe in. Ask Him to tell me what to do. But all I hear is the icy breath of the forest, and my own heart pounding in my chest.

When I open my eyes again, I see the boy and the woman teetering on the edge of the cliff. The boy opens his mouth as if he wants to say something, but remains silent. Then they fall down toward the ground. I hear branches cracking and several loud thuds.

Then silence.

It's almost as if they were never here.

# Malin

There's a thud from inside the forest, followed by a cracking sound, as if someone were breaking a bundle of sticks with a well-aimed kick.

Andreas's grip on my arm tightens, and he whispers in my ear: "Shit. I think somebody fell down from that cliff."

"*Ättestupan?*"

"Yes, I think I saw someone or something falling."

"Oh God," I say. "No one could survive that fall."

We run toward the cliff.

"But what about the man?" Andreas pants. "Your cousin."

"Magnus? I don't know what he's doing here, but he's harmless. We can talk to him later."

"Are you sure?"

I think of Magnus. Of his big body and thick red lips. Of how he keeps his eyes glued to the ground whenever I try to talk to him.

"He's as gentle as a lamb."

We trudge between the trees, in the direction of Orm Mountain and Ättestupan. The snow flurries around our legs as we do our best to hurry.

The body is lying on top of a bush, next to the vertical mountain wall. The legs are bent backward in an unnatural position. A twig sticks out through one pants leg, at knee height. One foot is turned upward, revealing the yellow rubber sole of a boot. In the middle of the sole, I see the outline of a five-pointed star.

It looks just like the star in the footprint outside Mom's front door. I know it's important, but my reasoning goes no further than that. I'm not capable of understanding its significance right now.

"*Fuck*," Andreas murmurs, and stops mid-step. "*Fucking hell.*"

I follow the contours of that small, sinewy body in the snow—the outdated coat, the hat with little hearts on it that Mom gave her last Christmas. The reflective tag in the shape of an owl dangling from one of her pockets. My eyes fasten on the twig sticking out of her snow pants, and it takes me a moment to realize what it is.

That's no twig—it's bone.

I turn around to vomit, but nothing comes out. Just dry heaves and something bitter that I spit into the snow.

"Malin!" Andreas says. "*She's alive!*"

I bend down, take a fistful of snow, and rub it around my mouth. Then I turn back and rush over to Margareta.

"It's my aunt," I say, and feel tears arriving.

Andreas gapes.

"*What?* Is this her? Magnus's mother? What's she doing out here?"

I don't respond.

"Look after her," Andreas says. "I'm calling an ambulance."

I nod and squat down next to Margareta. Take off my gloves and search for a pulse on her throat. Do all the things I was taught to do during first-aid training.

Margareta opens her eyes and looks at me. Her mouth forms a silent word: "Malin."

I stroke her cheek, trying to keep her calm. Trying to push away my own panic.

*Margareta.*

She's always been there, like Ormberg. I've always taken her for granted—Magnus, Mom, and Margareta.

They're the only family I have.

Will I lose her now?

"Don't move," I say, stroking her cheek. "We've called for help."

Margareta opens her mouth again, but this time there are no words, just a string of saliva mixed with bloody bubbles. It drips down onto the snow. She coughs.

"*Shhh,*" I whisper. "What in the *hell* were you doing up there on Orm Mountain?"

Margareta closes her eyes.

My tears arrive, and I wipe them away with the back of my hand.

"Malin," she whispers, and turns her head back and forth a little.

And then, barely audible:

"I'm sorry."

Sorry? What's she talking about?

She coughs again; the snow around her head is spotted by blood.

"*Don't talk!* And stay still!"

I hear Andreas speaking to someone in the distance, but I can't hear what they're saying. Or, maybe my brain just can't decode their meaning.

Then he comes back. Hunches down next to me, puts a hand on my shoulder, and looks at Margareta.

"They're on their way. Best not move her."

I nod.

"What was she doing up there?" he asks.

"No clue."

I stroke Margareta gently on the cheek again. The skin is cold and a little rough.

Margareta opens her eyes and looks at me, and at that moment I have just one thought in my head, as obvious as it is selfish: *Don't die, goddamnit. Mom needs you here. So does Magnus.*

We hear steps in the forest.

"Are they here *already*?" I ask.

"No, it must be somebody else," Andreas says.

The steps get closer, and two people arrive—an older woman and a boy. The boy has a large wound across one cheek, and blood is smeared on his chin.

It takes a few seconds for me to recognize them.

It's Hanne and Jake Birgersson—Stefan Birgersson's son. I remember the terror in his eyes the last time I saw him, when we picked up his father for interrogation.

Jake points to Margareta and opens his mouth as if he intends to say something, but no words come. Instead, he stops, stands in silence. Hanne nods, as if she knows what Jake is trying to say.

"She . . . tried to kill us," Hanne says, gesturing at Margareta.

I shake my head and smile involuntarily.

"No," I say. "Of course she didn't."

Andreas puts a hand on my arm.

"Wait a minute, Malin," he says, and turns to Hanne. "What happened?"

Hanne seems unsure and looks at Jake as if seeking his support.

"She pulled down . . ."

Hanne looks uncertain, points to Jake.

"She pulled him off the cliff," she continues, as if struggling to make sense of what happened.

"*Margareta?*" I say. "There must be some misunderstanding. Why would she—"

"*Quiet*, Malin," Andreas says, with a sharpness in his voice that both bothers and surprises me.

"But," I say. "Why are they saying Margareta pulled him off the cliff? They're standing right there."

Jake meets my eyes. His are dark and expressionless. He tugs on something that's hanging down from under his coat. It looks like a ball of pink yarn. Long threads hang between his fingers and drag in the snow.

Then he looks down at his hand and wrinkles his forehead.

"It was the sweater," he says. "It catches on everything."

"It caught on a branch a meter below the edge," Hanne clarifies. "I managed to pull him up again. If it hadn't been for that . . ."

Hanne leaves the sentence unfinished.

"They killed that cop," Jake says quietly, nodding at Margareta. "And she kept the woman with long hair captive in her basement."

I shake my head and stand up.

The forest is spinning around me, and my nausea returns. The cold disappears and my thighs and neck start to pour out sweat.

"No," I say. "You must have . . . They would never . . ."

I'm almost laughing, it's so absurd. My chest feels tight, and my fingers are tingling.

Jake and Hanne watch me in silence.

"How do you know this?" Andreas asks, looking at Jake.

"She . . ."

Jake seems to hesitate, takes a deep breath, then continues:

"Hanne told me."

"Is that right, Hanne?" Andreas asks.

Hanne looks unsure. Her eyes flicker back and forth from me to Andreas. She puts a hand to her hat and adjusts it a little.

"Yes. No. Or, yes. I think so."

At that very moment a figure rushes out from the darkness.

*Magnus.*

He hurls himself at Hanne and slams something hard against her head. I think it's a rock. The sound it makes when it crashes into her head is alarmingly dull.

Hanne screams loudly and shrilly, like an animal.

Andreas reacts immediately, throwing himself at Magnus and

trying to grab hold of his arms. But Magnus is strong, far too strong for his own good. He raises the rock and slams it against Hanne's head again.

And again.

As for me, I stand frozen in the snow. Can't move, can't speak. Can barely even think. But above all, I can't understand what's happening in front of my eyes. That my aunt—a harmless old lady in her seventies—lies severely injured in the snow, while my mentally handicapped cousin tries to kill Hanne.

Then Jake comes running with a big branch in his hand. He stands wide, raises the branch, and swings it at Magnus.

It hits Magnus's head with a loud crack.

Magnus rolls to the side and falls into the snow. Andreas grabs his arms and puts them in cuffs. Then he looks at me.

"*For fuck's sake,* Malin. Were you planning to stand there and watch him kill Hanne? What's *wrong* with you?"

Andreas goes over to Hanne and helps her sit up. Pulls off her hat and runs his fingers along her head. Her gray hair is matted with blood.

"*Owwww,*" Hanne whimpers, and grimaces.

"I think it's superficial," Andreas says, deflating a little as if from relief. Then he sits down in the snow with a heavy thud and puts his head in his hands.

"I'm sorry," I say.

Andreas doesn't answer. He shakes his head back and forth.

"I'm sorry," I say again.

# Jake

The cop whose name is Manfred pours some hot tea into a small plastic mug and pushes it slowly across the table to me.

It feels strange to be sitting in the old grocery store.

We're sitting at a table in a room behind the shop. The walls are covered with photographs, documents, and handwritten notes. They form a kind of patchwork quilt. There are Post-it notes here and there. A laptop sits on one of the chairs.

Manfred is special.

I don't know if I like him—I hardly know him. But he has an elegant style, as if he actually cares about what he's wearing—even though he's a man.

He's wearing an olive green wool suit with leather buttons. The fabric has a slight pink pattern, and a pale pink handkerchief sticks up from his breast pocket. His beard is red, as is his hair, which is a bit damp and stuck to his temples.

I sip on the tea and touch the bandage that covers my cheek.

Manfred drove me to the hospital in Katrineholm. They said I probably had a mild concussion and should take it easy for the next few days. I got three stitches as well, and they promised the scar would barely be visible in a few weeks.

I didn't tell them I wanted that scar, that it's important to me because it proves what I did for Hanne.

I want it to be there forever, like a silent reminder whenever I look in the mirror.

Hanne also had to go to the hospital, but she didn't need stitches. I think one of the other police officers drove her back to Berit's later.

What happened to Margareta and Magnus I don't know.

"Now let's try this again, then I'll take you home," Manfred says. "Okay?"

"Okay."

"Did you meet Hanne in the woods the night she was found?"

"Yes. It was a Saturday."

"Saturday the second of December," Manfred says, running a hand over his beard and making a scraping sound.

"I think so. I didn't check the date."

"And when you did, she mentioned that Magnus or Margareta had hurt Peter."

I consider how honest I should be.

I've decided *not* to mention the diary. Hanne wouldn't want Manfred and the other police officers to read about how sad and ill she was, even if the book contains important information.

But now Margareta and Magnus have been caught. The policemen have found Magnus's disgusting *murder basement* and Peter's frozen body. And apparently P's car was in Margareta's barn. So Hanne's diary can't really be that important anymore. They have all the evidence they need.

"She said that, yes."

Manfred nods and writes something in his notebook.

"And then she told you Magnus had kept a woman prisoner in his basement?"

I nod.

Manfred lays down his pen and massages his temples. His

hands are huge. When Dad sees hands that big he usually calls them "toilet lids."

Manfred puts his toilet lids on the table, meets my eyes, and I immediately feel nervous, because his expression is so stern. Just like Dad when he's about to chew me out.

"I have to ask," he says.

I nod, because I already know what's coming. I've been thinking about it since I left the Katrineholm hospital. Twisting and turning it in my head like a Rubik's Cube.

"Why didn't you tell anyone? You *must* have known it was important. That Margareta and Magnus were suspected of very serious crimes."

Manfred looks at me.

"The truth, Jake," he says quietly. "You have to tell the truth. Do you have a problem with that?"

I don't respond.

Instead, I look down on the worn surface of the desk. At the hundreds of tiny scratches that came from all the people who ever sat here: men, women. Maybe even children.

But nobody like me.

No one *aberrant*.

"I thought that police officer was already dead," I say, and trace one of the scratches with my finger.

Manfred sighs a little.

"Yes. He probably was already dead. But still. You couldn't know that for sure. Right?"

"No."

"So why didn't you say anything, Jake? *Why?* I think you know a lot more than you're saying. And I believe you told someone else, too. Someone who called the police and tipped us off."

I shiver, but not from the cold—I'm still wearing my coat and Manfred has the floor heater on full blast, and it's pointed right at us.

"*Jake?*"

I shake my head slowly. I want to say it, but it's as if the words get stuck in my mouth and refuse to come out. As if all my strength and determination fell off that cliff along with Margareta.

Manfred sighs again. Stands up, walks over to the wall, and grabs a small paper box. Then he comes back, sits down, and puts it on the table.

The box is brown and maybe ten centimeters long and five centimeters wide.

He meets my eyes, opens the box, puts a hand in it, and takes out a small, transparent plastic bag. Places it in front of me on the table.

I lean forward to get a better look.

At first I think it's empty, but then I see it.

A small gold-colored sequin glitters inside the bag.

"Jake?"

Manfred's voice isn't angry; instead, it sounds almost pleading.

I close my eyes, because I don't want to look at the sequin. But there's no way to shut the images out: the glittering dress, the lipstick, and Hanne's soaking-wet, injured body creeping out between the bushes. It almost feels like I'm standing there again, that I'm back in the woods, surrounded by the smell of wet soil and rotting leaves, the rain whipping against my face. Yes, I can actually see Hanne in front of me. But she looks different now. She smiles at me and stretches out her hand.

I saved her, I think. I did that.

I look at Manfred, at his elegant suit and his pale pink handkerchief. At his rosy round cheeks, and his tired eyes.

Maybe he'll understand?

He raises one eyebrow.

"*Jake?*" he repeats, as if it were a question.

And then my thoughts scatter again—flying away like birds or butterflies, whispering to me that maybe everyone is sick or weird, if you look closely enough. Or that maybe there's no such thing as sick or healthy. And that maybe there's nothing wrong with wearing a dress, even if your name is Jake, and you live in a backwater like Ormberg, and unfortunately one day you'll grow up to be a man.

A dress is just a dress. A piece of fabric that you can like if you want to.

But killing somebody?

That's wrong for real, because death lasts a very long time.

"Yes, it was me," I say. "I like dresses. *Do you have a problem with that?*"


Manfred drops me off in the driveway of Ormberg's most beautiful house. Before I get out of the car, he puts a hand on my shoulder.

"Well done, Jake," he says. *"Well done!"*

Only that, then he falls silent.

I open the door and jump out of his big car. I throw my bag over my shoulder, squinting in the bright morning light, and start to make my way to the house. The snow crunches under my feet, and the front door opens just as Manfred pulls away.

Dad is standing inside.

He takes a step out into the snow, and then another down the stairs, even though he's not wearing shoes. Then he starts running toward me, throws his arms around me, and hugs me harder than I can remember him ever doing before.

"Jake, *goddamnit*. You scared the shit out of me!"

"I'm sorry," I say.

We stand there for a moment. Dad's breath is warm and smells like beer.

"We can't stand out here," he says finally. "I'll freeze my ass off. And my toes. Come on, let's go inside!"

Everything looks like usual at home. I don't know what I was expecting, but it feels like something should have changed. As soon as we step into the hall, I start to worry what Melinda will say when she sees me. I've pushed that thought out of my mind for the last few hours, but now it comes back, roaring like a jet into my head.

"Melinda?" I ask.

"With Markus," Dad says. "Do you want something to eat?"

"No, thanks. We had a hot dog on our way back from Katrine-holm."

Dad nods, and looks at me. Reaches a hand toward the bandage on my cheek, but freezes before touching me.

"Damn! I just can't believe it. You saved that old lady's life."

"Yes."

"Honestly, I didn't think you had it in you."

"Have *what* in me?"

Dad shakes his head.

"Oh, forget it. But I wanna hear everything later. You probably wanna rest for a while. You probably didn't get any sleep."

I nod and head up the stairs.

My room looks the same, as well: The soft, thick carpet tickles my feet, and the posters, hung on the wall with tape, have come loose here and there and flutter a bit in the draft from my windows. Even the unmade bed and the dirty socks and the underwear lying in a pile on the floor are exactly the same.

I sit down on the mattress and feel the fatigue overtaking me. My head and cheek ache, my legs are stiff, and nausea lurks just below my throat.

Slowly I let my body sink down into the mattress. Pull the blanket over me without taking off my clothes. Close my eyes.

I'm so tired. I think I could sleep for days.

When I turn on my side, I feel something hard against my neck, like a Lego. I sit up on my elbow and examine the object. Turn on my bedside lamp and hold it up to the light.

It's a small package, not much bigger than a matchbox, and

wrapped in gold paper. "To Jake from Melinda" stands in round, slanted handwriting. And Melinda has drawn a heart next to it. The pen must have stopped working when she did it, because sections have been filled in with a different-color marker.

I take off the paper and throw it on the floor.

Inside is a small box.

I open the box and see a bottle with a pink top. I take it out and hold it closer to the light.

It's nail polish with tiny gold flakes in it. When I shake it, the glittery particles hover in the liquid. It reminds me of those glass globes with a miniature winter landscape inside, where the plastic snow swirls when you turn it over.

# Malin

**M**om is sitting at the kitchen table when I come home the next morning. Her eyes are red-rimmed, and a balled-up tissue sits on the tablecloth in front of her. When she sees me, she rises and smooths down the blouse that's stretched over her heavy bust.

I go over to her and give her a hug, but she doesn't hug me back. Instead, she pats me on the back, as if I were a football player who's just scored. The top of her head barely reaches my shoulder, and I feel a sudden tenderness for her.

"Malin," she says, pushing a lock of hair out of my face. *"Sweet baby."*

I sit down on the chair next to her and wonder how much my colleagues told her about what happened. But I suppose she knows most of it, since Manfred sent two people to interview her as soon as he got to Ättestupan.

When it became clear that my aunt and cousin were murder suspects, I was pulled off the investigation. Hanne and Peter must have been on their trail. Of course, they didn't tell the rest of us, because my family was involved.

I don't know what's going to happen now, but Manfred told

me to go home and rest up. Still, I stayed in the woods for a long time, walked in circles around the cairn before continuing on to the ironworks. Then spent the rest of the night in the office, reading preliminary investigation protocols.

I think I was trying to understand.

I don't know if I feel any wiser. Margareta and Magnus are surely guilty of terrible crimes, and I've lived my life here, side by side with them, and never suspected a thing.

What does that say about me?

Not just as a cop, but as a human being. There must have been clues, cracks in the façade that could have told me something was wrong. Could people truly be such monsters without showing it? Surely your own family, the people you trust and build your life around, couldn't dupe you so completely?

What hurts most is that Magnus was involved. I've always felt so protective of him, despite his obvious problems, or maybe because of them. My whole life I've defended him from the kids in the village—verbally, but also physically when the need arose.

And all that time, I thought he was the victim.

Mom picks up her tissue and blows her nose.

"Shall we leave?" I ask.

Margareta is in intensive care, and the doctor made it clear that we needed to get there as soon as possible.

He said it was just a matter of time.

Mom sobs, and fidgets with the little ball of tissue. A thin strip of paper falls onto the tablecloth, like a wilted flower petal.

"We have to talk first," she says with her eyes on her tissue.

"The doctor said we needed to hurry—"

"I *know*," Mom interrupts me. "But we have to talk. First."

"Yes?"

I look at the clock and then back at Mom. I find it hard to understand what could be so urgent, what couldn't be handled in the car on the way to the hospital.

"About what?" I ask.

Mom blinks several times, then wipes a tear off her cheek.

"This is so hard," she says.

"She might make it."

Mom shakes her head and laughs. It's a short, dry laugh that makes me uncomfortable. It feels inappropriate: There's nothing to laugh about.

"No. Sweetheart. It's not Margareta I'm talking about. We have to talk about us."

"About *us*?"

I start to feel a creeping uneasiness that I can't quite put my finger on. As if I know what's coming can't be good.

Not good at all.

The red felt Christmas Star I made in middle school is hanging in the window. The glitter and sequins have come loose and hang by strands of dry glue.

"You know that I love you more than anything in the world? Nobody means more to me than you."

"Yes," I say, wondering where she's going with this.

The minutes are ticking by, and Margareta is dying in intensive care. Even if she is a monster, she and Magnus are the only relatives we have.

I'm sure Mom would want to see her one last time.

"We had such a hard time having a baby," Mom says. "We tried for so many years, your dad and me. I don't know how many miscarriages I had. It was so horrible; it ate us up from the inside, like a cancer. And you should know that I never knew anything about *how* it happened. How he kept her in that basement. How could a person do something like that? Magnus, who's so nice. And Margareta—can you believe she protected him this whole time? Even if he is her son, I don't understand it."

"Wait a second. I'm not following you."

Mom starts sobbing uncontrollably. Tears flow down her cheeks. She unfolds the snotty tissue and blows again. Then she takes a deep breath and continues:

"We just wanted to help. We thought we were doing the right thing."

"What are you talking about? What do you mean, 'doing the right thing'?"

Mom sobs again; her words are choked by it.

"That woman, the refugee that Magnus took care of—well, that's how Margareta explained it to us anyway. She was pregnant. But she either couldn't or didn't want to take care of the child."

"I don't understand . . ."

"And me and your dad, we longed for one. And we had a good home and could take care of a child."

Something cold and sticky spreads inside as I realize what it is she's trying to say.

"No," I say. "You can't . . . *mean* . . ."

My voice fades away. The only sound is Mom's sobbing and the old fridge droning in the corner. A sparrow lands on the windowsill and pecks at the tallow ball Mom's put there.

"We thought we were helping her," she whispers. "And Margareta took care of all the details. She'd done a lot of home deliveries before, since she's a registered midwife, and she was able to arrange the whole thing: the birth certificate, the paperwork that had to be sent to the Swedish Tax Agency. She took care of it all. And we loved you from the first moment, Malin. We loved you as our own child. You were ours. Our beloved baby."

*"No! Stop!"*

I stand up so quickly my chair falls back on the floor. It lands with a crash.

But Mom, who's sitting shrunken up in front of me, doesn't react. She doesn't even move. All she does is pull tiny pieces of paper off her tissue.

And suddenly I understand.

The pieces fall inexorably into place, one by one. I remember how Margareta mumbled "Sorry" to me as she lay in the snow beneath Ättestupan with a bone sticking out of her old snow pants. Then I think of Magnus, who has never been able to look me in the eyes. Who always looked down at the ground when we met, as if he were afraid of me, or ashamed.

And finally: the conversation from Manfred. How he called and asked about Azra's medallion. "Did you touch it? The hair, that is. I got a call from the technicians . . ."

The room is spinning.

I don't want to follow that thought to its conclusion, but I force myself to do it anyway: Azra had a lock of hair inside that medallion. Manfred probably asked if I'd touched it because the technicians found my DNA there—the technicians swabbed me when we found Azra's body, and my DNA would have then been put into the Elimination Register, to ensure that we hadn't contaminated the evidence.

They must have made a match with me.

But the reason the hair contained my DNA was not that I'd touched it, or that the test was "a snafu," as Manfred put it, but because the hair was mine.

The room spins faster, and my heart races. I open and close my mouth several times without getting out a word.

Mom looks up at me.

In her face is a despair so deep it terrifies me. A desperation as intense as the one I remember from the day Dad died on his way to the barn with a washing machine in his arms.

*Little Mom.*

So different from me. Short where I'm tall. Blond where my hair is dark. Calm where I'm impulsive and emotional.

*We are so different you might think they found me in the woods, with the trolls.*

And she's heavyset—so it's quite possible people around here thought she was pregnant even though she wasn't.

I have to grab on to the table in order not to fall over.

*"You stole a child?"* I whisper.

"No," Mom screams. "No! We thought we were helping her, we thought she didn't want you. I thought I was giving you a home, I thought you had nowhere to go, and I loved you so much."

She buries her head in her hands and sniffs. Then she stiffens, lifts her head, and meets my eyes.

The expression on her face is imploring.

"Malin," she says quietly. "Nobody needs to know about this. It won't help anyone. And Magnus won't tell, Margareta saw to that. It's up to you now."

I turn around and stumble into the hall, open the front door, and let in the bitingly cold wind. Squint at the sun where it hangs above the treetops, as if the world hadn't just ended.

As if I weren't the daughter of a murdered Bosnian Muslim woman with no face. As if the skeleton I found in the cairn weren't my sister. As if Esma with her broken hands and faded Polaroid pictures of a family that no longer exists were not my aunt.

Maybe Sump-Ivar was right: Maybe he did see a naked infant at the cairn—and that infant was me.

*And the hair.*

The nausea rolls over me when I think about it: how that soft, brittle hair in the medallion felt against my fingertips. Azra must have cut a lock from her newborn daughter and put it in the medallion before Margareta stole her child.

*Before she stole the baby, who was me.*

I fall and fall, and it never ends.

I fall through the earth and into hell and then I keep falling, because there's no longer anyone left to catch me.

Tears run down my cheeks to my lips. Filling my mouth with the salty taste of a false past.

# Malin

P lease," I say. "I need to know. I can't handle it otherwise. I . . ."

The words die out, get stuck in my throat, even though I'm doing everything I can to push down the sadness and despair sitting in my chest.

Outside, the snow is falling. Heavy, wet flakes float quickly to the ground and melt immediately on the black asphalt.

I've been paralyzed since Margareta died. All I've been able to think about is what Mom told me, that I'm the daughter of Azra Malkoc.

I've been forced to rethink everything I thought I knew about myself, about my family, and I don't know where that process will end. But one thing I am sure of: I need to know what happened that winter when my biological mother and sister disappeared from the refugee camp.

I have to understand.

And then I have to decide: Should I tell Manfred what Mom said? Should I crush what little family I have left, to seek out justice for Azra and Nermina, or will I keep that terrible secret buried forever?

I think of Mom—I haven't even spoken to her since Margareta died, though she's tried to contact me every day.

I've wanted to call her, but I can't.

I've told myself she's the woman who took care of me, raised me as her own, and loved me every moment of it.

I've tried to convince myself that Margareta persuaded her and Dad to take care of me. That she had no idea Magnus was holding my biological mother prisoner in his basement.

That she just wanted to help.

I've really tried.

But it's impossible.

All I feel is a despair and a hate so intense and bottomless, it terrifies me. Every time I think of Mom, I remember that faceless, bloody body in the snow at the cairn . . . the woman who was robbed of both her children and her life.

I wish there were someone I could talk to about this, but there isn't. Everyone I'm close to is either gone or touched by the evil that's been sprouting in Ormberg.

Max, I don't want back. And what I want from Andreas I don't even have the energy to think about yet.

*"Please!"* I repeat.

Manfred rubs his temples and shakes his head slowly.

"I can't. I can't share the details with anyone outside of the investigation, and you've been reassigned. I'm sorry, I can't even imagine how this must feel for you, but I can't do it."

Manfred falls silent. Clears his throat and then continues in a softer tone of voice:

"Listen. Malin. I know I'm not always the easiest person to work with. Tough to please, reluctant to praise. Et cetera, et cetera. If it's any comfort, I want you to know you're a damned fine cop. I would gladly work with you again."

I lean forward.

"I *have to* know," I say.

Manfred sighs and rolls his eyes.

On the floor next to the wall stands a black overnight bag and a briefcase. I guess he's on his way home to Stockholm: to his wife and his tiny daughter, who no longer has ear infections all the time. To a life that will go on as usual, which has nothing to do with the evil in Ormberg.

*"Please!"*

My voice is a whisper that almost drowns in the air coming through the vents of the police station.

Manfred slaps his hands on his knees.

*"Damn it!"*

And then:

"Do you know how much shit I'll get if this comes out?"

I don't respond.

He opens his laptop, turns it to face me, and meets my eyes. Then he shakes his head and pushes the computer toward me.

"I have to go take care of a few things. It will take me a half hour. Do you understand? *A half hour.*"

I nod silently.

He stands up, smooths down his perfectly tailored suit, and runs a hand through his reddish brown hair. Then he leaves the room without looking at me.

With trembling hands, I pull the laptop closer. On the screen, I see Magnus, in a chair. Opposite him, Svante sits with his arms crossed and his head leaning so that his beard rests against his chest. A microphone hangs from a cord above a table.

The recording must have been made at the interrogation room here at the police station.

I press *Play*, and Svante and Magnus come to life.

"Where did you first meet Azra and Nermina Malkoc?" Svante asks.

Magnus rocks back and forth a little in his chair.

"At the refugee camp. With Mom."

"And what were you two doing there?" Svante asks.

Magnus's eyes roll up toward the ceiling.

"Mom wanted to talk to somebody who was in charge of the snowplowing. She wanted the boss to sign a list. And then we met Assa and started to talk."

"You mean Azra?"

"I called her Assa."

"But she had a name. And that name was Azra, not Assa."

Magnus falls silent, stares down at the table. Shrugs his shoulders.

"What happened then?" Svante asks.

Magnus stretches a bit.

"We . . . we met Assa more times. She told me about herself and Nermina. They probably wouldn't get to stay in Sweden, she said. I said they could live in my basement."

"And what did your mother say to that?"

Magnus pushes his lower lip out defiantly. Everything about him—his body language, gestures, way of speaking—remind me of a giant child.

"Mom got super mad."

"Why?"

"Cuz. She said we had enough of our own problems. That we couldn't have immigrants living in the basement. You can't have immigrants in the basement just because you have a basement. She said."

"And what did you do then?"

Magnus sucks in his lower lip, seems to be chewing on it.

"Said I'd move. To Katrineholm. Like *Lill-Leffe.*"

Svante makes a few notes, then waits for Magnus to meet his eyes.

"What did your mother say when you said you were going to move?"

Magnus looks to the side, toward the wall. The tendons in his neck are stretched taut, and his cheeks are spotted red.

"That I couldn't. She always said I couldn't when I wanted to move. She got super super mad."

Svante scribbles something in his notebook before meeting Magnus's eyes again.

"And what did you say then?"

Magnus squirms a little.

"That I was gonna move this time. For real."

The room is silent for a moment.

"And?" Svante says. "What happened then?"

Magnus slowly rocks back and forth in his chair.

"She changed her mind. Said they could stay there for a little while. Until they went to Stockholm. So. They moved in. But even though we did everything we could to make them comfortable, they just wanted to leave all the time. Even though Mom bought them ice cream and chips and . . . They weren't at all grateful. They just wanted to leave, even though they'd just moved in. One night, Nermina disappeared. I'd forgotten to lock the door, and she just disappeared."

"She escaped?"

"*Escaped?*"

Magnus looks confused, as if he hadn't ever considered that he was holding them captive. In the end, he nods, acknowledging Svante's description.

"And what did you do then?" Svante asks.

Magnus looks confused. His eyes flit; he licks his lips.

"I followed her. Into the woods."

Then silence.

"Did you find her?" Svante asks quietly.

Magnus nods.

"At the cairn. She was standing in the clearing. And I didn't want to. I didn't want to. Hurt her."

"What happened?"

Magnus mumbles something inaudible, and even though I know he's a monster, I can't help feeling a little sorry for him. In many ways, he's a child. The more I think about it, the more convinced I am that Margareta is the one morally responsible for what happened.

I've thought a lot about why she did it. Why she allowed Magnus to keep Azra and Nermina locked up in the basement.

I know Margareta had a hard life. Her first child died before he turned one, and Lill-Leffe left her when she was pregnant with Magnus. I think that's why she protected him, because she had no one else, because she was so deeply afraid he'd move and leave her all alone.

I would guess that Magnus will be evaluated to determine if he's suffering from a serious mental disorder. And if he is, he'll be sentenced to legal psychiatric care.

"*What happened?*" Svante asks again.

"I was just trying to catch her, but she struggled so much that she fell back and hit her head on one of the rocks. And I sort of . . . fell on top of her. And when I got up, she wasn't breathing anymore."

Magnus stares down at his round stomach.

"I didn't mean to," he continues. "I'm just so big and clumsy. I didn't want to hurt her. It was different with Assa. I couldn't catch up with her. I *had to* shoot her. But I just wanted to catch Nermina. I couldn't let her tell . . ."

"*What?*" Svante asks.

Magnus looks down at the table and shrugs a little.

"Then everyone would think we'd kidnapped them."

"Didn't you?"

"Well. What do you mean?"

"*Didn't* you kidnap them?"

"No. We were just . . . trying to help them."

"Then why didn't you let them go? If you just wanted to help them?"

Magnus squirms again. He rubs his hands together, and his forehead wrinkles.

"*But* . . ." he says.

And a few seconds later:

"But I *liked* her."

"Azra?"

Magnus looks down at the table. The big head starts to bob up and down. His bald spot flashes under the fluorescent lights.

"Yes," he says, sniffing loudly. "And Mom said nobody would notice if a few Yugos went missing. She said it didn't matter. Not in the grand scheme of things. She said I could keep her as long as I lived at home. But then . . . after Nermina . . . *disappeared*, Assa was different. She stopped talking and didn't want to leave the basement anymore. She just sat there on her bed. So. Everything was good. At least until that police officer and that bitch from Stockholm came and scared her away. The policeman was really angry. I got so scared. It was awful, but I had to. To protect myself, that is. And stop Assa. But that old lady disappeared. The one from Stockholm."

Silence again.

I sense Svante's shock—even though the screen is blurry and the sound is scratchy, I can feel it vibrating through my body.

He's sitting with his mouth open, as if he can't really take in what Magnus is saying.

"Were you in love with Azra?" Svante asks in the end.

Magnus's head bobs even more, and he sniffs again.

"*Love?*"

"Yes. Were you in love? Did you want to be close to her? Were you attracted to her? Was that why you kept her?"

"No," he says, and sniffs again. "She was more like a pet."

My stomach clenches in shock, and I push *Pause*. It's hard to breathe.

*He called her a pet.*

*My mother, Magnus's pet.*

Tears start to flow down my cheeks, and I remember all those times I spent with them when I was little.

I remember I used to run into Magnus's house and hide under the kitchen table, when we were playing hide-and-seek. I'd lie on my stomach with my cheek pressed against the cool linoleum floor. Breathing in the smell of cooking grease and cigarette smoke, swallowing my giggles while I waited to be found.

She was there, below me.

My bare feet ran over her head.

My ear was pressed to the floor that was her ceiling.

And I didn't notice anything.

Esma's words come back to me, the Bosnian saying she mentioned when we visited her.

*Those who sow the wind, harvest the storm.*

The storm is here now. The evil seeds Margareta sowed that winter when they offered shelter to Azra and Nermina have grown into a raging storm.

I hear a scraping sound from outside. The door opens, and Manfred comes in.

He sits down opposite me, meets my eyes, and nods slowly as if to confirm that the horror I've just witnessed is actually true.

I think of what Andreas said when we were arguing about refugees in front of Manfred, when I tried to explain why the people of Ormberg were so unkind to them. I remember doing my best to explain why we, the people from here, deserved more help and support than the refugees. As if my origin were a currency that could be exchanged for sympathy and privilege.

I will never forget his words; they're carved into my memory.

*Malin, it could have been you . . . It could have been you who had to flee from war and starvation.*

And I responded, it could never have been me.

I was from Ormberg, I wasn't some fucking Muslim who'd

crossed the Mediterranean in a patched-up rubber boat hoping to take advantage of the Swedish welfare system.

*But that's exactly who I was.*

At that moment, I know what I have to do, what I owe Azra, Nermina, and Esma, and also myself.

"Manfred," I say. "I have to tell you something."

# Jake

*Four months later*

Berit puts tea and buns on the table.

I look out the window.

The sun has burned away the snow, revealing large, dark gashes in the field outside. Next to the small mound of stones at the edge of the farmland a brave little coltsfoot is growing.

Berit's buns smell delicious.

I can't remember the last time I ate freshly baked buns. It must have been before Mom died—she used to bake sometimes. Mostly sugar cakes, because those are easy to make, but now and then she baked buns, too, with cinnamon and crispy pearls of sugar on top.

Dad can't cook or bake, but that doesn't matter if you have a microwave.

Hanne looks at Berit and wrinkles her forehead.

"Please, Berit. I can set the table."

"No, sit," Berit says. "I'll take care of it. Then the two of you can have some time to chat. Joppe needs a walk."

"Then I'll do the dishes," Hanne says.

"No you won't."

"Of course I will."

"That's out of the question," Berit says.

They almost sound married.

Dad and Mom used to sound like that, squabbling about little things like who was gonna take out the garbage or what TV show they should watch on Friday nights.

Maybe Berit and Hanne like each other, like Mom and Dad did. Even if they're not in love with each other.

Dad says that it's a "scandal" that the county is letting Hanne stay with Berit. He says it would be both cheaper and safer to put her in a home, but I don't agree. I can't imagine Hanne among a lot of old, confused people, locked in a rest home.

Berit limps out into the hall, and Joppe saunters loyally behind her, throwing a last longing glance at the buns before reluctantly disappearing.

The front door closes, and we're sitting face-to-face.

Hanne smiles a little.

She's not as thin as I remember her, and her face has a lot more color. Her hair is thick and shiny and falls in soft waves onto her shoulders.

"I hear I owe you a thank-you," Hanne says. "They say you saved my life."

My cheeks feel hot, and I look down at the table.

She holds out the plate, and I grab the biggest bun. I take a bite and meet her eyes again.

She looks curious, and even though she's so old, she reminds me of a child when she looks at me like that.

"I have to admit I don't remember what happened," she says. "But they've told me the story. Several times, in fact."

She laughs a bit when she says the last.

"Is it hard not to be able to remember stuff?" I ask.

Hanne nods and grabs a bun for herself. She holds it in the palm of her hand, observing it as if trying to figure out how much it weighs or what it's made of.

"Yes. Sometimes it's very difficult. Though I think it's gotten a little better. I started taking a new medicine. And now my life isn't so *dramatic* anymore."

She raises her eyebrows and smiles when she says "dramatic."

"I remember more now," she continues. "I still don't remember everything that happened when Peter disappeared, but I know he's . . ."

She blinks a few times.

"Dead?" I say.

Hanne nods, but says nothing. She gazes out through the window.

"Do you wish you could remember everything that happened here in Ormberg?" I ask.

Hanne puts the bun on the table, straightens up, and looks at me.

"I'm not really sure," she says. "It depends. Sometimes ignorance is a blessing."

And then:

"And what about you? Is it hard to be as brave as you are?"

I feel embarrassed again, don't know what to say.

"Nah. Or, I guess. Maybe a little."

"In what way?" she asks, taking a bite of her bun.

I consider it a bit before I answer.

"It's hard to find the courage to be the person you are inside. I think everyone could be brave, if they found their courage."

Hanne nods.

"You're not just brave, you're wise, too. And how did you find your courage?"

I look out the window again. Berit disappears between the trees, Joppe jumping around her legs. Water drips from the roof and down to the windowsill.

"I was very afraid at first," I say.

"*Mmhhhm.*" Hanne nods again as if she understands just what I mean, as if courage is her specialty.

It's so strange to be sitting here telling her all this. Because I've never talked to any adult about these things. But with Hanne, I have to be honest, I just know it. When I read her diary, I learned so much about her—it's only right that she learns a little about me, too.

It's a question of balance.

"Courage is in short supply these days," Hanne says, looking out toward the church.

Maybe she's thinking about what lies beyond it, of the refugee camp.

The story of how Magnus held a refugee woman and her children captive in a basement has been in the newspapers and on television every day since Margareta fell off Ättestupan and died. And when it came out that Malin was the daughter of the refugee woman, journalists from all over the world came here.

They call Magnus "The Ormberg Butcher," and his basement "The Chamber of Death." Apparently, someone is even going to write a book called *The Pet* about what happened.

That's what Ballsack-Magnus called Azra during his police interrogation.

Saga said that was the most twisted thing she'd ever heard. And our social studies teacher told us that Magnus and Margareta probably didn't think of Azra and Nermina as having the same *human dignity as them* because they were from a different background.

Foreign journalists even called Dad and offered us money to interview me.

He told them all to go to hell.

You can't trust journalists. Especially if they come from big cities like Stockholm, Berlin, London, and Paris.

We talk for a while, then Berit comes back with her dog and starts to clear the table.

"Please, Berit," Hanne says. "I'll take care of all this later."

"No you won't," Berit says.

"I'll help you," Hanne says, starting to get up.

"You sit," Berit says, limping around the table and pushing Hanne down into her chair again.

I feel good when I leave Hanne and Berit.

Before I start my moped, I take out my phone and text:

"See you in five."

Then I put on my helmet and head toward the old highway. I drive with my visor up; the air on my face is lukewarm. Dirty snow still lies in drifts on the side of the road, and glassy puddles of snowmelt stand in the deep potholes on the gravel road.

I turn right after Orm Mountain and continue a few hundred meters, then stop and park my moped.

The forest around me is awakening after a long, cold winter. Small, rolled-up ferns shoot up out of last year's grass. The birds are singing. The sun is hot, and everything smells like wet earth and spruce trees.

Saga is already there.

She's standing in the middle of the road with her hands pushed deep into her jean pockets. The wind plays with her blue hair.

I give her a quick hug, and she hugs back. Then I take out the diary and flip through it. Stop near the end, near one of Hanne's bloody handprints.

I put my hand over it. They fit exactly.

Saga does the same.

I think again about how grateful I am that she forgave me and kept the diary secret. And about how lucky it is that her mom stopped dating that asshole Björn, and that she won't end up killed in a sauna.

I flip back a few pages. Read that spindly, familiar hand-writing.

I'm going to burn this diary when this is all over. Erase the last two weeks of my life. Forget Ormberg and all that happened here. Until we got here life was perfect, despite the disease.

Dear God, I ask of you only this: Help me forget!

"Shall I?" Saga asks.

I nod and think of what Hanne said.

*Sometimes ignorance is a blessing.*

Saga digs in her pocket and takes out a lighter, flicks the little wheel with her thumb, and holds the flame to the book.

It sparks as fire grabs hold of those brittle pages. The flames lick the pages, and for a moment it seems as if the text were floating freely in the air, receiving a new life, released from that mottled parchment-like paper.

As if Hanne's story no longer needed a diary in order to exist.

I put the burning book on the gravel road and watch the fire eat it page by page, until it finally swallows everything, cover to cover. The paper darkens, and flimsy, black flakes float away in the wind.

Saga's hand slips into mine, squeezes tight.

"Ready to go?" she asks.

# About *After She's Gone*

We live in a difficult time. More people have been displaced from their homes than ever before in history. And this stream of refugees has been met with xenophobia, conflict, and fear.

My Ormberg isn't a real place, but it exists all around us. Maybe you live in Ormberg, and don't even know it, or maybe you drive through it on your way to work, or visit your relatives there. Ormberg is a state of mind, not a geographic location— a condition that arises when large changes sweep through, like forest fires. Ormberg is what grows out of the ashes of the old ironworks. It takes its nourishment from dejection, dissatisfaction, or maybe just sadness.

"It could have been you who had to flee from war and starvation," Andreas says to Malin. And it's this simple but important message that I want to convey in *After She's Gone*.

# Acknowledgments

I'd like to offer my sincere thanks to everyone who helped me during the writing of *After She's Gone,* especially my editor, Anne Speyer; the team at Ballantine Books, including Jennifer Hershey, Kim Hovey, and Kara Welsh; and my agents at Ahlander Agency, Christine Edhäll and Astri von Arbin Ahlander. In addition, I'm eternally grateful to Åsa Torlöf, who read the manuscript and contributed important insights about police work; Martina Nilsson, who generously shared her knowledge of DNA analyses; and Lejla Hastor, who answered my questions about Bosnia. Finally, I'd like to thank my family and friends for their understanding and encouragement while I was writing this book. Without your love and patience, no book!

## ABOUT THE AUTHOR

CAMILLA GREBE was born in 1968 in Alvsjo, Sweden. She holds a degree from the Stockholm School of Economics and was a cofounder of the audiobook publisher Storyside. With her sister Åsa Träff, Grebe has written five celebrated crime novels, the first two of which were nominated for Best Swedish Crime Novel of the Year. Grebe is also the cowriter of the popular Moscow Noir trilogy.

@CamillaGrebe

This book was set in Sabon, a typeface designed by the well-known German typographer Jan Tschichold (1902–74). Sabon's design is based upon the original letter forms of sixteenth-century French type designer Claude Garamond and was created specifically to be used for three sources: foundry type for hand composition, Linotype, and Monotype. Tschichold named his typeface for the famous Frankfurt typefounder Jacques Sabon (c. 1520–80).

# ITALIAN
## PHRASE BOOK AND DICTIONARY

by Charles A. Hughes

A GD/PERIGEE BOOK

Perigee Books
are published by
The Putnam Publishing Group
200 Madison Avenue
New York, New York 10016

LC: 75-144062
ISBN 0-399-50795-7

First Perigee printing, 1982
Printed in the United States of America

*Seventh Impression*

# CONTENTS

# INTRODUCTION

In this phrase book for travel in Italy, we have tried to incorporate features that will make it convenient and easy for you to use in actual situations. Every phrase and word is translated into proper Italian and then respelled to guide you in its pronunciation.

The book is also "programmed" to help you with two of the basic problems of the novice in a language — an inability to comprehend the spoken word and a certain hesitancy in speaking out. To solve the first problem, questions have been avoided, to the extent possible, in the phrases. When they could not be avoided, they have been worded so that a yes or no answer may be expected. And sometimes, when even this solution is impossible, the anticipated answer is given. To solve the problem of hesitancy, the contents of the book have been arranged so that a minimal command of basic phrases, salutations, weather, numbers-time, statements of need and desire, may be acquired in the first sections. The pronunciation guides printed under the Italian translations should also give you confidence that you will be understood. If your listener should indicate that he doesn't understand, merely try again. A slight mispronunciation is no embarrassment.

Finally, to aid you in finding a phrase that you wish to use, the Dictionary has been partially indexed. The Dictionary itself is comprehensive enough so that you will not lack the basic words for any usual situation.

# TIPS ON PRONUNCIATION AND ACCENT

The pronunciation of each word in this phrase book is indicated by a respelling that approximates the sounds of Italian, according to the following system:

The vowels:

| | |
|---|---|
| ah | Pronounced like "a" in f*a*ther |
| eh | Pronounced like "ay" in m*ay*be |
| e | Pronounced like "e" in m*e*t |
| ee | Pronounced like "ee" in s*ee*n |
| o | Pronounced like "o" in b*o*y |
| oh | Pronounced like "o" in *o*ver |
| oo | Pronounced like "oo" in s*oo*n |
| ah-ee | Pronounced like the pronoun *I* or the word *eye* |
| ow | Pronounced like "ow" in n*ow* |
| wah | Pronounced like "wa" in w*a*ter |
| woh | Pronounced like "wo" in w*o*n't |
| oy | Pronounced like "oy" in b*oy* |

Consonants are sounded approximately as in English, with these exceptions:

"c" before "a," "o" and "u" sounds like "c" in *c*an; it is represented in the pronunciations by "k."

"c" before "e" and "i" sounds like "ch" in *ch*urch.

"ch" sounds like "k" in s*k*ate.

"g" before "a," "o" and "u" sounds like "g" in *g*o.

"g" before "e" and "i" sounds like "g" in *g*em or "j" in *j*oy.

"gh" sounds like "g" in *g*o.

"gl" sounds like "lli" in mi*lli*on.

"gn" sounds like "ny" in ca*ny*on.

"h" is always silent.

"r" is always trilled.

"s" between vowels and before voiced consonants sounds like "z" in *z*ebra.

"s" when it is initial, or is doubled in writing, or comes before voiceless consonants sounds like "ss" in mi*ss*.

"z" sounds like "ts" in ca*ts* or like "dz" in a*dz*e.

All consonants written double in Italian are pronounced twice as long as their single counterparts.

In the pronunciations, the stress or main accent in a word is indicated by an accent mark (') after the stressed syllable.

**brother,** fratello *frah-tel'-loh*
**four,** quattro *kwaht'-troh*
**city,** città *cheet-tah'*
**lightning,** fulmine *fool'-mee-neh*

# Salutations and Greetings

Even before you learn anything else in a foreign language, you will want to learn how to greet people. Here are some short expressions that you will find easy to learn and to use when you meet people in a foreign land or along the way, perhaps on the ship or the plane.

**Good morning.**
Buon giorno.
*Bwon jor'-noh*

**Good day.**
Buon giorno
*Bwon jor'-noh.*

**Good afternoon.**
Buon giorno.
*Bwon jor'-noh.*

**Good evening.**
Buona sera.
*Bwoh'-nah seh'-rah.*

**Good-bye.**
Addio.
*Ad-dee'-yoh.*

**Good-night.**
Buona notte.
*Bwoh'-nah not'-teh.*

**How are you?**
Come sta?
*Ko'-meh stah?*

**Well, thank you. And you?**
Bene, grazie. E Lei?
*Beh'-neh, grah'-tsee-yeh. Eh leh'-ee?*

**How is Mr. . . . ?**
Come sta il signor . . . ?
*Ko'-meh stah eel seen-yor' . . ?*

**How is Mrs. . . . ?**
Come sta la signora . . . ?
*Ko'-meh stah lah seen-yoh'-rah . . . ?*

**Is Miss . . . well?**
Sta bene la signorina . . . ?
*Stah beh'-neh lah seen-yoh-ree'-nah . . . ?*

**May I present my wife?**
Posso presentare mia moglie?
*Pos'-soh preh-zen-tah'-reh mee'-yah mo'-lyeh?*

**This is my husband.**
Questo è mio marito.
*Kwehs'-toh e mee'-yoh mah-ree'-toh.*

**Pleased to meet you.**
Piacere di conoscerla.
*Pyah-che'-reh dee ko-no'-sher-lah.*

**This is my friend.**
Questo è il mio amico (m).
*Kwehs'-toh e eel mee'-yoh ah-mee'-koh.*

**This is my friend.**
Questa è la mia amica (f).
*Kwehs'-tah e lah mee'-yah ah-mee'-kah.*

**This is my mother and my father.**
Questa è mia madre e questo è mio padre.
*Kwehs'-tah e mee'-yah mah'-dreh eh kwes'-toh e mee'-yoh pah'-dreh.*

**This is my sister and my brother.**
Questa è mia sorella e questo è mio fratello.
*Kwes'-tah e mee'-yah so-rel'-lah eh kwes'-toh e mee'-yoh frah-tel'-loh.*

**Is this your daughter?**
È questa Sua figlia?
*E kwes'-tah soo'-ah feel'-yah?*

**Is this your son?**
È questo Suo figlio?
*E kwes'-toh soo-oh feel'-yoh?*

**I hope that we will meet again.**
Spero che ci incontriamo di nuovo.
*Spe'-roh keh chee een-kon-tree-yah'-moh dee nwoh'-voh.*

**I'll be seeing you.**
Arrivederci.
*Ahr-ree-veh-der'-chee.*

**I'll see you tomorrow.**
Ci vediamo domani.
*Chee veh-dee-yah'-moh doh-mah'-nee.*

**Excuse me.**
Mi scusi.
*Mee skoo'-zee.*

**Pardon me.**
Scusi.
*Skoo'-zee.*

**I'm very sorry.**
Mi dispiace molto. / Mi rincresce molto.
*Mee dees-pyah'-cheh mol'-toh. / Mee reen-kre'-sheh mol'-toh*

**Don't mention it.**
Non c'è di che.
*Non che dee keh.*

**You're welcome.**
Prego.
*Preh'-goh.*

**Please.**
Per favore. / Per piacere.
*Per fah-voh'-reh. / Per pyah-
cheh'-reh.*

**With pleasure.**
Con piacere.
*Kon pyah-cheh'-reh.*

**Good luck!**
Buona fortuna.
*Bwoh'-nah for-too'-nah!*

# The Weather

The weather is one thing everyone has in common, and it is a universal topic of conversation. The phrases given here — combined with a bit of added vocabulary — are easily mastered.

**It's nice weather today.**
Oggi fa bel tempo.
*Oj'-jee fah bel tem'-poh.*

**It's bad weather today.**
Oggi fa brutto tempo.
*Oj'-jee fah broot'-toh tem'-poh.*

**It's cold.**
Fa freddo.
*Fah frehd'-doh.*

**It's warm.**
Fa caldo.
*Fah kahl'-doh.*

**Is it raining?**
Piove?
*Pyo'-veh?*

**Yes, it's raining.**
Sì, piove.
*See, pyo'-veh.*

**No, it's not raining.**
No, non piove.
*Noh, non pyo'-veh.*

**It's snowing.**
Nevica.
*Neh'-vee-kah.*

**It rains (snows) here every day.**
Qui piove (nevica) tutti i giorni.
*Kwee pyo'-veh (neh'-vee-kah) toot'-tee ee jor'-nee.*

**It's beginning to rain (to snow).**
Comincia a piovere (nevicare).
*Ko-meen'-chah ah pyo'-veh-reh (neh-vee-kah'-reh).*

**It often rains (snows) here.**
Qui piove (nevica) spesso.
*Kwee pyo'-veh (neh'-vee-kah) spes'-soh.*

**It will rain (snow) tomorrow.**
Domani pioverà (nevicherà).
*Doh-mah'-nee pyo-ve-rah' (neh-vee-ke-rah').*

**It rained (snowed) yesterday.**
Ha piovuto (nevicato) ieri.
*Ah pyo-voo'-toh (neh-vee-kah'-toh) ye'-ree.*

**It has stopped raining (snowing).**
Ha cessato di piovere (nevicare).
*Ah ches-sah'-toh dee pyo'-ve-reh (neh-vee-kah'-reh).*

**It's windy.**
Tira vento.
*Tee'-rah ven'-toh.*

**There's a lot of fog.**
C'è molta nebbia.
*Che mol'-tah nehb'-byah.*

**The sun is rising.**
Il sole si leva.
*Eel so'-leh see leh'-vah.*

**The sun is setting.**
Il sole tramonta.
*Eel so'-leh trah-mon'-tah.*

**How is the weather?**
Che tempo fa?
*Keh tem'-poh fah?*

**I need an umbrella.**
Ho bisogno d'un ombrello.
*Oh bee-zo'-nyoh doon om-brel'-loh.*

| I see . . . | I like . . . | I'm afraid of . . |
|---|---|---|
| Vedo . . . | Mi piace . . . | Ho paura di . . . |
| *Veh'-doh . . .* | *Mee pyah'-cheh...* | *Ah pah-oo'-rah dee . . .* |

**the rain.**
la pioggia.
*lah pyoj'-jah.*

**the wind.**
il vento.
*eel ven'-toh.*

**the snow.**
la neve.
*lah neh'-veh.*

**the ice.**
il ghiaccio.
*eel gyahch'-choh.*

**the sky.**
il cielo.
*eel chyeh'-loh.*

**the sun.**
il sole.
*eel soh'-leh.*

**the moon.**
la luna.
*la loo'-nah.*

**the stars.**
le stelle.
*leh stel'-leh.*

**a star.**
una stella.
*oo'-nah stel'-lah.*

**a rainbow.**
un arcobaleno.
*oon ahr-koh-bah-leh'-noh.*

**a cloud.**
una nuvola.
*oo'-nah noo'-voh-lah.*

**the clouds.**
le nuvole.
*leh noo'-voh-leh.*

**the lightning.**
il fulmine, i lampi.
*eel fool'-mee-neh, ee lahm'-pee.*

**the thunder.**
il tuono.
*eel twoh'-noh.*

**the storm.**
la tempesta, il temporale.
*lah tem-pe'-stah, eel tem-poh-rah'-leh.*

**Will it be cool there?**
Farà fresco là?
*Fah-rah' fres'-koh lah?*

**Will it be damp there?**
Ci sarà umidità?
*Chee sah-rah' oo-mee-dee-tah'?*

**Should I take a sweater?**
Dovrei prendere un maglione?
*Dov-reh'-ee pren'-deh-reh oon mah-lyoh'-neh?*

**a jacket?**
una giacca?
*oo'-nah jahk'-kah?*

**a raincoat?**
un impermeabile?
*oon eem-per-meh-yah'-bee-leh?*

**It's lightning.**
Lampeggia.
*Lahm-pej'-jah.*

**It's thundering.**
Tuona.
*Twoh'-nah.*

**Warm weather.**
Tempo caldo.
*Tem'-poh kahl'-doh.*

**Cold weather.**
Tempo freddo.
*Tem'-poh frehd'-doh.*

**Warm water.**
Acqua calda.
*Ahk'-kwah kahl'-dah.*

**Hot water.**
Acqua caldissima.
*Ahk'-kwah kahl-dees'-see-mah.*

**Cold water.**
Acqua fredda.
*Ahk'-kwah frehd'-dah.*

# General Expressions

In this section you will find the most useful expressions —
the ones you will use over and over again. They are the
phrases that you should have on the tip of the tongue,
ready for immediate use — particularly those that express
desire or volition. Here they have been kept short for
easy acquisition and speedy communication. You will
see them appear again and again in other sections of this
book, where they are used in particular situations.

**What is your name?**
Come si chiama Lei?
*Ko'-meh see kyah'-mah*
*leh'-ee?*

**My name is . . .**
Mi chiamo . . .
*Mee kyah'-moh . . .*

**What is his (her) name?**
Come si chiama lui (lei)?
*Ko'-meh see kyah'-mah*
*loo'-ee (leh'-ee)?*

**I don't know.**
Non lo so.
*Non loh soh.*

His (her) name is . . .
Si chiama . . .
*See kyah'-mah . . .*

**Do you know him (her)?**
Lo (La) conosce?
*Loh (lah) ko-no'-sheh?*

**Yes, I know him (her).**
Sí, lo (la) conosco.
*See, loh (lah) ko-nos'-koh.*

**No, I don't know him (her).**
No, non lo (la) conosco.
*Noh, non loh (lah) ko-nos'-koh.*

**I know you.**
La conosco.
*Lah ko-nos'-koh.*

**Where do you live?**
Dove abita Lei?
*Do'-veh ah'-bee-tah leh'-ee?*

**I live here.**
Abito qui.
*Ah'-bee-toh kwee.*

**At which hotel are you staying?**
A quale albergo scende?
*Ah kwah'-leh ahl-ber'-goh shen'-deh?*

**She's a beautiful woman.**
È una bella donna.
*E oo'-nah bel'-lah don'-nah.*

**She's a pretty girl.**
È una ragazza graziosa.
*E oo'-nah rah-gaht'-tsah grah-tsyoh'-zah.*

**He's a handsome man.**
È un bell'uomo.
*E oon bel-lwoh'-moh.*

**I love you.**
Ti amo.
*Tee ah'-moh.*

**I love her.**
L'amo.
*Lah'-moh.*

**I love him.**
Lo amo.
*Loh ah'-moh.*

**Do you know where he lives?**
Sa dove lui abita?
*Sah do'-veh loo'-ee ah'-bee-tah?*

**Do you speak English?**
Parla Lei inglese?
*Pahr'-lah leh'-ee een-gleh'-zeh?*

**Please say it in English.**
Lo dica in inglese, per favore.
*Loh dee'-kah een een-gleh'-zeh, per fah-voh'-reh.*

**Is there anyone here who speaks English?**
C'è qualcuno qui che parla inglese?
*Che kwahl-koo'-noh kwee keh pahr'-lah een-gleh'-zeh?*

**Do you understand?**
Capisce?
*Kah-pee'-sheh?*

**Yes, I understand.**
Sì, capisco.
*See, kah-pees'-koh.*

**No, I don't understand.**
No, non capisco.
*Noh, non kah-pees'-koh.*

**I understand a little.**
Capisco un poco.
*Kah-pees'-koh oon poh'-koh.*

**I don't understand everything.**
Non capisco tutto.
*Non kah-pees'-koh toot'-toh.*

**Please speak more slowly.**
Parli più lentamente (adagio), per favore.
*Pahr'-lee pyoo len-tah-men'-teh (ah-dah'-joh) per fah-voh'-reh.*

**Please repeat.**
Ripeta, per favore.
*Ree-peh'-tah, per fah-voh'-reh.*

**What did you say?**
Che cosa ha detto?
*Keh ko'-zah ah det'-toh?*

**How do you say that in Italian?**
Come si dice questo in italiano?
*Ko'-meh see dee'-cheh kwes'-toh een ee-tah-lyah'-noh?*

**What does that mean?**
Che significa questo?
*Keh see-nyee'-fee-kah
kwes'-toh?*

**What do you mean?**
Che vuol dire?
*Keh vwohl dee'-reh?*

**You are right (wrong).**
Lei ha ragione (torto).
*Leh'-ee ah rah-joh'-neh
(tor'-toh).*

**He is right (wrong).**
Lui ha ragione (torto).
*Loo'-ee ah rah-joh'-neh
(tor'-toh).*

**Without doubt.**
Senza dubbio.
*Sehn'-tsah doob'-byoh.*

**Where are you going?**
Dove va Lei? Dove va?
*Do'-veh vah leh'-ee?*

**Where is he going?**
Dove va lui? Dove va?
*Do'-veh vah loo'-ee?*

**Where are we going?**
Dove andiamo?
*Do'-veh ahn-dyah'-moh?*

**I will wait here.**
Aspetterò qui.
*Ah-spet-te-roh' kwee.*

**How long must I wait?**
Quanto tempo devo aspettare?
*Kwahn'-toh tem'-poh deh'-voh ah-spet-tah'-reh?*

**Wait here until I come back.**
Aspetti qui finchè torni.
*Ah-spet'-tee kwee feen-keh' tor'-nee.*

**Come here.**
Venga qua.
*Ven'-gah kwah.*

**Is it near here?**
È qui vicino?
*E kwee vee-chee'-noh?*

**Come in.**
Avanti.
*Ah-vahn'-tee.*

**Is it far from here?**
È lontano da qui?
*E lon-tah'-noh dah kwee?*

**Bring me . . .**
Mi porti . . .
*Mee por'-tee . . .*

**Tell me . . .**
Mi dica . . .
*Mee dee'-kah . . .*

**Give me . . .**
Mi dia . . .
*Mee dee'-yah . . .*

**Show me . . .**
Mi mostri . . .
*Mee mos'-tree . . .*

**Send me . . .**
Mi mandi . . .
*Mee mahn'-dee . . .*

**Write to me . . .**
Mi scrıva . . .
*Mee skree'-vah . .*

**I need . . .**
Ho bisogno di . . .
*Oh bee-zo'-nyoh dee . . .*

**I would like . . .**
Vorrei . . .
*Vor-reh'-ee . . .*

**I want . . .**
Voglio (Desidero) . . .
*Vo'-lyoh (deh-zee'-de-roh) . . .*

**I don't want . . .**
Non voglio (desidero) . .
*Non vo'-lyoh (deh-zee'-de-roh) . . .*

**I can do that.**
Posso fare questo.
*Pos'-soh fah'-reh kwes'-toh.*

**I cannot do that.**
Non posso fare questo.
*Non pos'-soh fah'-reh kwes'-toh.*

**Have you . . . ?**
Ha Lei . . . ?
*Ah leh'-ee . . . ?*

**Are you . . . ?**
È Lei . . . ?
*E leh'-ee . . . ?*

**Where is . . . ?**
Dov'è . . . ?
*Do-ve' . . . ?*

**Where are . . . ?**
Dove sono . . . ?
*Do'-veh soh'-noh . . . ?*

**It's possible.**
È possibile.
*E pos-see'-bee-leh.*

**It's impossible.**
E impossibile.
*È eem-pos-see'-bee-leh.*

# Emergencies

You will probably never need to use any of the brief cries, entreaties, or commands that appear here, but accidents do happen, items may be mislaid or stolen, and mistakes do occur. If an emergency does arise, it will probably be covered by one of these expressions.

**Help!**
Aiuto! Al soccorso!
*Ah-yoo'-toh*! *Ahl sok-kor'-soh*!

**Help me!**
Mi aiuti!
*Mee ah-yoo'-tee*!

**There has been an accident!**
C'è stato un incidente!
*Che stah'-toh oon een-chee-den'-teh*!

**Stop!**
Alt! Fermate!
*Ahlt*! *Fer-mah'-teh*!

**Hurry up!**
Faccia presto!
*Fahch'-chah pres'-toh*!

**Look out!**
Attenzione!
*Aht-ten-tsyoh'-neh*!

**Send for a doctor!**
Faccia venire un medico!
*Fahch'-chah veh-nee'-reh oon meh'-dee-koh!*

**Fire!**
Fuoco!
*Fwoh'-koh!*

**What happened?**
Che cosa è successo?
*Keh ko'-zah e sooch-chehs'-soh?*

**Don't worry!**
Non si preoccupi!
*Non see preh-ok'-koo-pee!*

**I missed the train (bus) (plane).**
Ho perduto il treno (autobus) (aeroplano).
*Oh per-doo'-toh eel treh'-noh (ow-toh-boos') (ah-eh-roh-plah'-noh).*

**I've been robbed!**
Sono stato derubato!
*Soh'-noh stah'-toh deh-roo-bah'-toh!*

**That man stole my money!**
Quell'uomo mi ha rubato il denaro!
*Kwel-lwoh'-moh mee ah roo-bah'-toh eel deh-nah'-roh!*

**Call the police!**
Chiami la polizia!
*Kyah'-mee lah poh-lee-tsee'-yah!*

**I have lost my money!**
Ho perduto il mio denaro!
*Oh per-doo'-toh eel mee-yoh deh-nah'-roh!*

**Poison!**
Veleno!
*Veh-leh'-noh!*

**Police!**
Polizia!
*Poh-lee-tsee'-yah!*

**What's the matter?**
Che c'è?
*Keh che?*

**I have lost my passport!**
Ho perduto il mio passaporte!
*Oh per-doo'-toh eel mee'-yoh pahs-sah-por'-teh!*

**It's an American (British) passport.**
È un passaporte americano (inglese).
*E oon pahs-sah-por'-teh ah-meh-ree-kah'-noh (een-gleh'-zeh).*

**Stay where you are!**
Rimanete dove siete!
*Ree-mah-neh'-teh do'-veh sye'-teh!*

**Don't move!**
Non si muova!
*Non see mwoh'-vah!*

# Signs and Notices

You could probably get along in a foreign land without speaking a word if only you could read the signs and notices that are posted and displayed as directions and advertising. A sign is an immediate communication to him who can read it, and the pronunciation doesn't matter. Here are the messages of some common signs. Some will help you to avoid embarrassment, and others danger. And some of them will merely make life more pleasant.

**A DESTRA,** To the right
**A SINISTRA,** To the left
**ALT,** Stop
**ALLARME D'INCENDIO,** Fire alarm
**APERTO,** Open
**APPARTAMENTI MOBIGLIATI D'AFFITTARE**
    Furnished rooms to let
**ASCIUGAMANI,** Hand towels

**ASPETTATE,** Wait
**ATTENZIONE,** Caution
**AVANTI,** Go
**AVVISO,** Warning
**CALDO,** Warm
**CASSIERE,** Cashier
**CHIESA,** Church
**CHIUSO,** Closed
**COLLINA,** Hill
**CURVA,** Curve
**CURVA PERICOLOSA,** Dangerous curve
**DEVIAZIONE,** Detour
**DIVIETO DI SOSTA,** No parking
**DONNE,** Women
**ENTRATA,** Entrance
**ENTRATA LIBERA,** Admission free
**È PERICOLOSO,** It's dangerous
**È PROIBITO PASSARE,** No thoroughfare
**È VIETATO L'INGRESSO,** Keep out
**È VIETATO FUMARE,** No smoking
**FREDDO,** Cold
**GABINETTO,** Lavatory, toilet
**INCROCIO FERROVIA,** Railroad crossing
**INCROCIO PERICOLOSO,** Dangerous crossroad
**INFORMAZIONI,** Information
**INGRESSO,** Entrance
**LAVORI IN CORSO,** Men working
**LA VIA CHIUSA,** No thoroughfare
**LIBERO,** Free
**NON BEVETE L'ACQUA,** Do not drink the water
**NON ENTRATE,** Do not enter
**NON GIRATE A DESTRA,** No right turn
**NON GIRATE A SINISTRA,** No left turn

**NON TOCCATE,** Do not touch
**OCCUPATO,** Occupied
**PEDAGGIO,** Toll
**PERICOLO,** Danger
**PONTE STRETTO,** Narrow bridge
**POSTEGGIO,** Parking
**PROIBITO,** Forbidden
**RALLENTARE,** Slow, Go slow
**RITIRATA,** Toilet
**SALA D'ASPETTO,** Waiting room
**SALA DA PRANZO,** Dining room
**SCUOLA,** School
**SENSO UNICO,** One way
**SIGNORE,** Women
**SIGNORI,** Men
**SI PERMETTE FUMARE,** Smoking allowed
**SPINGETE,** Push
**STANZA DA BAGNO,** Bathroom
**STRADA STRETTA,** Narrow road
**SUONATE,** Ring
**TENETE LA DESTRA,** Keep to the right
**TIRATE,** Pull
**UOMINI,** Men
**USCITA,** Exit
**VIETATO,** Forbidden
**VIETATO IL POSTEGGIO,** No parking

# Numbers, Time and Dates

You may only want to count your change or make an appointment or catch a train, but you will need to know the essentials of counting and telling time if you wish to stay on schedule, buy gifts, or pay for accommodations. In Europe, you should remember, time is told by a twenty-four hour system. Thus 10 P.M. in Italy is 2200 and 10:30 P.M. is 2230.

## *Cardinal Numbers*

**one**
uno, una, un, un'
*oo'-noh, oo'-nah, oon, oon'*

**two**
due
*doo'-eh*

**three**
tre
*tre*

**four**
quattro
*kwaht'-troh*

**five**
cinque
*cheen'-kweh*

**six**
sei
*seh'-ee*

**seven**
sette
*set'-teh*

**eight**
otto
*ot'-toh*

**nine**
nove
*no'-veh*

**ten**
dieci
*dyeh'-chee*

**eleven**
undici
*oon'-dee-chee*

**twelve**
dodici
*do'-dee-chee*

**thirteen**
tredici
*tre'-dee-chee*

**fourteen**
quattordici
*kwaht-tor'-dee-chee*

**fifteen**
quindici
*kween'-dee-chee*

**sixteen**
sedici
*seh'-dee-chee*

**seventeen**
diciassette
*dee-chahs-set'-teh*

**eighteen**
diciotto
*dee-chot'-toh*

**nineteen**
diciannove
*dee-chahn-no'-veh*

**twenty**
venti
*ven'-tee*

**twenty-one**
ventuno
*ven-too'-noh*

**twenty-two**
ventidue
*ven-tee-doo'-eh*

**thirty**
trenta
*tren'-tah*

**thirty·one**
trentuno
*tren-too'-noh*

**forty**
quaranta
*kwah-rahn'-tah*

**fifty**
cinquanta
*cheen-kwahn'-tah*

**sixty**
sessanta
*ses-sahn'-tah*

**seventy**
settanta
*set-tahn'-tah*

**eighty**
ottanta
*ot-tahn'-tah*

**ninety**
novanta
*no-vahn'-tah*

**one hundred**
cento
*chen'-toh*

**two hundred**
duecento
*doo-eh-chen'-toh*

**three hundred**
trecento
*tre-chen'-toh*

**five hundred**
cinquecento
*cheen-kweh-chen'-toh*

**one thousand**
mille
*meel'-leh*

**one million**
un milione
*oon mee-lyoh'-neh*

**nineteen hundred seventy- . . .**
mille novecento settanta- . . .
*meel'-leh no-veh-chen'-toh set-tahn'-tah- . . .*

**one man**
un uomo
*oon woh'-moh*

**one woman**
una donna
*oo'-nah don'-nah*

**one child**
un bambino (un fanciullo)
*oon bahm-bee'-noh (fahn-choolʼ-loh)*

**two children**
due bambini (fanciulli)
*doo'-eh bahm-bee'-nee (fahn-choolʼ-lee).*

**two women**
due donne
*doo'-eh don'-neh*

**two men**
due uomini
*doo'-eh woh'-mee-nee*

## Some Ordinal Numbers

**the first**
il primo
*eel pree'-moh*

**the second**
il secondo
*eel seh-kon'-doh*

**the third**
il terzo
*eel ter'-tsoh*

**the fourth**
il quarto
*eel kwahr'-toh*

**the fifth**
il quinto
*eel kween'-toh*

**the sixth**
il sesto
*eel ses'-toh*

**the seventh**
il settimo
*eel set'-tee-moh*

**the eighth**
l'ottavo
*lot-tah'-voh*

**the ninth**
il nono
*eel noh'-noh*

**the tenth**
il decimo
*eel deh'-chee-moh*

**the first man**
il primo uomo
*eel pree'-moh woh'-moh*

**the first woman**
la prima donna
*lah pree'-mah don'-nah*

**the first child**
il primo bambino
*eel pree'-moh bahm-bee'-noh*

**the fifth floor**
il quinto piano
*eel kween'-toh pyah'-noh*

**the third day**
il terzo giorno
*eel ter'-tsoh johr'-noh*

**the fourth street**
la quarta strada
*lah kwahr'-tah strah'-dah*

**the second building**
il secondo edifizio
*eel seh-kohn'-doh eh-dee-fee'-tsyoh*

## Telling Time

**What time is it?**
Che ora è?
*Keh oh'-rah e?*

**It's one o'clock.**
È l'una.
*E loo'-nah.*

**It's two o'clock.**
Sono le due.
*Soh'-noh leh doo'-eh.*

**It's a quarter after two.**
Sono le due e un quarto.
*Soh'-noh leh doo'-eh eh
    oon kwahr'-toh.*

**It's half-past two.**
Sono le due e mezza.
*Soh'-noh leh doo'-eh eh med'-dzah.*

**It's a quarter till two.**
Sono le due meno un quarto.
*Soh'-noh leh doo'-eh meh'-noh oon kwahr'-toh.*

**It's ten after two.**
Sono le due e dieci.
*Soh'-noh leh doo'-eh eh
    dyeh'-chee.*

**It's ten till two.**
Sono le due meno dieci.
*Soh'-noh leh doo'-eh meh'-
    noh dyeh'-chee.*

**It's five o'clock.**
Sono le cinque.
*Soh'-noh leh cheen'-kweh.*

**It's ten o'clock.**
Sono le dieci.
*Soh'-noh leh dyeh'-chee.*

**It's noon.**
È mezzogiorno.
*E med-dzoh-jor'-noh.*

**It's midnight.**
È mezzanotte.
*E med-dzah-not'-teh.*

**It's early.**
È presto.
*E pre-stoh.*

**It's late.**
È tardi.
*E tahr'-dee.*

**one second**
un secondo
*oon seh-kon'-doh*

**five seconds**
cinque secondi
*cheen'-kweh seh-kon'-dee*

**one minute**
un minuto
*oon mee-noo'-toh*

**five minutes**
cinque minuti
*cheen'-kweh mee-noo'-tee*

**one quarter hour**
un quarto d'ora
*oon kwahr'-toh doh'-rah*

**one half hour**
una mezz'ora
*oo'-nah med-dzoh'-rah*

**one hour**
un'ora
*oon oh'-rah*

**five hours**
cinque ore
*cheen'-kweh oh'-reh*

**At what time are you leaving?**
A che ora parte?
*Ah keh oh'-rah pahr'-teh?*

**When do you arrive?**
Quando arriva?
*Kwahn'-doh ahr-ree'-vah?*

**When do you arrive?**
Quando arriva?
*Kwahn'-doh ahr-ree'-vah?*

**When will we arrive?**
Quando arriveremo?
*Kwahn'-doh ahr-ree-veh-reh'-moh?*

**When shall we meet?**
Quando ci incontreremo?
*Kwahn'-doh chee een-kon-treh-reh'-moh?*

**Meet me here at five o'clock.**
M'incontri qui alle cinque.
*Meen-kon'-tree kwee ahl'-leh cheen'-kweh.*

**At what time do you get up?**
A che ora si alza?
*Ah keh oh'-rah see ahl'-tsah?*

**At what time do you go to bed?**
A che ora si corica?
*Ah keh oh'-rah see koh'-ree-kah?*

## Dates

**today**
oggi
*oj'-jee*

**tomorrow**
domani
*doh-mah'-nee*

**yesterday**
ieri
*ye'-ree*

**one day**
un giorno
*oon jor'-noh*

**two days**
due giorni
*doo'-eh jor'-nee*

**five days**
cinque giorni
*cheen'-kweh jor'-nee*

**the day after tomorrow**
dopo domani
*doh'-poh doh-mah'-nee*

**the day before yesterday**
l'altro ieri
*lahl'-troh ye'-ree*

**the morning**
la mattina
*lah maht-tee'-nah*

**the afternoon**
il pomeriggio
*eel poh-me-reej'-joh*

**the evening**
la sera
*lah seh'-rah*

**the night**
la notte
*lah not'-teh*

**the week**
la settimana
*lah set-tee-mah'-nah*

**the month**
il mese
*eel meh'-zeh*

**the year**
l'anno
*lahn'-noh*

**last week**
la settimana scorsa
*lah set-tee-mah'-nah skor'-sah*

**last month**
il mese scorso
*eel meh'-zeh skor'-soh*

**last year**
l'anno scorso
*lahn'-noh skor'-soh*

**this week**
questa settimana
*kwes'-tah set-tee-mah'-nah*

**this month**
questo mese
*kwes'-toh meh'-zeh*

**this year**
quest'anno
*kwest-ahn'-noh*

**next week**
la settimana ventura (prossima)
*lah set-tee-mah'-nah ven-too'-rah (pros'-see-mah)*

**next month**
il mese venturo (prossimo)
*eel meh'-zeh ven-too'-roh
   (pros'-see-moh)*

**next year**
l'anno venturo (prossimo)
*lahn'-noh ven-too'-roh
   (pros'-see-moh)*

**this morning**
stamattina
*stah-maht-tee'-nah*

**yesterday morning**
ieri mattina
*ye'-ree maht-tee'-nah*

**tomorrow morning**
domani mattina
*doh-mah'-nee maht-tee'-nah*

**this evening**
stasera
*stah-seh'-rah*

**yesterday evening**
ieri sera
*ye'-ree seh'-rah*

**tomorrow evening**
domani sera
*doh-mah'-nee seh'-rah*

**every day**
tutti i giorni (ogni giorno)
*toot'-tee ee jor'-nee (oh'-
   nyee jor'-noh)*

**two days ago**
due giorni fa
*doo'-eh jor'-nee fah*

## *The Days of the Week*

**Monday**
lunedì
*loo-neh-dee'*

**Tuesday**
martedì
*mahr-teh-dee'*

**Wednesday**
mercoledì
*mer-koh-leh-dee'*

**Thursday**
giovedì
*joh-veh-dee'*

**Friday**
venerdì
*ve-ner-dee'*

**Saturday**
sabato
*sah'-bah-toh*

**Sunday**
domenica
*doh-meh'-nee-kah*

## *The Months of the Year*

**January**
gennaio
*jen-nah'-yoh*

**February**
febbraio
*feb-brah'-yoh*

**March**
marzo
*mahr'-tsoh*

**April**
aprile
*ah-pree'-leh*

**May**
maggio
*mahj'-joh*

**June**
giugno
*joo'-nyoh*

**July**
luglio
*loo'-lyoh*

**August**
agosto
*ah-go'-stoh*

**September**
settembre
*set-tem'-breh*

**October**
ottobre
*ot-to'-breh*

**November**
novembre
*no-vem'-breh*

**December**
dicembre
*dee-chem'-breh*

## The Seasons

**the spring**
la primavera
*lah pree-mah-veh'-rah*

**the summer**
l'estate
*le-stah'-teh*

**the autumn**
l'autunno
*low-toon'-noh*

**the winter**
l'inverno
*leen-ver'-noh*

# Changing Money

Whether poet or businessman, you will need cash as you travel. Sooner or later every traveler meets the problem of how to manage the exchange. The following phrases cover most situations you will encounter. You will help yourself if you obtain the latest official exchange rate before you leave home, and it can do no harm if you familiarize yourself with the sizes, shapes, and even colors of the various coins and bills. It is wise, too, to take along a small amount of the foreign currency for immediate use on arrival.

**Where is the nearest bank?**
Dov'è la banca più vicina?
*Do-ve' lah bahn'-kah pyoo vee-chee'-nah?*

**Please write the address.**
Scriva l'indirizzo, per piacere
*Skree'-vah leen-dee-reet'-tsoh, per pyah-cheh'-reh.*

**I would like to cash this check.**
Vorrei incassare quest'assegno.
*Vor-reh'-ee een-kahs-sah'-reh kwest-ahs-seh'-nyoh.*

**Will you cash this check?**
Vuole scontarmi quest'assegno?
*Vwoh'-leh skon-tahr'-mee kwest-ahs-seh'-nyoh?*

**Do you accept travelers' checks?**
Accettate assegni di viaggio?
*Ahch-chet-tah'-teh ahs-seh'-nyee dee vyahj'-joh?*

**I want to change some money.**
Voglio cambiare del denaro.
*Voh'-lyoh kahm-byah'-reh del deh-nah'-roh.*

**What kind?**
Che specie?
*Keh speh'-chyeh?*

| **Dollars.** | **Pounds.** |
|---|---|
| Dollari. | Libbre. |
| *Dol'-lah-ree.* | *Leeb'-breh.* |

**What is the rate of exchange for the dollar (pound)?**
Qual'è il cambio in dollari (libbre)?
*Kwahl-e' eel kahm'-byoh een dol'-lah-ree (leeb'-breh)?*

**Your passport, please.**
Il Suo passaporto, per piacere.
*Eel soo'-woh pahs-sah-por'-toh, per pyah-cheh'-reh.*

**How much do you wish to change?**
Quanto desidera cambiare?
*Kwahn'-toh deh-zee'-deh-rah kahm-byah'-reh?*

**I want to change ten dollars.**
Voglio cambiare dieci dollari.
*Voh'-lyoh kahm-byah'-reh dyah'-chee dol'-lah-ree.*

**Go to that clerk's window.**
Vada allo sportello di quell'impiegato.
*Vah'-dah ahl'-loh spor-tel'-loh dee kwel'-leem-pyeh-gah'-toh.*

**Here's the money.**
Ecco il denaro.
*Ek'-koh eel deh-nah'-roh.*

**Please give me some small change.**
Per piacere, mi dia della moneta spicciola.
*Per pyah-cheh'-reh, mee dee'-yah del'-lah moh-neh'-tah speech'-choh-lah.*

**Here's your change.**
Ecco il resto.
*Ek'-koh eel res'-toh.*

**Please count to see if it's right.**
Lo conti, per favore, per vedere se è giusto.
*Loh kon'-tee, per fah-voh'-reh, per veh-deh'-reh seh e joos'-toh.*

**Please sign this receipt.**
Firmi questa ricevuta, per piacere.
*Feer'-mee kwes'-tah ree-cheh-voo'-tah, per pyah-cheh'-reh.*

**Can I change money here at the hotel?**
Posso cambiare denaro qui in albergo?
*Pos'-soh kahm-byah'-reh deh-nah'-roh kwee een ahl-ber'-goh?*

**I'm expecting some money by mail.**
Aspetto denaro per la posta.
*Ah-spet'-toh deh-nah'-roh per lah pos'-tah.*

# Customs

Your first experience with Italian may be with the personnel or fellow passengers on a ship or a plane, but you will really begin to use the language when you come to customs. Here are some phrases that will speed your entry into the country and get you on your way again.

**Have you anything to declare?**
Ha qualcosa da dichiarare?
*Ah kwahl-ko'-zah dah dee-kyah-rah'-reh?*

**I have nothing to declare.**
Non ho niente da dichiarare.
*Non oh nyen'-teh dah dee-kyah-rah'-reh.*

**Your passport, please.**
Il passaporto, prego.
*Eel pahs-sah-por'-toh, preh'-goh.*

**Here is my passport.**
Ecco il mio passaporto.
*Ek'-koh eel mee'-yoh pahs-sah-por'-toh.*

**Are these your bags?**
Sono queste le Sue valige?
*Soh'-noh kwes'-teh leh soo'-weh vah-lee'-jeh?*

**Yes, and here are the keys.**
Sì, ed ecco le chiavi.
*See, ed ek'-koh leh kyah'-vee.*

| | |
|---|---|
| **Open this box.** | **Close your bags.** |
| Apra questa scatola. | Chiuda le valige. |
| *Ah'-prah kwes'-tah skah'-toh-lah.* | *Kyoo'-dah leh vah-lee'-jeh.* |

**Have you any cigarettes or tobacco?**
Ha delle sigarette o tabacco?
*Ah del'-leh see-gah-ret'-teh oh tah-bahk'-koh?*

**I have only some cigarettes.**
Ho soltanto qualche sigaretta.
*Oh sol-tahn'-toh kwahl'-keh see-gah-ret'-teh.*

**You must pay duty.**
Lei deve pagare dazio.
*Leh'-ee deh'-veh pah-gah'-reh dah'-tsyoh.*

**They are for my personal use.**
Sono per il mio uso personale.
*Soh'-noh per eel mee'-yoh oo'-zoh per-soh-nah'-leh.*

| | |
|---|---|
| **How much must I pay?** | **You must pay . . .** |
| Quanto devo pagare? | Deve pagare . . . |
| *Kwahn'-toh deh'-voh pah-gah'-reh?* | *Deh'-veh pah-gah'-reh . . .* |

**May I go now?**
Posso andare adesso?
*Pos'-soh ahn-dah'-reh ah-dehs'-soh?*

**Is that all?**
Questo è tutto?
*Kwes'-toh e toot'-toh?*

**Porter, please carry this luggage.**
Facchino, per piacere, porti questo bagaglio.
*Fahk-kee'-noh, per pyah-cheh'-reh por'-tee kwes'-toh bah-gahl'-yoh.*

# At the Hotel

Your accommodations may be a deluxe hotel, a modest hotel, a pension, or whatever, but it is important to be able to express your needs to be sure you get what you want. Outside of the cities, of course, few people are likely to be able to help you if you do not speak Italian, so we have given you the most useful expressions to cover most situations. They may make the difference between getting the room you want and having to settle for something less.

**Which is the best hotel?**
Qual'è il miglior albergo?
*Kwahl-e' eel meel-yohr'*
*ahl-ber'-goh?*

**This is a good hotel.**
Questo è un buon albergo.
*Kwes'-toh e oon bwon ahl-*
*ber'-goh.*

**I like this hotel.**
Mi piace quest'albergo.
*Mee pyah'-cheh kwest-ahl-ber'-goh.*

**I would like to have a room here.**
Vorrei prendere una camera qui.
*Vor-reh'-ee pren'-de-reh oo'-nah kah'-meh-rah kwee.*

**A single room.**
Una camera a un letto.
*Oo'-nah kah'-meh-rah ah oon let'-toh.*

**A double room.**
Una camera a due letti.
*Oo'-nah kah'-meh-rah ah doo'-eh let'-tee.*

**A room with (without) bath.**
Una camera con (senza) bagno.
*Oo'-nah kah'-meh-rah kon (sehn'-tsah) bah'-nyoh.*

**May I see the room?**
Posso vedere la camera?
*Pos'-soh veh-deh'-reh lah kah'-meh-rah?*

**Is there a shower?**
C'è una doccia?
*Che oo'-nah doch'-chah?*

**This is a large room.**
Questa è una camera grande.
*Kwes'-tah e oo'-nah kah'-meh-rah grahn'-deh.*

**This room is too small.**
Questa camera è troppo piccola.
*Kwes'-tah kah'-meh-rah e trop'-poh peek'-koh-lah.*

**The room faces the street.**
La camera dà sulla strada.
*Lah kah'-meh-rah dah sool'-lah strah'-dah.*

**Do you have a quieter room?**
Ha una camera più silenziosa?
*Ah oo'-nah kah'-meh-rah pyoo see-len-tsyoh'-zah?*

**Do you have a room with a view of the ocean (court)?**
Ha una camera con vista sull'oceano (sul cortile)?
*Ah oo'-nah kah'-meh-rah kon vees'-tah sool-loh-cheh'-ah-noh (sool kor-tee'-leh)?*

**What is the price of this room?**
Qual'è il prezzo di questa camera?
*Kwahl-e' eel preht'-tsoh dee kwes'-tah kah'-meh-rah?*

**That's much too expensive.**
È troppo cara.
*E trop'-poh kah'-rah.*

**That's very good.**
È molto buono.
*E mol'-toh bwoh'-noh.*

**Does the price include breakfast?**
È compresa la prima colazione nel prezzo?
*Eh kom-preh'-zah lah pree'-mah koh-lah-tsyoh'-neh nel pret'-tsoh?*

**Do you have a restaurant in the hotel?**
C'è un ristorante nell'albergo?
*Cheh oon rees-toh-rahn'-teh nel-lahl-ber'-goh?*

**Must we eat our meals in the hotel restaurant?**
Dobbiamo mangiare i pasti nel ristorante dell'albergo?
*Dob-byah'-moh mahn-jah'-reh ee pahs'-tee nel rees-toh-rahn'-teh del-lahl-ber'-goh?*

**Where is the dining room?**
Dov'è la sala da pranzo?
*Do-ve' lah sah'-lah dah prahn'-dzoh?*

**We will stay here.**
Rimarremo qui.
*Ree-mahr-reh'-moh kwee.*

**How long will you stay?**
Quanto tempo rimarrà?
*Kwahn'-toh tem'-poh ree-mahr-rah'?*

**I will stay three weeks.**
Rimarrò tre settimane.
*Ree-mahr-roh'-tre set-tee-mah'-neh.*

**We will stay three weeks.**
Rimarremo tre settimane.
*Ree-mahr-reh'-moh tre set-tee-mah'-neh.*

**Please fill out this card.**
Riempia questa carta, per favore.
*Ree-em-pee'-yah kwes'-tah kahr'-tah, per fah-voh'-reh.*

**My key, please.**
La mia chiave, prego.
*Lah mee'-yah kyah'-veh,
    preh'-goh.*

**What number, sir?**
Che numero, signore?
*Keh noo'-me-roh, see-
    nyoh'-reh?*

**I have lost my key.**
Ho perduto la mia chiave.
*Oh per-doo'-toh lah mee'-
    yah kyah'-veh.*

**Where is the elevator?**
Dov'è l'ascensore?
*Do-ve' lah-shen-soh'-reh?*

**Where is the key to my room?**
Dov'è la chiave della mia camera?
*Do-ve' lah kyah'-veh del'-lah mee-yah kah'-meh-rah?*

**Take my suitcase to my room.**
Porti la mia valigia alla mia camera.
*Por'-tee lah mee'-yah vah-lee'-jah ahl'-lah mee'-yah kah'-
    meh-rah.*

**Where is the bathroom?**
Dov'è la stanza da bagno?
*Do-ve' lah stahn'-tsah dah bah'-nyoh?*

**Open the window, please.**
Apra la finestra, per favore.
*Ah'-prah lah fee-nes'-trah, per fah-voh'-reh.*

**Close the window, please.**
Chiuda la finestra, per favore.
*Kyoo'-dah lah fee-nes'-trah, per fah-voh'-reh.*

**Please call the chambermaid.**
Chiami la cameriera, per favore.
*Kyah'-mee lah kah-meh-ree-ye'-rah, per fah-voh'-reh.*

**I want to have these shirts washed.**
Desidero far lavare queste camice.
*Deh-zee'-de-roh fahr lah-vah'-reh kwes'-teh kah-mee'-cheh.*

**This is not my handkerchief.**
Questo non è il mio fazzoletto.
*Kwes'-toh non e eel mee'-yoh fahz-tsoh-let'-toh.*

**I want a towel and some soap.**
Desidero un asciugamano e del sapone.
*Deh-zee'-de-roh oon ah-shoo-gah-mah'-noh eh del sah-poh'-neh.*

**I want a clean towel.**
Voglio un asciugamano pulito.
*Vohl'-yoh oon ah-shoo-gah-mah'-noh poo-lee'-toh.*

**Please wake me at seven o'clock.**
Per favore, mi svegli alle sette.
*Per fah-voh'-reh, mee zve'-lyee ahl'-leh set'-teh.*

**We are leaving tomorrow.**
Partiamo domani.
*Pahr-tyah'-moh doh-mah'-nee.*

**Take my luggage down.**
Faccia scendere il mio bagaglio.
*Fahch'-chah shen'-de-reh eel mee'-yoh bah-gahl'-yoh.*

**Are there any letters for me?**
Ci sono delle lettere per me?
*Chee soh'-noh del'-leh let'-te-reh per meh?*

**I need some postage stamps.**
Ho bisogno di alcuni francobolli.
*Oh bee-zoh'-nyoh dee ahl-koo'-nee frahn-koh-bol'-lee.*

# Using the Telephone

Many visitors to foreign lands avoid using the telephone when they should not. Of course, gesturing and pointing are of no avail when you cannot see the person to whom you are speaking and have to depend entirely on what you hear and say. Still, it is possible to communicate if you make an effort. If there is difficulty, remember to ask the other person to speak slowly. It's your best assurance that the message will get through.

**Where is there a telephone?**
Dove c'è un telefono?
*Do'-veh che oon te-le'-foh-noh?*

**I would like to telephone.**
Vorrei telefonare.
*Vor-reh'-ee te-le-foh-nah'-reh.*

**I would like to make a (long-distance) call to . . .**
Vorrei fare una telefonata (interurbana) a . . .
*Vor-reh'-ee fah'-reh oo'-nah te-le-foh-nah'-tah (een-ter-oor-bah'-nah) ah . .*

**What is the telephone number?**
Qual'è il numero telefonico?
*Kwahl-e' eel noo'-me-roh te-le-foh'-nee-koh?*

**Where is the telephone book?**
Dov'è l'elenco telefonico?
*Do-ve' leh-lehn'-koh te-le-foh'-nee-koh?*

**My number is . . .**
Il mio numero è . . .
*Eel mee'-yoh noo'-me-roh eh . . .*

**Operator!**
Telefonista!
*Te-le-foh-nees'-tah!*

**I want number . . .**
Desidero il numero . . .
*Deh-zee'-de-roh eel noo'-me-roh . . .*

**Can I dial this number?**
Posso fare questo numero?
*Pos'-soh fah'-reh kwes'-toh noo'-me-roh?*

**How much is a telephone call to . . . ?**
Quanto costa una chiamata telefonica a . . . ?
*Kwahn'-toh kos'-tah oo'-nah kyah-mah'-tah te-le-foh'-nee-kah ah . . . ?*

**I am ringing.**
Sto suonando.
*Stoh swoh-nahn'-doh.*

**Please do not hang up.**
Un momento, per favore.
*Oon moh-men'-toh, per fah-voh'-reh.*

**Deposit coins.**
Depositi della moneta.
*Deh-poh'-zee-tee del'-lah moh-neh'-tah.*

**They do not answer.**
Non rispondono.
*Non ree-spon'-doh-noh.*

**Please dial again.**
Faccia il numero di nuovo, per piacere.
*Fahch'-chah eel noo'-me-roh dee nwoh'-voh, per pyah-cheh'-reh.*

**The line is busy.**
La linea è occupata.
*Lah lee'-neh-yah e ok-koo-pah'-tah.*

**Who is speaking?**
Chi parla?
*Kee pahr'-lah?*

**May I speak to . . . ?**
Posso parlare con . . . ?
*Pos'-soh pahr-lah'-reh kon . . . ?*

**He (she) is not in.**
Non c'è.
*Non che.*

**Please speak more slowly.**
Parli più lentamente (adagio), per favore.
*Pahr'-lee pyoo len-tah-men'-teh (ah-dah'-joh), per fah-voh'-reh.*

# Getting Around by Taxi and Bus

The drivers of taxis and buses almost never speak English, which may be fortunate when you relish a few peaceful moments. However, you will have to tell them where you're going, or want to go, and for that we've provided some handy phrases.

**Call a taxi, please.**
Chiami un tassì, per piacere.
*Kyah'-mee oon tahs-see', per pyah-cheh'-reh.*

**Put my luggage into the taxi.**
Metta il mio bagaglio nel tassì.
*Met'-tah eel mee'-yoh bah-gahl'-yoh nel tahs-see'.*

**Driver, are you free?**
Autista, è libero?
*Ow-tees'-tah, e lee'-be-roh?*

**Where do you wish to go?**
Dove desidera andare?
*Do'-veh deh-zee'-de-rah ahn-dah'-reh?*

**Drive to the railroad station (airport).**
Mi conduca alla stazione ferroviaria (all'aeroporto).
*Meek on-doo'-kah ahl'-lah stah-tsyoh'-neh fer-roh-vee'-yah-ree-yah (ahll-ah-eh-roh-por'-toh).*

**How much is the ride from here to the hotel?**
Quanto costa la passeggiata da qui all'albergo?
*Kwahn'-toh kos'-tah lah pahs-sehj-jah'-tah dah kwee ahl-ahl-ber'-goh?*

**Stop here!**
Fermi qui!
*Fer'-mee kwee!*

**I want to get out here.**
Voglio scendere qui.
*Vohl'-yoh shen'-de-reh kwee.*

**Wait until I come back.**
Aspetti finchè torni.
*Ahs-pet'-tee feen-keh' tor'-nee.*

**Wait for me here.**
Mi aspetti qui.
*Mee ahs-pet'-tee kwee.*

**Drive a little farther.**
Vada un po' più avanti.
*Vah'-dah oon po pyoo ah-vahn'-tee.*

**Please drive carefully.**
Vada con cura, per favore.
*Vah'-dah kon koo'-rah, per fah-voh'-reh.*

**Please drive slowly.**
Vada adagio, per favore.
*Vah'-dah ah-dah'-joh, per fah-voh'-reh.*

**Turn to the left (right) here.**
Giri a sinistra (destra) qui.
*Jee'-ree ah see-nees'-trah (des'-trah) kwee.*

**Drive straight ahead.**
Vada sempre diritto.
*Vah'-dah sem'-preh dee-reet'-toh.*

**How much is the fare?**
Quanto è la tariffa?
*Kwahn'-toh e lah tah-reef'-fah?*

**Which bus goes downtown?**
Quale autobus va al centro della città?
*Kwah'-leh ow-toh-boos' vah ahl chen'-troh del'-lah cheet-tah'?*

**Bus number . . .**
L'autobus numero . . .
*Low-toh-boos' noo'-me-roh . . .*

**Does the bus stop here?**
L'autobus si ferma qui?
*Low-toh-boos' see fer'-mah kwee?*

**Which bus goes to . . . ?**
Quale autobus va a . . . ?
*Kwah'-leh ow-toh-boos' vah ah . . . ?*

**Get on the bus here.**
Salga nell'autobus qui.
*Sahl'-gah nell-ow-toh-boos' kwee.*

**Get off the bus here.**
Scenda dall'autobus qui.
*Shen'-dah dahll-ow-toh-boos' kwee.*

**Please tell me when we arrive at . . . street.**
Mi dica, per piacere, quando arriveremo alla via . . .
*Mee dee'-kah per pyah-cheh'-reh kwahn'-doh ahr-ree-ve-reh'-moh ahl'-lah vee'-yah . . .*

**Does this bus go to the museum?**
Va quest'autobus al museo?
*Vah kwest-ow-toh-boos' ahl moo-zeh'-oh?*

**Where must I transfer?**
Dove devo trasferire?
*Do'-veh deh'-voh trahs-fe-ree'-reh?*

**When does the last bus leave?**
Quando parte l'ultimo autobus?
*Kwahn'-doh pahr'-teh lool'-tee-moh ow-toh-boos'?*

# Eating and Drinking

Merely going abroad is thrill enough for some persons; for others the high points are likely to be the hours spent at the table. Getting to know and appreciate the national cuisine and learning how to order native dishes are extra thrills for many travelers. Here, to the phrases that are necessary to order your meals, we have added a menu reader of the most typical dishes of the cuisine in the countries where Italian is spoken.

| | |
|---|---|
| **I'm hungry.** | **I'm thirsty.** |
| Ho fame. | Ho sete. |
| *Oh fah'-meh.* | *Oh seh'-teh.* |
| | |
| **Are you hungry?** | **Are you thirsty?** |
| Ha fame? | Ha sete? |
| *Ah fah'-meh?* | *Ah seh'-teh?* |

**I'm not hungry.**
Non ho fame.
*Non oh fah'-meh.*

**I'm not thirsty.**
Non ho sete.
*Non oh seh'-teh.*

**Do you want to eat now?**
Vuole mangiare adesso?
*Vwoh'-leh mahn-jah'-reh ah-dehs'-soh?*

**Let's eat now.**
Mangiamo adesso.
*Mahn-jah'-moh ah-dehs'-soh.*

**Where is there a good restaurant?**
Dove c'è un buon ristorante?
*Do'-veh che oon bwon ree-stoh-rahn'-teh?*

**The meals.**
I pasti.
*Ee pahs'-tee.*

**breakfast**
la prima colazione
*lah pree'-mah koh-lah-tsyoh'-neh*

**lunch**
la seconda colazione
*lah seh-kon'-dah koh-lah-tsyoh'-neh*

**dinner**
il pranzo
*eel prahn'-dzoh*

**supper**
la cena
*lah cheh'-nah*

**At what time is breakfast (lunch, dinner)?**
A che ora si serve la prima colazione (la seconda colazione, il pranzo)?
*Ah keh oh'-rah see ser'-veh lah pree'-mah koh-lah-tsyoh'-neh (lah seh-kon'-dah koh-lah-tsyoh'-neh, eel prahn'-dzoh)?*

**I want breakfast in my room.**
Desidero la prima colazione nella mia camera.
*Deh-zee'-deh-roh lah pree'-mah koh-lah-tsyoh'-neh nel'-lah mee'-yah kah'-mee-rah.*

**I would like . . .**
Vorrei . . .
*Vor-reh'-ee . . .*

**eggs**
uova
*woh'-vah*

**fried eggs**
uova fritte, uova alpiatto
*woh'-vah freet'-teh, woh'-vah ahl pyaht'-toh*

**scrambled eggs**
uova strapazzate
*woh'-vah strah-pahd-dzah'-teh*

**two soft-boiled eggs**
due uova bollite
*doo'-eh woh'-vah bol-lee'-teh*

**a poached egg**
un uovo affogato
*oon woh'-voh ahf-foh-gah'-toh*

**bacon**
pancetta, lardo
*pahn-chet'-tah, lahr'-doh*

**bread and butter**
pane e burro
*pah'-neh eh boor'-roh*

**black coffee**
caffè nero
*kahf-fe' neh'-roh*

**coffee with milk**
caffè latte
*kahf-fe' laht'-teh*

**coffee without milk**
caffè senza latte
*kahf-fe' sehn'-tsah laht'-teh*

**milk**
il latte
*el laht'-teh*

**tea**
il tè
*eel te*

**ham**
prosciutto
*proh-shoot'-toh*

**cold meat**
carne fredda
*kahr'-neh frehd'-dah*

**rolls**
panini
*pah-nee'-nee*

**Breakfast is ready.**
La prima colazione è servita.
*Lah pree'-mah koh-lah-
   tsyoh'-neh e ser-vee'-tah.*

**Dinner is being served.**
Il pranzo è servito.
*Eel prahn'-dzoh e ser-vee'-
   toh.*

**A table for two, please.**
Una tavola per due, per favore.
*Oo'-nah tah'-voh-lah per doo'-eh, per fah-voh'-reh.*

**Where is the waitress?**
Dov'è la cameriera?
*Do-ve' lah kah-me-ree-yeh'-rah?*

**Waiter (waitress), the menu, please.**
Cameriere (cameriera), la lista, per favore.
*Kah-me-ree-yeh'-reh (kah-me-ree-yeh'-rah), lah lees'-tah,
   per fah-voh'-reh.*

**Waiter, please bring an ashtray.**
Cameriere, porti un portacenere, per favore.
*Kah-me-ree-yeh'-reh, por'-tee oon por-tah-cheh'-neh-reh,
   per fah-voh'-reh.*

**What do you recommend?**
Che raccomanda? / Che mi consiglia?
*Keh rahk-koh-mahn'-dah? / Keh mee kon-seel'-yah?*

**Do you recommend . . . ?**
Raccomanda . . . ? / Mi consiglia . . . ?
*Rahk-koh-mahn'-dah . . . ? / Mee kon-seel'-yah . . . ?*

**Bring me some coffee now, please.**
Mi porti un po' di caffè adesso, per favore.
*Mee por'-tee oon po dee kahf-fe' ah-dehs'-soh, per fah-voh'-
   reh.*

**More butter, please.**
Più burro, per favore.
*Pyoo boor'-roh, per fah-voh'-reh.*

**Bring some more sugar.**
Porti più zucchero.
*Por'-tee pyoo dzook'-ke-roh.*

**Bring me a glass of water, please.**
Mi porti un bicchiere d'acqua, per favore.
*Mee por'-tee oon beek-kee-ye'-reh dahk'-kwah, per fah-voh'-reh.*

**This coffee is cold.**
Questo caffè è freddo.
*Kwes'-toh kahf-fe' e frehd'-doh.*

**Do you take milk and sugar?**
Prende latte e zucchero?
*Pren'-deh laht'-teh eh dzook'-ke-roh?*

---

### *The Condiments*

| | |
|---|---|
| **the salt** | **the pepper** |
| il sale | il pepe |
| *eel sah'-leh* | *eel peh'-peh* |
| **the sugar** | **the oil** |
| lo zucchero | l'olio |
| *loh dzook'-ke-roh* | *loh'-lyoh* |
| **the vinegar** | |
| l'aceto | |
| *lah-cheh'-toh* | |
| **the mustard** | |
| il senape, la mostarda | |
| *eel seh'-nah-peh, lah mos-tahr'-dah* | |

**No sugar, thank you.**
Niente zucchero, grazie.
*Nyen'-teh dzook'-ke-roh, grah'-tsee-yeh.*

**We eat only fruit for breakfast.**
Mangiamo solo frutta alla prima colazione.
*Mahn-jah'-moh soh'-loh froot'-tah ahl'-lah pree'-mah koh-lah-tsyoh'-neh.*

**This butter is not fresh.**
Questo burro non è fresco.
*Kwes'-toh boor'-roh non e fres'-koh.*

**This milk is warm.**
Questo latte è caldo.
*Kwes'-toh laht'-teh e kahl'-doh.*

**This milk is sour.**
Questo latte è acido.
*Kwes'-toh laht'-teh e ah'-chee-doh.*

**I would like a glass of cold milk.**
Vorrei un bicchiere di latte freddo.
*Vor-reh'-ee oon beek-kee-ye'-reh dee laht'-teh frehd'-doh.*

---

### Foods and Beverages

**the fish**
il pesce
*eel peh'-sheh*

**fruit**
la frutta
*lah froot'-tah*

**the meat**
la carne
*lah kahr'-neh*

**the water**
l'acqua
*lahk'-kwah*

**vegetables**
i legumi
*ee leh-goo'-mee*

**the beer**
la birra
*lah beer'-rah*

**the wine**
il vino
*eel vee'-noh*

**the bread**
il pane
*eel pah'-neh*

**Another cup of coffee?**
Un'altra tazza di caffè?
*Oon ahl'-trah taht'-tsah dee kahf-fe'?*

**Another cup of tea?**
Un'altra tazza di tè?
*Oon ahl'-trah taht'-tsah dee te?*

**Do you want some more tea?**
Vuole più tè?
*Vwoh'-leh pyoo te?*

**Nothing more, thank you.**
Nient'altro, grazie.
*Nyent-ahl'-troh, grah'-tsee-yeh.*

**At what time are the meals in this hotel?**
A che ora si servono i pasti in quest'albergo?
*Ah keh oh'-rah see ser'-voh-noh ee pahs'-tee een kwest-ahl-ber'-goh?*

**We dine at seven o'clock.**
Pranziamo alle sette.
*Prahn-dzyah'-moh ahl'-leh set'-teh.*

---

**the cheese**
il formaggio
*eel for-mahj'-joh*

**the milk**
il latte
*eel laht'-teh*

**the butter**
il burro
*eel boor'-roh*

**the honey**
il miele
*eel myeh'-leh*

**the jam**
la confettura
*lah kon-fet-too'-rah*

**the salad**
l'insalata
*leen-sah-lah'-tah*

**the soup**
la zuppa, la minestra
*lah dzoop'-pah, lah mee-nes'-trah*

**Here they dine at eight o'clock.**
Qui mangiano alle otto.
*Kwee mahn'-jah-noh ahl'-leh ot'-toh.*

**Please reserve a table for us.**
Prenoti una tavola per noi, per piacere.
*Preh-noh'-tee oo'-nah tah'-voh-lah per noy, per pyah-cheh'-reh.*

**Do you want soup?**
Vuole zuppa?
*Vwoh'-leh dzoop'-pah?*

---

### The Setting

**a spoon**
un cucchiaio
*oon kook-kee-ah'-ee-yoh*

**a small spoon**
un cucchiaino
*oon kook-kee-ah-ee'-noh*

**a knife**
un coltello
*oon kol-tel'-loh*

**a small knife**
un coltello piccolo
*oon kol-tel'-loh peek'-koh-loh*

**a fork**
una forchetta
*oo'-nah for-ket'-tah*

**a small fork**
una forchetta piccola
*oo'-nah for-ket'-tah peek'-koh-lah*

**a plate**
un piatto
*oon pyaht'-toh*

**a tray**
un vassoio
*oon vahs-soh'-yoh*

**a napkin**
un tovagliolo
*oon toh-vahl-yoh'-loh*

**Bring me a fork (a knife, a spoon).**
Mi porti una forchetta (un coltello, un cucchiaio).
*Mee por'-tee oo'-nah for-ket'-tah (oon kol-tel'-loh, oon kook-kee-ah'-ee-yoh).*

**This fork is dirty.**
Questa forchetta è sporca.
*Kwes'-tah for-ket'-tah e spor'-kah.*

**This spoon isn't clean.**
Questo cucchiaio non è pulito.
*Kwes'-toh kook-kee-ah'-ee-yoh non e poo-lee'-toh.*

**Please bring me a napkin.**
Mi porti un tovagliolo, per favore.
*Mee por'-tee oon toh-vahl-yoh'-loh, per fah-voh'-reh.*

**I would like a glass of wine.**
Vorrei un bicchiere di vino.
*Vor-reh'-ee oon beek-kee-ye'-reh dee vee'-noh.*

**A glass of red (white) wine.**
Un bicchiere di vino rosso (bianco).
*Oon beek-kee-ye'-reh dee vee'-noh ros'-soh (byahn'-koh).*

**A bottle of wine.**
Una bottiglia di vino.
*Oo'-nah bot-teel'-yah dee vee'-noh.*

| **This wine is too warm.** | **A half-bottle.** |
| --- | --- |
| Questo vino è troppo caldo. | Una mezza bottiglia. |
| *Kwes'-toh vee'-noh e trop'-poh kahl'-doh.* | *Oo'-nah med'-dzah bot-teel'-yah.* |

**Please bring some ice.**
Porti un po' di ghiaccio, per favore.
*Por'-tee oon po dee gyahch'-choh, per fah-voh'-reh.*

**I didn't order this.**
Non ho ordinato questo.
*Non oh or-dee-nah'-toh kwes'-toh.*

**A glass of beer.**
Un bicchiere di birra.
*Oon beek-kee-ye'-reh dee beer'-rah.*

**A bottle of beer.**
Una bottiglia di birra.
*Oo'-nah bot-teel'-yah dee beer'-rah.*

**To your health!**
Alla Sua (Vostra) salute!
*Ahl'-lah Soo'-wah (Vos'-trah) sah-loo'-teh!*

**Enjoy your meal!**
Buon appetito!
*Bwon ahp-peh-tee'-toh!*

**This tablecloth is not clean.**
Questa tovaglia non è pulita.
*Kwes'-tah toh-vahl'-yah non e poo-lee'-tah.*

**Do you eat fish?**
Mangia pesce?
*Mahn'-jah peh'-sheh?*

**He doesn't eat meat.**
Lui non mangia carne.
*Loo'-ee non mahn'-jah kahr'-neh.*

**I don't eat dessert.**
Io non mangio dolci.
*Ee'-yoh non mahn'-joh dohl'-chee.*

**He would like some ice cream.**
Vorrebbe gelato.
*Vor-reb'-beh jeh-lah'-toh.*

**Waiter, the check, please.**
Cameriere, il conto, per favore.
*Kah-me-ree-yeh'-reh, eel kon'-toh, per fah-voh'-reh.*

**How much do I owe you?**
Quento Le devo?
*Kwahn'-toh Leh deh'-voh?*

**Is the tip included?**
È compreso il servizio?
*E kom-preh-zoh eel ser-*
*vee'-tsee-yoh*?

**Where do I pay?**
Dove pago?
*Do'-veh pah'-goh*?

**At the cashier's booth.**
Alla cassa.
*Ahl'-lah kahs'-sah.*

**I have already paid.**
Ho già pagato.
*Oh jah pah-gah'-toh.*

**Here is a tip.**
Ecco una mancia.
*Ek'-koh oo'-nah mahn'-chah.*

**I left the tip on the table.**
Ho lasciato la mancia sulla tavola.
*Oh lah-shah'-toh lah mahn'-chah sool'-lah tah'-voh-lah.*

**There is a mistake in the bill.**
C'è uno sbaglio nel conto.
*Che oo'-noh zbahl'-yoh nel kon'-toh.*

# Menu
# Reader

*Zuppe ed Antipasti* Soups and Appetizers

**Antipasto** (*ahn-tee-pahs'-toh*) Hor d'oeuvres.

**Brodo** (*broh'-doh*) Consomme.

**Minestrone** (*mee-nes-troh'-neh*) Vegetable soup with various regional additions.

**Pastina in brodo** (*pahs-tee'-nah een broh'-doh*) Pasta in soup broth.

**Zuppa alla pavese** (*dzoop'-pah ahl'-lah pah-veh'-zeh*) Egg soup.

**Zuppa di pesce** (*dzoop'-pah dee peh'-sheh*) Fish soup.

*Farinacei* Pasta Dishes

**Cannelloni** (*kahn-nel-loh'-nee*) Meat-filled pasta, baked in cheese and tomato sauce.

**Ravioli alla fiorentina** (*rah-vyoh'-lee ahl'-lah fyoh-ren-tee'-nah*) Cheese ravioli.

**alla vegetariana** (*ahl'-lah veh-jeh-tah-ree-yah'-nah*) Ravioli with tomato sauce.

**fatti in casa** (*faht-tee een kah-zah*) Home-made ravioli.

**Spaghetti alla Bolognese** (*spah-get'-tee ahl'-lah boh-lohn-yeh'-zeh*) Spaghetti with meat sauce.

**alla bosaiola** (*ahl'-lah boh-zah-yoh'-lah*) Spaghetti with tuna, mushrooms and cheese.

**alla carbonara** (*ahl'-lah kahr-boh-nah'-rah*) Spaghetti cooked in egg and bacon.

**al pomodoro** (*ahl poh-moh-doh'-roh*) Spaghetti with tomato sauce.

**al sugo di carne** (*ahl soo'-goh dee kahr'-neh*) Spaghetti with meat sauce.

**alle vongole** (*ahl-leh von-goh-leh*) Spaghetti with clam sauce.

**Taglierini, fettuccine** (*tahl-yeh-ree'-nee, fet-tooch-chee'-neh*) Noodles.

## *Pesce* Fish

**Acciughe** (*ahch-choo'-geh*) Anchovies.

**Aragosta** (*ah-rah-gos'-tah*) Lobster.

**Filetto di sogliola** (*fee-let'-toh dee sohl'-yoh-lah*) Filet of sole.

**Fritto misto** (*freet'-toh mees'-toh*) Assorted tiny fried fish. Italian specialty.

**Gamberi** (*gahm'-beh-ree*) Shrimps.

**Ostriche** (*os'-tree-keh*) Oysters.

**Sgombro** (*zgom'-broh*) Mackerel.

**Tonno** (*ton'-noh*) Tuna fish.

**Trotta** (*trot'-tah*) Trout.

## *Carne* Meat

**Bistecca** (*bees-tek'-kah*) Steak.

**all'inglese** (*ahl-leen-gleh'-zeh*) Rare.

**ben cotta** (*ben kot'-tah*) Well done.

**Cervello** (*cher-vel'-loh*) Brains.

**Cotoletta alla bolognese** (*koh-toh-let'-tah ahl'-lah boh-lohn-yeh'-zeh*) Veal cutlet with melted cheese.

    **alla Milanese** (*ahl'-lah mee-lah-neh'-zeh*) Breaded veal cutlet

**Fegato** (*feh'-gah-toh*) Liver.

**Maiale** (*mah-yah'-leh*) Pork.

**Manzo lesso** (*mahn'-dzoh les'-soh*) Boiled beef.

**Pancetta** (*pahn-chet'-tah*) Bacon.

**Pollo alla cacciatora** (*pol'-loh ahl'-lah kahch-chah-toh'-rah*) Stewed chicken.

    **alla diavolo** (*ahl'-lah dyah'-voh-loh*) Chicken broiled with herbs.

**Prosciutto** (*proh-shoot'-toh*) Thinly sliced, dark spicy ham.

**Rosbif** (*roz-beef'*) Roast beef.

**Salsicce** (*sahl-seech'-cheh*) Sausages.

**Saltimbocca** (*sahl-teem-bok'-kah*) Veal and ham dish. Italian specialty.

**Spezzatino di manzo** (*spet-tsah-tee'-noh dee mahn'-dzoh*) Beef stew.

**Vitello al forno** (*vee-tel'-loh ahl for'-noh*) Roast veal.

*Verdura ed Insalata* Vegetables and Salads

**Asparagi** (*ahs-pah'-rah-jee*) Asparagus.

**Carciofi** (*kahr-choh'-fee*) Artichokes.

**Cavolo** (*kah'-voh-loh*) Cabbage.

**Cetrioli** (*cheh-tree-yoh'-lee*) Cucumbers.

**Cipolle** (*chee-pol'-leh*) Onions.

**Fagiolini** (*fah-joh-lee'-nee*) String beans.

**Finocchio** (*fee-nok'-kyoh*) Type of celery.

**Funghi** (*foon'-gee*) Mushrooms.

**Insalata mista** (*een-sah-lah'-tah mees'-tah*) Mixed salad.

**Insalata verde** (*een-sah-lah'-tah ver'-deh*) Lettuce salad.

**Lattuga** (*laht-too'-gah*) Lettuce.

**Melanzana** (*meh-lahn-dzah'-nah*) Eggplant.

**Olive** (*oh-lee'-veh*) Olives.

**Peperoni** (*peh-peh-roh'-nee*) Green peppers.

**Pomodori** (*poh-moh-doh'-ree*) Tomatoes.
**Spinaci** (*spee-nah'-chee*) Spinach.
**Zucchini** (*dzook-kee'-nee*) Summer squash.

*Frutte e Dolci* Fruits and Desserts

**Ananasso** (*ah-nah-nahs'-soh*) Pineapple.
**Arance** (*ah-rahn'-cheh*) Oranges.
**Banane** (*bah-nah'-neh*) Bananas.
**Cassata** (*kahs-sah'-tah*) Ice cream with fruit.
**Ciliegie** (*chee-lee-yeh'-jeh*) Cherries.
**Composta di frutta** (*kom-pos'-tah dee froot'-tah*) Stewed
  fruit.
**Formaggio** (*for-mahj'-joh*) Cheese.
**Gelato** (*jeh-lah'-toh*) Ice cream.
**Mela** (*meh'-lah*) Apple.
**Pasticceria** (*pahs-teech-cheh-ree'-yah*) Pastry.
**Pesca alla melba** (*pes'-kah ahl'-lah mel'-bah*) Peach melba.
**Pere** (*peh'-reh*) Pears.
**Pompelmo** (*pom-pel'-moh*) Grapefruit.
**Torta** (*tor'-tah*) Cake.
**Uva** (*oo'-vah*) Grapes.

*Bibite* Beverages

**Acqua** (*ahk'-kwah*) Water.
**Aranciata** (*ah-rahn-chah'-tah*) Orangeade.
**Birra** (*beer'-rah*) Beer.
**Caffè** (*kahf-feh'*) Coffee.
  **caffè latte** (*kahf-feh' laht'-teh*) Coffee with milk.
**Latte** (*laht'-teh*) Milk.
**Limonata** (*lee-moh-nah'-tah*) Lemonade.
**Sherry dolce** (*sher'-ree dol'-cheh*) Sweet sherry.
**Sherry secco** (*sher'-ree sek'-koh*) Dry sherry.
**Succhi di frutta** (*sook'-kee dee froot'-tah*) Fruit juices.
**Tè** (*teh*) Tea.
**Vino bianco** (*vee'-noh byahn'-koh*) White wine.
**Vino rosso** (*vee'-noh ros'-soh*) Red wine.

# Shopping

Shopping abroad is always an adventure and frequently a delight. It's not only the varied merchandise that you may buy to take home as gifts, but the sheer pleasure of making yourself understood. It's important to know, and to be able to explain, exactly what it is that you want since, obviously, you won't be able to trot downtown a week later to make an exchange. You'll discover, too, that sizes and weights are different; so we have included conversion tables here. Here are the typical questions that you or the salesman might ask or the statements you may make during your shopping trips.

**I would like to go shopping.**
Vorrei fare delle compre.
*Vor-reh'-ee fah'-reh del'-leh kom'-preh.*

**At what time do the stores open?**
A che ora si aprono i negozi?
*Ah keh oh'-rah see ah'-proh-noh ee neh-goh'-tsee?*

**At what time do the stores close?**
A che ora si chiudono i negozi?
*Ah keh oh'-rah see kyoo'-doh-noh ee neh-goh'-tsee?*

**Where is there . . . ?**
Dove c'è . . . ?
*Do'-veh che . . . ?*

**an antique shop.**
un negozio di antichità.
*oon neh-goh'-tsyoh dee ahn-tee-kee-tah'.*

**a book store.**
una libreria.
*oo'-nah lee-bre-ree'-yah.*

**a candy store.**
una confetteria.
*oo'-nah kon-fet-te-ree'-yah.*

**a department store.**
un grande magazzino.
*oon grahn'-deh mah-gahd-dzee'-noh.*

**a dressmaker.**
una sarta.
*oo'-nah sahr'-tah.*

**a druggist.**
un droghiere.
*oon droh-gyeh'-reh.*

**a drugstore.**
una farmacia.
*oo'-nah fahr-mah-chee'-yah.*

**a florist.**
un fioraio.
*oon fee-yoh-rah'-yoh.*

**a grocery.**
una bottega di comestibili.
*oo'-nah bot-teh'-gah dee ko-mes-tee'-bee-lee.*

**a greengrocer.**
un verduraio.
*oon ver-doo-rah'-yoh.*

**May I help you?**
Posso servirLe?
*Pos'-soh ser-veer'-leh?*

**Will you help me, please?**
Per piacere, mi aiuterà?
*Per pyah-cheh'-reh, mee ah-yoo-te-rah'?*

**Are you being served?** (m)
È stato servito?
*Eh stah'-toh ser-vee'-toh?*

**Are you being served?** (f)
È stata servita?
*E stah'-tah ser-vee'-tah?*

**What do you wish?**
Che cosa desidera?
*Keh ko'-zah deh-zee'-deh-rah?*

---

**a hat shop.**
una cappelleria.
*oo'-nah kahp-pel-le-ree'-yah.*

**a jewelry store.**
una gioielleria.
*oo'-nah joy-el-le-ree'-yah.*

**a perfumery.**
una profumeria.
*oo'-nah proh-fee-me-ree'-yah.*

**a photography shop.**
un negozio di fotografia.
*oon neh-goh'-tsyoh dee foh-toh-grah-fee'-yah.*

**a shoe store.**
una calzoleria.
*oo'-nah kahl-tsoh-le-ree'-yah.*

**a tailor.**
un sarto.
*oon sahr'-toh.*

**a tobacconist.**
una tabaccaio.
*oo'-nah tah-bahk-kah'-yoh.*

**a toy store.**
un negozio di giocattoli.
*oon neh-goh'-tsyoh dee joh-kaht'-toh-lee.*

**a watchmaker.**
un orologiaio.
*oon oh-roh-loh-jah'-yoh.*

**I would like . . .**
Vorrei . . .
*Vor-reh'-ee . . .*

---

**a brassiere.**
un reggipetto.
*oon rej-jee-pet'-toh.*

**a handkerchief.**
un fazzoletto.
*oon faht-tshoh-let'-toh.*

**panties.**
mutandine.
*moo-tahn-dee'-neh.*

**shoes.**
scarpe.
*skahr'-peh.*

**a skirt.**
una gonna.
*oo'-nah gon'-nah.*

**socks.**
calzette.
*kahl-tset'-teh.*

**a suit.**
un abito.
*oon ah'-bee-toh.*

**a tie.**
una cravatta.
*oo'-nah krah-vaht'-tah.*

**underwear.**
biancheria.
*byahn-ke-ree'-yah.*

**gloves.**
dei guanti.
*deh'-ee gwahn'-tee.*

**a hat.**
un cappello.
*oon kahp-pel'-loh.*

**a shirt.**
una camicia.
*oo'-nah kah-mee'-chah.*

**shorts.**
mutande.
*moo-tahn'-deh.*

**a slip.**
una sottana.
*oo'-nah sot-tah'-nah.*

**stockings.**
calze.
*kahl'-tseh.*

**a sweater.**
un maglione.
*oon mah-lyoh'-neh.*

**an undershirt.**
una camiciola.
*oo'-nah kah-mee'-choh-lah.*

**I would like to buy . . .**
Vorrei comprare . . .
*Vor-reh'-ee kom-prah'-reh . . .*

**a battery.**
una batteria.
*oo'-nah baht-te-ree'-yah.*

**a camera.**
una macchina fotografica.
*oo'-nah mahk'-kee-nah
foh-toh-grah'-fee-kah.*

**film.**
pellicola, film.
*pel-lee'-koh-lah, feelm.*

**flashbulbs.**
lampadine fotografiche.
*lahm-pah-dee'-neh foh-
toh-grah'-fee-keh.*

**a pen.**
una penna.
*oo'-nah pen'-nah.*

**a pencil.**
una matita.
*oo'-nah mah-tee'-tah.*

**postcards.**
cartoline postali.
*kahr-toh-lee'-neh pos-
tah'-lee.*

**stamps.**
francobolli.
*frahn-koh-bol'-lee.*

**lotion.**
lozione.
*loh-tsyoh'-neh.*

**powder.**
cipria.
*cheep'-ree-yah.*

**razor blades.**
lame da rasoio.
*lah'-meh dah rah-zoh'-
yoh.*

**shampoo.**
shampoo, frizionamento.
*shahm-poo', free-tsyoh-
nah-men'-toh.*

**shaving cream.**
crema da barba.
*kreh'-mah dah bahr'-bah.*

**soap.**
sapone.
*sah-poh'-neh.*

**toothbrush.**
spazzolino da denti.
*spaht-tshoh-lee'-noh dah
den'-tee.*

**toothpaste.**
pasta dentifricia.
*pahs'-tah den-tee-free'-
chah.*

**Do you sell . . . ?**
Vendete . . . ?
*Ven-deh'-teh . . . ?*

**Do you have . . . ?**
Ci avete . . . ?
*Chee ah-veh'-teh . . . ?*

**Please show me some . . .**
Per piacere, mi mostri . . .
*Per pyah-cheh'-reh, mee mos'-tree . . .*

**What size, please?**
Che misura, per favore?
*Keh mee-zoo'-rah, per fah-voh'-reh?*

**Try on these . . .**
Provi questi . . .
*Proh'-vee kwes'-tee . . .*

**How much does it cost?**
Quanto costa?
*Kwahn'-toh kos'-tah?*

**How much do they cost?**
Quanto costano?
*Kwahn'-toh kos'-tah-noh?*

**That is too expensive.**
Questo è troppo caro.
*Kwes'-toh e trop'-poh kah'-roh.*

**That is cheap.**
Questo è a buon mercato.
*Ques'-toh e ah bwon mer-kah'-toh.*

**I like this one.**
Questo mi piace.
*Kwes'-toh mee pyah'-cheh.*

**I will take this one.**
Prenderò questo.
*Pren-de-roh' kwes'-toh.*

---

**cigar.**
sigaro.
*see'-gah-roh.*

**cigarettes.**
sigarette.
*see-gah-ret'-teh.*

**flint.**
pietra focaia.
*pye'-trah foh-kah'-yah.*

**fluid.**
benzina.
*ben-dzee'-nah.*

**lighter.**
accendi-sigari.
*ahch-cheh'-dee-see'-gah-ree.*

**matches.**
fiammiferi.
*fee-yahm-mee'-fe-ree.*

**I don't like this color.**
Questo colore non mi piace.
*Kwes'-toh koh-loh'-reh non mee pyah'-cheh.*

---

**I prefer it in . . .**
Lo preferisco in . . .
*Loh preh-fe-rees'-koh een . . .*

---

| black | blue | brown | gray |
|-------|------|-------|------|
| nero | azzurro | bruno, marrone | grigio |
| *neh'-roh* | *ahd-dzoor'-roh* | *broo'-noh, mahr'-roh'-neh* | *gree'-joh* |

| green | red | white | yellow |
|-------|-----|-------|--------|
| verde | rosso | bianco | giallo |
| *ver'-deh* | *ros'-soh* | *byahn'-koh* | *jahl'-loh* |

| dark | light |
|------|-------|
| scuro | chiaro |
| *skoo'-roh* | *kyah'-roh* |

---

**Sale**
Vendita
*Ven'-dee-tah*

**For Sale**
Da vendere
*Dah ven'-deh-reh*

**Clearance Sale**
Vendita a stralcio, svendita
*Ven'-dee-tah ah strahl'-choh, sven'-dee-tah*

**This dress is too short.**
Questo vestito è troppo corto.
*Kwes'-toh ves-tee'-toh e trop'-poh kor'-toh.*

**This skirt is too long.**
Questa gonna è troppo lunga.
*Kwes'-tah gon'-nah e trop'-poh loon'-gah.*

**I would like to see a white shirt.**
Vorrei vedere una camicia bianca.
*Vor-reh'-ee veh-deh'-reh oo'-nah kah-mee'-chah byan'-kah.*

**He would like to see some white shirts.**
Lui vorrebbe vedere alcune camice bianche.
*Loo'-ee vor-reb'-beh veh-deh'-reh ahl-koo'-neh kah-mee'-cheh byan'-keh.*

**The sleeves are too wide.**
Le maniche sono troppo larghe.
*Leh mah'-nee-keh soh'-noh trop'-poh lahr'-geh.*

**The sleeves are too narrow.**
Le maniche sono troppo strette.
*Leh mah'-nee-keh soh'-noh trop'-poh stret'-teh.*

**I would like to see some shoes.**
Vorrei vedere delle scarpe.
*Vor-reh'-ee veh-deh'-reh del'-leh skahr'-peh.*

**A pair of black (brown) shoes.**
Un paio di scarpe nere (marroni).
*Oon pah'-yoh dee skahr'-peh neh'-reh (mahr-roh'-nee).*

| **Try this pair on.** | **They are too narrow.** |
|---|---|
| Provi questo paio. | Sono troppo strette. |
| *Proh'-vee kwes'-toh pah'-yoh.* | *Soh'-noh trop'-poh stret'-teh.* |

**They are too (tight, loose, long, short).**
Sono troppo (strette, sciolte, lunghe, corte).
*Soh'-noh trop'-poh (stret'-teh, shol'-teh, loon'-geh, kor'-teh).*

**They are not big enough.**
Non sono abbastanza grandi.
*Non soh'-noh ahb-bahs-tahn'-tsah grahn'-dee.*

**Do you sell cigarettes?**
Vendete sigarette?
*Ven-deh'-teh see-gah-ret'-
teh?*

**Do you have matches?**
Avete fiammiferi?
*Ah-veh'-teh fee-yahm-mee'-
fe-ree?*

**I want to buy needles, pins, and some thread.**
Voglio comprare aghi, spilli e del filo.
*Vohl'-yoh kom-prah'-reh ah'-gee, speel'-lee eh del fee'-loh.*

**How many do you want?**
Quanti ne vuole?
*Kwahn'-tee neh vwoh'-leh?*

**Anything else?**
Qualche altra cosa?
*Kwahl'-keh ahl'-trah ko'-
zah?*

**No, thank you. That's all.**
No, grazie. Questo è tutto.
*Noh, grah'-tsee-yeh. Kwes'-
toh e toot'-toh.*

**I'll take it (them) with me.**
Lo (Li) prenderò con me.
*Loh (lee) pren-de-roh' kon
meh.*

**Will you wrap it, please?**
Vuole avvolgerlo, per favore?
*Vwoh'-leh ahv-vol'-jer-loh, per fah-voh'-reh?*

**Send it to the hotel.**
Lo mandi in albergo.
*Loh mahn'-dee een ahl-ber'-goh.*

**Pack it (them) for shipment to . . .**
Lo (Li) impacchi per spedizione a . . .
*Loh (lee) eem-pahk'-kee per speh-dee-tsyoh'-neh ah . . .*

**Here is the bill.**
Ecco la fattura.
*Ek'-koh lah faht-too'-rah.*

**Is there a discount?**
C'è uno sconto?
*Cheh oo'-noh skon'-toh?*

**I will pay cash.**
Pagherò in denaro contante.
*Pah-ge-roh' een deh-nah'-roh kon-tahn'-teh.*

## CLOTHING SIZE CONVERSIONS: *Women*

### Dresses, Suits and Coats

| American: | 8 | 10 | 12 | 14 | 16 | 18 |
|---|---|---|---|---|---|---|
| British: | 30 | 32 | 34 | 36 | 38 | 40 |
| Continental: | 36 | 38 | 40 | 42 | 44 | 46 |

### Blouses and Sweaters

| American: | 32 | 34 | 36 | 38 | 40 | 42 | 44 |
|---|---|---|---|---|---|---|---|
| British: | 34 | 36 | 38 | 40 | 42 | 44 | 46 |
| Continental: | 40 | 42 | 44 | 46 | 48 | 50 | 52 |

### Stockings

| American & British: | 8 | 8½ | 9 | 9½ | 10 | 10½ | 11 |
|---|---|---|---|---|---|---|---|
| Continental: | 35 | 36 | 37 | 38 | 39 | 40 | 41 |

### Shoes

| American: | 5 | 5½ | 6 | 6½ | 7 | 7½ | 8 | 8½ | 9 |
|---|---|---|---|---|---|---|---|---|---|
| British: | 3½ | 4 | 4½ | 5 | 5½ | 6 | 6½ | 7 | 7½ |
| Continental: | 35 | 35 | 36 | 37 | 38 | 38 | 38½ | 39 | 40 |

### Gloves

American, British and Continental sizes are the same.

## CLOTHING SIZE CONVERSIONS: *Men*

### Suits, Sweaters and Overcoats

| American & British: | 34 | 36 | 38 | 40 | 42 | 44 | 46 | 48 |
|---|---|---|---|---|---|---|---|---|
| Continental: | 44 | 46 | 48 | 50 | 52 | 54 | 56 | 58 |

### Shirts

| American & British: | 14 | 14½ | 15 | 15½ | 16 | 16½ | 17 | 17½ |
|---|---|---|---|---|---|---|---|---|
| Continental: | 36 | 37 | 38 | 39 | 40 | 41 | 42 | 43 |

### Socks

| American and British: | 9½ | 10 | 10½ | 11 | 11½ | 12 | 12½ |
|---|---|---|---|---|---|---|---|
| Continental: | 39 | 40 | 41 | 42 | 43 | 44 | 45 |

### Shoes

| American: | 7 | 7½ | 8 | 8½ | 9 | 9½ | 10 | 10½ | 11 | 11½ |
|---|---|---|---|---|---|---|---|---|---|---|
| British: | 6½ | 7 | 7½ | 8 | 8½ | 9 | 9½ | 10 | 10½ | 11 |
| Continental: | 39 | 40 | 41 | 42 | 43 | 43 | 44 | 44 | 45 | 45 |

# Getting
# Around by
# Automobile

Since few attendants who work at garages and stations speak English, some ability in Italian will be very useful. Your car will need gasoline, of course, and probably some regular servicing. And should there be some problem with it, a lot of time and energy will be saved if you can explain your needs.

**I would like to hire a car.**
Vorrei noleggiare una macchina.
*Vor-reh'-ee noh-lej-jah'-reh oo'-nah mahk'-kee-nah.*

**How much does a car cost per day?**
Quanto costa una macchina al giorno?
*Kwahn'-toh kos'-tah oo'-nah mahk'-kee-nah ahl jor'-noh?*

**How much per kilometer?**
Quanto per chilometro?
*Kwahn'-toh per kee-loh'-meh-troh?*

**Is gasoline expensive in this country?**
È cara la benzina in questo paese?
*E kah'-rah lah ben-dzee'-nah een kwes'-toh pah-eh'-zeh?*

**Is there a deposit?**
C'è un deposito?
*Cheh oon deh-poh'-zee-toh?*

**I would like a car with seatbelts and an outside mirror, please.**
Vorrei una macchina con cinture di posto e uno specchio esteriore, per favore.
*Vor-reh'-ee oo'-nah mahk'-kee-nah kon cheen-too'-reh dee pos'-toh eh oo'-noh spek'-kyoh es-te-ree-yoh'-reh, per fah-voh'-reh.*

**I will (will not) take the car out of the country.**
Prenderò (Non prenderò) la macchina fuori del paese.
*Pren-deh-roh' (non pren-deh-roh') lah mahk'-kee-nah fwoh'-ree del pah-eh'-zeh.*

**I want to leave it in . . .**
Voglio lasciarla a . . .
*Vohl'-yoh lah-shahr'-lah ah . . .*

**How much is the insurance per day?**
Quanto è l'assicurazione al giorno?
*Kwahn'-toh eh las-see-koo-rah-tsyoh'-neh ahl jor'-noh?*

**Here is the registration and the key.**
Ecco la registrazione e la chiave.
*Ek'-koh lah reh-jees-trah-tsyoh'-neh eh lah kyah'-veh.*

**Where is there a gas station?**
Dove c'è una pompa di benzina?
*Do'-veh che oo'-nah pom'-pah dee ben-dzee'-nah?*

**a garage?**
un'autorimessa, un garage?
*oon ow-toh-ree-mes'-sah, oon gah-rah'-jeh?*

**Fill it up.**
Lo riempia.
*Loh ree-em-pee'-yah.*

**Premium.**
Superiore.
*Soo-peh-ree-yoh'-reh.*

**Regular.**
Ordinario.
*Ord-dee-nah'-ree-yoh.*

**I want twenty liters of gasoline.**
Voglio venti litri di benzina.
*Vohl'-yoh ven'-tee lee'-tree dee ben-dzee'-nah.*

**I also need some oil.**
Anche mi occorre un po' d'olio.
*Ahn'-keh mee ok-kor'-reh oon po doh'-lyoh.*

**Please put in some water.**
Metta dentro un po' d'acqua, per favore.
*Met'-tah den'-troh oon po dahk'-kwah, per fah-voh'-reh.*

**Wash the car, please.**
Lavi la macchina, per piacere.
*Lah'-vee lah mahk'-kee-nah, per pyah-cheh'-reh.*

**Please inspect the tires.**
Esamini le gomme (i pneumatici), per favore.
*Eh-zah-mee'-nee leh gom'-meh (ee pneh-oo-mah'-tee-chee), per fah-voh'-reh.*

**Put in some air.**
Metta dentro un po' d'aria.
*Met'-tah den'-troh oon po dah'-ree-yah.*

**Is there a mechanic here?**
C'è un meccanico qui?
*Che oon mek-kah'-nee-koh kwee?*

**Can you fix a flat tire?**
Può riparare una gomma forata?
*Pwoh ree-pah-rah'-reh oo'-nah gom'-mah foh-rah'-tah?*

**How long will it take?**
Quanto tempo ci vorrà?
*Kwahn'-toh tem'-poh chee vor-rah'?*

**Have you a road map?**
Ha una carta stradale?
*Ah oo'-nah kahr'-tah strah-dah'-leh?*

**Where does this road go to?**
Dove va questa strada?
*Do'-veh vah kwes'-tah strah'-dah?*

**Is this the road to . . . ?**
È questa la strada per . . . ?
*E kwes'-tah lah strah'-dah per . . ?*

**Is the road good?**
È buona la strada?
*E bwoh'-nah lah strah'-dah?*

**A narrow road.**
Una strada stretta.
*Oo'-nah strah'-dah stret'-tah.*

**A wide road.**
Una strada larga.
*Oo'-nah strah'-dah lahr'-gah.*

**A narrow bridge.**
un ponte stretto.
*Oon pon'-teh stret'-toh.*

**A bad road.**
Una cattiva strada.
*Oo'-nah kaht-tee'-vah strah'-dah.*

**This road is slippery when it's wet.**
Questa strada è scivolosa quando è bagnata.
*Kwes'-tah strah'-dah e shee-voh-loh'-zah kwahn'-doh e bah-nyah'-tah.*

**Is there a speed limit here?**
C'è un limite di velocità qui?
*Che oon lee'-mee-teh dee veh-loh-chee-tah' kwee?*

**You were driving too fast.**
Lei conduceva troppo veloce.
*Leh'-ee kon-doo-cheh'-vah trop'-poh veh-loh'-cheh.*

**You must pay the fine.**
Lei deve pagare la multa.
*Leh'-ee deh'-veh pah-gah'-reh lah mool'-tah.*

**May I leave the car here?**
Posso lasciare la macchina qui?
*Pos'-soh lah-sha'-reh lah mahk'-kee-nah kwee?*

**May I park here?**
Posso parcheggiare qui?
*Pos'-soh pahr-kehj-jah'-reh kwee?*

**Where is the nearest garage?**
Dov'è l'autorimessa più vicina?
*Do-ve' low-toh-ree-mes'-sah pyoo vee-chee'-nah?*

**This car isn't running well.**
Questa macchina non va bene.
*Kwes'-tah mahk-kee'-nah non vah beh'-neh.*

**I have a driver's license.**
Ho un patente.
*Oh oon pah-ten'-teh.*

**Can you fix it?**
Può ripararlo?
*Pwoh ree-pah-rahr'-loh?*

**Your car is ready.**
La Sua macchina è pronta.
*Lah Soo'-wah mahk'-kee-nah e pron'-tah.*

**Please check . . .**
Per piacere, esamini . . .
*Per pyah-cheh'-reh eh-zah-mee'-nee . . .*

**How long will it take?**
Quanto tempo ci vorrà?
*Kwahn'-toh tem'-poh chee vor-rah'?*

**Drive carefully!**
Conduca con cura!
*Kon-doo'-kah kon koo'-rah!*

**Please wipe the windshield.**
Per piacere, pulisca la parabrezza.
*Per pyah-cheh'-reh, poo-lees'-kah lah pah-rah-bret'-tsah.*

**I don't know what the matter is.**
Non so ciò che c'è.
*Non soh choh keh che.*

| **I think it's . . .** | **Is it . . . ?** |
|---|---|
| Credo che è | È . . . ? |
| *Creh'-doh keh e . . .* | *E . . . ?* |

**the accelerator.**
l'acceleratore.
*lahch-cheh-leh-rah-toh'-reh.*

**the air filter.**
il filtro d'aria.
*eel feel'-troh dah'-ree-yah.*

**the battery.**
la batteria.
*lah baht-teh-ree'-yah.*

**the brakes.**
i freni.
*ee freh'-nee.*

**the carburetor.**
il carburatore.
*eel kahr-boo-rah-toh'-reh.*

**the clutch.**
la frizione.
*lah free-tsyoh'-neh.*

**the lights.**
i fari.
*ee fah'-ree.*

**the motor.**
il motore.
*eel moh-toh'-reh.*

**the spark plugs.**
le candele.
*leh kahn-deh'-leh.*

**the tires.**
le gomme, i pneumatici.
*leh gom'-meh, ee pneh-oo-mah'-tee-chee.*

**the wheel.**
la ruota.
*lah rwoh'-tah.*

**the wheels.**
le ruote.
*leh rwoh'-teh.*

**the front wheel.**
la ruota anteriore.
*lah rwoh'-tah ahn-te-ree-yoh'-reh.*

**the back wheel.**
la ruota posteriore.
*lah rwoh'-tah pos-te-ree-yoh'-reh.*

Priority road ahead

## Some International Road Signs

 = RED

 = BLUE

= BLACK

Stop

Dangerous curve

Right curve

Double curve

Intersection

Intersection with secondary road

Railroad crossing
with gates

Railroad crossing
without gates

Road work

Pedestrian
crossing

Children

Road narrows

Uneven road

Slippery road

Traffic circle
ahead

Danger

Closed to
all vehicles

No entry

No left turn

No U turn

Overtaking
prohibited

Speed limit

Customs

No parking

Direction to
be followed

Traffic circle

No parking

# Getting Around by Train

The railroad is the most frequently used means of transportation by travelers abroad. Schedules and timetables are usually readily understandable — if they are available and visible — but otherwise, in arranging your travel by train, you will need to use some of these phrases.

**The railroad station.**
La stazione ferroviaria.
*Lah stah-tsyoh'-neh fer-roh-vee-yah'-ree-yah.*

**The train.**
Il treno.
*Eel treh'-noh.*

**Drive to the railroad station.**
Mi conduca alla stazione ferroviaria.
*Mee kon-doo'-kah ahl'-lah stah-tsyoh'-neh fer-roh-vee-yah'-ree-yah.*

**I need a porter.**
Mi occorre un facchino.
*Mee ok-kor'-reh oon fahk-kee'-noh.*

**Porter, here is my luggage.**
Facchino, ecco il mio bagaglio.
*Fahk-kee'-noh, ek'-koh eel mee'-yoh bah-gahl'-yoh.*

**These are my bags.**
Queste sono le mie valige.
*Kwes'-teh soh'-noh leh mee'-yeh vah-lee'-jeh.*

**Here are the baggage checks.**
Ecco gli scontrini.
*Ek'-koh lyee skon-tree'-nee.*

**Where is the ticket window?**
Dov'è lo sportello dei biglietti?
*Do-ve' loh spor-tel'-loh deh'-ee bee-lyet'-tee?*

**Have you a timetable?**
Avete un orario?
*Ah-veh'-teh oon oh-rah'-ree-yoh?*

**When does the train leave?**
Quando parte il treno?
*Kwahn'-doh pahr'-teh eel treh'-noh?*

**From which platform?**
Da che piattaforma?
*Dah keh pyaht-tah-for'-mah?*

**I want to check this baggage.**
Desidero registrare questo bagaglio.
*Deh-zee'-de-roh reh-jees-trah'-reh kwes'-toh bah-gahl'-yoh.*

**I must pick up a ticket.**
Devo prendere un biglietto.
*Deh-voh pren'-de-reh oon bee-lyet'-toh.*

**I want a ticket to . . .**
Voglio un biglietto per . . .
*Vohl'-yoh oon bee-lyet'-toh per . . .*

**First class.**
Prima classe.
*Pree'-mah klahs'-seh.*

**Second class.**
Seconda classe.
*Seh-kon'-dah klahs'-seh.*

**One way.**
Andata solo.
*Ahn-dah'-tah soh'-loh.*

**Round trip.**
Andata e ritorno.
*Ahn-dah'-tah eh ree-tor'-noh.*

**Is there a dining car?**
C'è una carrozza ristorante?
*Che oo'-nah kahr-rot'-tsah rees-toh-rahn'-teh?*

**Does this train go to . . . ?**
Va questo treno a . . . ?
*Vah kwes'-toh treh'-noh ah . . . ?*

**Does this train stop at . . . ?**
Si ferma questo treno a . . . ?
*See fer'-mah kwes'-toh treh'-noh ah . . . ?*

**Is the train late?**
È in ritardo il treno?
*E een ree-tahr'-doh eel treh'-noh?*

**Is this seat occupied?**
È occupato questo posto?
*E ok-koo-pah'-toh kwes'-toh pos'-toh?*

**What is the name of this station?**
Come si chiama questa stazione?
*Ko'-meh see kyah'-mah kwes'-tah stah-tsyoh'-neh?*

**How long do we stop here?**
Quanto tempo ci fermiamo qui?
*Kwahn'-toh tem'-poh chee fer-myah'-moh kwee?*

**May I open the window?**
Posso aprire il finestrino?
*Pos'-soh ah-pree'-reh eel fee-nes-tree'-noh?*

**Please close the door.**
Per piacere, chiuda lo sportello.
*Per pyah-cheh'-reh, kyoo'-dah loh spor-tel'-loh.*

**I have missed the train!**
Ho perduto il treno!
*Oh per-doo'-toh eel treh'-noh!*

**When does the next train leave?**
Quando parte il prossimo treno?
*Kwahn'-doh pahr'-teh eel pros'-see-moh treh'-noh?*

**Where is the waiting room?**
Dov'è la sala d'aspetto?
*Do-ve' lah sah'-lah dahs-pet'-toh?*

**Where is the lavatory?**
Dov'è il gabinetto?
*Do-ve' eel gah-bee-net'-toh?*

**The train is arriving now.**
Il treno arriva adesso.
*Eel treh'-noh ahr-ree-vah ah-dehs'-soh.*

**Tickets, please.**
I biglietti, prego.
*Ee bee-lyet'-tee, preh'-goh.*

**All aboard!**
In carrozza!
*Een kahr-rot'-tsah!*

**The train is leaving.**
Il treno è in partenza.
*Eel treh'-noh e een pahr-tehn'-tsah.*

**Arrivals.**
Arrivi.
*Ahr-ree'-vee.*

**Departures.**
Partenze.
*Pahr-tehn'-tseh.*

**Express train.**
Il treno diretto. / Direttissimo.
*Eel treh-noh dee-ret'-toh. / Dee-ret-tees'-see-moh.*

**Local train.**
Il treno accelerato.
*Eel treh'-noh ahch-cheh-leh-rah'-toh.*

# Getting Around by Ship and Plane

If you go abroad on a ship or airplane, your first chance to use your Italian will come in transit. Being able to speak with the personnel can be an exciting start to a journey. They will be more helpful, too, if you make an effort to speak to them in their language. And your efforts will be rewarded.

**There's the harbor (the port).**
Ecco il porto.
*Ek'-koh eel por'-toh.*

**Where is the pier?**
Dov'è il molo?
*Do-ve' eel moh'-loh?*

**When does the ship sail?**
Quando parte la nave?
*Kwahn'-doh pahr'-teh lah nah'-veh?*

**Let's go on board!**
Andiamo a bordo!
*Ahn-dyah'-moh ah bor'-doh!*

**Where is cabin number . . . ?**
Dov'è la cabina numero . . . ?
*Do-ve' lah kah-bee'-nah noo'-me-roh . . . ?*

**Is this my cabin?**
È questa la mia cabina?
*E kwes'-tah lah mee'-yah kah-bee'-nah?*

**Steward, do you have the key to my cabin?**
Cameriere, ha la chiave della mia cabina?
*Kah-meh-ree-ye'-reh, ah lah kyah'-veh del'-lah mee'-yah kah-bee'-nah?*

**I'm looking for the dining room.**
Cerco la sala da pranzo.
*Cher'-koh lah sah'-lah dah prahn'-dzoh.*

**We want a table for two.**
Vogliamo una tavola per due.
*Vohl-yah'-moh oo'-nah tah'-voh-lah per doo'-eh.*

**A first-class cabin.**
Una cabina di prima classe.
*Oo'-nah kah-bee'-nah dee pree'-mah klahs'-seh.*

**A second-class cabin.**
Una cabina di seconda classe.
*Oo'-nah kah-bee'-nah dee seh-kon'-dah klahs'-seh.*

**Let's go on deck.**
Andiamo sul ponte.
*Ahn-dyah'-moh sool pon'-teh.*

**I would like a deck chair.**
Vorrei una sedia a sdraio.
*Vor-reh'-ee oo'-nah seh'-dyah ah zdrah'-yoh.*

**I would like to eat by the swimming pool.**
Vorrei mangiare vicino alla piscina.
*Vor-reh'-ee mahn-jah'-reh vee-chee'-noh ahl'-lah pee-shee'-nah.*

**The ship arrives at seven o'clock.**
La nave arriva alle sette.
*Lah nah'-veh ahr-ree'-vah ahl'-leh set'-teh.*

**When do we go ashore?**
Quando scendiamo a terra?
*Kwahn'-doh shen-dyah'-moh ah ter'-rah*?

**Where is the gangplank?**
Dov'è la passerella (lo scalandrone)?
*Do-ve' lah pahs-se-rel'-lah (loh skah-lahn-droh'-neh)*?

**The landing card, please.**
Il permesso (cartoncino) di sbarco, prego.
*Eel per-mes'-soh (kahr-ton-chee'-noh) dee zbahr'-koh, preh'-goh.*

**I wasn't seasick at all!**
Non avevo mal di mare affatto!
*Non ah-veh'-voh mahl dee mah'-reh ahf-faht'-toh!*

**Have a good trip!**
Buon viaggio!
*Bwon vyahj'-joh!*

**I want to go to the airport.**
Voglio andare all'aeroporto.
*Vohl'-yoh ahn-dah'-reh ahll-ah-eh-roh-por'-toh.*

**Drive me to the airport.**
Mi conduca all'aeroporto.
*Mee kon-doo'-kah ahll-ah-eh-roh-por'-toh.*

**When does the plane leave?**    **When does it arrive?**
Quando parte l'aeroplano?    Quando arriva?
*Kwahn'-doh pahr'-teh lah-eh-roh-plah'-noh*?    *Kwahn'-doh ahr-ree'-vah*?

**Flight number . . . leaves at . . .**
Il volo numero . . . parte alle . . .
*Eel voh'-loh noo'-me-roh . . . pahr'-teh ahl'-leh . . .*

**From which gate?**
Da che porta?
*Dah keh por'-tah?*

**I want to reconfirm my flight.**
Voglio riconfirmare il mio volo.
*Vohl'-yoh ree-kon-feer-mah'-reh eel mee'-yoh voh'-loh.*

**Ticket, please.**
Il biglietto, prego.
*Eel bee-lyet'-toh, preh'-goh.*

**Boarding pass, please.**
Il permesso d'imbarco, prego.
*Eel per-mes'-soh deem-bahr'-koh, preh'-goh.*

**Please fasten your seat belts.**
Attaccate le cinture, prego.
*Aht-tahk-kah'-teh leh cheen-too'-reh, preh'-goh.*

**No smoking.**
Vietato fumare.
*Vyeh-tah'-toh foo-mah'-reh.*

**Stewardess, a small pillow, please.**
Hostess, un guanciale piccolo, per piacere.
*Ohs-tess, oon gwahn-chah'-leh peek'-koh-loh, per pyah-cheh'-reh.*

**I fly to Europe every year.**
Io volo all'Europa ogni anno.
*Ee'-yoh voh'-loh ahll-eh-oo-roh'-pah oh'-nyee ahn'-noh.*

**The airplane is taking off!**
L'aeroplano decolla.
*Lah-eh-roh-plah'-noh deh-kol'-lah.*

**Is a meal served during this flight?**
Si serve un pasto durante questo volo?
*See ser'-veh oon pahs'-toh doo-rahn'-teh kwes'-toh voh'-loh?*

**The airplane will land in ten minutes.**
L'aeroplano atterrerà fra dieci minuti.
*Lah-eh-roh-plah'-noh aht-ter-re-rah' frah dyeh'-chee mee-noo'-tee.*

**There will be a delay.**
Ci sarà un ritardo.
*Chee sah-rah' oon ree-tahr'-doh.*

**There's the runway!**
Ecco la pista!
*Ek'-koh lah pees'-tah!*

**We have arrived.**
Siamo arrivati.
*Syah'-moh ahr-ree-vah'-tee.*

# Health

We hope you will never need the phrases you will find in this section; but emergencies do arise, and sickness does overwhelm. Since a physician's diagnosis often depends on what you, the patient, can tell him, you will want to make your woes clearly understood. If you have a chronic medical problem, you will want to have prescriptions or medical descriptions of the difficulty in hand or translated before you leave on your trip.

**I need a doctor.**
Ho bisogno d'un medico.
*Oh bee-zoh'-nyoh doon meh'-dee-koh.*

**Send for a doctor.**
Faccia venire un medico.
*Fahch'-chah veh-nee'-reh oon meh'-dee-koh.*

**Send for a doctor.**
Mandi chiamare un medico.
*Mahn'-dee kyah-mah'-reh oon meh'-dee-koh.*

**Are you the doctor?**
È Lei il medico?
*E leh'-ee eel meh'-dee-koh?*

**What is the matter with you?**
Che cosa ha?
*Keh ko'-zah ah?*

**I don't feel well.**
Non mi sento bene.
*Non mee sen'-toh beh'-neh.*

**I am sick.**
Sono ammalato (*m*) / ammalata (*f*).
*Soh'-noh ahm-mah-lah'-toh (m) / -tah (f).*

**How long have you been sick?**
Da quanto tempo è ammalato?
*Dah kwahn'-toh tem'-poh e ahm-mah-lah'-toh?*

| **I have a headache.** | **Where is the hospital?** |
| Ho mal di testa. | Dov'è l'ospedale? |
| *Oh mahl dee tes'-tah.* | *Do-ve' los-peh-dah'-leh?* |

**Is there a drugstore near here?**
C'è una farmacia qui vicino?
*Che oo'-nah fahr-mah-chee'-yah kwee vee-chee'-noh?*

| **I have a stomach ache.** | **Where does it hurt?** |
| Ho mal di stomaco. | Dove Le duole? |
| *Oh mahl dee stoh'-mah-koh.* | *Do'-veh leh dwoh'-leh?* |

**My leg hurts.**
La gamba mi fa male.
*Lah gahm'-bah mee fah mah'-leh.*

**My finger is bleeding.**
Il mio dito sanguina.
*Eel mee'-yoh dee'-toh sahn'-gwee-nah.*

**Do I have a fever?**
Ho una febbre?
*Oh oo'-nah feb'-breh?*

---

**the arm, the arms**
il braccio, le braccia
*eel brahch'-choh, leh brahch-chah.*

**the back**
la schiena
*lah skyeh'-nah*

**the bladder**
la vescica
*lah veh-shee'-kah*

**the bone**
l'osso
*los'-soh*

**the chest**
il petto
*eel pet'-toh*

**the ear, the ears**
l'orecchio, gli orecchi
*loh-rek'-kyoh, lyee oh-rek'-kee.*

**the elbow**
il gomito
*eel goh'-mee-toh*

**the eye, the eyes**
l'occhio, gli occhi
*lok'-kyoh, lyee ok'-kee*

**the face**
il viso, la faccia
*eel vee'-zoh, lah fahch'-chah*

**the finger**
il dito
*eel dee'-toh*

**the foot, the feet**
il piede, i piedi
*eel pyeh'-deh, ee pyeh'-dee*

**the forehead**
la fronte
*lah fron'-teh*

**I have burned myself.**
Mi sono bruciato (*m*) / bruciata (*f*).
*Mee soh'-noh broo-chah'-toh (m) / -tah (f).*

**You must stay in bed.**
Deve stare a letto.
*Deh'-veh stah'-reh ah let'-toh.*

**How long?**
Quanto tempo?
*Kwahn'-toh tem'-poh?*

---

**the hair**
i capelli
*ee kah-pel'-lee*

**my hair**
i miei capelli
*ee myeh'-ee kah-pel'-lee*

**the hand, the hands**
la mano, le mani
*lah mah'-noh, leh mah'-nee*

**the head**
la testa
*lah tes'-tah*

**the heart**
il cuore
*eel kwoh'-reh*

**the hip**
l'anca
*lahn'-kah*

**the joint**
la giuntura
*lah joon-too'-rah*

**the kidneys**
i reni
*ee reh'-nee*

**the knee**
il ginocchio
*eel jee-nok'-kyoh*

**the leg, the legs**
la gamba, le gambe
*lah gahm'-bah, leh gahm'-beh*

**the liver**
il fegato
*eel feh'-gah-toh*

**the lung, the lungs**
il polmone, i polmoni
*eel pol-moh'-neh, ee pol-moh'-nee*

**At least two days.**
Al meno due giorni.
*Ahl meh'-noh doo'-eh jor'-nee.*

**Show me your tongue.**
Mi mostri la lingua.
*Mee mos'-tree lah leen'-gwah.*

---

**the mouth**
la bocca
*lah bok'-kah*

**the muscle**
il muscolo
*eel moos'-koh-loh*

**the neck**
il collo
*eel kol'-loh*

**the nose**
il naso
*eel nah'-zoh*

**the shoulder**
la spalla
*lah spahl'-lah*

**the skin**
la pelle
*lah pel'-leh*

**the skull**
il cranio
*eel krah'-nyoh*

**the spine**
la spina dorsale
*lah spee'-nah dor-sah'-leh*

**the stomach**
lo stomaco
*loh stoh'-mah-koh*

**the thigh**
la coscia
*lah ko'-shah*

**the throat**
la gola
*lah goh'-lah*

**the thumb**
il pollice
*eel pol'-lee-cheh*

**the toe**
il dito del piede
*eel dee'-toh del pyeh'-deh*

**the tooth, the teeth**
il dente, i denti
*eel den'-teh, ee den'-tee*

**the waist**
la vita
*lah vee'-tah*

**the wrist**
il polso
*eel pol'-soh*

**Lie down.**
Si corichi.
*See koh'-ree-kee.*

**Get up.**
Si alzi.
*See ahl'-tsee.*

**I have a cold.**
Sono raffreddato (*m*) / raffreddata (*f*).
*Soh'-noh rahf-frehd-dah'-toh (m) / -tah (f).*

**Do you smoke?**
Fuma?
*Foo'-mah?*

**Yes, I smoke.**
Sì, fumo.
*See, foo'-moh.*

**No, I don't smoke.**
No, non fumo.
*Noh, non foo'-moh.*

**Do you sleep well?**
Dorme bene?
*Dor'-meh beh'-neh?*

**No, I don't sleep well.**
No, non dormo bene.
*Noh, non dor'-moh beh'-neh.*

**I cough frequently.**
Tossisco spesso.
*Tos-sees'-koh spehs'-soh.*

**Take this medicine three times a day.**
Prenda questa medicina tre volte al giorno.
*Pren'-dah kwes'-tah meh-dee-chee'-nah tre vol'-teh ahl jor'-noh.*

**Here is a prescription.**
Ecco una prescrizione.
*Ek'-koh oo'-nah preh-skree-tsyoh'-neh.*

**Can you come again tomorrow?**
Può venire di nuovo domani?
*Pwoh veh-nee'-reh dee nwoh'-voh doh-mah'-nee?*

**Yes, I can come.**
Sì, posso venire.
*See, pos'-soh veh-nee'-reh.*

**I will come later.**
Verrò più tardi.
*Ver-roh' pyoo tahr'-dee.*

**He's a good doctor.**
Lui è un buon medico.
*Loo'-ee e oon bwon meh'-dee-koh.*

# Sightseeing

No phrase book can possibly supply you with all the phrases you might want in the infinite number of situations, emotions, likes, and dislikes you will encounter in your travels. The basics are here, but they can only be a beginning. The dictionary at the back of this book will supply you with a larger vocabulary to use with the phrases given here. In addition, local bilingual or multilingual guides are usually very helpful in supplying other language information concerning a given situation. If an unusual phrase is required, ask him and it will be given to you gladly.

**I would like to go sightseeing.**
Vorrei girare per vedere delle curiosità.
*Vor-reh'-ee jee-rah'-reh per veh-deh'-reh del'-leh koo-ree-yoh-zee-tah'.*

**How long does the tour last?**
Quanto tempo dura il giro?
*Kwahn'-toh tem-poh doo'-rah eel jee'-roh?*

**It lasts three hours.**
Dura tre ore.
*Doo'-rah tre oh'-reh.*

**Are you the guide?**
È Lei la guida?
*E leh'-ee lah gwee'-dah?*

**What is the name of this place?**
Come si chiama questo luogo?
*Ko'-meh see kyah'-mah kwes'-toh lwoh'-goh?*

**Are the museums open today?**
Sono aperti i musei oggi?
*Soh'-noh ah-per'-tee ee moo-zeh'-ee oj'-jee?*

**No, the museums are closed today.**
No, i musei sono chiusi oggi.
*Noh, ee moo-zeh'-ee soh'-noh kyoo'-zee oj'-jee.*

**The stores are open.**
I negozi sono aperti.
*Ee neh-goh'-tsee soh'-noh ah-per'-tee.*

**I would like to visit an art museum.**
Vorrei visitare un museo d'arte.
*Vor-reh'-ee vee-zee-tah'-reh oon moo-zeh'-oh dahr'-teh.*

**Is there an exhibition there now?**
C'è un' esposizione lì adesso?
*Che oon es-poh-zee-tsyoh'-neh lee ah-des'-soh?*

**I would like to see the city.**
Vorrei vedere la città.
*Vor-reh'-ee veh-deh'-reh lah cheet-tah'.*

**What is the name of that church?**
Come si chiama quella chiesa?
*Ko'-meh see kyah'-mah kwel'-lah kyeh'-zah?*

**May we go in?**
Possiamo entrare?
*Pos-syah'-moh en-trah'-reh?*

**Is the old church closed this morning?**
È chiusa la vecchia chiesa stamattina?
*E kyoo'-zah lah vek'-kyah kyeh'-zah stah-maht-tee'-nah?*

**Will it be open this evening?**
Sarà aperta stasera?
*Sah-rah' ah-per'-tah stah-seh'-rah?*

**This is the main square of the city.**
Questa è la piazza principale della città.
*Kwes'-tah e lah pyaht'-tsah preen-chee-pah'-leh del'-lah cheet-tah'.*

**May I take pictures here?**
Posso fare delle fotografie qui?
*Pos'-soh fah'-reh del'-leh fot-toh-grah-fee'-yeh kwee?*

**We have walked a lot.**
Abbiamo camminato molto.
*Ahb-byah'-moh kahm-mee-nah'-toh mol'-toh.*

| **I am tired.** | **Let's sit down.** |
|---|---|
| Sono stanco (*m*) / stanca (*f*). | Sediamoci. |
| *Soh'-noh stahn'-koh (m) / -kah (f).* | *Seh-dyah'-moh-chee.* |

**Where does this street lead to?**
Dove va questa strada?
*Do'-veh vah kwes'-tah strah'-dah?*

**To the cathedral.**
Alla cattedrale.
*Ahl'-lah kaht-teh-drah'-leh.*

**What is that monument?**
Qual'è quel monumento?
*Kwahl-e' kwel moh-noo-men'-toh?*

**Is that a theater?**
È quello un teatro?
*E kwel'-loh oon teh-yah'-troh?*

**It's a movie house.**
È un cinema.
*E oon chee'-neh-mah.*

**What is the name of this park?**
Come si chiama questo parco?
*Ko'-meh see kyah'-mah kwes'-toh pahr'-koh?*

**We cross the street here.**
Attraversiamo la strada qui.
*Aht-trah-ver-syah'-moh lah strah'-dah kwee.*

**Will we visit a castle?**
Visiteremo un castello?
*Vee-zee-teh-reh'-moh oon kahs-tel'-loh?*

**We will visit a palace.**
Visiteremo un palazzo.
*Vee-zee-teh-reh'-moh oon pah-laht'-tsoh.*

**Who lives in this palace?**
Chi abita questo palazzo?
*Kee ah'-bee-tah kwes'-toh pah-laht'-tsoh?*

**Nobody lives here.**
Nessuno abita qui.
*Nes-soo'-noh ah'-bee-tah kwee.*

**What is the name of this river?**
Come si chiama questo fiume?
*Ko'-meh see kyah'-mah kwes'-toh fyoo'-meh?*

**This is the longest bridge in the city.**
Questo è il ponte più lungo della città.
*Kwes'-toh e eel pon'-teh pyoo loon'-goh del'-lah cheet-tah'.*

**There's too much water in the boat.**
C'è tropp'acqua nella barca.
*Che trop-pahk'-kwah nel'-lah bahr'-kah.*

**Is our hotel near the river?**
È il nostro albergo vicino al fiume?
*E eel nos'-troh ahl-ber'-goh vee-chee'-noh ahl fyoo'-meh?*

**This is the shopping center.**
Questo è il centro di compre.
*Kwes'-toh e eel chen'-troh dee kom'-preh.*

**Is it far from here to the beach?**
È lontano da qui alla spiaggia?
*E lon-tah'-noh dah kwee ahl'-lah spyahj'-jah?*

**I would like to go swimming this morning.**
Vorrei andare a fare il bagno stamattina.
*Vor-reh'-ee ahn-dah'-reh ah fah'-reh eel bah'-nyoh stah-maht-tee'-nah.*

**If it doesn't rain, we'll go there.**
Se no piove, ci andremo.
*Seh non pyo'-veh, chee ahn-dreh'-moh.*

**Thank you for an interesting tour.**
Grazie per un giro interessante.
*Grah'-tsee-yeh per oon jee'-roh een-te-res-sahn'-teh.*

**Thank you very much for it.**
La ringrazio molto.
*Lah reen-grah'-tsyoh mol'-toh.*

| | |
|---|---|
| **I like it.** | **I liked it.** |
| Mi piace. | Mi è piaciuto. |
| *Mee pyah'-cheh.* | *Mee e pyah-choo'-toh.* |

# DICTIONARY

# Some Tips On Italian Grammar

*Gender* Nouns in Italian are either masculine or feminine. This is important to know since the form of other parts of speech (articles, adjectives, pronouns) depends on whether they modify or appear in connection with a masculine or feminine noun. The indefinite and definite articles and adjectives, always agree with the noun in number and gender.

As a rule, nouns ending in "o" are masculine and those ending in "a" are feminine. Nouns ending in "e" in the singular may be either masculine or feminine, and the correct gender must be learned when the word is first encountered.

The definite articles (*the*) are *il* for the masculine singular nouns beginning with a single consonant (except "z") or with two consonants (except "s" plus consonant), and *lo* for masculine singular nouns beginning with "z" or with "s" plus consonant. The definite article *l'* is used before masculine and feminine singular nouns beginning with a vowel. The definite article *la* is used before feminine singular nouns beginning with a consonant or consonants. In plural nouns, *i* replaces the article *il*, and *gli* replaces *lo* and *l'* with masculins nouns. *Le* replaces *la* and *l'* with feminine noune. Notice the following:

| | |
|---|---|
| il fiume (the river) | i fiumi (the rivers) |
| il vestito (the dress) | i vestiti (the dresses) |
| l'uomo (the man) | gli uomini (the men) |
| lo zio (the uncle) | gli zii (the uncles) |
| lo spillo (the pin) | gli spilli (the pins) |
| la donna (the woman) | le donne (the women) |
| l'acqua (the water) | le acque (the waters) |

The indefinite articles (*a, an*) are *un* or *uno* for masculine singular nouns and *una* for feminine singular nouns.

un fiume (a river)

una donna (a woman)

Adjectives vary in gender according to the nouns they modify. Notice the following:

un fiume lung*o* (a long river)

fiumi lungh*i* (long rivers)

una spiaggia lung*a* (a long beach)

spiagge lungh*e* (long beaches)

When a woman or girl speaks of herself or refers to another female, the feminine form of the adjective must be used:

| | |
|---|---|
| Sono ammalato. | **I am sick.** (a man speaking) |
| Sono ammalata. | **I am sick.** (a woman speaking) |
| È ammalato. | **He is sick.** |
| È ammalata. | **She is sick.** |
| Sono ammalati. | **They are sick.** (men or men and women) |
| Sono ammalate. | **They are sick.** (women only) |

*Plurals* The plurals of nouns and adjectives are formed by substituting -*i* for masculine singular -*o* and masculine and feminine singular -*e*. Feminine plurals substitute -*e* for singular -*a*.

| | |
|---|---|
| mela (apple) | mele (apples) |
| dente (tooth) | denti (teeth) |
| libro (book) | libri (books) |
| arancia (orange) | arance (oranges) |
| ponte (bridge) | ponti (bridges) |
| matita (pencil) | matite (pencils) |

*Word Order* The order of words in Italian is much the same as in English, with two prime exceptions. In Italian the adjective usually follows the noun:

| | |
|---|---|
| un fiume lungo | **a long river** |
| lo spillo piccolo | **the small pin** |
| il vestito nero | **the black dress** |

And the indirect and direct object pronouns, in an affirmative statement, precede the verb:

| | |
|---|---|
| He gave me the money. | Mi ha dato il denaro. |
| He gave it to me. | Me l'ha dato. |

*Verbs* Person is indicated in Italian verbs by endings attached to the verb stem. In regular verbs, the verb stem is got by dropping the *-are*, *-ere*, and *-ire* from the infinite form. (Some verb stems are irregular.) Notice the following:

parl*are*, **to speak**
parl*o*, **I speak**
parl*a*, **he, she speaks; you** (polite) **speak**
parl*iamo*, **we speak**
parl*ate*, **you** (pl., polite) **speak**
parl*ano*, **they speak**

prend*ere*, **to take**
prend*o*, **I take**
prend*e*, **he, she takes; you** (polite) **take**
prend*iamo*, **we take**
prend*ete*, **you** (pl., polite) **take**
prend*ono*, **they take**

part*ire*, **to leave**
part*o*, **I leave**
part*e*, **he, she leaves; you** (polite) **leave**
part*iamo*, **we leave**
part*ite*, **you** (pl., polite) **leave**
part*ono*, **they leave**

fin*ire*, **to finish**
fin*isco*, **I finish**
fin*isce*, **he, she finishes; you** (polite) **finish**
fin*iamo*, **we finish**
fin*ite*, **you** (pl., polite) **finish**
fin*iscono*, **they finish**

There is a set of personal subject pronouns that indicate person with verbs, but they are used largely for emphasis:

| | |
|---|---|
| parlo, I speak | io parlo, *I* speak |
| ho parlato, I spoke | io ho parlato, *I* spoke |
| parlano, they speak | essi parlano, *they* speak |

The reflexive pronouns used with reflexive verbs (those ending in -*si* in the Dictionary) follow the same rule for word order given above.

**a,** uno, una, un, un' *oo'-noh, oo'nah, oon, oon*
**able: to be able,** potere *poh-teh'-reh*
**aboard,** a bordo *ah bor'-doh*
**about** *adv.*, quasi *kwah'-zee*
**about** *prep.*, circa *cheer'-kah*
**above,** sopra *soh'-prah*
**abroad,** all'estero *ahl-les'-te-roh*
**absolutely,** assolutamente *ahs-soh-loo-tah-men'-teh*
**accelerate,** accelerare *ahch-cheh-leh-rah'-reh*
**accelerator,** acceleratore *ahch-cheh-leh-rah-toh'-reh*
**accent** *n.*, accento *ahch-chen'-toh*
**accept** *v.*, accettare *ahch-chet-tah'-reh* [31]
**accident,** incidente *een-chee-den'-teh* [14]
**according to,** secondo *seh-kon'-doh*
**account** *n.*, conto *kon'-toh*
**ache** *n.*, dolore *doh-loh'-reh*
**ache** *v.*, far male, dolere *fahr mah'-leh, doh-leh'-reh*
**acquaintance,** conoscenza *koh-noh-shehn'-tsah*
**across,** attraverso *aht-trah-ver'-soh*
**act** *n.*, atto *aht'-toh*
**act** [do] *v.*, agire, fare *ah-jee'-reh, fah'-reh*; [drama], recitare *reh-chee-tah'-reh*
**active,** attivo *aht-tee'-voh*
**actor,** attore *aht-toh'-reh*
**actress,** attrice *aht-tree'-cheh*
**actual,** attuale *aht-too-ah'-leh*
**add,** sommare, aggiungere *som-mah'-reh, ahj-joon'-geh-reh*
**address** *n.*, indirizzo *een-dee-reet'-tsoh* [30]
**admiration,** ammirazione (f) *ahm-mee-rah-tsyoh'-neh*
**admire,** ammirare *ahm-mee-rah'-reh*
**admission,** ammissione (f) *ahm-mees-syoh'-neh*
**admit,** ammettere *ahm-met'-teh-reh*
**adorable,** adorabile *ah-doh-rah'-bee-leh*
**advance** *v.*, avanzare *ah-vahn-tsah'-reh*
**advantage,** vantaggio *vahn-tahj'-joh*

**adventure,** avventura *ahv-ven-too'-rah*

**advertisement,** pubblicità *poob-blee-chee-tah'*

**advice,** consiglio *kon-seel'-yoh*

**advise,** consigliare *kon-seel-yah'-reh*

**affectionate,** affettuoso *ahf-fet-too-oh'-zoh*

**afraid: to be afraid,** aver paura *ah-vehr' pah-oo'-rah*

**after,** dopo *doh'-poh*

**afternoon,** pomeriggio *poh-meh-reej'-joh*

**afterwards,** dopo *doh'-poh*

**again,** di nuovo *dee nwoh'-voh*

**against,** contro *kon'-troh*

**age,** età *eh-tah'*

**agent,** agente *ah-jen'-teh*

**ago,** fa *fah*

**agree: to be in accord,** essere d'accordo *es'-seh-reh dahk-kor'-doh*

**agreeable** [pleasing], gradevole *grah-deh'-voh-leh*

**agreement,** accordo *ahk-kohr'-doh*

**ahead: straight ahead,** sempre diritto *sem'-preh dee-reet'-toh*

**air,** aria *ah'-ree-yah* [74]

**air filter,** filtro d'aria *feel'-troh dah'-ree-yah*

**air line,** linea aerea *lee'-neh-yah ah-eh'-reh-yah*

**airmail,** posta aerea *pos'-tah ah-eh'-reh-yah*

**airplane,** aereo, aeroplano *ah-eh'-reh-oh, ah-eh-roh-plah'-noh* [89, 90]

**airport,** aeroporto *ah-eh-roh-por'-toh* [45, 88]

**alarm,** allarme (m) *ahl-lahr'-meh*

**alarm clock,** sveglia *zvehl'-yah*

**alcohol,** alcool *ahl-koh-ohl'*

**alike,** simile, somigliante *see'-mee-leh, soh-meel-yahn'-teh*

**alive,** vivo *vee'-voh*

**all,** tutto *toot'-toh* **not at all** [none], niente affatto *nyen'-teh ahf-faht'-toh*; [it's nothing], non c'è di che *non che dee keh* **after all,** dopo tutto *doh'-poh toot'-toh*

**allergy,** allergia *ahl-ler-jee'-yah*

**allow,** permettere *per-met'-teh-reh*

**almond,** mandorla *mahn'-dor-lah*

**almost,** quasi *kwah'-zee*

**alone,** solo *soh'-loh*

**along,** lungo *loon'-goh*

**already,** già *jah* [57]

**also,** anche *ahn'-keh*

**altar,** altare (m) *ahl-tah'-reh*

**alter,** modificarsi *moh-dee-fee-kahr'-see*

**alteration** [of clothing], alterazione *ahl-teh-rah-tsyoh'-neh*

**although,** sebbene, benchè *seb-beh'-neh, ben-keh'*

**altogether,** interamente *een-teh-rah-men'-teh*

**always,** sempre *sem'-preh*

**am: I am,** sono, sto, io sono *soh'-noh, stoh, ee'-yoh soh'-noh*

**ambassador,** ambasciatore (m) *ahm-bah-shah-toh'-reh*

**American,** americano *ah-meh-ree-kah'-noh*

**amount,** somma *som'-mah*

**amusement,** divertimento *dee-ver-tee-men'-toh*

**amusing,** divertente *dee-ver-ten'-teh*

**an,** uno, una, un, un' *oo'-noh, oo'-nah, oon, oon*

**and,** e, ed *eh, ehd*

**anger** n., rabbia, collera *rahb'-byah, kol'-leh-rah*

**angry,** arrabbiato, adirato *ahr-rahb-byah'-toh, ah-dee-rah'-toh*

**animal,** animale (m) *ah-nee-mah'-leh*

**ankle,** caviglia *kah-veel'-yah*

**announce,** anunziare *ah-noon-tsyah'-reh*

**annoy,** annoiare *ahn-noh-yah'-reh*

**another,** un altro, un'altra *oon ahl'-troh, oon ahl'-trah*

**answer** n., risposta *rees-pos'-tah*

**answer** v., rispondere *rees-pon'-deh-reh* [42]

**antique shop,** negozio di antichità *neh-goh'-tsyoh dee ahn-tee-kee-tah'*

**anxious,** ansioso *ahn-syoh'-zoh*

**any,** alcuno *ahl-koo'-noh*

**anyone,** chiunque *kee-yoon'-kweh*

**anyhow,** comunque, in ogni modo *koh-moon'-kweh, een on'-yee moh'-doh*

**anything,** qualunque cosa, qualsiasi cosa *kwah-loon'-kweh ko'-zah, kwahl-see'-yah-zee ko'-zah*

**anywhere,** dovunque, ovunque *doh-voon'-kweh, oh-voon'-kweh*

**apartment,** appartamento *ahp-pahr-tah-men'-toh*

**apologize,** scusarsi *skoo-zahr'-see*

**apology,** apologia *ah-poh-loh-jee'-yah*

**appear** apparire *ahp-pah-ree'-reh*

**appendicitis,** appendicite *ahp-pen-dee-chee'-teh*

**appendix,** appendice *ahp-pen'-dee-cheh*

**appetite,** appetito *ahp-peh-tee'-toh*

**appetizer,** antipasto *ahn-tee-pahs'-toh*

**apple,** mela *meh'-lah*

**appointment,** appuntamento *ahp-poon-tah-men'-toh*

**appreciate,** apprezzare *ahp-pret-tsah'-reh*

**approve,** approvare *ahp-proh-vah'-reh*

**approximately,** approssimativamente *ahp-pros-see-mah-tee-vah-men'-teh*

**April,** aprile *ah-pree'-leh*

**arch,** arco *ahr'-koh*

**architect,** architetto *ahr-kee-tet'-toh*

**architecture,** architettura *ahr-kee-tet-too'-rah*

**are: you are,** tu sei, Lei è *too say, leh'-ee e* **you** (pl), **they are,** voi siete, essi sono *voy syeh'-teh, es'-see soh'-noh* **we are,** noi siamo *noy syah'-moh*

**area,** area *ah'-reh-yah*

**argue,** disputare *dees-poo-tah'-reh*

**arm,** braccio *brahch'-choh*

**around,** intorno *een-tor'-noh*

**arrange,** regolare *reh-goh-lah'-reh*

**arrest** *v.*, arrestare *ahr-res-tah'-reh*

**arrival,** arrivo *ahr-ree'-voh* [85]

**arrive,** arrivare *ahr-ree-vah'-reh* [25, 46, 85, 87, 88, 90]

**art,** arte (f) *ahr'-teh* [99]

**artichoke,** carciofo *kahr-choh'-foh*

**article,** articolo *ahr-tee'-koh-loh*

**artificial,** artificiale *ahr-tee-fee-chah'-leh*

**artist,** artista *ahr-tees'-tah*

**as,** come *ko'-meh*

**ashamed,** vergognoso *ver-gon-yoh'-zoh*

**ashore,** a terra *ah ter'-rah* [88]

**ashtray,** portacenere (m) *por-tah-cheh'-neh-reh* [50]

**ask,** domandare *doh-mahn-dah'-reh*

**asleep,** addormentato *ahd-dor-men-tah'-toh*

**asparagus,** asparagi (m, pl) *ahs-pah'-rah-jee*

**aspirin,** aspirina *ahs-pee-ree'-nah*

**assist,** assistere *ahs-sees'-teh-reh*

**assistant,** assistente *ahs-sees-ten'-teh*

**associate** *n.*, socio *soh'-choh*

**association,** associazione (f) *ahs-soh-chah-tsyoh'-neh*

**assure,** assicurare *ahs-see-koo-rah'-reh*

**at** *prep.*, a, ad *ah, ahd*

**Atlantic,** Atlantico *aht-lahn'-tee-koh*

**attach,** accludere *ahk-kloo'-deh-reh*

**attain** [reach], ottenere *ot-teh-neh'-reh*

**attempt** *v.*, provare, tentare *proh-vah'-reh, ten-tah'-reh*

**attend,** attendere, assistere *aht-ten'-deh-reh, ahs-sees'-teh-reh*

**attention,** attenzione (f) *aht-ten-tsyoh'-neh*

**attract,** attirare *aht-tee-rah'-reh*

**audience,** udienza *oo-dyen'-tsah*

**August,** agosto *ah-gos'-toh*

**aunt,** zia *dzee'-yah*

**author,** autore (m) *ow-toh'-reh*

**authority,** autorità *ow-toh-ree-tah'*

**automobile,** automobile (f), macchina *ow-toh-moh'-bee-leh, mahk'-kee-nah*

**autumn,** autunno *ow-toon'-noh*

**available,** disponibile *dees-poh-nee'-bee-leh*
**avenue,** via, viale (m) *vee'-yah, vee-yah'-leh*
**avoid,** evitare *eh-vee-tah'-reh*
**await,** aspettare *ah-spet-tah'-reh*
**awake** *adj.,* sveglio *zvehl'-yoh*
**awake** *v.,* svegliarsi *zvehl-yahr'-see*
**away,** via, lontano *vee'-yah, lon-tah'-noh*
**axle,** asse (f) *ahs'-seh*

**baby,** bambino, bimbo *bahm-bee'-noh, beem'-boh*
**bachelor,** celibe (m) *cheh'-lee-beh*
**back** *adv.,* dietro *dyeh'-troh* **to go back,** tornare *tohr-nah'-reh*
**back** *n.,* schiena *skyeh'-nah*
**bacon,** pancetta, lardo *pahn-chet'-tah, lahr'-doh*
**bad,** cattivo *kaht-tee'-voh*
**badly,** male *mah'-leh*
**bag,** sacco, borsa *sahk'-koh, bor'-sah*; [suitcase], valigia *vah-lee'-jah* [34, 83]
**baggage,** bagaglio *bah-gahl'-yoh* [83]
**baggage check,** scontrino *skon-tree'-noh* [83]
**bakery,** panetteria *pah-net-teh-ree'-yah*
**balcony,** galleria, balcone (m) *gahl-leh-ree'-yah, bahl-koh'-neh*
**ball,** palla *pahl'-lah*
**banana,** banana *bah-nah'-nah*
**band** [music], banda *bahn'-dah*
**bandage,** benda *ben'-dah*
**bank,** banca *bahn'-kah* [30]
**bar,** bar (m) *bahr*
**barber,** barbiere (m) *bahr-byeh'-reh*
**bargain** *n.,* occasione (f) *ok-kah-zyoh'-neh*
**basket,** cestino *ches-tee'-noh*
**bath,** bagno *bahn'-yoh* [37]
**bathe,** bagnarsi, fare il bagno *bahn-yahr'-see, fah'-reh eel bahn'-yoh*

**bathing suit,** costume da bagno (m) *kos-too'-meh dah bahn'-yoh*

**bathroom,** stanza da bagno *stahn'-tsah dah bahn'-yoh* [39]

**battery,** batteria *baht-teh-ree'-yah*

**bay,** baia *bah'-yah*

**be,** essere, stare *es'-seh-reh, stah'-reh*

**beach,** spiaggia *spyahj'-jah* [102]

**beans,** fagioli *fah-joh'-lee*

**beard,** barba *bahr'-bah*

**beautiful,** bello *behl'-loh* [10]

**beauty parlor,** salone di bellezza *sah-loh'-neh dee bel-leht'-tsah*

**because,** perchè *per-keh'*

**become,** diventare *dee-ven-tah'-reh*

**bed,** letto *let'-toh* [94]  **to go to bed,** andare al letto *ahn-dah'-reh ahl let'-toh*

**bedroom,** camera da letto *kah'-meh-rah dah let'-toh*

**bee,** ape (f) *ah'-peh*

**beef,** manzo *mahn'-dzoh*

**beefsteak,** bistecca *bee-stek'-kah*

**beer,** birra *beer'-rah* [56]

**beet,** barbabietola *bahr-bah-byeh'-toh-lah*

**before** [time], prima (di) *pree'-mah (dee)*; [place], davanti a *dah-vahn'-tee ah*

**begin,** cominciare *ko-meen-chah'-reh*

**beginning,** principio *preen-chee'-pyoh*

**behind,** dietro a *dyeh'-troh ah*

**believe,** credere *kreh'-deh-reh*

**bell,** campana *kahm-pah'-nah*

**belong,** appartenere *ahp-pahr-teh-neh'-reh*

**belt,** cintura *cheen-too'-rah* [73, 89]

**beside,** accanto a, al lato di *ahk-kahn'-toh ah, ahl lah'-toh dee*

**besides,** inoltre, di più *een-ohl'-treh, dee pyoo*

**best,** ottimo *ot'-tee-moh*

**better** *adj.*, migliore *meel-yoh'-reh*
**better** *adv.*, meglio *mehl'-yoh*
**between,** tra, fra *trah, frah*
**big,** grande, grosso *grahn'-deh, gros'-soh* [69]
**bill,** conto *kon'-toh* [57]
**bird,** uccello *ooch-chel'-loh*
**birth,** nascita *nah'-shee-tah*
**birthday,** compleanno *kom-pleh-ahn'-noh*
**bit: a bit,** un poco *oon poh'-koh*
**bite** *v.*, mordere *mor'-deh-reh*
**black,** nero *neh'-roh*
**blanket,** coperta *koh-per'-tah*
**bleed,** sanguinare *sahn-gwee-nah'-reh* [93]
**blind,** cieco *chyeh'-koh*
**blister,** bolla *bol'-lah*
**block** *n.*, masso *mahs'-soh*
**blonde,** biondo *byon'-doh*
**blood,** sangue (m) *sahn'-gweh*
**blouse,** blusa, camicetta *bloo'-zah, kah-mee-chet'-tah*
**blue,** azzurro *ahd-dzoor'-roh*
**board; room and board,** camera con vitto *kah'-meh-rah kon veet'-toh*
**boarding house,** pensione (f) *pen-syoh'-neh*
**boarding pass,** permesso d'imbarco *per-mes'-soh deem-bahr'-koh* [89]
**boat,** barca *bahr'-kah* [101]
**body,** corpo *kor'-poh*
**boil** *v.*, bollire *bol-lee'-reh*
**bone,** osso *os'-soh*
**book,** libro *leeb'-roh*
**bookstore,** libreria *leeb-reh-ree'-yah*
**booth,** cabina *kah-bee'-nah*
**boot,** stivale (m) *stee-vah'-leh*
**border** *n.*, frontiera, confine (m) *fron-tyeh'-rah, kon-fee'-neh*

**born,** nato *nah'-toh*

**borrow,** prendere a prestito *pren'-deh-reh ah pres'-tee-toh*

**both,** tutti e due (m), tutte e due (f) *toot'-tee eh doo'-eh, toot'-teh eh doo'-eh*

**bottle,** bottiglia *bot-teel'-yah* [55, 56]

**bottle opener,** cavatappi (m) *kah-vah-tahp'-pee*

**bottom,** fondo *fon'-doh*

**box,** scatola *skah'-toh-lah* [34]

**boy,** ragazzo *rah-gaht'-tsoh*

**bracelet,** braccialetto *brahch-chah-let'-toh*

**brake** *n.,* freno *freh'-noh*

**brandy,** acquavite (m), cognac *ahk-kwah-vee'-teh, kon-yahk'*

**brassiere,** reggipetto *rej-jee-pet'-toh*

**brave,** coraggioso *koh-rahj-joh'-zoh*

**bread,** pane (m) *pah'-neh*

**break** *v.,* rompere *rom'-peh-reh*

**breakfast,** prima colazione (f) *pree'-mah koh-lah-tsyoh'-neh* [38, 48, 50, 52]

**breast,** seno *seh'-noh*

**breath,** respiro *res-pee'-roh*

**breathe,** respirare *res-pee-rah'-reh*

**bridge,** ponte (m) *pon'-teh* [101]

**bright,** chiaro *kyah'-roh*

**bring,** portare *por-tah'-reh* [13, 50, 51, 55]

**broken,** rotto *rot'-toh*

**brother,** fratello *frah-tel'-loh* [3]

**brown,** marrone, bruno *mahr-roh'-neh, broo'-noh*

**bruise** *n.,* bernoccolo *ber-nok'-koh-loh*

**brush** *n.,* spazzola *spaht'-tsoh-lah*

**brunette,** bruno *broo'-noh*

**build** *v.,* costruire *kos-troo-ee'-reh*

**building,** edifizio *eh-dee-fee'-tsyoh*

**burn** *n.,* bruciatura *broo-chah-too'-rah*

**burn** *v.,* bruciare *broo-chah'-reh* [94]

**burst,** scoppiare *skop-pyah'-reh*

**bus,** autobus, pullman *ow'-toh-boos, pool'-mahn* [15, 46]

**business,** affari (m, pl) *ahf-fah'-ree*

**busy,** occupato *ok-koo-pah'-toh* [43]

**but,** ma *mah*

**butter,** burro *boor'-roh* [49, 50, 51]

**button,** bottone (m) *bot-toh'-neh*

**buy,** comprare *kom-prah'-reh* [66, 70]

**by,** da *dah*

**cabbage,** cavolo *kah'-voh-loh*

**cabin,** cabina *kah-bee'-nah* [86, 87]

**café,** caffè (m) *kahf-feh'*

**cake,** torta *tor'-tah*

**call** *n.,* chiamata *kyah-mah'-tah* [41, 42]

**call** *v.,* chiamare *kyah-mah'-reh* [15, 40, 44]

**camera,** macchina fotografica *mahk'-kee-nah foh-toh-grah'-fee-kah*

**can** *n.,* latta *laht'-tah*

**can: to be able,** potere *poh-teh'-reh* **I can,** posso *pos'-soh*

**canal,** canale (m) *kah-nah'-leh*

**cancel** *v.,* annullare *ahn-nool-lah'-reh*

**candy,** caramella, dolci *kah-rah-mel'-lah, dol'-chee*

**candy store,** confetteria *kon-fet-teh-ree'-yah*

**capital,** capitale (f) *kah-pee-tah'-leh*

**car,** automobile (f), macchina *ow-toh-moh'-bee-leh, mahk'-kee-nah* [72, 73, 74, 76]

**carburetor,** carburatore (m) *kahr-boo-rah-toh'-reh*

**card,** cartolina *kahr-toh-lee'-nah*

**care,** *n.,* cura *koo'-rah*

**care** *v.,* preoccuparsi (di) *preh-ok-koo-pahr'-see (dee)*

**careful,** cauto *kow'-toh*

**carpet,** tappeto *tahp-peh'-toh*

**carrot,** carota *kah-roh'-tah*

**carry,** portare *por-tah'-reh* [35]

**cash** *n.,* denaro contante *deh-nah'-roh kon-tahn'-teh* [70]

**cashier,** cassiere (m) *kahs-syeh'-reh* [57]

**castle,** castello *kahs-tehl'-loh* [101]

**cat,** gatto *gaht'-toh*

**catch** *v.*, prendere, acchiappare *pren'-deh-reh, ahk-kyahp-pah'-reh*

**cathedral,** cattedrale (f), duomo *kaht-teh-drah'-leh, dwoh'-moh* [100]

**Catholic,** cattolico *kaht-toh'-lee-koh*

**catsup,** salsa di pomodori *sahl'-sah dee poh-moh-doh'-ree*

**cattle,** bestiame (m) *bes-tee-yah'-meh*

**cauliflower,** cavolfiore (m) *kah-vol-fyoh'-reh*

**caution,** precauzione (f) *preh-kow-tsyoh'-neh*

**cave,** caverna, grotta *kah-ver'-nah, grot'-tah*

**ceiling,** soffitto *sof-feet'-toh*

**celery,** sedano *seh'-dah-noh*

**cellar,** cantina *kahn-tee'-nah*

**cemetary,** cimitero *chee-mee-teh'-roh*

**center,** centro *chen'-troh*

**centimeter,** centimetro *chen-tee'-meh-troh*

**century,** secolo *seh'-koh-loh*

**ceremony,** cerimonia *cheh-ree-moh-nee'-yah*

**certain,** certo *cher'-toh*

**certainly,** certo *cher'-toh*

**chair,** sedia *seh'-dyah* [87]

**chambermaid,** cameriera *kah-me-ree-yeh'-rah* [40]

**champagne,** sciampagna *shahm-pahn'-yah*

**chance** *n.*, caso, azzardo *kah'-zoh, ahd-dzahr'-doh*

**change** [coins], cambio *kahm'-byoh* [32]

**change** *v.*, cambiare *kahm-byah'-reh* [31, 32]

**chapel,** cappella *kahp-pehl'-lah*

**charge** *v.*, mettere sul conto *met'-teh-reh sool kon'-toh*

**charming,** grazioso, incantevole *grah-tsyoh'-zoh, een-kahn-teh'-voh-leh*

**chauffeur,** autista (m) *ow-tees'-tah*

**cheap,** a buon mercato *ah bwon mer-kah'-toh* [67]

**check** *n.*, assengo *ahs-sehn'-yoh* [31] **traveler's check,** assegno di viaggio *ahs-sehn'-yoh dee vyahj'-joh* [31]

**check** [one's luggage], spedire una valigia *speh-dee'-reh oo'-nah vah-lee'-jah* [83]

**check** [inspect], esaminare, verificare *eh-zah-mee-nah'-reh, veh-ree-fee-kah'-reh* [76]

**cheek,** guancia *gwahn'-chah*

**cheese,** formaggio *fohr-mahj'-joh*

**cherry,** ciliegia *chee-lee-yeh'-jah*

**chest,** petto *pet'-toh*

**chicken,** pollo *pol'-loh*

**child,** bambino, fanciullo *bahm-bee'-noh, fahn-chool'-loh*

**chin,** mento *men'-toh*

**chocolate,** cioccolata *chok-koh-lah'-tah*

**choose,** scegliere *shehl'-yeh-reh*

**chop,** costoletta *kos-toh-let'-tah*

**Christmas,** Natale (m) *nah-tah'-leh*

**church,** chiesa *kyeh'-zah* [99, 100]

**cigar,** sigaro *see'-gah-roh*

**cigarette,** sigaretta *see-gah-ret'-tah* [34, 70]

**cinema,** cinema *chee'-neh-mah*

**circle,** circolo *cheer'-koh-loh*

**citizen,** cittadino *cheet-tah-dee'-noh*

**city,** città *cheet-tah'* [99, 100, 101]

**class,** classe (f) *klahs'-seh* **first class,** prima classe *pree'-mah klahs'-seh* **second class,** seconda classe *seh-kon'-dah klahs'-seh*

**classify,** classificare *klahs-see-fee-kah'-reh*

**clean** *adj.*, pulito *poo-lee'-toh* [40, 55, 56]

**clean** *v.*, pulire *poo-lee'-reh*

**cleaners,** lavanderia a secco *lah-vahn-deh-ree'-yah ah sek'-koh*

**clear,** chiaro *kyah'-roh*

**climb,** salire, arrampicarsi *sah-lee'-reh, ahr-rahm-pee-kahr'-see*

**clock,** orologio *oh-roh-lohj'-joh*

**close** [near], vicino *vee-chee'-noh*

**close** *v.,* chiudere *kyoo'-deh-reh* [34, 39, 62, 84, 99, 100]

**closed,** chiuso *kyoo'-zoh* [99, 100]

**closet,** armadio *ahr-mah'-dyoh*

**cloth,** tela *teh'-lah*

**clothes,** vestiti *ves-tee'-tee*

**cloud,** nuvola *noo'-voh-lah* [7]

**clutch** [of a car], frizione (f) *free-tsyoh'-neh*

**coast,** costa *kos'-tah*

**coat,** cappotto, soprabito *kahp-pot'-toh, soh-prah'-bee-toh*

**cocktail,** cocktail *kok'-tehl*

**coffee,** caffè (m) *kahf-feh'* [49, 50, 51, 53]

**cognac,** cognac (m) *kon-yahk'*

**coin,** moneta *moh-neh'-tah* [42]

**cold** *adj.,* freddo *frehd'-doh* [51, 52]   **I am cold,** ho freddo *oh frehd'-doh*   **it is cold,** fa freddo *fah frehd'-doh*

**cold** *n.,* raffreddore (m) *rahf-frehd-doh'-reh* [96]

**collar,** colletto *kol-let'-toh*

**collect,** raccogliere *rahk-kohl'-yeh-reh*

**collection,** collezione (f) *kol-leh-tsyoh'-neh*

**college,** università, collegio *oo-nee-ver-see-tah', kol-lehj'-joh*

**collide,** scontrarsi *skon-trahr'-see*

**color,** colore (m) *koh-loh'-reh* [68]

**comb,** pettine (m) *pet'-tee-neh*

**come,** venire *veh-nee'-reh* [12, 96, 97]

**comfortable,** comodo *koh'-moh-doh*

**company,** compagnia, ditta *kom-pahn-yee'-yah, deet'-tah*

**comparison,** paragone (m), confronto *pah-rah'-goh-neh, kon-fron'-toh*

**compartment,** compartimento *kom-pahr-tee-men'-toh*

**complain,** lamentarsi, lagnarsi *lah-men-tahr'-see, lahn-yahr'-see*

**complete** *adj.,* completo *kom-pleh'-toh*

**compliment** n., complimento *kom-plee-men'-toh*
**concert**, concerto *kon-cher'-toh*
**condition**, condizione (f) *kon-dee-tsyoh'-neh*
**confuse**, confondere *kon-fon'-deh-reh*
**congratulations**, congratulazioni (f, pl) *kon-grah-too-lah-tsyoh'-nee*
**connect**, connettere *kon-net'-teh-reh*
**consent** v., consentire *kon-sen-tee'-reh*
**consider**, considerare *kon-see-deh-rah'-reh*
**constipated**, costipato *kos-tee-pah'-toh*
**consul**, console (m) *kon'-soh-leh*
**consulate**, consolato *kon-soh-lah'-toh*
**contagious**, contagioso *kon-tah-joh'-zoh*
**contain**, contenere *kon-teh-neh'-reh*
**contented**, contento *kon-ten'-toh*
**continue**, continuare *kon-tee-noo-ah'-reh*
**contrary**, contrario *kon-trah'-ree-yoh* **on the contrary**, al contrario *ahl kon-trah'-ree-yoh*
**convenient**, conveniente *kon-veh-nyen'-teh*
**conversation**, conversazione (f) *kon-ver-sah-tsyoh'-neh*
**cook** n., cuoco *kwoh'-koh*
**cook** v., cuocere *kwoh'-cheh-reh*
**cool**, fresco *fres'-koh* [8]
**copy**, copia *koh'-pyah*
**corkscrew**, cavatappi (m) *kah-vah-tahp'-pee*
**corn**, frumento *froo-men'-toh*
**corner**, angolo *ahn'-goh-loh*
**correct** adj., corretto *kor-ret'-toh*
**cost** n., costo *kos'-toh*
**cost** v., costare *kos-tah'-reh* [67, 72]
**cotton**, cotone (m) *koh-toh'-neh*
**cough** n., tosse (f) *tos'-seh*
**cough** v., tossire *tos-see'-reh* [96]
**count** v., contare *kon-tah'-reh* [32]
**country** [nation], paese (m) *pah-eh'-zeh* [73]; [not city], campagna *kahm-pahn'-yah*

**courage,** coraggio *koh-rahj-joh*

**course,** corso *kor'-soh* **of course,** certo *cher'-toh* **main course,** piatto principale *pyaht'-toh preen-chee-pah'-leh*

**court,** tribunale (m) *tree-boo-nah'-leh*

**courtyard,** cortile (m) *kor-tee'-leh* [37]

**cover** *v.,* coprire *koh-pree'-reh*

**cow,** vacca, mucca *vahk'-kah, mook'-kah*

**crab,** granchio *grahn'-kyoh*

**cramp,** crampo *krahm'-poh*

**crazy,** pazzo, matto *paht'-tsoh, maht'-toh*

**cream,** crema, panna *kreh'-mah, pahn'-nah*

**cross** *n.,* croce (f) *kroh'-cheh*

**cross** *v.,* attraversare *aht-trah-ver-sah'-reh* [101]

**crossing,** incrocio *een-kroh'-choh;* [by ship], traversata *trah-ver-sah'-tah*

**crossroads,** incrocio, bivio *een-kroh'-choh, bee'-vee-yoh*

**crowd,** folla *fol'-lah*

**cry** *v.,* piangere *pyahn-jeh'-reh*

**cucumber,** cetriolo *cheh-tree-yoh'-loh*

**cup,** tazza *taht'-tsah* [53]

**curve,** curva *koor'-vah*

**custard,** crema *kreh'-mah*

**customer,** cliente (m) *klee-yen'-teh*

**customs,** dogana *doh-gah'-nah*

**cut** [injury], piaga *pyah'-gah*

**cut** *v.,* tagliare *tahl-yah'-reh*

**cutlet,** costoletta *kos-toh-let'-tah*

**daily** *adj.,* quotidiano *kwoh-tee-dyah'-noh*

**daily** *adv.,* ogni giorno *oh'-nyee johr'-noh*

**damage** *v.,* danneggiare *dahn-nehj-jah'-reh*

**damaged,** danneggiato *dahn-nehj-jah'-toh*

**damp,** umido *oo'-mee-doh* [8]

**dance** *n.,* ballo *bahl'-loh*

**dance** *v.,* ballare *bahl-lah'-reh*

**danger,** pericolo *peh-ree'-koh-loh*

**dangerous,** pericoloso *peh-ree-koh-loh'-zoh*

**dare** *v.,* osare *oh-zah'-reh*

**dark,** scuro, buio *skoo'-roh, boo'-ee-yoh*

**darkness,** oscurità *oh-skoo-ree-tah'*

**date** [time], data *dah'-tah;* [appointment], appuntamento *ahp-poon-tah-men'-toh*

**daughter,** figlia *feel'-yah* [3]

**day,** giorno *johr'-noh* **per day, a day,** al giorno *ahl johr'-noh*

**dead,** morto *mor'-toh*

**dear** [endearment], caro *kah'-roh*

**December,** dicembre *dee-chem'-breh*

**decide,** decidere *deh-chee'-deh-reh*

**deck,** ponte *pon'-teh* [87]

**declare,** dichiarare *dee-kyah-rah'-reh* [33]

**deep,** profondo *proh-fon'-doh*

**deer,** cervo *cher'-voh*

**delay** *n.,* ritardo *ree-tahr'-doh* [90]

**delicious,** delizioso *deh-lee-tsyoh'-zoh*

**delighted,** felicissimo *feh-lee-chees'-see-moh*

**deliver,** consegnare *kon-sehn-yah'-reh*

**dentist,** dentista (m) *den-tees'-tah*

**deodorant,** deodorante (m) *deh-oh-doh-rahn'-teh*

**department store,** grande magazzino *grahn'-deh mah-gahd-dzee'-noh*

**departure,** partenza *pahr-tehn'-tsah* [85]

**deposit** *v.,* depositare *deh-poh-zee-tah'-reh* [42]

**descend,** scendere *shen'-deh-reh*

**describe,** descrivere *deh-skree'-veh-reh*

**desert** *n.,* deserto *deh-zer'-toh*

**desert** *v.,* disertare, abbandonare *dee-zer-tah'-reh, ahb-bahn-doh-nah'-reh*

**desire** *v.,* desiderare *deh-zee-deh-rah'-reh*

**desk,** scrivania *skree-vah-nee'-yah*

**dessert,** dessert, dolci *dehs-ser', dohl'-chee* [56]

**destroy,** distruggere *dee-strooj'-jeh-reh*

**detour,** deviazione (f) *deh-vee-yah-tsyoh'-neh*
**develop,** sviluppare *zvee-loop-pah'-reh*
**dial** *v.,* fare il numero *fah'-reh eel noo'-meh-roh* [42, 43]
**diamond,** diamante (m) *dee-yah-mahn'-teh*
**diaper,** pannilino *pahn-nee-lee'-noh*
**diarrhea,** diarrea *dee-yahr-reh'-yah*
**dictionary,** dizionario *dee-tsee-yoh-nah'-ree-yoh*
**die,** morire *moh-ree'-reh*
**difference,** differenza *deef-feh-rehn'-tsah*
**different,** differente *deef-feh-rehn'-teh*
**difficult,** difficile *deef-fee'-chee-leh*
**dine,** pranzare *prahn-dzah'-reh* [53]
**dining car,** carrozza ristorante *kahr-rot'-tsah rees-toh-rahn'-teh* [84]
**dining room,** sala da pranzo *sah'-lah dah prahn'-dzoh* [38, 87]
**dinner,** pranzo *prahn'-dzoh* [48, 50]
**direct,** diretto *dee-ret'-toh*
**direction,** direzione (f) *dee-reh-tsyoh'-neh*
**director,** direttore (m) *dee-reht-toh'-reh*
**dirty,** sporco *spor'-koh* [55]
**disappear,** sparire *spah-ree'-reh*
**discount** *n.,* sconto *skon'-toh* [70]
**discuss,** discutere *dee-skoo'-teh-reh*
**disease,** malattia *mah-laht-tee'-yah*
**dish,** piatto *pyaht'-toh*
**disinfect,** disinfettare *dee-seen-fet'-tah'-reh*
**distance,** distanza *dee-stahn'-tsah*
**district,** distretto *dee-stret'-toh*
**disturb,** disturbare *dee-stoor-bah'-reh*
**divorced,** divorziato *dee-vohr-tsyah'-toh*
**do,** fare *fah'-reh*   **how do you do?** come sta? *ko'-meh stah*
**dock,** molo *moh'-loh*
**doctor,** medico, dottore *meh'-dee-koh, dot-toh'-reh* [51, 91]
**dog,** cane (m) *kah'-neh*
**doll,** bambola *bahm'-boh-lah*

**dollar,** dollaro *dol'-lah-roh* [31]

**done,** fatto *faht'-toh*

**donkey,** asino *ah'-zee-noh*

**door,** porta *por'-tah*

**dose,** dose (f) *doh'-zeh*

**double,** doppio *dop'-pyoh*

**doubt,** dubbio *doob'-byoh* **without doubt,** senza dubbio *sehn'-tsah doob'-byoh* **no doubt,** nessun dubbio *nes-soon' doob'-byoh*

**down,** giù *joo* **to go down,** scendere *shen'-deh-reh*

**downtown,** centro città *chen'-troh chee-tah'* [46]

**dozen,** dozzina *dod-dzee'-nah*

**drawer,** cassetto *kahs-set'-toh*

**dress** *n.*, vestito *ves-tee'-toh* [68]

**dress** [oneself], vestirsi *ves-teer'-see*

**dressmaker,** sarta *sahr'-tah*

**drink** *n.*, bibita, bevanda *bee'-bee-tah, beh-vahn'-dah*

**drink** *v.*, bere *beh'-reh*

**drive** *v.*, condurre *kon-door'-reh* [45, 75, 76]

**driver,** autista *ow-tees'-tah* [44]

**drop** *v.*, lasciar cadere *lah-shar' kah-deh'-reh*

**druggist,** farmacista (m) *fahr-mah-chees'-tah*

**drugstore,** farmacia *fahr-mah-chee'-yah* [92]

**drunk,** ubriaco *oo-bree-yah'-koh*

**dry,** secco *sek'-koh*

**duck,** anitra *ah'-nee-trah*

**during,** durante *doo-rahn'-teh*

**dust,** polvere (f) *pol'-veh-reh*

**duty,** dovere (m) *doh-veh'-reh* [34]

**dysentery,** dissenteria *dees-sen-teh-ree'-yah*

**each** ciascuno, ciascun *chahs-koo'-noh, chahs-koon'*

**each one,** ciascuno *chahs-koo'-noh*

**eager,** avido *ah'-vee-doh*

**ear,** orecchio *oh-rek'-kyoh*

**earache,** mal d'orecchi *mahl doh-rek'-kee*

**early**, presto, di buon'ora *pres'-toh, dee bwon-oh'-rah* [24]
**earn**, guadagnare *gwah-dahn-yah'-reh*
**earrings**, orecchini *oh-rek-kee'-nee*
**earth**, terra *ter'-rah*
**easily**, facilmente *fah-cheel-men'-teh*
**east**, est (m) *est*
**Easter**, Pasqua *pahs'-kwah*
**easy**, facile *fah'-chee-leh*
**eat**, mangiare *mahn-jah'-reh* [38, 48, 52, 56, 87]
**edge**, orlo *ohr'-loh*
**egg**, uovo *woh'-voh*
**eight**, otto *ot'-toh*
**eighteen**, diciotto *dee-chot'-toh*
**eighth**, ottavo *ot-tah'-voh*
**eighty**, ottanta *ot-tahn'-tah*
**either**, l'uno o l'altro *loo'-noh oh lahl'-troh*
**either . . . or . . .** , o . . . o . . . *oh . . . oh . . .*
**elbow**, gomito *goh'-mee-toh*
**electric**, elettrico *eh-let'-tree-koh*
**elevator**, ascensore (m) *ah-shen-soh'-reh* [39]
**eleven**, undici *oon'-dee-chee*
**else: nobody else**, nessun altro *nes-soon' ahl'-troh* **nothing else**, nient'altro *nyent-ahl'-troh* **something else**, qualcosa d'altro *kwahl-ko'-zah dahl'-troh*
**elsewhere**, altrove *ahl-troh'-veh*
**embark**, imbarcarsi *eem-bahr-kahr'-see*
**embarrassed**, imbarazzato *eem-bah-rahd-dzah'-toh*
**embassy**, ambasciata *ahm-bah-shah'-tah*
**embrace** *v.*, abbracciare *ahb-brach-chah'-reh*
**emergency**, emergenza *eh-mer-jehn'-tsah*
**empty**, vuoto *vwoh'-toh*
**end** *n.*, fine (f) *fee'-neh*
**engaged** [busy], occupato *ok-koo-pah'-toh*
**engine**, motore (m) *moh-toh'-reh*
**English**, inglese *een-gleh'-zeh* [11]
**enjoy** godere *goh-deh'-reh*

**enormous,** enorme *eh-nohr'-meh*

**enough,** abbastaza *ahb-bahs-tahn'-tsah* **that's enough,** basta *bahs-tah*

**enter,** entrare *en-trah-reh*

**entertaining,** divertente *dee-ver-ten'-teh*

**entire,** intero *een-teh'-roh*

**entrance,** entrata, ingresso *en-trah'-tah, een-gres'-soh*

**envelope,** busta *boos'-tah*

**equal,** uguale *oo-gwah'-leh*

**equipment,** equipaggiamento *eh-kwee-pahj-jah-men'-toh*

**error,** errore (m) *er-roh'-reh*

**Europe,** Europa *eh-oo-roh'-pah*

**even** *adv.,* anche, perfino *ahn'-keh, per-fee'-noh*

**even** [number], pari *pah'-ree*

**evening,** sera *seh'-rah* [100] **good evening,** buona sera *bwoh'-nah seh'-rah*

**ever,** sempre, mai *sem'-preh, mah'-ee*

**every,** ogni *ohn'-yee*

**everyone,** ognuno *ohn-yoo'-noh*

**everything,** ogni cosa, tutto *ohn'-yee ko'-zah, toot'-toh*

**everywhere,** dappertutto *dahp-per-toot'-toh*

**evidently,** evidentemente *eh-vee-den-teh-men'-teh*

**exact,** esatto *eh-zaht'-toh*

**examination,** esame (m) *eh-zah'-meh*

**examine,** esaminare *eh-zah-mee-nah'-reh*

**example,** esempio *eh-zem'-pyoh* **for example,** per esempio *per eh-zem'-pyoh*

**excellent,** eccellente *ech-chel-len'-teh*

**except,** eccetto *ech-chet'-toh*

**exchange** *v.,* cambiare, scambiare *kahm-byah'-reh, skahm-byah'-reh*

**exchange rate,** cambio *kahm'-byoh* [31]

**excursion,** escursione (f) *es-koor-zyoh'-neh*

**excuse** *v.,* scusare *skoo-zah'-reh* **excuse me,** (mi) scusi *(mee) skoo'-zee*

**exercise,** esercizio *eh-zer-chee'-tsyoh*

**exhibition,** esposizione (f) *es-poh-zee-tsyoh'-neh* [99]

**exit,** uscita *oo-shee'-tah*

**expect,** sperare *speh-rah'-reh* [32]

**expensive,** costoso, caro *kos-toh'-zoh, kah'-roh* [38, 67]

**explain,** spiegare *spyeh-gah'-reh*

**explanation,** spiegazione (f) *spyeh-gah-tsyoh'-neh*

**export** *v.,* esportare *es-por-tah'-reh*

**express** *adj.,* espresso *es-pres'-soh*

**extra,** extra, suppletivo *es'-trah, soop-pleh-tee'-voh*

**extraordinary,** straordinario *strah-ohr-dee-nah'-ree-yoh*

**eye,** occhio *ok'-kyoh*


**face,** faccia, viso *fahch-chah, vee'-zoh*

**factory,** fabbrica *fahb'-bree-kah*

**faint** *v.,* svenire *zveh-nee'-reh*

**fair** [market], fiera *fyeh'-rah*

**fall** [season], autunno *ow-toon'-noh*

**fall** *n.,* caduta *kah-doo'-tah*

**fall** *v.,* cadere *kah-deh'-reh*

**false,** falso *fahl'-soh*

**family,** famiglia *fah-meel'-yah*

**famous,** famoso *fah-moh'-zoh*

**fan,** ventilatore (m), ventaglio *ven-tee-lah-toh'-reh, ven-tahl'-yoh*

**far,** lontano *lon-tah'-noh* **so far,** così lontano *ko-see' lon-tah'-noh* **how far is it?** a quanta distanza è? *ah kwahn'-tah dees-tahn'-tsah eh?*

**fare** [cost], tariffa *tah-reef'-fah* [45]

**farewell,** addio *ahd-dee'-yoh*

**farm,** podere (m), fattoria *poh-deh'-reh, faht-toh-ree'-yah*

**farmer,** agricoltore (m) *ah-gree-kol-toh'-reh*

**farther,** più lontano *pyoo lon-tah'-noh*

**fashion,** moda *moh'-dah*

**fast** [quick], veloce *veh-loh'-cheh*

**fasten,** attaccare *aht-tahk-kah'-reh* [89]

**fat**, grasso *grahs'-soh*
**father**, padre *pah'-dreh* [3]
**father-in-law**, suocero *swoh'-cheh-roh*
**fault**, colpa *kol'-pah*
**favor**, favore (m) *fah-voh'-reh*
**favorite** *adj. & n.*, favorito *fah-voh-ree'-toh*
**fear: to be afraid**, temere, aver paura *teh-meh'-reh, ah-vehr' pah-oo'-rah*
**feather**, piuma, penna *pyoo'-mah, pen'-nah*
**February**, febbraio *feb-brah'-yoh*
**fee**, onorario *oh-noh-rah'-ree-yoh*
**feel**, sentire *sen-tee'-reh* [92]
**feeling**, sentimento *sen-tee-men'-toh*
**female**, femmina *fem'-mee-nah*
**fence**, steccato *stek-kah'-toh*
**fender**, parafango *pah-rah-fahn'-goh*
**ferry** [boat], nave-traghetto *nah'-veh trah-get'-toh*
**fever**, febbre (f) *feb'-breh* [93]
**few**, pochi, poche *poh'-kee, poh'-keh*
**field**, campo *kahm'-poh*
**fifteen**, quindici *kween'-dee-chee*
**fifth**, quinto *kween'-toh*
**fifty**, cinquanta *cheen-kwahn'-tah*
**fight** *n.*, lotta *lot'-tah*
**fight** *v.*, combattere *kom-baht'-teh-reh*
**fill** *v.*, riempire *ree-em-pee'-reh* [39, 74]
**filling** [for a tooth], piombatura *pyom-bah-too'-rah*
**film**, pellicola, film *pel-lee'-koh-lah, feelm*
**final**, finale *fee-nah'-leh*
**finally**, finalmente *fee-nah'-men'-teh*
**find**, trovare *troh-vah'-reh*
**fine** *adj.*, bene *beh'-neh*
**fine** *n.*, multa *mool'-tah* [75]
**finger**, dito *dee'-toh* [93]
**finish** *v.*, finire *fee-nee'-reh*
**fire**, fuoco *fwoh'-koh* [15]

**first,** primo *pree'-moh* **first class,** prima classe *pree'-mah klahs'-seh* [83, 87]

**fish,** pesce (m) *peh'-sheh* [56]

**fish** v., pescare *pes-kah'-reh*

**fish-bone,** lisca *lees'-kah*

**fit** [seizure], convulsione (f) *kon-vool-syoh'-neh*

**fit** v., andar bene *ahn-dahr' beh'-neh*

**fitting** [of a garment], prova *proh'-vah*

**five,** cinque *cheen'-kweh*

**fix** v., reparare, aggiustare *reh-pah-rah-reh, ahj-joos-tah'-reh* [74, 76]

**flag,** bandiera *bahn-dyeh'-rah*

**flashbulb,** lampadina fotografica *lahm-pah-dee'-nah fot-toh-grah'-fee-kah*

**flat,** piano *pyah'-noh*

**flat tire,** gomma forata *gom'-mah foh-rah'-tah* [74]

**flavor,** sapore (m) *sah-poh'-reh*

**flight,** volo *voh'-loh* [88, 89, 90]

**flint,** pietra focaia *pyeh'-trah foh-kah'-yah*

**flirt** v., civettare *chee-vet-tah'-reh*

**flood,** inondazione (f) *ee-non-dah-tsyoh'-neh*

**floor,** pavimento *pah-vee-men'-toh;* [storey], piano *pyah'-noh*

**florist,** fioraio *fyoh-rah'-yoh*

**flower,** fiore (m) *fyoh'-reh*

**fluid,** fluido, liquido *floo-ee'-doh, lee'-kwee-doh*

**fly** [insect], mosca *mos'-kah*

**fly** v., volare *voh-lah'-reh* [89]

**fog,** nebbia *nehb'-byah* [6]

**follow,** seguire *seh-gwee-reh*

**food,** cibo, vitto *chee'-boh, veet'-toh*

**foot,** piede (m) *pyeh'-deh*

**for,** per *per*

**forbid,** proibire, vietare *proh-ee-bee'-reh, vyeh-tah'-reh*

**forbidden,** proibito, vietato *proh-ee-bee'-toh, vyeh-tah'-toh*

**forehead,** fronte (f) *fron'-teh*

**foreign,** estero, straniero *es'-teh-roh, strah-nyeh'-roh*

**foreigner,** straniero, forestiere *strah-nyeh'-roh, foh-res-tyeh'-reh*

**forest,** selva, foresta *sel'-vah, foh-res'-tah*

**forget,** dimenticare *dee-men-tee-kah'-reh*

**forgive,** perdonare *per-doh-nah'-reh*

**fork,** forchetta *fohr-ket'-tah* [55]

**form,** forma *for'-mah*

**former,** precedente *preh-cheh-den'-teh*

**formerly,** prima *pree'-mah*

**fort,** forte (m) *for'-teh*

**fortunate,** fortunato *for-too-nah'-toh*

**fortunately,** fortunatamente *for-too-nah-tah-men'-tah*

**forty,** quaranta *kwah-rahn'-tah*

**forward,** avanti *ah-vahn'-tee*

**fountain,** fontana *fon-tah'-nah*

**four,** quattro *kwaht'-troh*

**fourteen,** quattordici *kwaht-tor'-dee-chee*

**fourth,** quarto *kwahr'-toh*

**fracture** *n.,* frattura *fraht-too'-rah*

**fragile,** fragile *frah'-jee-leh*

**free,** libero *lee'-beh-roh* [44]

**freedom,** libertà *lee-ber-tah'*

**freeze,** gelare *jeh-lah'-reh*

**frequently,** frequentemente *freh-kwen-teh-men'-teh*

**fresh,** fresco *fres'-koh* [52]

**Friday,** venerdì *ve-ner-dee'*

**fried,** fritto *freet'-toh*

**friend,** amico *ah-mee'-koh*, [2]

**friendly,** amichevole *ah-mee-keh'-voh-leh*

**from,** da *dah*

**front,** fronte (f) *fron'-teh* **in front of,** davanti a *dah-vahn'-tee ah*

**frozen,** congelato *kon-jeh-lah'-toh*

**fruit,** frutta *froot'-tah* [52]

**full,** pieno *pyeh'-noh*

**fun,** divertimento *dee-ver-tee-men'-toh*

**function,** funzione (f) *foon-tsyoh'-neh*

**funnel,** imbuto *eem-boo'-toh*

**funny,** comico *koh'-mee-koh*

**fur,** pelo *peh'-loh*

**furnished,** ammobiliato *ahm-moh-bee-lee-yah'-toh*

**furniture,** mobili *moh'-bee-lee*

**further,** inoltre, di più *een-ol'-treh, dee pyoo*

**future,** futuro, avvenire (m) *foo-too'-roh, ahv-veh-nee'-reh*


**gain** *v.,* guadagnare *gwah-dahn-yah'-reh*

**gamble** *v.,* giocare *joh-kah'-reh*

**game,** gioco *joh'-koh*

**gangplank,** passerella, scalandrone (m) *pahs-seh-rehl'-lah, skah-lahn-droh'-neh* [88]

**garage,** autorimessa *ow-toh-ree-mes'-sah* [73, 76]

**garden,** giardino *jahr-dee'-noh*

**garlic,** aglio *ahl'-yoh*

**gas,** gas *gahs*

**gasoline,** benzina *ben-dzee'-nah* [73, 74]

**gas station,** stazione di servizio *stah-tsyoh'-neh dee ser-vee'-tsyoh* [73]

**gate,** cancello, porta *kahn-chel'-loh, por'-tah* [89]

**gather** [collect], raccogliere *rahk-kol'-yeh-reh*

**gay,** gaio *gah'-yoh*

**general** *adj.,* generale *jeh-neh-rah'-leh* **generally, in general,** generalmente *jeh-neh-rahl-men'-teh*

**generous,** generoso *jeh-neh-roh'-zoh*

**gentleman,** signore *seen-yoh'-reh*

**get,** ottenere *ot-teh-neh'-reh* **get in, get on,** salire *sah-lee'-reh* [46] **get off,** scendere *shen'-deh-reh* [46] **get up,** alzarsi *ah-tsahr'-see* [96]

**gift,** regalo *reh-gah'-loh*

**gin,** gin *jeen*

**girl,** ragazza *rah-gaht'-tsah* [10]

**give,** dare *dah'-reh* [13, 32]

**glad,** contento *kon-ten'-toh*

**gladly,** con piacere, volentieri *kon-pyah-cheh'-reh, voh-len-tyeh'-ree*

**glass** [for drinking], bicchiere *beek-kyeh'-reh* [51, 52, 55]

**glasses** [for the eyes], occhiali (m, pl) *ok-kyah'-lee*

**glove,** guanto *gwahn'-toh*

**go,** andare *ahn-dah'-reh* [12, 35, 44, 46, 88, 102] **go back,** tornare *tohr-nah'-reh* **go in,** entrare *en-trah'-reh* **go out,** uscire *oo-shee'-reh*

**God,** Dio *dee'-yoh*

**gold,** oro *oh'-roh*

**good,** buono *bwoh'-noh*

**good-bye,** arrivederci *ahr-ree-veh-der'-chee*

**government,** governo *goh-ver'-noh*

**grandfather,** nonno *non'-noh*

**grandmother,** nonna *non'-nah*

**grape(s),** uva *oo'-vah*

**grapefruit,** pompelmo *pom-pel'-moh*

**grass,** erba *er'-bah*

**grateful,** grato *grah'-toh*

**gray,** grigio *gree'-joh*

**grease** *n.,* grasso *grahs'-soh*

**great,** grande *grahn'-deh*

**green,** verde *ver'-deh*

**grocery,** bottega bi comestibili *bot-teh'-gah dee koh-mes-tee'-bee-lee*

**ground,** terra *ter'-rah*

**group,** gruppo *groop'-poh*

**grow,** crescere *kreh'-sheh-reh*

**guard** *n.,* guardia *gwahr'-dyah*

**guest,** ospite (m) *os'-pee-teh*

**guide** *n.,* guida *gwee'-dah* [99]

**guilty,** colpevole *kol-peh'-voh-leh*

**guitar,** chitarra *kee-tahr'-rah*

**gum** [chewing], gomma da masticare *gom'-mah dah mahs-tee-kah'-reh*

**gun,** fucile (m) *foo-chee'-leh*

**habit,** abitudine (f) *ah-bee-too'-dee-neh*

**hair,** capelli (m, pl) *keh-pel'-lee*

**haircut,** taglio di capelli *tahl'-yoh dee kah-pel'-lee*

**hairdresser,** parrucchiere (m) *pahr-rook-kyeh'-reh*

**hairpin,** forcella *for-chel'-lah*

**half** *adj.,* mezzo *med'-dzoh*

**half** *n.,* metà *meh-tah'*

**hall,** corridoio *kor-ree-doh'-yoh*

**ham,** proscuitto *proh-shoot'-toh*

**hand,** mano (f) *mah'-noh*

**handkerchief,** fazzoletto *faht-tsoh-let'-toh* [40]

**hand-made,** fatto a mano *faht'-toh ah mah'-noh*

**handsome,** bello *bel'-loh* [10]

**hang,** impiccare *eem-peek-kah'-reh* **hang up,** appendere *ahp-pen-deh'-reh*

**hanger** [for clothing], attaccapanni *aht-tahk-kah-pahn'-nee*

**happen,** succedere *sooch-cheh'-deh-reh* [15]

**happy,** felice *feh-lee'-cheh*

**harbor,** porto *por'-toh* [86]

**hard,** duro *doo'-roh*

**hardly,** appena *ahp-peh'-nah*

**harm** *n.,* male (m) *mah'-leh*

**harm** *v.,* far male *fahr mah'-leh*

**harmful,** nocivo *noh-chee'-voh*

**haste,** fretta *fret'-tah*

**hat,** cappello *kahp-pel'-loh*

**hat shop,** cappelleria *kahp-pel-leh-ree'-yah*

**hate** *v.,* odiare *oh-dee-yah'-reh*

**have,** avere *ah-veh'-reh* **I have,** ho *oh* **have you?** ha Lei? *ah leh'-ee*

**he,** egli. lui *ehl'-yee, loo'-ee*

**head,** testa *tes'-tah*

**headache,** mal di testa *mahl dee tes'-tah* [92]

**health,** salute (f) *sah-loo'-teh* [56]

**hear,** udire, sentire *oo-dee'-reh, sen-tee'-reh*

**heart,** cuore (m) *kwoh'-reh*

**heat** *n.,* calore (m) *kah-loh'-reh*

**heavy,** pesante *peh-zahn'-teh*

**heel,** tacco *tahk'-koh*

**hello,** ciao, buon giorno *chow, bwon johr'-noh*

**help** *n.,* aiuto, soccorso *ah-yoo'-toh, sok-kor'-soh*

**help** *v.,* aiutare *ah-yoo-tah'-reh* [14, 64]

**helpful,** soccorrevole *sok-kor-reh'-voh-leh*

**hem** *n.,* orlo *ohr'-loh*

**hen,** gallina *gahl-lee'-nah*

**her,** la, lei *lah, leh'-ee*

**here,** qui, qua *kwee, kwah*

**hers,** suo, sua *soo'-oh, soo'-ah*

**high,** alto *ahl'-toh*

**hill,** collina *kol-lee'-nah*

**him,** lo, lui *loh, loo'-ee*

**hip,** anca *ahn'-kah*

**hire,** noleggiare *noh-lej-jah'-reh* [72]

**his,** suo, sua *soo'-oh, soo'-ah*

**history,** storia *stoh'-ree-yah*

**hit** *v.,* colpire *kol-pee'-reh*

**hold,** tenere *teh-neh'-reh*

**hole,** buco *boo'-koh*

**holiday,** giorno festivo, giorno di festa *johr'-noh fes-tee'-voh, johr'-noh dee fes'-tah*

**holy,** santo *sahn'-toh*

**home,** casa *kah'-zah*

**honest,** onesto *oh-nes'-toh*

**honey** [food], miele (m) *myeh'-leh*

**honor,** onore (m) *oh-noh'-reh*

**hope** *n.,* speranza *speh-rahn'-tsah*

**hope** *v.,* sperare *speh-rah'-reh* [3]

**horn** [automobile], tromba *trom'-bah*

**hors d'oeuvres**, antipasto *ahn-tee-pahs'-toh*

**horse**, cavallo *kah-vahl'-loh*

**hospital**, ospedale (m) *os-peh-dah'-leh* [92]

**host**, oste (m) *os'-teh*

**hot**, caldo *kahl'-doh*

**hotel**, albergo *ahl-ber'-goh* [10, 32, 36, 38, 45, 53, 70, 102]

**hour**, ora *oh'-rah*

**house**, casa *kah'-zah*

**how**, come *ko'-meh* **how are you?** come sta? *ko'-meh stah* **how far?** quanto lontano? *kwahn'-toh lon-tah'-noh* **how long?** quanto tempo? *kwahn'-toh tem'-poh* **how many?** quanti? quante? *kwahn'-tee, kwahn'-teh* **how much?** quanto? *kwahn'-toh*

**hug** *n.*, abbraccio *ahb-brahch'-choh*

**human**, umano *oo-mah'-noh*

**humid**, umido *oo'-mee-doh*

**hundred**, cento *chen'-toh*

**hunger**, fame (f) *fah'-meh*

**hungry: to be hungry**, aver fame *ah-vehr' fah'-meh* [47, 48]

**hurry** *v.*, affrettarsi *ahf-fret-tahr'-see* **to be in a hurry,** aver fretta *ah-vehr' fret'-tah*

**hurt**, far male *fahr mah'-leh* [93]

**husband**, marito *mah-ree'-toh* [2]

**I**, io *ee'-yoh*

**ice**, ghiaccio *gyahch'-choh* [55]

**ice cream**, gelato *jeh-lah'-toh* [56]

**idea**, idea *ee-deh'-yah*

**identification**, identificazione (f) *ee-den-tee-fee-kah-tsyoh'-neh*

**if**, se *seh*

**ill**, ammalato *ahm-mah-lah'-toh*

**illegal**, illegale *eel-leh-gah'-leh*

**illness**, malattia *mah-laht-tee'-yah*

**imagine,** immaginare, figurarsi *eem-mah-jee-nah'-reh, fee-goo-rahr'-see*

**immediately,** immediatamente, subito *eem-meh-dee-yah-tah-men'-teh, soo'-bee-toh*

**important,** importante *eem-por-tahn'-teh*

**impossible,** impossibile *eem-pos-see'-bee-leh* [13]

**improve,** migliorare *meel-yoh-rah'-reh*

**improvement,** miglioramento *meel-yoh-rah-men'-toh*

**in,** in *een*

**incident,** incidente (m) *een-chee-den'-teh*

**included,** incluso, compreso *een-kloo'-zoh, kom-preh'-zoh* [57]

**incomplete,** incompleto *een-kom-pleh'-toh*

**inconvenient,** inconveniente *een-kon-veh-nyen'-teh*

**incorrect,** inesatto *een-eh-zaht'-toh*

**increase** *v.,* aumentare *ow-men-tah'-reh*

**incredible,** incredibile *een-kreh-dee'-bee-leh*

**indeed,** in verità *een veh-ree-tah'*

**independence,** indipendenza *een-dee-pen-den'-tsah*

**independent,** indipendente *een-dee-pen-den'-teh*

**indicate,** indicare *een-dee-kah'-reh*

**indigestion,** indigestione (f) *een-dee-jes-tyoh'-neh*

**indoors,** dentro *den'-troh*

**industrial,** industriale *een-doos-tree-yah'-leh*

**inexpensive,** a buon mercato *ah bwon mehr-kah'-toh*

**infection,** infezione (f) *een-feh-tsyoh'-neh*

**infectious,** infettivo *een-fet-tee'-voh*

**inform,** informare *een-fohr-mah'-reh*

**information,** informazioni (f, pl) *een-fohr-mah-tsyoh'-nee*

**injection,** iniezione (f) *een-yeh-tsyoh'-neh*

**injury,** ferita, danno, lesione (f) *feh-ree'-tah, dahn'-noh, leh-zyoh'-neh*

**injustice,** ingiustizia *een-joos-tee'-tsyah*

**ink,** inchiostro *een-kyohs'-troh*

**inn,** taverna *tah-ver'-nah*

**inquire,** domandare, informarsi *doh-mahn-dah'-reh, een-fohr-mahr'-see*

**inside,** dentro *den'-troh*

**insist,** insistere *een-sees'-teh-reh*

**inspect,** ispezionare *ee-speh-tsee-yoh-nah'-reh*

**instead of,** invece di *een-veh'-cheh dee*

**institution,** istituzione (f) *ee-stee-toot-syoh'-neh*

**insurance,** assicurazione (f) *ahs-see-koo-rah-tsyoh'-neh*

**insure,** assicurare *ahs-see-koo-rah'-reh*

**intelligent,** intelligente *een-tel-lee-jen'-teh*

**intend,** intendere *een-ten'-deh-reh*

**intense,** intenso *een-ten'-soh*

**intention,** intenzione (f) *een-ten-tsyoh'-neh*

**interest** *n.,* interesse (m) *een-teh-res'-seh*

**interest** *v.,* interessare *een-teh-res-sah'-reh*

**interesting,** interessante *een-teh-res-sahn'-teh* [102]

**intermission,** intervallo *een-ter-vahl-loh*

**internal,** interno *een-ter'-noh*

**international,** internazionale *een-ter-nah-tsee-yoh-nah'-leh*

**interpret,** interpretare *een-ter-preh-tah'-reh*

**interpreter,** interprete (m) *een-ter'-preh-teh*

**interview** *n.,* intervista *een-ter-vees'-tah*

**into,** in *een*

**introduce,** presentare *preh-zen-tah'-reh*

**introduction,** presentazione (f) *preh-zen-tah-tsyoh'-neh*

**investigate,** investigare *een-ves-tee-gah'-reh*

**invitation,** invito *een-vee'-toh*

**invite,** invitare *een-vee-tah'-reh*

**iron** [for ironing], ferro da stiro *fer'-roh dah stee'-roh*

**iron** [metal], ferro *fer'-roh*

**iron** *v.,* stirare *stee-rah'-reh*

**is:** è, sta *eh, stah* **he is,** lui è *loo'-ee eh* **she is,** lei è *leh'-ee eh* **it is,** è *eh*

**island,** isola *ee'-zoh-lah*

**itch** *v.,* prudere *proo'-deh-reh*

**jacket,** giacca *jahk'-kah* [8]

**jail,** carcere (m) *kahr'-cheh-reh*

**jam,** confettura *kon-fet-too'-rah*

**January,** gennaio *jen-nah'-yoh*

**jaw,** mandibola *mahn-dee'-boh-lah*

**jelly,** gelatina *jeh-lah-tee'-nah*

**jewelry,** gioielli (m, pl) *joh-yel'-lee*

**jewelry store,** gioielleria *joh-yel-leh-ree'-yah*

**job,** compito, lavoro *kom'-pee-toh, lah-voh'-roh*

**joke,** scherzo *sker'-tsoh*

**juice,** succo *sook'-koh*

**July,** luglio *lool'-yoh*

**jump** *v.,* saltare *sahl-tah'-reh*

**June,** giugno *joon'-yoh*

**just,** giusto *joos'-toh*

**justice,** giustizia *joos-tee'-tsee-yah*


**keep,** mantenere *mahn-teh-neh'-reh*

**key,** chiave (f) *kyah'-veh* [34, 39, 73, 87]

**kidneys,** reni *reh'-nee*

**kill,** uccidere, ammazzare *och-chee'-deh-reh, ahm-mahd-dzah'-reh*

**kilogram,** chilogrammo *kee-loh-grahm'-moh*

**kilometer,** chilometro *kee-loh'-me-troh* [72]

**kind** *adj.,* gentile *jen-tee'-leh*

**kind** *n.,* specie (f) *speh'-chyeh* [31]

**king,** re *reh*

**kiss** *n.,* bacio *bah'-choh*

**kiss** *v.,* baciare *bah-chah'-reh*

**kitchen,** cucina *koo-chee'-nah*

**knee,** ginocchio *jee-nok'-kyoh*

**knife,** coltello *kol-tel'-loh* [55]

**knock** *v.,* bussare *boos-sah'-reh*

**know** [something], sapere *sah-peh'-reh* [9]; [someone], conoscere *koh-noh'-sheh-reh* [10]

**laborer,** lavoratore (m), operaio *lah-voh-rah-toh'-reh, oh-peh-rah'-yoh*

**lace,** merletto *mer-let'-toh*

**ladies' room,** gabinetto da signore *gah-bee-net'-toh dah seen-yoh'-reh*

**lady,** signora *seen-yoh'-rah*

**lake,** lago *lah'-goh*

**lamb,** agnello *an-yel'-loh*

**lame,** zoppo *dzop'-poh*

**lamp,** lampada *lahm'-pah-dah*

**land** *n.,* terra *ter'-rah*

**land** *v.,* atterrare *aht-ter-rah'-reh* [90]

**landing card,** cartoncino (permesso) di sbarco *kahr-ton-chee'-noh (per-mes'-soh) dee zbahr'-koh* [88]

**language,** lingua *leen'-gwah*

**large,** grande, grosso *grahn'-deh, gros'-soh*

**last** *adj.,* ultimo *ool'-tee-moh*

**last** *v.,* durare *doo-rah'-reh* [99]

**late,** tardi *tahr'-dee* [24, 84]

**laugh** *v.,* ridere *ree'-deh-reh*

**laughter,** riso *ree'-zoh*

**laundry,** lavanderia *lah-vahn-deh-ree'-yah*

**lavatory,** gabinetto *gah-bee-net'-toh* [85]

**law,** legge (f) *lej-jeh*

**lawyer,** avvocato *ahv-voh-kah'-toh*

**lazy,** pigro *peeg'-roh*

**lead** *v.,* condurre *kon-door'-reh*

**leaf,** foglia *fohl'-yah*

**leak** *n.,* perdita *per'-dee-tah*

**learn,** imparare *eem-pah-rah'-reh*

**least,** minimo *mee'-nee-moh*

**leather,** cuoio *kwoh'-yoh*

**leave,** partire, andarsene *pahr-tee'-reh, ahn-dahr'-seh-neh* [25, 40, 46, 83, 85, 88]

**left,** sinistro *see-nees'-troh* [45]

**leg,** gamba *gahm'-bah* [93]

**lemon,** limone (m) *lee-moh'-neh*

**lend,** prestare *pres-tah'-reh*

**length,** lunghezza *loon-get'-tsah*

**lens,** lente (f) *len'-teh*   **contact lens,** lente (f) *len'-teh*

**less,** meno *meh'-noh*

**let,** lasciare *lah-shah'-reh*

**letter,** lettera *let'-teh-rah* [40]

**lettuce,** lattuga *laht-too'-gah*

**liberty,** libertà *lee-ber-tah'*

**library,** biblioteca *bee-blee-oh-teh'-kah*

**license,** licenza, patente (f) *lee-chen'-tsah, pah-ten'-teh* [76]

**lie** [untruth], bugia, menzogna *boo-jee'-yah, men-tsohn'-yah*

**lie: to lie down,** coricarsi *koh-ree-kahr'-see* [96]

**life,** vita *vee'-tah*

**lift** v., sollevare *sol-leh-vah'-reh*

**light** [weight], leggero *lej-jeh'-roh;* [color], chiaro *kyah'-roh*

**light** n., luce (f) *loo'-cheh*

**lighter** [cigarette], accendi-sigari (m) *ahch-chen'-dee see'-gah-ree*

**lightning,** lampo, fulmine (m) *lahm'-poh, fool'-mee-neh* [00]

**like** adv., come *ko'-meh*

**like** v., piacere a *pyah-cheh'-reh ah* [7, 36, 67, 102]   **I would like,** vorrei *vor-reh'-ee* [37, 52, 69, 98]

**line,** linea *lee'-neh-ah*

**linen,** lino *lee'-noh*

**lip,** labbro *lahb'-broh*

**lipstick,** matita per le labbra *mah-tee'-tah per leh lahb'-brah*

**liqueur,** liquore (m) *lee-kwoh'-reh*

**list,** lista *lees'-tah*

**listen,** ascoltare *ahs-kol-tah'-reh*

**liter,** litro *leet'-roh* [74]

**little,** piccolo *peek'-koh-loh* **a little,** un poco *oon poh'-koh* [11]

**live** *v.*, vivere, abitare *vee'-veh-reh, ah-bee-tah'-reh* [10]

**liver,** fegato *feh'-gah-toh*

**lobby,** atrio *ah'-tree-yoh*

**lobster,** aragosta *ah-rah-gos'-tah*

**long,** lungo *loon'-goh* [68, 69]

**look** *v.*, guardare *gwahr-dah'-reh*

**loose,** sciolto *shol'-toh* [69]

**lose,** perdere *per'-deh-reh* [16, 39]

**lost,** perduto *per-doo'-toh*

**lot: a lot of,** molto *mol'-toh*

**lotion,** lozione (f) *loh-tsyoh'-neh*

**loud,** ad alta voce *ahd ahl'-tah voh'-cheh*

**love** *n.*, amore (m) *ah-moh'-reh*

**love** *v.*, amare *ah-mah'-reh* [10]

**low,** basso *bahs'-soh*

**lubricate** *v.*, lubricare *loo-bree-kah'-reh*

**luck,** fortuna *for-too'-nah* **good luck,** buona fortuna *bwoh'-nah for-too'-nah*

**lucky,** fortunato *for-too-nah'-toh* **to be lucky,** essere fortunato *es'-seh-reh for-too-nah'-toh*

**luggage,** bagaglio *bah-gahl'-yoh* [35, 40, 44, 48]

**lunch,** seconda colazione *seh-kon'-dah koh-lah-tsyoh'-neh* [48]

**lung,** polmone (m) *pol-moh'-neh*


**machine,** macchina *mahk'-kee-nah*

**madam,** signora *seen-yoh'-rah*

**magazine,** rivista *ree-vees'-tah*

**mail** *n.*, posta *pos'-tah* [32]

**mailbox,** buca da lettere, cassetta postale *boo'-kah dah let'-teh-reh, kahs-set'-tah pos-tah'-leh*

**main,** principale *preen-chee-pah'-leh* **main course,** piatto principale *pyaht'-toh preen-chee-pah'-leh*

**major,** maggiore *mahj-joh'-reh*

**make,** fare *fah'-reh*

**male,** maschio, maschile (m) *mahs'-kyoh, mahs-kee'-leh*

**man,** uomo *woh'-moh* [10, 15]

**manager,** gerente (m), *direttore* (m) *jeh-ren'-teh, dee-ret-toh'-reh*

**manicure,** manicure (f) *mah-nee-koo'-reh*

**manner,** maniera *mah-nyeh'-rah*

**manufactured,** fabbricato *fahb-bree-kah'-toh*

**many,** molti, molte *mol'-tee, mol'-teh*

**map,** carta geografica *kahr'-tah jeh-oh-grah'-fee-kah* [75]

**marble,** marmo *mahr'-moh*

**March,** marzo *mahr'-tsoh*

**mark,** marca *mahr'-kah*

**market,** mercato *mer'-kah-toh*

**marketplace,** mercato *mer-kah'-toh*

**marmalade,** marmellata *mahr-mel-lah'-tah*

**married,** sposato *spoh-zah'-toh*

**marry,** sposarsi *spoh-zahr'-see*

**marvelous,** meraviglioso *meh-rah-veel-yoh'-zoh*

**mass** [church], messa *mes'-sah*

**massage** *n.*, massaggio *mahs-sahj'-joh*

**match,** fiammifero *fyahm-mee'-feh-roh* [70]

**material,** materiale (m) *mah-teh-ree-yah'-leh*

**matter: no matter,** non importa *non eem-por'-tah* **what is the matter?** che c'è? *keh cheh*

**May,** maggio *mahj'-joh*

**may,** potere *poh-teh'-reh* **I may,** posso *pos'-soh* **may I?** posso? *pos'-soh*

**maybe,** forse *for'-seh*

**me,** me, mi *meh, mee* **to me,** mi, me *mee, meh*

**meal,** pasto *pahs'-toh* [38, 48, 53, 90]

**mean** *v.*, significare, voler dire *seen-yee-fee-kah'-reh, voh-lehr' dee'-reh* [12]

**measure** *n.*, misura *mee-zoo'-rah*

**measure** *v.*, misurare *mee-zoo-rah'-reh*

**meat,** carne (f) *kahr'-neh* [56]

**mechanic,** meccanico *mek-kah'-nee-koh* [74]

**medicine,** medicina *meh-dee-chee'-nah* [96]

**medium,** medio *meh'-dyoh*

**meet,** incontrare *een-kon-trah'-reh* [3]

**melon,** melone (m) *meh-loh'-neh*

**member,** membro *mem'-broh*

**memory,** memoria *meh-moh'-ree-yah*

**mend,** rammendare *rahm-men-dah'-reh*

**men's room,** gabinetto per signori *gah-bee-net'-toh per seen-yoh'-ree*

**mention** *v.,* menzionare *men-tsee-yoh-nah'-reh*

**menu,** lista *lees'-tah* [50]

**message,** messaggio *mes-sahj-joh*

**messenger,** messaggero *mes-sahj-jeh'-roh*

**metal,** metallo *meh-tahl'-loh*

**meter** [measure], metro *meh'-troh*

**middle,** mezzo *med'-dzoh*

**midnight,** mezzanotte *med-dzah-not'-teh* [24]

**mild,** mite *mee'-teh*

**milk,** latte (m) *laht'-teh* [52, 53]

**milliner,** modista *moh-dees'-tah*

**million,** milione *meel-yoh'-neh*

**mind,** mente (f) *men'-teh*

**mine,** mio *mee'-yoh*

**mineral,** minerale *mee-neh-rah'-leh*

**mineral water,** acqua minerale *ahk'-kwah mee-neh-rah'-leh*

**minute,** minuto *mee-noo'-toh*

**mirror,** specchio *spek'-kyoh* [73]

**misfortune,** disgrazia *dees-grah'-tsee-yah*

**Miss,** signorina *seen-yoh-ree'-nah*

**missing,** manca, mancante *mahn'-kah, mahn-kahn'-teh*

**mistake** *n.,* sbaglio *zbahl'-yoh* [57]

**mistaken,** sbagliato *zbah-lyah'-toh*

**mix** *v.,* mescolare *mes-koh-lah'-reh*

**mixed,** mescolato, misto *mes-koh-lah'-toh, mees'-toh*
**model,** modello *moh-del'-loh*
**modern,** moderno *moh-der'-noh*
**modest,** modesto *moh-des'-toh*
**moment,** momento *moh-men'-toh*
**Monday,** lunedì *loo-neh-dee'*
**money,** denaro *deh-nah'-roh* [15, 31, 32]
**money order,** vaglia *vahl'-yah*
**monk,** monaco *moh'-nah-koh*
**month,** mese (m) *meh'-zeh* **per month, a month,** al mese *ahl meh'-zeh*
**monument,** monumento *moh-noo-men'-toh* [101]
**moon,** luna *loo'-nah* [7]
**more,** più *pyoo*
**morning,** mattina, mattino *maht-tee'-nah, maht-tee'-noh* [100] **good morning,** buon giorno *bwon johr'-noh*
**mosquito,** zanzara *dzahn-dzah'-rah*
**mosquito net,** zanzariera *dzahn-dzah-ree-yeh'-rah*
**most,** il più (m), la più (f) *eel pyoo, lah pyoo* **most of,** la maggior parte di, la maggioranza di *lah mahj-johr' pahr'-teh dee, lah mahj-joh-rahn'-tsah dee*
**mother,** madre *mah'-dreh* [3]
**motion,** mozione (f), moto, movimento *moh-tsyoh'-neh, moh'-toh, moh-vee-men'-toh*
**motor,** motore (m) *moh-toh'-reh*
**mountain,** montagna *mon-tahn'-yah*
**mouth,** bocca *bok'-kah*
**move** *v.*, muovere, trasferire *mwoh'-veh-reh, trahs-feh-ree'-reh* [16]
**movie,** cinema (m) *chee'-neh-mah* [101]
**Mr.,** signore *seen-yoh'-reh*
**Mrs.,** signora *seen-yoh'-rah*
**much,** molto, molta *mol'-toh, mol-tah* **very much,** moltissimo *mol-tees'-see-moh* **too much,** troppo *trop'-poh* **how much?** quanto? *kwahn'-toh*
**mud,** fango *fahn'-goh*

**muffler,** silenziatore (m) *see-len-tsee-yah-toh'-reh*
**muscle,** muscolo *moos'-koh-loh*
**museum,** museo *moo-zeh'-oh* [46, 99]
**mushroom,** fungo *foon'-goh*
**music,** musica *moo'-zee-kah*
**musician,** musicista *moo-zee-chees'-tah*
**must,** dovere *doh-veh'-reh* **I must,** devo *deh'-voh*
**mustache,** baffi (pl) *bahf'-fee*
**mustard,** mostarda, senape (m) *mos-tahr'-dah, seh'-nah-peh*
**mutton,** montone (m) *mon-toh'-neh*
**my,** mio *mee'-yoh*
**myself,** io stesso *ee'-yoh stes'-soh*

**nail** [fingernail], unghia *oon'-gyah*
**nailfile,** lima da unghie *lee'-mah dah oon'-gyeh*
**naked,** nudo *noo'-doh*
**name,** nome (m) *noh'-meh* [9, 10] **last name,** cognome (m) *kon-yoh'-meh* **what is your name?** come si chiama Lei? *ko'-meh see kyah'-mah leh'-se* **my name is . . . ,** mi chiamo . . . *mee kyah'-moh . . .*
**napkin,** tovagliolo *toh-vahl-yoh'-loh* [55]
**narrow,** stretto *stret'-toh* [69, 75]
**nation,** nazione (f) *nah-tsyoh'-neh*
**national,** nazionale *nah-tsyoh-nah'-leh*
**nationality,** nazionalità *nah-tsyoh-nah-lee-tah'*
**native,** nativo *nah-tee'-voh*
**natural,** naturale *nah-too-rah'-leh*
**naturally,** naturalmente *nah-too-rahl-men'-teh*
**nature,** natura *nah-too'-rah*
**near,** vicino *vee-chee'-noh*
**nearly,** circa, quasi *cheer'-kah, kwah'-zee*
**necessary,** necessario *neh-chehs-sah'-ree-yoh*
**neck,** collo *kol'-loh*
**necklace,** collana *kol-lah'-nah*
**necktie,** cravatta *krah-vaht'-tah*

**need** *v.*, aver bisogno di *ah-vehr' bee-zon'·yoh dee*
   **I need,** ho bisogno di, mi occorre *oh bee-zon'-yoh dee, mee ok-kor'-reh*
**needle,** ago *ah'-goh* [70]
**neighbor,** vicino *vee-chee'-noh*
**neighborhood,** vicinato *vee-chee-nah'-toh*
**neither . . . nor . . . ,** nè . . . nè . . . *neh . . . neh . . .*
**nephew,** nipote (m) *nee-poh'-teh*
**nerve,** nervo *ner'-voh*
**nervous,** nervoso *ner-voh'-zoh*
**never,** mai, non . . . mai . . . *mah'-ee, non . . . mah'-ee*
**nevertheless,** tuttavia *toot-tah-vee'-yah*
**new,** nuovo *nwoh'-voh*
**news,** notizia, notizie *noh-tee'-tsyah, noh-tee'-tsyeh*
**newspaper,** giornale (m) *johr-nah'-leh*
**next** *adj.,* prossimo *pros'-see-moh*
**next,** *adv.,* quindi *kween'-dee* [85]
**nice,** simpatico *seem-pah'-tee-koh*
**niece,** nipote (f) *nee-poh'-teh*
**night,** notte (f) *not'-teh* **good night,** buona notte *bwoh'-nah not'-teh*
**nightclub,** locale notturno (m) *loh-kah'-leh not-toor'-noh*
**nightgown,** camicia da notte *kah-mee'-chah dah not'-teh*
**nine,** nove *noh'-veh*
**nineteen,** diciannove *dee-chahn-noh'-veh*
**ninety,** novanta *noh-vahn'-tah*
**ninth,** nono *noh'-noh*
**no,** no *noh*
**noise,** rumore (m) *roo-moh'-reh*
**noisy,** rumoroso *roo-moh-roh'-zoh*
**none,** nessuno *nes-soo'-noh*
**noodles,** taglierini (m,pl), fettuccine (f, pl) *tahl-yeh-ree'-nee, fet-tooch-chee'-neh*
**noon,** mezzogiorno *med-dzoh-johr'-noh* [24]
**no one,** nessuno *nes-soo'-noh*
**north,** nord (m) *nord*

**northeast,** nord-est *nord-est'*
**northwest,** nord-ovest *nord-oh'-vest*
**nose,** naso *nah'-zoh*
**not,** non *non*
**notebook,** quaderno *kwah-dehr'-noh*
**nothing,** niente *nyen'-teh* **nothing else,** nient'altro *nyent-ahl'-troh*
**notice** n., avviso *ahv-vee'-zoh*
**notice** v., notare *noh-tah'-reh*
**notify,** notificare *noh-tee-fee-kah'-reh*
**novel** [book], romanzo *roh-mahn'-dzoh*
**November,** novembre *noh-vem'-breh*
**novocaine,** novocaina *noh-voh-kah-ee'-nah*
**now,** adesso, ora *ah-des'-soh, oh'-rah*
**nowhere,** in nessun luogo *een nes-soon' lwoh'-goh*
**number,** numero *noo'-meh-roh* [39, 42, 88]
**nun,** monaca *moh'-nah-kah*
**nurse,** infermiera *een-fer-myeh'-rah*
**nursemaid,** governante (f) *goh-ver-nahn'-teh*
**nut, nuts,** noce, noci (f) *noh'-cheh, noh'-chee*

**obey,** obbedire *ob-beh-dee'-reh*
**obliged,** obbligato *ohb-blee-gah'-toh*
**obtain,** ottenere *ot-teh-neh'-reh*
**obvious,** ovvio *ov'-vyoh*
**occasionally,** occasionalmente, di tempo in tempo *ok-kah-zyoh-nahl-men'-teh, dee tem'-poh een tem'-poh*
**occupation,** occupazione (f) *ok-koo-pah-tsyoh'-neh*
**occupied,** occupato *ok-koo-pah'-toh* [86]
**ocean,** oceano *oh-cheh'-ah-noh* [37]
**October,** ottobre *ot-toh'-breh*
**odd** [unusual], raro *rah'-roh*
**odd** [number], dispari *dees'-pah-ree*
**of,** di *dee*
**offer** v., offrire *of-free'-reh*
**office,** ufficio *oof-fee'-choh*

**official** *adj.*, ufficiale *oof-fee-chah'-leh*

**often,** spesso *spes'-soh*

**oil,** olio *oh'-lyoh* [74]

**old,** vecchio, anziano *vek'-kyoh, ahn-tsyah'-noh*

**olive,** oliva *oh-lee'-vah*

**omelet,** frittata, omeletta *freet-tah'-tah, oh-meh-let'-tah*

**on,** su *soo*

**once,** una volta *oo'-nah vol'-tah*

**one,** uno, un, una, un' *oo'-noh, oon, oo'-nah, oon*

**one-way** [street], senso unico *sen'-soh oo'-nee-koh*; [ticket], solo andata *soh'-loh ahn-dah'-tah* [84]

**onion,** cipolla *chee-pol'-lah*

**only,** soltanto, solamente *sol-tahn'-toh, soh-lah-men'-teh*

**open** *adj.*, aperto *ah-per'-toh* [100]

**open** *v.*, aprire *ah-pree'-reh* [34, 39, 62, 84, 99, 100]

**opera,** opera *oh'-peh-rah*

**operation,** operazione (f) *oh-peh-rah-tsyoh'-neh*

**operator** [telephone], telefonista, centralino *teh-leh-foh-nees'-tah, chen-trah-lee'-noh*

**opinion,** opinione (f) *oh-pee-nyoh'-neh*

**opportunity,** occasione, opportunità (f) *ok-kah-zyoh'-neh, oppor-too-nee-tah'*

**opposite,** opposto *op-pos'-toh*

**optician,** ottico *ot'-tee-koh*

**or,** o, od *oh, ohd*

**orange,** arancia *ah-rahn'-chah*

**order** *v.*, ordinare *or-dee-nah'-reh* [56]   **in order to,** per *per*

**ordinary,** ordinario *or-dee-nah'-ree-yoh*

**oriental,** orientale *oh-ree-en-tah'-leh*

**original,** originale *oh-ree-jee-nah'-leh*

**ornament,** ornamento *or-nah-men'-toh*

**other,** altro *ahl'-troh*

**ought,** dovere *doh-veh'-reh*

**our, ours,** nostro, il nostro *nos'-troh, eel nos'-troh*

**out** *adv.*, fuori *fwoh'-ree*

**outdoor,** all'aperto *ahl-lah-per'-toh*

**out of order,** non funziona *non foon-tsyoh'-nah*

**outside** *adv.*, fuori *fwoh'-ree* **outside of,** fuori di *fwoh'-ree dee*

**over** [ended] *adj.*, finito *fee-nee'-toh*

**over** [above] *prep.*, sopra *so'-prah*

**overcharge** *n.*, prezzo eccessivo *pret'-tsoh ech-ches-see'-voh*

**overcoat,** soprabito *so-prah'-bee-toh*

**overcooked,** troppo cotto *trop'-poh kot'-toh*

**overhead,** in alto, di sopra *een ahl'-toh, dee so'-prah*

**overturn,** capovolgere *kah-poh-vol'-jeh-reh*

**owe,** dovere *doh-veh'-reh* [56]

**own** *adj.*, proprio *proh'-pree-yoh*

**owner,** proprietario *proh-pree-yeh-tah'-ree-yoh*

**oyster,** ostrica *os'-tree-kah*


**pack** *v.*, impaccare *eem-pahk-kah'-reh* [70]

**package,** pacco *pahk'-koh*

**page,** pagina *pah'-jee-nah*

**paid,** pagato *pah-gah'-toh*

**pain,** dolore (m) *doh-loh'-reh*

**paint,** pittura *peet-too'-rah*

**paint** *v.*, dipingere *dee-peen'-jeh-reh*

**painting,** pittura *peet-too'-rah*

**pair,** paio *pah'-yoh* [69]

**palace,** palazzo *pah-laht'-tsoh* [101]

**pale,** pallido *pahl'-lee-doh*

**palm,** palmo *pahl'-moh*

**pants,** pantaloni (m, pl) *pahn-tah-loh'-nee*

**paper,** carta *kahr'-tah*

**parcel,** pacco *pahk'-koh*

**pardon,** scusa *skoo'-zah* **pardon me,** mi scusi *mee skoo'-zee*

**parents,** genitori *jeh-nee-toh'-ree*

**park,** parco *pahr'-koh* [101]

**park** [a car] *v.*, posteggiare, parcheggiare *pos-tej-jah'-reh, pahr-kej-jah'-reh* [76]

**parsley,** prezzemolo *pred-dzeh'-moh-loh*

**part,** parte (f) *pahr'-teh*

**part** [leave], partire *pahr-tee'-reh*

**particular,** particolare *pahr-tee-koh-lah'-reh*

**partner** [business], socio, *soh'-choh*

**party,** festa *fes'-tah*

**pass** *v.*, passare *pahs-sah'-reh*

**passage,** passaggio *pahs-sahj'-joh*

**passenger,** passeggero *pahs-sej-jeh'-roh*

**passport,** passaporto *pahs-sah-por'-toh* [16, 31, 33, 34]

**past** *adj. & n.*, passato *pahs-sah'-toh*

**pastry,** pasticceria *pahs-teech-cheh-ree'-yah*

**path,** sentiero *sen-tyeh'-roh*

**patient** *adj. & n.*, paziente *pah-tsyen'-teh*

**pay** *v.*, pagare *pah-gah'-reh* [34 ,57, 75]  **to pay cash,** pagare in contante *pah-gah'-reh een kon-tahn'-teh* [70]

**payment,** pagamento *pah-gah-men'-toh*

**pea,** pisello *pee-zel'-loh*

**peace,** pace (f) *pah'-cheh*

**peaceful,** pacifico *pah-chee'-fee-koh*

**peach,** pesca *pes'-kah*

**peak,** picco *peek'-koh*

**peanut,** arachide (f) *ah-rah'-kee-deh*

**pear,** pera *peh'-rah*

**pearl,** perla *per'-lah*

**peasant,** contadino *kon-tah-dee'-noh*

**peculiar,** strano *strah'-noh*

**pen,** penna *pen'-nah*  **fountain pen,** penna stilografica *pen'-nah stee-loh-grah'-fee-kah*

**penalty,** pena *peh'-nah*

**pencil,** matita *mah-tee'-tah*

**penny,** centesimo *chen-teh'-zee-moh*

**people,** gente (f) *jen'-teh*

**pepper** [spice], pepe (m) *peh'-peh*

**peppermint,** menta *men'-tah*
**per,** al, alla *ahl, ahl'-lah*
**perfect,** perfetto *per-fet'-toh*
**performance,** rappresentazione (f) *rahp-preh-zen-tah-tsyoh'-neh*
**perfume,** profumo *proh-foo'-moh*
**perfumery,** profumeria *proh-foo-meh-ree'-yah*
**perhaps,** forse *for'-seh*
**period,** periodo *peh-ree'-oh-doh*
**permanent,** permanente *per-mah-nen'-teh*
**permission,** permesso *per-mes'-soh*
**permit** *v.,* permettere *per-met'-teh-reh*
**person,** persona *per-soh'-nah*
**personal,** personale *per-soh-nah'-leh* [34]
**perspiration,** sudore (m) *soo-doh'-reh*
**petrol,** petrolio *peh-trohl'-yoh*
**petticoat,** sottoveste (f) *sot-toh-ves'-teh*
**pharmacist,** farmacista (m) *fahr-mah-chees'-tah*
**pharmacy,** farmacia *fahr-mah-chee'-yah*
**photograph,** fotografia *foh-toh-grah-fee'-yah*
**photographer,** fotografo *foh-toh'-grah-foh*
**photography,** fotografia *foh-toh-grah-fee'-yah*
**photography shop,** negozio di fotografia *neh-goh'-tsyoh dee foh-toh-grah-fee'-yah*
**piano,** pianoforte (m) *pee-yah-noh-for'-teh*
**pick up,** cogliere *kohl'-yeh-reh*
**picture,** quadro *kwah'-droh*
**pie,** torta *tor'-tah*
**piece,** pezzo *pet'-tsoh*
**pier,** molo *moh'-loh* [86]
**pig,** maiale, porco *mah-yah'-leh, por'-koh*
**pigeon,** piccione (m) *peech-choh'-neh*
**pile,** catasta, mucchio *kah-tahs'-tah, mook'-kyoh*
**pill,** pillola *peel'-loh-lah*
**pillar,** pilastro *pee-lahs'-troh*
**pillow,** guanciale (m) *gwahn-chah'-leh* [89]

**pilot,** pilota (m) *pee-loh'-tah*

**pin,** spillo *speel'-loh* [70]  **safety pin,** spillo di sicurezza *speel'-loh dee see-koo-ret'-tsah*

**pineapple,** ananasso *ah-nah-nahs'-soh*

**pink,** rosa *roh'-zah*

**pipe** [tobacco], pipa *pee'-pah*

**place** *n.,* posto, luogo *pos'-toh, lwoh'-goh* [99]

**place** *v.,* mettere, collocare *met'-teh-reh, kol-loh-kah'-reh*

**plain** [simple], semplice *sem'-plee-cheh*

**plan** *n.,* piano *pyah'-noh*

**plant,** pianta *pyahn'-tah*

**plastic,** plastico *plahs'-tee-koh*

**plate,** piatto *pyaht'-toh*

**platform,** piattaforma *pyaht-tah-for'-mah* [83]

**play** *v.,* giocare *joh-kah'-reh*

**pleasant,** piacevole *pyah-cheh'-voh-leh*

**please** [suit or satisfy], piacere a *pyah-cheh'-reh ah*  **if you please,** per favore, per piacere *per fah-voh'-reh, per pyah-cheh'-reh*

**pleasure,** piacere (m) *pyah-cheh'-reh* [4]

**plenty of,** molto, molti *mol'-toh, mol'-tee*

**plum,** susina *soo-zee'-nah*

**pneumonia,** polmonite (f) *pohl-moh-nee'-teh*

**poached,** cotto in camicia *kot'-toh een kah-mee'-chah*

**pocket,** tasca *tahs'-kah*

**pocketbook** [wallet], portafoglio *por-tah-fohl'-yoh*; [purse], borsa *bor'-sah*

**point** *n.,* punto *poon'-toh*

**poison,** veleno *veh-leh'-noh*

**poisonous,** velenoso *veh-leh-noh'-zoh*

**police,** polizia (f) *poh-lee-tsee'-yah* [15]

**policeman,** poliziotto, carabiniere (m) *poh-lee-tsee-yot'-toh, kah-rah-bee-nyeh'-reh*

**police station,** questura *kwes-too'-rah*

**political,** politico *poh-lee'-tee-koh*

**pond,** stagno *stahn'-yoh*

**pool,** piscina *pee-shee'-nah*

**poor,** povero *poh'-veh-roh*

**popular,** popolare *poh-poh-lah'-reh*

**pork,** carne di maiale (f) *kahr'-neh dee mah-yah'-leh*

**port,** porto *por'-toh* [86]

**porter,** facchino *fahk-kee'-noh* [35, 82, 83]

**portrait,** ritratto *ree-traht'-toh*

**position,** posizione (f) *poh-zee-tsyoh'-neh*

**positive,** positivo *poh-zee-tee'-voh*

**possible,** possibile *pos-see'-bee-leh* [13]

**possibly,** possibilmente *pos-see-beel-men'-teh*

**postage,** affrancatura *ahf-frahn-kah-too'-rah*

**postage stamp,** francobollo *frahn-koh-bol'-loh* [40]

**postcard,** cartolina postale *kahr-toh-lee'-nah pos-tah'-leh*

**post office,** ufficio postale *oof-fee'-choh pos-tah'-leh*

**potato,** patata *pah-tah'-tah*

**pound** [money], libbra *leeb'-brah* [31]

**powder,** cipria *cheep'-ree-yah*

**power,** potenza *poh-ten'-tsah*

**powerful,** potente *poh-ten'-teh*

**practical,** pratico *prah'-tee-koh*

**practice** *n.*, pratica *prah'-tee-kah*

**prayer,** preghiera *preh-gyeh'-rah*

**precious,** prezioso *preh-tsyoh'-zoh*

**prefer,** preferire *preh-feh-ree'reh*

**preferable,** preferibile *preh-feh-ree'-bee-leh*

**pregnant,** incinta *een-cheen'-tah*

**premier,** primo ministro *pree'-moh mee-nees'-troh*

**preparation,** preparazione (f) *preh-pah-rah-tsyoh'-neh*

**prepare,** preparare *preh-pah-rah'-reh*

**prepay,** pagare anticipatamente *pah-gah'-reh ahn-tee-chee-pah-tah-men'-teh*

**prescription,** prescrizione (f) *preh-skree-tsyoh'-neh* [96]

**present** [gift], regalo *reh-gah'-loh*; [time], attuale *aht-too-ah'-leh*

**present** *v.*, regalare *reh-gah-lah'-reh* [2]

**press** [clothes] *v.*, stirare *stee-rah'-reh*
**pressure**, pressione (f) *pres-syoh'-neh*
**pretty**, bello, grazioso *bel'-loh, grah-tsyoh'-zoh* [10]
**prevent**, prevenire *preh-veh-nee'-reh*
**previous**, precedente *preh-cheh-den'-teh*
**price**, prezzo *pret'-tsoh* [38]
**priest**, prete *preh'-teh*
**principal**, principale *preen-chee-pah'-leh*
**prison**, prigione (f) *pree-joh'-neh*
**prisoner**, prigioniero *pree-joh-nyeh'-roh*
**private**, privato *pree-vah'-toh*
**prize**, premio *preh'-myoh*
**probable**, probabile *proh-bah'-bee-leh*
**probably**, probabilmente *proh-bah-beel-men'-teh*
**problem**, problema (m) *proh-bleh'-mah*
**produce** *v.*, produrre *proh-door'-reh*
**production**, produzione (f) *proh-doo-tsyoh'-neh*
**profession**, professione (f) *proh-fes-syoh'-neh*
**professor**, professore (m) *proh-fes-soh'-reh*
**profit**, profitto *proh-feet'-toh*
**program** *n.*, programma (m) *proh-grahm'-mah*
**progress** *n.*, progresso *proh-gres'-soh*
**promenade**, passeggiata *pahs-sej-jah'-tah*
**promise** *n.*, promessa *proh-mes'-sah*
**prompt**, pronto *pron'-toh*
**pronunciation**, pronunzia *proh-noon'-tsyah*
**proof**, prova *proh'-vah*
**proper**, appropriato *ahp-proh-pree-yah'-toh*
**property**, proprietà *proh-pree-eh-tah'*
**proposal**, proposta *proh-pos'-tah*
**proprietor**, proprietario *proh-pree-eh-tah'-ree-yoh*
**prosperity**, prosperità *proh-speh-ree-tah'*
**protect**, proteggere *proh-tej'-jeh-reh*
**protection**, protezione (f) *proh-teh-tsyoh'-neh*
**protestant**, protestante *proh-tes-tahn'-teh*
**proud**, orgoglioso *ohr-gohl-yoh'-zoh*

**provide,** provvedere *prov-veh-deh'-reh*
**province,** provincia *proh-veen'-chah*
**provincial,** provinciale *proh-veen-chah'-leh*
**provision,** disposizione (f) *dees-poh-zee-tsyoh'-neh*
**prune,** prugna secca, prugna *proon'-yah sek'-kah, proon'-nyah*
**public,** pubblico *poob'-blee-koh*
**publish,** pubblicare *poob-blee-kah'-reh*
**pull** *v.,* tirare *tee-rah'-reh*
**pump,** pompa *pom'-pah*
**punish,** punire *poo-nee'-reh*
**pupil,** alunno *ah-loon'-noh*
**purchase** *n.,* compera *kom'-peh-rah*
**purchase** *v.,* comprare *kom-prah'-reh*
**pure,** puro *poo'-roh*
**purple,** porpora *por'-poh-rah*
**purpose** *n.,* scopo *skoh'-poh*
**purse,** borsa *bor'-sah*
**purser,** commissario *kom-mees-sah'-ree-yoh*
**push** *v.,* spingere *speen'-jeh-reh*
**put,** mettere *met'-teh-reh* [74]

**quality,** qualità *kwah-lee-tah'*
**quantity,** quantità *kwahn-tee-tah'*
**quarrel** *n.,* alterco *ahl-ter'-koh*
**quarrel** *v.,* litigare *lee-tee-gah'-reh*
**quarter** *adj. & n.,* quarto *kwahr'-toh*
**queen,** regina *reh-jee'-nah*
**question** *n.,* domanda *doh-mahn'-dah*
**quick,** rapido, veloce *rah'-pee-doh, veh-loh'-cheh*
**quickly,** rapidamente *rah-pee-dah-men'-teh*
**quiet,** quieto, silenzioso *kwee-eh'-toh, see-len-tsyoh'-zoh* [38]
**quite,** molto, del tutto *mol'-toh, del toot'-toh*

**radio,** radio (f) *rah'-dyoh*

**railroad,** ferrovia *fer-roh-vee'-yah*

**railroad car,** vagone (m), carrozza *vah-goh'-neh, kahr-rot'-tsah*

**railroad station,** stazione ferroviaria *stah-tsyoh'-neh fer-roh-vee-yah'-ree-yah* [45, 82]

**rain** n., pioggia *pyoj'-jah* [7]

**rain** v., piovere *pyoh'-veh-reh* [102] **it's raining,** piove *pyoh'-veh*

**rainbow,** arcobaleno *ahr-koh-bah-leh'-noh* [7]

**raincoat,** impermeabile (m) *eem-per-meh-ah'-bee-leh* [8]

**raise** v., sollevare *sol-leh-vah'-reh*

**rapidly,** rapidamente *rah-pee-dah-men'-teh*

**rare,** raro *rah-roh*

**rash** n., eruzione cutanea (f) *eh-roo-tsyoh'-neh koo-tah-neh'-ah*

**raspberry,** lampone (m) *lahm-poh'-neh*

**rate,** tariffa *tah-reef'-fah*

**rather,** piuttosto, abbastanza *pyoot-tos'-toh, ahb-bahs-tahn'-tsah*

**raw,** crudo *kroo'-doh*

**razor,** rasoio *rah-zoh'-yoh*

**razor blade,** lametta (per la barba) *lah-met'-tah (per lah bahr'-bah)*

**reach** v., raggiungere *rahj-joon'-jeh-reh*

**read,** leggere *lej'-jeh-reh*

**ready,** pronto *pron'-toh* [75]

**real,** vero *veh'-roh*

**really,** veramente *veh-rah-men'-teh*

**rear,** di dietro *dee dyeh'-troh*

**reason** n., ragione (f) *rah-joh'-neh*

**reasonable,** ragionevole *rah-joh-neh'-voh-leh*

**receipt,** ricevuta *ree-cheh-voo'-tah* [32]

**receive,** ricevere *ree-cheh'-veh-reh*

**recent,** recente *reh-chen'-teh*

**reception desk,** ricevimento *ree-cheh-vee-men'-toh*

**recognize,** riconoscere *ree-koh-noh'-sheh-reh*

**recommend,** raccomandare *rahk-koh-mahn-dah'-reh* [50]

**reconfirm** [a flight], riconfirmare *ree-kon-feer-mah'-reh* [89]

**recover,** guarire *gwah-ree'-reh*

**red,** rosso *ros'-soh*

**reduce,** ridurre *ree-door'-reh*

**reduction,** riduzione (f) *ree-doo-tsyoh'-neh*

**refreshments,** rinfreschi (m, pl) *reen-fres'-kee*

**refund** *v.,* rimborsare *reem-bohr-sah'-reh*

**refuse** *v.,* rifiutare *ree-fyoo-tah'-reh*

**region,** regione (f) *reh-joh'-neh*

**register** *n.,* registro *reh-jees'-troh*

**register** [a letter], raccomandare *rahk-koh-mahn-dah'-reh*; [at a hotel], iscriversi sul registro *ees-kree'-vehr-see sool reh-jees'-troh*

**regret** *v.,* dispiacersi *dees-pyah-chehr'-see*

**regular,** regolare *reh-goh-lah'-reh*

**regulation,** regolamento *reh-goh-lah-men'-toh*

**relative** [kin], parente (m) *pah-ren'-teh*

**religion,** religione (f) *reh-lee-joh'-neh*

**remark** *n.,* osservazione (f) *os-ser-vah-tsyoh'-neh*

**remember,** ricordarsi di *ree-kor-dahr'-see dee*

**remove,** rimuovere *ree-mwoh'-veh-reh*

**renew,** rinnovare *reen-noh-vah'-reh*

**rent** *v.,* affittare *ahf-feet-tah'-reh*

**repair** *v.,* riparare *ree-pah-rah'-reh*

**repeat** *v.,* ripetere *ree-peh'-teh-reh* [11]

**replace** [put back], ricollocare *ree-kol-loh-kah'-reh*

**reply** *n.,* risposta *rees-pos'-tah*

**republic,** repubblica *reh-poob'-blee-kah*

**request** *v.,* chiedere *kyeh'-deh-reh*

**rescue** *v.,* salvare *sahl-vah'-reh*

**reservation,** prenotazione (f) *preh-noh-tah-tsyoh'-neh*

**reserve** *v.,* prenotare, riservare *preh-noh-tah'-reh, ree-zer-vah'-reh* [54]

**reserved,** riservato *ree-zer-vah'-toh*

**residence,** residenza *reh-zee-den'-tsah*

**resident,** residente *reh-zee-den'-teh*

**responsible,** responsabile *reh-spon-sah'-bee-leh*

**rest** *n.,* riposo *ree-poh'-zoh*

**rest** *v.,* riposarsi *ree-poh-zahr'-see*

**restaurant,** ristorante (m) *rees-toh-rahn'-teh* [38, 48]

**restless,** irrequieto *eer-reh-kwee-eh'-toh*

**rest room,** gabinetto *gah-bee-net'-toh*

**result** *n.,* risultato *ree-zool-tah'-toh*

**return** *v.,* ritornare, tornare *ree-tohr-nah'-reh, tohr-nah'-reh*

**return ticket,** biglietto di ritorno *beel-yet'-toh dee ree-tohr'-noh*

**review** *n.,* rivista *ree-vees'-tah*

**reward,** ricompensa *ree-kom-pen'-sah*

**rib,** costola *kos'-toh-lah*

**ribbon,** nastro *nahs'-troh*

**rice,** riso *ree'-zoh*

**rich,** ricco *reek'-koh*

**ride** *n.,* corsa, passeggiata *kor'-sah, pahs-sej-jah'-tah* [45]

**right** [correct], corretto *kor-ret'-toh* **to be right,** aver ragione *ah-vehr' rah-joh'-neh* [12] **all right,** molto bene, va bene *mol'-toh beh'-neh, vah beh'-neh*

**right** [direction], a destra *ah des'-trah*

**ring** *n.,* anello *ah-nel'-loh*

**ring** *v.,* suonare *swoh-nah'-reh* [44]

**ripe,** maturo *mah-too'-roh*

**rise** *v.,* sorgere *sor'-jeh-reh*

**river,** fiume (m) *fyoo'-meh* [101, 102]

**road,** strada, cammino *strah'-dah, kahm-mee'-noh* [75]

**roast,** arrosto *ahr-rohs'-toh*

**rob,** rubare *roo-bah'-reh* [15]

**robber,** ladro *lah'-droh*

**rock,** roccia *roch'-chah*

**roof,** tetto *tet'-toh*

**roll** [bread], panino *pah-nee'-noh*

**roll** *v.*, rotolare *roh-toh-lah'-reh*

**room** [of a house], stanza, camera *stahn'-tsah, kah'-meh-rah* [7]; [in a hotel], camera *kah'-meh-rah* [37, 38, 48]

**rope,** corda *kor'-dah*

**rose,** rosa *roh'-zah*

**rouge,** rossetto *ros-set'-toh*

**rough,** ruvido, aspro *roo'-vee-doh, ahs'-proh*

**round,** rotondo *roh-ton'-doh*

**round trip,** andata e ritorno *ahn-dah'-tah eh ree-tor'-noh* [84]

**royal,** reale *reh-ah'-leh*

**rubber,** gomma *gom'-mah*

**rude,** rude, rozzo, sgarbato *roo'-deh, rot'-tsoh, zgahr-bah'-toh*

**rug,** tappeto *tahp-peh'-toh*

**ruin** *v.*, rovinare *roh-vee-nah'-reh*

**rum,** rum (m) *room*

**run** *v.*, correre *kor'-reh-reh*

**runway,** pista *pees'-tah* [90]

**sad,** triste *trees'-teh*

**safe,** sicuro *see-koo'-roh*

**safety pin,** spillo di sicurezza *speel'-loh dee see-koo-ret'-tsah*

**sail** *v.*, navigare, veleggaiare, partire *nah-vee-gah'-reh, veh-lej'-jah-reh, pahr-tee'-reh* [86]

**sailor,** marinaio *mah-ree-nah'-yoh*

**saint,** santo *sahn'-toh*

**salad,** insalata *een-sah-lah'-tah*

**sale,** vendita *ven'-dee-tah* [68]  **for sale,** da vendere *dah ven'-deh-reh*

**salesgirl,** venditrice (f) *ven-dee-tree'-cheh*

**salesman,** commesso, venditore *kom-mes'-soh, ven-dee-toh'-reh*

**salmon,** salmone (m) *sahl-moh'-neh*

**salt,** sale (m) *sah'-leh*

**same,** stesso *stes'-soh*  **the same as,** lo stesso come *loh stes'-soh ko'-meh*

**sample** *n.,* campione (m) *kahm-pyoh'-neh*

**sand,** sabbia *sahb'-byah*

**sandwich,** panino imbottito *pah-nee'-noh eem-bot-tee'-toh*

**sanitary,** sanitario *sah-nee-tah'-ree-yoh*

**sanitary napkin,** pannilino igienico *pahn-nee-lee'-noh ee-jyeh'-nee-koh*

**satin,** raso *rah'-zoh*

**satisfactory,** soddisfacente *sod-dees-fah-chen'-teh*

**satisfied,** soddisfatto *sod-dees-faht'-toh*

**satisfy,** soddisfare *sod-dees-fah'-reh*

**Saturday,** sabato *sah'-bah-toh*

**sauce,** salsa *sahl'-sah*

**saucer,** piattino *pyaht-tee'-noh*

**sausage,** salsiccia *sahl-seech'-chah*

**save,** risparmiare *rees-pahr-myah'-reh*; [rescue], salvare *sahl-vah'-reh*

**say,** dire *dee'-reh* [11]

**scale,** bilancia *bee-lahn'-chah*

**scar** *n.,* cicatrice (f) *chee-kah-tree'-cheh*

**scarce,** scarso *skahr'-soh*

**scarcely,** appena *ahp-peh'-nah*

**scare** *v.,* spaventare *spah-ven-tah'-reh*

**scarf,** sciarpa *shahr'-pah*

**scenery,** paesaggio *pah-eh-zahj'-joh*

**scent** *n.,* promfumo, fiuto *proh-foo'-moh, fyoo'-toh*

**schedule** *n.,* orario *oh-rah'-ree-yoh*

**school,** scuola *skwoh'-lah*

**science,** scienza *shyen'-tsah*

**scientist,** scienziato *shyen-tsyah'-toh*

**scissors,** forbici (f, pl) *for'-bee-chee*

**scratch** *n.,* graffio *grahf'-fyoh*

**sculpture,** scultura *skool-too'-rah*

**sea,** mare (m) *mah'-reh*

**seafood,** pesce e frutti di mare *peh'-sheh eh froot'-tee dee mah'-reh*

**seagull,** gabbiano *gahb-byah'-noh*

**seam,** cucitura *koo-chee-too'-rah*

**seaport,** porto di mare *por'-toh dee mah'-reh*

**search** v., cercare *cher-kah'-reh*

**seasick,** soffrendo mal di mare *sof-fren'-doh mahl dee mah'-reh* [88]

**season,** stagione (f) *stah-joh'-neh*

**seat,** posto *pos'-toh* [84]

**second,** secondo *seh-kon'-doh* **second class,** seconda classe *seh-kon'-dah klahs'-seh* [83, 87]

**secret** adj. & n., segreto *seh-greh'-toh*

**secretary,** segretario *seh-greh-tah'-ree-yoh*

**section** sezione (f) *seh-tsyoh'-neh*

**see,** vedere *veh-deh'-reh* [3, 7, 99]

**seem,** sembrare, parere *sem-brah'-reh, pah-reh'-reh*

**select** v., scegliere *shehl'-yeh-reh*

**selection,** selezione (f) *seh-leh-tsyoh'-neh*

**self,** stesso, stessa *stes'-soh, stes'-sah*

**sell,** vendere *ven'-deh-reh* [67, 70]

**send,** mandare, spedire *mahn-dah'-reh, speh-dee'-reh* [13, 70]

**sensible,** ragionevole *rah-joh-neh'-voh-leh*

**separate** adj., separato *seh-pah-rah'-toh*

**separate** v., separare *seh-pah-rah'-reh*

**September,** settembre (m) *set-tem'-breh*

**series,** serie (f) *seh'-ree-yeh*

**serious,** serio *seh'-ree-yoh*

**servant,** servo, domestico *ser'-voh, doh-mes'-tee-koh*

**serve** v., servire *ser-vee'-reh* [50, 64, 90]

**service,** servizio *ser-vee'-tsee-yoh*

**service charge,** spese di servizio (f, pl) *speh'-zeh dee ser-vee'-tsee-yoh*

**set** [fixed], fissato *fees-sah'-toh*

**set** [place] *v.*, mettere *met'-teh-reh*

**seven**, sette *set'-teh*

**seventeen**, diciassette *dee-chahs-set'-teh*

**seventh**, settimo *set'-tee-moh*

**seventy**, settanta *set-tahn'-tah*

**several**, parecchi *pah-rek'-kee*

**severe**, severo *seh-veh'-roh*

**sew**, cucire *koo-chee'-reh*

**shade**, ombra *om'-brah*

**shampoo**, shampoo *shahm-poo'*

**shape** *n.*, forma *for'-mah*

**share** *v.*, condividere *kon-dee-vee'-deh-reh*

**shark**, pescecane (m) *peh-sheh-kah'-neh*

**sharp**, affilato, aguzzo *ahf-fee-lah'-toh, ah-goot'-tsoh*

**shave** *v.*, farsi la barba, radersi *fahrsee lah bahr'-bah, rah'-der-see*

**shaving cream**, crema per la barba *kreh'-mah per lah bahr'-bah*

**she**, ella, essa, lei *el'-lah, es'-sah, leh'-ee*

**sheep**, pecora *peh'-koh-rah*

**sheet** [of paper], foglio *fohl'-yoh* **bedsheet**, lenzuolo *len-tswoh'-loh*

**shellfish**, frutti di mare *froot'-tee dee mah'-reh*

**shelter**, rifugio *ree-foo'-joh*

**sherry**, vino di Xeres *vee'-noh dee sheh'-rehs*

**shine** *v.*, lustrare *loos-trah'-reh*

**ship** *n.*, nave (f) *nah'-veh* [86, 87]

**ship** *v.*, spedire *speh-dee'-reh* [70]

**shirt**, camicia *kah-mee'-chah* [40, 69]

**shiver** *v.*, tremare *treh-mah'-reh*

**shock** *n.*, colpo *kol'-poh*

**shoe**, scarpa *skahr'-pah* [69]

**shoelace**, laccio *lahch'-choh*

**shoeshine**, lustro di scarpe *loos'-troh dee skahr'-peh*

**shoestore**, calzoleria *kahl-tsoh-leh-ree'-yah*

**shoot** *v.*, sparare *spah-rah'-reh*

**shop** *n.*, negozio *neh-goh'-tsyoh*

**shop: to go shopping,** fare delle compere *fah'-reh del'-leh kom'-peh-reh* [62]

**shopping center,** centro di compere *chen'-troh dee kom'-peh-reh* [102]

**shore,** sponda, riva *spon'-dah, ree'-vah*

**short,** corto *kor'-toh* [68, 69]

**shorts,** mutande (f, pl) *moo-tahn'-deh*

**shoulder,** spalla *spahl'-lah*

**show** *n.*, spettacolo *spet-tah'-koh-loh*

**show** *v.*, mostrare *mos-trah'-reh* [13, 67, 95]

**shower** [bath], doccia *doch'-chah* [37]

**shrimp,** gambero *gahm'-beh-roh*

**shut** *adj.*, chiuso *kyoo'-zoh*

**shut** *v.*, chiudere *kyoo'-deh-reh*

**shy,** timido *tee'-mee-doh*

**sick,** ammalato *ahm-mah-lah'-toh* [92]

**side,** lato, fianco *lah'-toh, fyahn'-koh*

**sidewalk,** marciapiede (m) *mahr-chah-pyeh'-deh*

**sight,** vista *vees'-tah*

**sightseeing,** girare per vedere le curiosità *jee-rah'-reh per veh-deh'-rah leh koo-ree-yoh-zee-tah'* [98]

**sign** *n.*, insegna *een-sehn'-yah*

**sign** *v.*, firmare *feer-mah'-reh* [32]

**signature,** firma *feer'-mah*

**silence,** silenzio *see-len-tsee'-yoh*

**silent,** silenzioso *see-len-tsee-yoh'-zoh*

**silk,** seta *seh'-tah*

**silly,** sciocco, stolto *shok'-koh, stol'-toh*

**silver,** argento *ahr-jen'-toh*

**similar,** simile *see'-mee-leh*

**simple,** semplice *sem'-plee-cheh*

**since,** da, dacchè, siccome *dah, dahk-keh', seek-ko'-meh*

**sing,** cantare *kahn-tah'-reh*

**single,** singolo *seen'-goh-loh*

**sir,** signore *seen-yoh'-reh*

**sister,** sorella *soh-rel'-lah* [3]
**sit,** sedersi *seh-dehr'-see* [100]
**situation,** situazione (f) *see-too-ah-tsyoh'-neh*
**six,** sei *seh'-ee*
**sixteen,** sedici *seh'-dee-chee*
**sixth,** sesto *ses'-toh*
**sixty,** sessanta *ses-sahn'-tah*
**size,** misura, *mee-zoo'-rah* [67]
**skilled, skillful,** abile *ah'-bee-leh*
**skin,** pelle (f) *pel'-leh*
**skirt,** gonna, gonnella *gon'-nah, gon-nel'-lah* [68]
**skull,** cranio *krah'-nee-yoh*
**sky,** cielo *chyeh'-loh*
**sleep** *n.,* sonno *son'-noh*
**sleep** *v.,* dormire *dor-mee'-reh* [96]
**sleeve,** manica *mah'-nee-kah* [69]
**slice** *n.,* fetta *fet'-tah*
**slice** *v.,* affettare *ahf-fet-tah'-reh*
**slight,** leggero *lej-jeh'-roh*
**slip** [garment], sottogonna *sot-toh-gon'-nah*
**slip** *v.,* scivolare *shee-voh-lah'-reh*
**slippers,** pantofole (f, pl) *pahn-toh'-foh-leh*
**slippery,** sciovoloso, sdruccievole *shee-voh-loh'-zoh,*
  *zdrooch-chyeh'-voh-leh* [75]
**slow,** lento *len'-toh*
**slowly,** lentamente, adagio, pian piano *len-tah-men'-teh,*
  *ah-dah'-joh, pyahn pyah'-noh* [11, 45]
**small,** piccolo *peek'-koh-loh*
**smart,** svelto *zvel'-toh*
**smell** *n.,* odore *oh-doh'-reh*
**smell** *v.,* odorare *oh-doh-rah'-reh*
**smile** *n.,* sorriso *sor-ree'-zoh*
**smile** *v.,* sorridere *sor-ree'-deh-reh*
**smoke** *n.,* fumo *foo'-moh*
**smoke** *v.,* fumare *foo-mah'-reh* [89, 96]
**smooth,** liscio *lee'-shoh*

**snack,** spuntino *spoon-tee'-noh*

**snow,** neve (f) *neh'-veh* **it's snowing,** nevica *neh'-vee-kah*

**so,** così *koh-see'* **so as,** così che *koh-see' keh* **so that,** affinchè *ahf-feen-keh'*

**soap,** sapone (m) *sah-poh'-neh* [40]

**social,** sociale *soh-chah'-leh*

**sock,** calzino *kahl-tsee'-noh*

**soda,** soda *soh'-dah*

**soft,** soffice, morbido, molle *sof'-fee-cheh, mor'-bee-doh, mol'-leh*

**sold,** venduto *ven-doo'-toh*

**solid,** solido *soh'-lee-doh*

**some,** del, della, dei *del, del'-lah, deh'-ee*

**somehow,** in qualche modo *een kwahl'-keh moh'-doh*

**someone,** qualcuno *kwahl-koo'-noh*

**something,** qualche cosa, qualcosa *kwahl'-keh ko'-zah, kwahl-ko'-zah*

**sometimes,** qualche volta *kwahl'-keh vol'-tah*

**somewhere,** in qualche luogo *een kwahl'-keh lwoh'-goh*

**son,** figlio *feel'-yoh* [3]

**song,** canzone (f) *kahn-tsoh'-neh*

**soon,** fra poco *frah poh'-koh*

**sore** *adj.,* dolente *doh-len'-teh*

**sore throat,** mal di gola *mahl dee goh'-lah*

**sorrow,** afflizione (f) *ahf-flee-tsyoh'-neh*

**sorry: to be sorry,** dispiacere a, rincrescere a *dees-pyah-cheh'-reh ah, reen-kreh'-sheh-reh ah* [3] **I'm sorry,** mi dispiace, mi rincresce *mee dees-pyah'-cheh, mee reen-kreh'-sheh*

**sort,** sorta *sor'-tah*

**soul,** anima *ah'-nee-mah*

**sound** *n.,* suono *swoh'-noh*

**soup,** zuppa, minestra *dzoop'-pah, mee-nes'-trah* [54]

**sour,** agro, acido *ah'-groh, ah'-chee-doh* [52]

**south,** sud (m) *sood*

**southeast,** sud-est *sood-est'*

**southwest**, sud-ovest *sood-oh'-vest*
**souvenir**, ricordo *ree-kor'-doh*
**space**, spazio *spah'-tsee-yoh*
**speak**, parlare *pahr-lah'-reh* [43]  **do you speak English?** parla Lei inglese? *pahr'- leh'-ee een-gleh'-zeh*
**special**, speciale *speh-chah'-leh*
**specialty**, specialità *speh-chah'-lee-tah*
**speed**, velocità *veh-loh-chee-tah'* [75]
**spell** *v.*, sillabare, scrivere *seel-lah-bah'-reh, skree'-veh-reh*
**spend**, spendere *spen'-deh-reh*
**spicy**, piccante *peek-kahn'-teh*
**spinach**, spinaci (m, pl) *spee-nah'-chee*
**spine**, spina dorsale *spee'-nah dor-sahl'-leh*
**splendid**, splendido *splen'-dee-doh*
**spoiled**, guasto *gwah'-toh*
**spoon**, cucchiaio *kook-kee-yah'-yoh* [55]
**spot** *n.*, macchia *mahk'-kee-yah*
**sprain** *n.*, storta *stor'-tah*
**spring** [season], primavera *pree-mah-veh'-rah*
**spring** [water], sorgente (f) *sor-jen'-teh*
**springs** [of a car], molla *mol'-lah*
**square** *adj.*, quadrato *kwah-drah'-toh*
**square** [public], piazza *pyaht'-tsah* [100]
**stairs**, scala *skah'-lah*
**stamp**, francobollo *frahn-koh-bol'-loh* [40]
**stand** *v.*, stare in piedi *stah'-reh een pyeh'-dee*
**star**, stella *stel'-lah* [7]
**starch**, amido *ah'-mee-doh*
**start** *n.*, principio *preen-chee'-pyoh*
**start** *v.*, cominciare *kom-een-chah'-reh*
**state**, stato *stah'-toh*
**stateroom**, cabina *kah-bee'-nah*
**station**, stazione (f) *stah-tsyoh'-neh* [82]
**statue**, statua *stah'-too-ah*
**stay** *v.*,    stare, rimanere *stah'-reh,   ree-mah-neh'-reh* [16, 38, 39, 94]

**steak,** bistecca *bees-tek'-kah*
**steal** *v.,* rubare *roo-bah'-reh* [15]
**steel,** acciaio *ahch-chah'-yoh*
**steep,** erto *er'-toh*
**step,** passo, gradino *pahs'-soh, grah-dee'-noh*
**stew,** stufato *stoo-fah'-toh*
**steward,** cameriere (m) *kah-mee-ree-yeh'-reh* [87]
**stick** *n.,* stecco *stek'-koh*
**stiff,** rigido *ree'-jee-doh*
**still** [quiet], tranquillo *trahn-kweel'-loh*
**still** [yet], tuttavia, eppure *toot-tah-vee'-yah, ep-poo'-reh*
**sting** *n.,* puntura *poon-too'-rah*
**sting** *v.,* pungere *poon'-jeh-reh*
**stockings,** calze (f, pl) *kahl'-tseh*
**stolen,** rubato *roo-bah'-toh*
**stomach,** stomaco *stoh'-mah-koh* [92]
**stone,** pietra *pyeh'-trah*
**stop** *n.,* fermata *fer-mah'-tah*
**stop** *v.,* fermarsi *fer-mahr'-see* [14, 45 46, 84]
**store** *n.,* negozio *neh-goh'-tsyoh* [62, 99]
**storey,** piano *pyah'-noh*
**storm,** tempesta, temporale (m) *tem-pes'-tah, tem-poh-rah'-leh*
**story,** storia *stoh'-ree-yah*
**straight,** diritto *dee-reet'-toh*
**straight ahead,** sempre diritto *sem'-preh dee-reet'-toh* [45]
**strange,** strano *strah'-noh*
**stranger,** straniero *strah-nyeh'-roh*
**strawberry,** fragola *frah'-goh-lah*
**stream,** corrente (f) *kor-ren'-teh*
**street,** strada, via *strah'-dah, vee'-yah* [37, 46, 100, 101]
**streetcar,** tranvia *trahn-vee'-yah*
**strength,** forza *for'-tsah*
**string,** spago *spah'-goh*
**strong,** forte *for'-teh*
**structure,** struttura *stroot-too'-rah*

**student,** studente *stoo-den'-teh*

**study** v., studiare *stoo-dee-yah'-reh*

**style,** stile (m) *stee'-leh*

**suburb,** sobborgo, dintorni (m, pl) *sob-bor'-goh, deen-tor'-nee*

**succeed** [follow], seguire *seh-gwee'-reh;* [attain one's goal], riuscire *ree-oo-shee'-reh*

**success,** successo *sooch-ches'-soh*

**such,** tale *tah'-leh*

**suddenly,** improvvisamente, ad un tratto *eem-prov-vee-zah-men'-teh, ahd oon traht'-toh*

**suffer,** soffrire *sof-free'-reh*

**sufficient,** sufficiente *soof-fee-chyen'-teh*

**sugar,** zucchero *dzook'-keh-roh* [51, 52]

**suggest,** suggerire *sooj-jeh-ree'-reh*

**suggestion,** suggerimento *sooj-jeh-ree-men'-toh*

**suit,** vestito, abito *vest-tee'-toh, ah'-bee-toh*

**suitcase,** valigia *vah-lee'-jah* [39]

**summer,** estate (f) *es-tah'-teh*

**sun,** sole (m) *soh'-leh* [6]

**sunburned,** bruciato dal sole *broo-chah'-toh dahl soh'-leh*

**Sunday,** domenica *doh-meh'-nee-kah*

**sunglasses,** occhiali da sole *ok-kyah'-lee dah soh'-leh*

**sunny,** soleggiato *soh-lej-jah'-toh*

**supper,** cena *chen'-nah* [51]

**sure,** sicuro *see-koo'-roh*

**surface,** superficie (f) *soo-per-fee'-chyeh*

**surprise** n., sorpresa *sor-preh'-zah*

**surprise** v., sorprendere *sor-pren'-deh-reh*

**suspect** v., sospettare *soh-spet-tah'-reh*

**suspicion,** sospetto *sos-pet'-toh*

**sweater,** maglione di lana (m) *mahl-yoh'-neh dee lah'-nah* [8]

**sweep,** spazzare, scopare *spaht-tsah'-reh, skoh-pah'-reh*

**sweet,** dolce *dol'-cheh*

**swim,** nuotare *nwoh-tah'-reh* [102]

**swollen,** gonfiato *gon-fyah'-toh*

**sword,** spada *spah'-dah*

**table,** tavola *tah'-voh-lah* [50, 54, 57, 87]

**tablecloth,** tovaglia *toh-vahl'-yah* [56]

**tailor,** sarto *sahr'-toh*

**take,** prendere *pren'-deh-reh* [51, 67]  **take off,** decollare *deh-kol-lah'-reh* [89]

**talk,** parlare *pahr-lah'-reh*

**tall,** alto *ahl'-toh*

**tank,** serbatoio *ser-bah-toh'-yoh*

**taste** *n.,* gusto *goos'-toh*

**taste** *v.,* assaggiare, gustare, saporare *ahs-saj-jah'-reh, goos-tah'-reh, sah-poh-rah'-reh*

**tax** *n.,* tassa *tahs'-sah*

**taxi,** tassì *tahs-see'* [44]

**tea,** tè (m) *teh* [53]

**teach,** insegnare *een-sehn-yah'-reh*

**teacher,** maestro *mah-ehs'-troh*

**tear** [drop], lagrima *lah'-gree-mah*

**tear** *v.,* strappare *strahp-pah'-reh*

**teaspoon,** cucchiaino *kook-kyah-ee'-noh*

**teeth,** denti (m, pl) *den'-tee*

**telegram,** telegramma (m) *teh-leh-grahm'-mah*

**telephone,** telefono *teh-leh'-foh-noh* [41]

**telephone booth,** cabina telefonica *kah-bee'-nah teh-leh-foh'-nee-kah*

**telephone operator,** telefonista, centralino *teh-leh-foh-nees'-tah, chen-trah-lee'-noh*

**television,** televisione (f) *teh-leh-vee-zyoh'-neh*

**tell,** dire, raccontare *dee'-reh, rahk-kon-tah'-reh* [13, 46]

**temperature,** temperatura *tem-peh-rah-too'-rah*

**temple,** tempio *tem'-pyoh*

**temporary,** provvisorio *prov-vee-zoh'-ree-yoh*

**ten,** dieci *dyeh'-chee*

**tent,** tenda *ten'-dah*

**tenth,** decimo *deh'-chee-moh*

**test,** prova *proh'-vah*

**than,** di, che *dee, keh*

**thank,** ringraziare *reen-grah-tsyah'-reh*    **thank you,** grazie *grah'-tsee-yeh*

**thankful,** grato *grah'-toh*

**that** *adj.,* quello, quel, quell', quella *kwel'-loh, kwel, kwel, kwel'-lah*

**that** *conj.,* che *keh*

**that** *pron.,* quello, quella *kwel'-loh, kwel'-lah*

**the,** il, la, l', lo i, le, gli *eel, lah, l, loh, ee, leh, lyee*

**theater,** teatro *teh-ah'-troh* [101]

**theft,** furto *foor'-toh*

**their,** loro *loh'-roh*

**theirs,** loro *loh'-roh*

**them,** loro, li, le *loh'-roh, lee, leh*

**then,** allora *ahl-loh'-rah*

**there** *adv.,* lì, là, ci *lee, lah, chee*    **there is, there are,** c'è, ci sono *cheh, chee soh'-noh*

**therefore,** perciò *per-choh'*

**thermometer,** termometro *ter-moh'-meh-troh*

**these** *adj., & pron.,* questi, queste *kwes'-tee, kwes'-teh*

**they,** loro, essi, esse *loh'-roh, es'-see, es'-seh*

**thick,** spesso *spes'-soh*

**thigh,** coscia *koh'-shah*

**thin,** sottile, magro *sot-tee'-leh, mah'-groh*

**thing,** cosa *ko'-zah*

**think,** pensare *pen-sah'-reh*

**third,** terzo *ter'-tsoh*

**thirst,** sete *seh'-teh*

**thirsty: to be thirsty,** aver sete *ah-vehr' seh'-teh* [47, 48]

**thirteen,** tredici *treh'-dee-chee*

**thirty,** trenta *tren'-tah*

**this** *adj.,* questo, questa, quest' *kwes'-toh, kwes'-tah, kwest*

**this** *pron.,* questo, questa *kwes'-toh, kwes'-tah*

**those** *adj.*, quelli, quelle, quegli, quei *kwel'-lee, kwel'-leh, kwel'-yee, kweh'-ee*

**those** *pron.*, quelli, quelle *kwel'-lee, kwel'-leh*

**thoroughfare,** strada principale *strah'-dah preen-chee-pah'-leh*

**thousand,** mille *meel'-leh*

**thread,** filo *fee'-loh* [70]

**three,** tre *treh*

**throat,** gola *goh'-lah*

**through** *prep.*, per, attraverso *per, aht-trah-ver'-soh*

**through** [finished], finito *fee-nee'-toh*

**throw,** lanciare, gettare *lahn-chah'-reh, jet-tah'-reh*

**thumb,** pollice (m) *pol'-lee-cheh*

**thunder,** tuono *twoh'-noh*

**Thursday,** giovedì *joh-veh-dee'*

**ticket,** biglietto *beel-yet'-toh* [83, 85, 89]

**ticket office,** sportello dei biglietti *spor-tel'-loh deh'-ee beel-yet'-tee* [83]

**tie** [bind], legare *leh-gah'-reh*

**tight,** stretto *stret'-toh* [69]

**tighten,** stringere *streen'-jeh-reh*

**till,** fino a, finchè *fee'-noh ah, feen-keh'*

**time,** tempo, volta *temp'-poh, vol'-tah*  **what time is it?** che ora è? *keh oh'-reh eh*  **on time,** a tempo *ah tem'-poh*

**timetable,** orario *oh-rah'-ree-yoh* [83]

**tip** [money], mancia *mahn'-chah* [57]

**tire** [of a car], gomma, pneumatico *gom'-mah, pneh-oo-mah'-tee-koh* [74]

**tire** *v.*, stancarsi *stahn-kahr'-see*

**tired,** stanco *stahn'-koh* [100]

**to,** a, ad *ah, ahd*

**toast,** pane tostato *pah'-neh tos-tah'-toh*

**tobacco,** tabacco *tah-bahk'-koh* [34]

**tobacconist,** tabaccaio *tah-bahk-kah'-yoh*

**today,** oggi *oj'-jee* [5, 99]

**toe,** dito del piede *dee'-toh del pyeh'-deh*

**together,** insieme *een-syeh'-meh*

**toilet,** gabinetto *gah-bee-net'-toh*

**toilet paper,** carta igienica *kahr'-tah ee-jyeh'-nee-kah*

**tomato,** pomodoro *poh-moh-doh'-roh*

**tomorrow,** domani *doh-mah'-nee* [3, 6, 40, 96]

**tongue,** linqua *leen'-gwah* [95]

**tonight,** questa notte, stasera *kwes'-tah not'-teh, stah-seh'-rah*

**tonsils,** tonsille (f, pl) *ton-seel'-leh*

**too** [excessive], troppo *trop'-poh;* [also], anche *ahn'-keh*

**tooth,** dente (m) *den'-teh*

**toothache,** dolor di denti *doh-lohr' dee den'-tee*

**toothbrush,** spazzolino da denti *spaht-tsoh-lee'-noh dah den'-tee*

**toothpaste,** pasta dentifricia *pahs'-tah den-tee-free'-chah*

**top,** cima *chee'-mah*

**torn,** strappato *strahp-pah'-toh*

**total,** totale *toh-tah'-leh*

**touch** *v.,* toccare *kok-kah'-reh*

**tough,** duro, resistente *doo'-roh, reh-zees-ten'-teh*

**tour,** giro *jee'-roh* [99, 102]

**tow,** rimorchiare *ree-mor-kyah'-reh*

**toward,** verso *ver'-soh*

**towel,** asciugamano *ah-shoo-gah-mah'-noh* [40]

**town,** città *sheet-tah'*

**toy,** giocattolo *joh-kaht'-toh-loh*

**toy shop,** negozio di giocattoli *neh-goh'-tsyoh dee joh-kaht'-toh-lee*

**trade,** commercio *kom-mer'-choh*

**traffic,** traffico *trahf'-fee-koh*

**train,** treno *treh'-noh* [15, 82, 83, 84, 85]

**transfer** *v.,* trasferire *trahs-feh-ree'-reh* [46]

**translate,** tradurre *trah-door'-reh*

**translation,** traduzione (f) *trah-doo-tsyoh'-neh*

**translator,** traduttore (m), traduttrice (f) *trah-doot-toh'-reh, trah-doot-tree'-cheh*

**transmission,** trasmissione (f) *trahz-mees-syoh'-neh*

**transportation,** trasporto *trahs-por'-toh*

**travel** *v.,* viaggiare *vyahj-jah'-reh*

**traveler,** viaggiatore (m) *vyahj-jah-toh'-reh*

**traveler's check,** assegno di viaggio *ahs-sehn'-yoh dee vyahj'-joh* [31]

**tray,** vassoio *vahs-soh'-yoh*

**tree,** albero *ahl'-beh-roh*

**trip,** viaggio *vyahj'-joh* [88]

**tropical,** tropicale *troh-pee-kah'-leh*

**trousers,** pantaloni (m, pl) *pahn-tah-loh'-nee*

**truck,** camione (m) *kah-myoh'-neh*

**true,** vero *veh'-roh*

**trunk,** baule (m) *bah-oo'-leh*

**truth,** verità *veh-ree-tah'*

**try** *v.,* tentare, cercare di *ten-tah'-reh, cher-kah'-reh dee*
  **try on,** provarsi *proh-vahr'-see* [67, 69]

**Tuesday,** martedì *mahr-teh-dee'*

**turn** *n.,* giro, voltata *jee'-roh, vol-tah'-tah*

**turn** *v.,* girare *jee-rah'-reh* [45]

**twelve,** dodici *doh'-dee-chee*

**twenty,** venti *ven'-tee*

**twice,** due volte *doo'-eh vol'-teh*

**twin beds,** letti gemelli *let'-tee jeh-mel'-lee*

**two,** due *doo'-eh*


**ugly,** brutto *broot'-toh*

**umbrella,** ombrello *om-brel'-loh* [6]

**uncle,** zio *dzee'-yoh*

**uncomfortable,** scomodo *skoh'-moh-doh*

**unconscious,** inconscio, privo di sensi *een-kon'-shoh, pree'-voh dee sen'-see*

**under** *prep.*, sotto *sot'-toh*
**underneath** *prep.*, disotto *dee-sot'-toh*
**undershirt,** camiciola *kah-mee-choh'-lah*
**understand,** capire *kah-pee-reh* [11]
**underwear,** maglia *mahl'-yah*
**undress** *v.*, svestirsi *zves-teer'-see*
**unequal,** ineguale *een-eh-gwah'-leh*
**unfair,** ingiusto *een-joos'-toh*
**unfortunate,** sfortunato *sfor-too-nah'-toh*
**unhappy,** infelice *een-feh-lee'-cheh*
**unhealthy,** malsano *mahl-sah'-noh*
**United States,** Stati Uniti (m, pl) *stah'-tee oo-nee'-tee*
**university,** università *oo-nee-ver-see-tah'*
**unless,** a meno che *ah meh'-noh keh*
**unlucky,** sfortunato *sfor-too-nah'-toh*
**unpack,** disfare le valige, sballare *dees-fah'-reh leh vah-lee'-jeh, zbahl-lah'-reh*
**unpleasant,** spiacevole *spyah-cheh'-voh-leh*
**unsafe,** non sicuro *non see-koo'-roh*
**until,** fino a, finchè *fee'-noh ah, feen-keh'*
**untrue,** falso *fahl'-soh*
**unusual,** insolito *een-soh'-lee-toh*
**up,** su *soo*
**upper,** superiore *soo-peh-ree-yoh'-reh*
**upstairs,** sopra *soh'-prah*
**urgent,** urgente *oor-jen'-teh*
**us,** noi, ci *noy, chee*
**use** *n.*, uso *oo'-zoh* [34]
**use** *v.*, usare *oo-zah'-reh*
**useful,** utile *oo'-tee-leh*
**useless,** inutile *een-oo'-tee-leh*
**usual,** usuale, solito *oo-zoo-ah'-leh, soh'-lee-toh*

**vacant,** libero *lee'-beh-roh*
**vacation,** vacanze (f, pl) *vah-kahn'-tseh*

**vaccination,** vaccinazione (f) *vahch-chee-nah-tsyoh'-neh*

**valuable,** prezioso, di valore *preh-tsyoh'-zoh, dee vah-loh'-reh*

**value** n., valore (m) *vah-loh'-reh*

**vanilla,** vaniglia *vah-neel'-yah*

**variety,** varietà *vah-ree-eh-tah'*

**veal,** vitello *vee-tel'-loh*

**vegetables,** legumi (m, pl) *leh-goo'-mee*

**very,** molto *mol'-toh*

**vest,** panciotto *pahn-chot'-toh*

**victim,** vittima *veet'-tee-mah*

**view** n., veduta, vista *veh-doo'-tah, vees'-tah* [37]

**village,** villaggio *veel-lahj'-joh*

**vinegar,** aceto *ah-cheh'-toh*

**visa,** visto *vees'-toh*

**visit** n., visita *vee'-zee-tah*

**visit** v., visitare *vee-zee-tah'-reh* [99, 101, 103]

**voice,** voce (f) *voh'-cheh*

**volcano,** vulcano *vool-kah'-noh*

**voyage** n., viaggio *vyahj'-joh*

**waist,** vita *vee'-tah*

**wait** v., aspettare *ahs-pet-tah'-reh* [12, 45]

**waiter,** cameriere (m) *kah-meh-ree-yeh'-reh* [50, 56]

**waiting room,** sala d'aspetto *sah'-lah dahs-pet'-toh* [85]

**waitress,** cameriera *kah-meh-ree-yeh'-rah* [50]

**wake up,** svegliare, svegliarsi *zvehl-yah'-reh, zvehl-yahr'-see*

**walk** n., passeggiata *pahs-sej-jah'-tah*

**walk** v., camminare *kahm-mee-nah'-reh* [100]

**wall,** muro, parete (f) *moo'-roh, pah-reh'-teh*

**wallet,** portafogli (m) *por-tah-fohl'-yee*

**want** v., volere *voh-leh-reh* **I want,** voglio *vohl'-yoh*

**warm,** caldo *kahl'-doh* [52, 55]

**warn,** avvertire *ahv-ver-tee'-reh*

**warning,** avvertimento, avvertenza *ahv-ver-tee-men'-toh, ahv-ver-ten'-tsah*

**wash** *v.*, lavare *lah-vah'-reh* [40, 74]

**wasp,** vespa *ves'-pah*

**watch** *n.*, orologio *oh-roh-loh'-joh*

**watch** *v.*, guardare, osservare *gwahr-dah'-reh, os-ser-vah'-reh*

**water,** acqua *ahk'-kwah* [8, 51, 74]

**waterfall,** cascata *kahs-kah'-tah*

**wave** [ocean], onda *on'-dah*

**way** [manner], maniera, modo *mah-nyeh'-rah, moh'-doh*

**we,** noi *noy*

**weak,** debole *deh'-boh-leh*

**wear** *v.*, indossare, portare *een-dos-sah'-reh, por-tah'-reh*

**weather,** tempo *tem'-poh* [5, 6, 7]

**Wednesday,** mercoledì *mer-koh-leh-dee'*

**week,** settimana *set-tee-mah'-nah* [38, 39]

**weigh,** pesare *peh-zah'-reh*

**weight,** peso *peh'-zoh*

**welcome** *n.*, benvenuto *ben-veh-noo'-toh*

**well,** bene *beh'-neh* **well done** [food], ben cotto *ben kot'-toh*

**well** [for water], pozzo *pot'-tsoh*

**west,** ovest (m) *oh'-vest*

**wet,** bagnato *bahn-yah'-toh* [75]

**what** *interr.*, che? che cosa? *keh, keh ko'-zah* **what else?** che altro? *keh ahl'-troh?*

**wheel,** ruota *rwoh'-tah*

**when,** quando *kwahn'-doh*

**whenever,** ogni volta che *ohn'-yee vol'-tah keh*

**where,** dove *do'-veh* **where is, where are,** dov'è, dove sono *do-ve', do'-veh son'-noh*

**wherever,** dovunque *do-voon'-kweh*

**which** *interr.*, quale? *kwah'-leh*

**while,** mentre *men'-treh*

**whip** *n.*, frusta *froos'-tah*
**white,** bianco *byahn'-koh* [69]
**who** *interr.*, chi? *kee*
**who** [*rel.*,] che *keh*
**whole,** intero *een-teh'-roh*
**whom** *interr.*, chi? *kee*
**whose** *interr.*, di chi? *dee kee*
**why** *interr.*, perchè? *per-keh'*
**wide,** largo *lahr'-goh* [69, 75]
**width,** larghezza *lahr-get'-tsah*
**wife,** moglie (f) *mohl'-yeh* [2]
**wild,** selvaggio *sel-vahj'-joh*
**willing,** disposto a *dees-pos'-toh ah*
**win** *v.*, vincere *veen'-cheh-reh*
**wind,** vento *ven'-toh* [6, 7]
**window,** finestra *fee-nes'-trah* [39, 84]
**windshield,** parabrezza *pah-rah-bret'-tsah* [76]
**wine,** vino *vee'-noh* [55]   **red wine,** vino rosso *vee'-noh ros'-soh*   **white wine,** vino bianco *vee'-noh byahn'-koh*
**wing,** ala *ah'-lah*
**winter,** inverno *een-ver'-noh*
**wipe,** pulire *poo-lee'-reh* [76]
**wise,** saggio *sahj'-joh*
**wish** *n.*, desiderio, augurio *deh-zee-deh'-ree-yoh, ow-goo'-ree-yoh*
**wish** *v.*, desiderare *deh-zee-deh-rah'-reh* [44, 64]
**with,** con *kon*
**without,** senza *sen'-tsah*
**woman,** donna *don'-nah* [10]
**wonderful,** meraviglioso *meh-rah-veel-yoh'-zoh*
**wood,** legno *lehn'-yoh*
**woods,** bosco *bos'-koh*
**wool,** lana *lah'-nah*
**word,** parola *pah-roh'-lah*
**work** *n.*, lavoro *lah-voh'-roh*
**work** *v.*, lavorare *lah-voh-rah'-reh*

**world,** mond *moon'-doh*
**worried,** preoccupato *preh-ok-koo-pah'-toh*
**worse,** peggiore, peggio *pej-joh'-reh, pej'-joh*
**worth,** valore *vah-loh'-reh*
**wound** [injury], ferita *feh-ree'-tah*
**wrap** *v.,* avvolgere *ahv-vol'-jeh-reh* [70]
**wrist,** polso *pol'-soh*
**wristwatch,** orologio da polso *oh-roh-loh'-joh dah pol'-soh*
**write,** scrivere *skree'-veh-reh* [13, 30]
**writing,** scrittura *skreet-too'-rah*
**wrong: to be wrong,** aver torto *ah-vehr' tor'-toh* [12]

**x ray,** raggi x *rahj'-jee eh-kees*

**yard,** cortile (m) *kor-tee'-leh*
**year,** anno *ahn'-noh* [89]
**yellow,** giallo *jahl'-loh*
**yes,** sì *see*
**yesterday,** ieri *yeh'-ree* [6]
**yet,** ancora *ahn-koh'-rah*
**you,** Lei, voi, tu *leh'-ee, voy, too*
**young,** giovane *joh'-vah-neh*
**your, yours,** suo, sua, vostro, vostra, tuo, tua *soo'-oh, soo'-ah vos'-troh, vos'-trah, too'-oh, too'-ah*

**zero,** zero *dzeh'-roh*
**zipper,** chiusura lampo *kyoo-zoo'-rah lahm'-poh*

## CONVERSION TABLES

### Length
1 centimetro (cm) = 0.39 inch
1 metro (m) = 39.36 inches
1 chilometro (km) = 0.62 mile
1 inch = 2.54 cm.
1 foot = 0.30 m.
1 mile = 1.61 km.

### Weight
1 grammo (gm) = 0.04 ounce
1 kilo (kg) = 2.20 pounds
1 ounce = 28.35 gm.
1 pound = 453.59 gm.

### Volume
1 litro = 0.91 dry quart
1 litro = 1.06 liquid quarts
1 pint liquid = 0.47 liter
1 US quart liquid = 0.95 liter
1 US gallon = 3.78 liters

### Temperature

| Celsius (°C): | −17.8 | 0 | 10 | 20 | 30 | 37 | 37.8 | 100 |
|---|---|---|---|---|---|---|---|---|
| Fahrenheit (°F): | 0 | 32 | 50 | 68 | 86 | 98.6 | 100 | 212 |

# Why We Make This Generous Offer

As a bonus to buyers of this book, Cortina Academy has arranged this special offer of a FREE Language Record and Lesson. Cortina Academy, the world-famous originator of the phonograph method of language learning, develops and publishes the most thorough and effective complete language courses available today. You have a special opportunity for introduction to these outstanding language materials—and there are several important reasons why you should take advantage of this opportunity *now*:

- Cortina's "learn-by-listening" Method is the *natural* way to learn;

- you learn almost without effort—at your own convenience;

- your rewards will be great—including the many business and travel opportunities available to speakers of foreign languages.

So take advantage of this unusual introductory offer. There is no obligation. Just mail the coupon today for your Free Language Record and Lesson.

**Cortina Institute of Languages, Dept. GD-P,**
**17 Riverside Ave., Westport, CT 06880**

---